CHOCOLAT

Joanne Harris

Doubleday

LONDON · NEW YORK · TORONTO · SYDNEY · AUCKLAND

TRANSWORLD PUBLISHERS
61–63 Uxbridge Road, London W5 5SA
a division of The Random House Group Ltd

RANDOM HOUSE AUSTRALIA (PTY) LTD
20 Alfred Street, Milsons Point, Sydney,
New South Wales 2061, Australia

RANDOM HOUSE NEW ZEALAND
18 Poland Road, Glenfield, Auckland 10, New Zealand

RANDOM HOUSE SOUTH AFRICA (PTY) LTD
Endulini, 5A Jubilee Road, Parktown 2193, South Africa

Published 1999 by Doubleday
a division of Transworld Publishers Ltd

A catalogue record for this book is
available from the British Library.

ISBN 0385 410646

Typeset in 10½ / 14 Goudy by
Deltatype Ltd, Birkenhead, Merseyside
Printed in Great Britain by
Mackays of Chatham plc, Chatham, Kent.

In memory of my
great-grandmother,
Marie André Sorin
(1892 - 1968)

Acknowledgements

Heartfelt thanks to everyone who helped to make this book possible: to my family for support, childminding and somewhat baffled encouragement; to Kevin for handling all the tedious paperwork; to Anouchka for the loan of Pantoufle. Thanks also to my indomitable agent Serafina Clarke and editor Francesca Liversidge, to Jennifer Luithlen and Lora Fountain, plus everyone at Doubleday who helped to make me so welcome. Finally, special thanks to fellow author Christopher Fowler for turning on the lights.

1

February 11
Shrove Tuesday

WE CAME ON THE WIND OF THE CARNIVAL. A WARM WIND for February, laden with the hot greasy scents of frying pancakes and sausages and powdery-sweet waffles cooked on the hotplate right there by the roadside, with the confetti sleeting down collars and cuffs and rolling in the gutters like an idiot antidote to winter. There is a febrile excitement in the crowds which line the narrow main street, necks craning to catch sight of the crêpe-covered *char* with its trailing ribbons and paper rosettes. Anouk watches, eyes wide, a yellow balloon in one hand and a toy trumpet in the other, from between a shopping-basket and a sad brown dog. We have seen carnivals before, she and I; a procession of two hundred and fifty of the decorated *chars* in Paris last Mardi Gras, a hundred and eighty in New York, two dozen marching bands in

Vienna, clowns on stilts, the *Grosses Têtes* with their lolling papier-mâché heads, drum majorettes with batons spinning and sparkling. But at six the world retains a special lustre. A wooden cart, hastily decorated with gilt and crêpe and scenes from fairy tales. A dragon's head on a shield, Rapunzel in a woollen wig, a mermaid with a Cellophane tail, a gingerbread house all icing and gilded cardboard, a witch in the doorway, waggling extravagant green fingernails at a group of silent children . . . At six it is possible to perceive subtleties which a year later are already out of reach. Behind the papier-mâché, the icing, the plastic, she can still see the real witch, the real magic. She looks up at me, her eyes, which are the blue-green of the Earth seen from a great height, shining.

'Are we staying? Are we staying here?' I have to remind her to speak French. 'But are we? Are we?' She clings to my sleeve. Her hair is a candyfloss tangle in the wind.

I consider. It's as good a place as any. Lansquenet-sous-Tannes, two hundred souls at most, no more than a blip on the fast road between Toulouse and Bordeaux. Blink once and it's gone. One main street, a double row of dun-coloured half-timbered houses leaning secretively together, a few laterals running parallel like the tines of a bent fork. A church, aggressively whitewashed, in a square of little shops. Farms scattered across the watchful land. Orchards, vineyards, strips of earth enclosed and regimented according to the strict apartheid of country farming: here apples, there kiwis, melons, endives beneath their black plastic shells, vines looking blighted and dead in the thin February sun but awaiting triumphant resurrection by March . . . Behind that, the Tannes, small tributary of the Garonne, fingers its way across the marshy pasture. And the people? They look much like all others we have known; a little pale perhaps in the unaccustomed sunlight, a little drab. Headscarves and berets are the colour of the hair beneath, brown, black or grey. Faces are lined like last summer's apples, eyes pushed into wrinkled flesh like marbles into old dough. A few children, flying colours of red and lime-green and yellow, seem like a different race. As the *char* advances ponderously along the street behind the old tractor which pulls it, a large woman with a square, unhappy face clutches a tartan coat about her shoulders and shouts something in the half-comprehensible local dialect; on the wagon a squat Santa Claus, out-of-season amongst the fairies and sirens and goblins, hurls sweets at the crowd with barely restrained aggression. An elderly small-featured man, wearing a felt hat rather than the round beret more common to the region, picks up the sad brown dog from between my legs with a look of polite apology. I see his thin graceful fingers moving in the dog's fur; the dog whines; the master's expression becomes complex with love, concern, guilt. No-one looks at us. We might as well be invisible; our clothing marks us as strangers, transients. They are polite,

3

so polite; no-one stares at us. The woman, her long hair tucked into the collar of her orange coat, a long silk scarf fluttering at her throat; the child in yellow wellingtons and sky-blue mac. Their colouring marks them. Their clothes are exotic, their faces – are they too pale or too dark? – their hair marks them other, foreign, indefinably strange. The people of Lansquenet have learned the art of observation without eye contact. I feel their gaze like a breath on the nape of my neck, strangely without hostility but cold nevertheless. We are a curiosity to them, a part of the carnival, a whiff of the outlands. I feel their eyes upon us as I turn to buy a *galette* from the vendor. The paper is hot and greasy, the dark wheat pancake crispy at the edges but thick and good in the centre. I break off a piece and give it to Anouk, wiping melted butter from her chin. The vendor is a plump, balding man with thick glasses, his face slick with the steam from the hot plate. He winks at her. With the other eye he takes in every detail, knowing there will be questions later.

'On holiday, Madame?' Village etiquette allows him to ask; behind his tradesman's indifference I see a real hunger. Knowledge is currency here; with Agen and Montauban so close, tourists are a rarity.

'For a while.'

'From Paris, then?' It must be our clothes. In this garish land the people are drab. Colour is a luxury; it wears badly. The bright blossoms of the roadside are weeds, invasive, useless.

'No, no, not Paris.'

The *char* is almost at the end of the street. A small band – two fifes, two trumpets, a trombone and a side drum – follows it, playing a thin unidentifiable march. A dozen children scamper in its wake, picking up the unclaimed sweets. Some are in costume; I see Little Red Riding Hood and a shaggy person who might be the wolf squabbling companionably over possession of a handful of streamers.

A black figure brings up the rear. At first I take him for a part of the parade – the Plague Doctor, maybe – but as he approaches I recognize the old-fashioned soutane of the country priest. He is in his thirties, though from a distance his rigid stance makes him seem older. He turns towards me, and I see that he too is a stranger, with the high cheekbones and pale eyes of the North and long pianist's fingers resting on the silver cross which hangs from his neck. Perhaps this is what gives him the right to stare at me, this alienness; but I see no welcome in his cold, light eyes. Only the measuring, feline look of one who is uncertain of his territory. I smile at him; he looks away, startled, beckons the two children towards him. A gesture indicates the litter which now lines the road; reluctantly the pair begin to clear it, scooping up spent streamers and sweet-wrappers in their arms and into a nearby bin. I catch the priest staring at me again as I turn away, a look which in another man might have been of appraisal.

There is no police station at Lansquenet-sous-Tannes, therefore no crime. I try to be like Anouk, to see beneath the disguise to the truth, but for now everything is blurred.

'Are we staying? Are we, *Maman*?' She tugs at my arm, insistently. 'I like it, I like it here. Are we staying?'

I catch her up into my arms and kiss the top of her head. She smells of smoke and frying pancakes and warm bedclothes on a winter's morning.

Why not? It's as good a place as any.

'Yes, of course,' I tell her, my mouth in her hair. 'Of course we are.'

Not quite a lie. This time it may even be true.

The carnival is gone. Once a year the village flares into transient brightness but even now the warmth has faded, the crowd dispersed. The vendors pack up their hotplates and awnings, the children discard their costumes and party-favours. A slight air of embarrassment prevails, of abashment at this excess of noise and colour. Like rain in midsummer it evaporates, runs into the cracked earth and through the parched stones, leaving barely a trace. Two hours later Lansquenet-sous-Tannes is invisible once more, like an enchanted village which appears only once every year. But for the carnival we should have missed it altogether.

We have gas but as yet no electricity. On our first night I made pancakes for Anouk by candlelight and we ate them by the fireside, using an old magazine for plates, as none of our things can be delivered until tomorrow. The shop was originally a bakery and still carries the baker's wheatsheaf carved above the narrow doorway, but the floor is thick with a floury dust, and we picked our way across a drift of junk mail as we came in. The lease seems ridiculously cheap, accustomed as we are to city prices; even so I caught the sharp glance of suspicion from the woman at the agency as I counted out the banknotes. On the lease document I am Vianne Rocher, the signature a hieroglyph which might mean anything. By the light of the candle we explored our new territory; the old ovens still surprisingly good beneath the grease and soot, the pine-panelled walls, the blackened earthen tiles. Anouk found the old awning folded away in a back-room and we dragged it out; spiders scattered from under the faded canvas. Our living area is above the shop; a bedsit and washroom, ridiculously tiny balcony, terracotta planter with dead geraniums . . . Anouk made a face when she saw it.

'It's so dark, *Maman*.' She sounded awed, uncertain in the face of so much dereliction. 'And it smells so sad.'

She is right. The smell is like daylight trapped for years

7

until it has gone sour and rancid, of mouse-droppings and the ghosts of things unremembered and unmourned. It echoes like a cave, the small heat of our presence only serving to accentuate every shadow. Paint and sunlight and soapy water will rid us of the grime, but the sadness is another matter, the forlorn resonance of a house where no-one has laughed for years. Anouk's face looked pale and large-eyed in the candlelight, her hand tightening in mine.

'Do we have to sleep here?' she asked. 'Pantoufle doesn't like it. He's afraid.'

I smiled and kissed her solemn golden cheek. 'Pantoufle is going to help us.'

We lit a candle for every room, gold and red and white and orange. I prefer to make my own incense, but in a crisis the bought sticks are good enough for our purposes, lavender and cedar and lemongrass. We each held a candle, Anouk blowing her toy trumpet and I rattling a metal spoon in an old saucepan, and for ten minutes we stamped around every room, shouting and singing at the top of our voices – *Out! Out! Out!* – until the walls shook and the outraged ghosts fled, leaving in their wake a faint scent of scorching and a good deal of fallen plaster. Look behind the cracked and blackened paintwork, behind the sadness of things abandoned, and begin to see faint outlines, like the after-image of a sparkler held in the hand – here a wall adazzle with golden paint, there an armchair, a little shabby, but coloured a triumphant orange, the old awning suddenly glowing as half-hidden colours slide out from beneath the layers of grime. *Out! Out! Out!* Anouk and Pantoufle stamped and sang and the faint images seemed to grow brighter – a red stool beside the vinyl counter, a string of bells against the front door. Of course, I know it's only a game. Glamours to comfort a frightened child. There'll have to be work done, hard work, before any of this becomes real. And yet for the moment it is enough to know that the house welcomes us, as we welcome it. Rock salt and bread by the doorstep to placate any resident gods. Sandalwood on our pillow, to sweeten our dreams.

Later Anouk told me Pantoufle wasn't frightened any more, so that was all right. We slept together in our clothes on the floury mattress in the bedroom with all the candles burning, and when we awoke it was morning.

2

February 12
Ash Wednesday

ACTUALLY THE BELLS WOKE US. I HADN'T REALIZED QUITE how close we were to the church until I heard them, a single low resonant drone falling into a bright carillon – *dómmm flá-di-dadi dómmmm* – on the downbeat. I looked at my watch. It was six o'clock. Grey-gold light filtered through the broken shutters onto the bed. I stood up and looked out onto the square, wet cobbles shining. The square white church tower stood out sharply in the morning sunlight, rising from a hollow of dark shopfronts; a bakery, a florist, a shop selling graveyard paraphernalia, plaques, stone angels, enamelled everlasting roses ... Above their discreetly shuttered façades the white tower is a beacon, the roman numerals of the clock gleaming redly at six-twenty to baffle the devil, the Virgin in her dizzy eyrie watching the square with a faintly sickened expression. At the tip of the short spire a weathervane turns – west to west-northwest – a robed man with a scythe. From the balcony with the dead geranium I could see the first arrivals to Mass. I recognized the woman in the tartan coat from the carnival; I waved to her, but she hurried on without an answering gesture, pulling her coat protectively around her. Behind her the felt-hatted man with his sad brown dog in tow gave me a hesitant smile. I called down brightly to him, but seemingly village etiquette did not allow for such informalities, for he did not respond, hurrying in his turn into the church, taking his dog with him.

After that no-one even looked up at my window, though I counted over sixty heads – scarves, berets, hats drawn down against an invisible wind – but I felt their studied, curious indifference. They had matters of importance to consider, said their hunched shoulders and lowered heads. Their feet dragged sullenly at the cobbles like the feet of children going to school. This one has given up smoking today, I knew; that one his weekly visit to the *café*, another will forgo her favourite foods. It's none of my business, of course. But I felt at that moment that if ever a place were in need of a little magic . . . Old habits never die. And when you've once been in the business of granting wishes the impulse never quite leaves you. And besides, the wind, the carnival wind was still blowing, bringing with it the dim scent of grease and candyfloss and gunpowder, the hot sharp scents of the changing seasons, making the palms itch and the heart beat faster. For a time, then, we stay. For a time. Till the wind changes.

We bought the paint in the general store, and with it brushes, rollers, soap and buckets. We began upstairs and worked downwards, stripping curtains and throwing broken fittings onto the growing pile in the tiny back garden, soaping floors and making tidal waves down the narrow sooty stairway so that both of us were soaked several times through. Anouk's scrubbing-brush became a submarine, and mine a tanker which sent noisy soap torpedoes scudding down the stairs and into the hall. In the middle of this I heard the doorbell jangle and looked up, soap in one hand, brush in the other, at the tall figure of the priest.

I'd wondered how long it would take him to arrive.

He considered us for a time, smiling. A guarded smile, proprietary, benevolent; the lord of the manor welcomes inopportune guests. I could feel him very conscious of my wet and dirty overalls, my hair caught up in a red scarf, my bare feet in their dripping sandals.

'Good morning.' There was a rivulet of scummy water heading for his highly polished black shoe. I saw his eyes flick towards it and back towards me.

'Francis Reynaud,' he said, discreetly sidestepping. 'Curé of the parish.' I laughed at that; I couldn't help it.

'Oh, that's it,' I said maliciously. 'I thought you were with the carnival.' Polite laughter; *heh, heh, heh.*

I held out a yellow plastic glove. 'Vianne Rocher. And the bombardier back there is my daughter Anouk.'

Sounds of soap explosions, and of Anouk fighting Pantoufle on the stairs. I could hear the priest waiting for details of Monsieur Rocher. So much easier to have everything on a piece of paper, everything official, avoid this uncomfortable, messy *conversation.*

'I suppose you are very busy this morning.'

I suddenly felt sorry for him, trying so hard, straining to make contact. Again the forced smile. 'Yes, we really need to get this place in order as soon as possible. It's going to take time! But we wouldn't have been at church this morning anyway, Monsieur le Curé. We don't attend, you know.' It was kindly meant, to show him where we stood, to reassure him; but he looked startled, almost insulted.

'I see.'

It was too direct. He would have liked us to dance a little, to circle each other like wary cats.

'But it's very kind of you to welcome us,' I continued brightly. 'You might even be able to help us make a few friends here.'

He is a little like a cat himself, I notice; cold, light eyes which never hold the gaze, a restless watchfulness, studied, aloof.

'I'll do anything I can.' He is indifferent now he knows we are not to be members of his flock. And yet his conscience pushes him to offer more than he is willing to give. 'Have you anything in mind?'

'Well, we could do with some help here,' I suggested. 'Not you, of course' – quickly, as he began to reply. 'But perhaps you know someone who could do with the extra money? A plasterer, someone who might be able to help with the decorating?' This was surely safe territory.

'I can't think of anyone.' He is guarded, more so than anyone I have ever met. 'But I'll ask around.' Perhaps he will. He knows his duty to the new arrival. But I know he will not find anyone. His is not a nature which grants favours graciously. His eyes flicked warily to the pile of bread and salt by the door.

'For luck.' I smiled, but his face was stony. He skirted the little offering as if it offended him.

'*Maman?*' Anouk's head appeared in the doorway, hair standing out in crazy spikes. 'Pantoufle wants to play outside. Can we?'

I nodded. 'Stay in the garden.' I wiped a smudge of dirt from the bridge of her nose. 'You look a complete urchin.' I saw her glance at the priest and caught her comical look just in time. 'This is Monsieur Reynaud, Anouk. Why don't you say hello?'

'Hello!' shouted Anouk on the way to the door. 'Goodbye!' A blur of yellow jumper and red overalls and she was gone, her feet skidding manically on the greasy tiles. Not for the first time, I was almost sure I saw Pantoufle disappearing in her wake, a darker smudge against the dark lintel.

'She's only six,' I said by way of explanation.

Reynaud gave a tight, sour smile, as if his first glimpse of my daughter confirmed every one of his suspicions about me.

3

Thursday, February 13

THANK GOD THAT'S OVER. VISITS TIRE ME TO THE BONE. I don't mean you, of course, *mon père*; my weekly visit to you is a luxury, you might almost say my only one. I hope you like the flowers. They don't look much, but they smell wonderful. I'll put them here, beside your chair, where you can see them. It's a good view from here across the fields, with the Tannes in the middle distance and the Garonne gleaming in the far. You might almost imagine we were alone. Oh, I'm not complaining. Not really. But you must know how heavy it is for one man to carry. Their petty concerns, their dissatisfactions, their foolishness, their thousand trivial problems ... On Tuesday it was the carnival. Anyone might have taken them for savages, dancing and screaming. Louis Perrin's youngest, Claude, fired a water-pistol at me, and what would his father say but that he was a youngster and needed to play a little? All I want is to guide them, *mon père*, to free them from their sin. But they fight me at every turn, like children refusing wholesome fare in order to continue eating what sickens them. I know you understand. For fifty years you held all this on your shoulders in patience and strength. You earned their love. Have times changed so much? Here I am feared, respected . . . but loved, no. Their faces are sullen, resentful. Yesterday they left the service with ash on their foreheads and a look of guilty relief. Left to their secret indulgences, their solitary vices. Don't they understand? The Lord sees everything. *I* see everything. Paul-Marie Muscat beats his wife. He pays ten *Avés* weekly in the confessional and leaves to begin again in exactly the same way. His wife steals. Last week she went to the market and stole trumpery jewellery from a vendor's stall. Guillaume Duplessis wants to know if animals have souls, and weeps when I tell him they don't. Charlotte Edouard thinks her husband has a mistress – I know he has three, but the confessional keeps me silent. What children they are! Their demands leave me bloodied and reeling. But I cannot afford to show weakness. Sheep are not the docile, pleasant creatures of the pastoral idyll. Any countryman will tell you that. They are sly, occasionally vicious, pathologically stupid. The lenient shepherd may find his flock unruly, defiant. I cannot afford to be lenient. That is why, once a week, I allow myself this one indulgence. Your mouth is as closely sealed, *mon père*, as that of the confessional. Your ears are always open, your heart always kind. For an hour I can lay aside the burden. I can be fallible.

We have a new parishioner. A Vianne Rocher, a widow, I take it, with a young child. Do you remember old Blaireau's bakery? Four years since he died, and the place has been going to ruin ever since. Well, she has taken the lease on it, and hopes to reopen by the end of the week. I don't expect it to last. We already have Poitou's bakery across the square, and, besides, she'll never fit in. A pleasant enough woman, but she has nothing in common with us. Give her two months, and she'll be back to the city where she belongs. Funny, I never did find out where she was from. Paris, I expect, or maybe even across the border. Her accent is pure, almost too pure for a Frenchwoman, with the clipped vowels of the North, though her eyes suggest Italian or Portuguese descent, and her skin . . . But I didn't really see her. She worked in the bakery all yesterday and today. There is a sheet of orange plastic over the window, and occasionally she or her little wild daughter appears to tip a bucket of dirty water into the gutter, or to talk animatedly with some workman or other. She has an odd facility for acquiring helpers. Though I offered to assist her, I doubted whether she would find many of our villagers willing. And yet I saw Clairmont early this morning, carrying a load of wood, then Pourceau with his ladders. Poitou sent some furniture; I saw him carrying an armchair across the square with the furtive look of a man who does not wish to be seen. Even that ill-tempered backbiter Narcisse, who flatly refused to dig over the churchyard last November, went over there with his tools to tidy up her garden. This morning at about eight-forty a delivery van arrived in front of the shop. Duplessis, who was walking his dog at the usual time, was just passing at that moment, and she called him over to help her unload. I could see he was startled by the request – for a second I was almost certain he would refuse – one hand halfway to his hat. She said something then – I didn't hear what it was – and I heard her laughter ringing across the cobbles. She laughs a great deal, and makes many extravagant, comical gestures with her arms. Again a city trait, I suppose. We are accustomed to a greater reserve in the people around us, but I expect she means well. A violet scarf was knotted gypsy-fashion around her head, but most of her hair had escaped from beneath it and was streaked with white paint. She didn't seem to mind. Duplessis could not recall later what she had said to him, but said in his diffident way that the delivery was nothing, only a few boxes, small but quite heavy, and some open crates containing kitchen utensils. He did not ask what was in the boxes, though he doubts such a small supply of anything would go very far in a bakery.

Do not imagine, *mon père*, that I spent my day watching the bakery. It is simply that it stands almost immediately opposite my own house – the one which was yours, *mon père*, before all this. Throughout the last day and a half there has been nothing but hammering and painting and whitewashing and scrubbing until in spite of myself I cannot help but be curious to see the result. I am not alone in this; I overheard Madame Clairmont gossiping self-importantly to a group of friends outside Poitou's of her husband's work; there was talk of *red shutters* before they noticed me and subsided into sly muttering. As if I cared. The new arrival has certainly provided food for gossip, if nothing else. I find the orange-covered window catches the eye at the strangest times. It looks like a huge bonbon waiting to be unwrapped, like a remaining slice of the carnival. There is something unsettling about its brightness and the way the plastic folds catch the sun; I will be happy when the work is finished and the place is a bakery once more.

The nurse is trying to catch my eye. She thinks I tire you. How can you bear them, with their loud voices and nursery manner? *Time for our rest, now, I think.* Her archness is jarring, unbearable. And yet she means kindly, your eyes tell me. *Forgive them, they know not what they do.* I am not kind. I come here for my own relief, not yours. And yet I like to believe my visits give you pleasure, keeping you in touch with the hard edges of a world gone soft and featureless. Television an hour a night, turning five times a day, food through a tube. To be talked over as if you were an object – *Can he hear us? Do you think he understands?* – your opinions unsought, discarded ... To be closed from everything, and yet to feel, to think. This is the truth of hell, stripped of its gaudy mediaevalisms. This loss of contact. And yet I look to you to teach me communication. Teach me hope.

4

𝔉𝔯𝔦𝔡𝔞𝔶, 𝔉𝔢𝔟𝔯𝔲𝔞𝔯𝔶 14
𝔖𝔱 𝔙𝔞𝔩𝔢𝔫𝔱𝔦𝔫𝔢

THE DOG-MAN'S NAME IS GUILLAUME. HE HELPED ME WITH the delivery yesterday and he was my first customer this morning. He had his dog, Charly, with him, and he greeted me with a shy politeness which was almost courtly.

'It looks wonderful,' he said, looking around. 'You must have been up all night doing this.'

I laughed.

'It's quite a transformation,' said Guillaume. 'You know, I'm not sure why, but I'd just assumed it was going to be another bakery.'

'What, and ruin poor Monsieur Poitou's trade? I'm sure he'd thank me for that, with his lumbago playing up the way it is, and his poor wife an invalid and sleeping so badly.'

Guillaume bent to straighten Charly's collar, but I saw his eyes twinkle.

'I see you've met,' he said.

'Yes. I gave him my recipe for bedtime *tisane*.'

'If it works, he'll be a friend for life.'

'It works,' I assured him. Then, reaching under the counter I pulled out a small pink box with a silver valentine bow on it. 'Here. For you. My first customer.' Guillaume looked little startled.

'Really, Madame, I—'

'Call me Vianne. And I insist.' I pushed the box into his hands. 'You'll like them. They're your favourite kind.'

He smiled at that. 'How do you know?' he enquired, tucking the box carefully into his coat pocket.

'Oh, I can just tell,' I told him mischievously. 'I know *everyone*'s favourite. Trust me, this is yours.'

The sign wasn't finished until about noon. Georges Clairmont came to hang it himself then, profusely apologetic at his lateness. The scarlet shutters look beautiful against the new whitewash and Narcisse, grumbling halfheartedly about the late frosts, brought some new geraniums from his nursery to put in my planters. I sent them both away with valentine boxes and similar expressions of bemused pleasure. After that, barring a few schoolchildren, I had few visitors. It is always the case when a new shop opens in such a small village; there is a strict code of behaviour governing such situations and people are reserved, pretending indifference though inwardly they burn with curiosity. An old lady ventured in, wearing the traditional black dress of the country widow. A man with dark, florid features bought three identical boxes without asking what was inside. Then for hours, no-one came. It was what I expected; people need time to adapt to change, and though I caught several sharp glances at my display window, no-one seemed inclined to go in. Behind the studied unconcern however, I sensed a kind of seething, a whispering of speculation, a twitching of curtains, gathering of resolve. When at last they came, it was together; seven or eight women, Caroline Clairmont, wife of the signmaker, amongst them. A ninth, arriving somewhat behind the group, remained outside, her face almost touching the window, and I recognized the woman in the tartan coat.

The ladies eyed everything, giggling like schoolgirls, hesitant, delighting in their collective naughtiness.

'And do you make them all yourself?' asked Cécile, who owns the pharmacy on the main street.

'I should be giving it up for Lent,' commented Caroline, a plump blonde with a fur collar.

'I won't tell a soul,' I promised. Then, observing the woman in the tartan coat still gazing into the window, 'Won't your friend join us?'

'Oh, she isn't with us,' replied Joline Drou, a sharp-featured woman who works at the local school. She glanced briefly at the square-faced woman at the window. 'That's Joséphine Muscat.' There was a kind of pitying contempt in her voice as she pronounced the name. 'I doubt she'll come in.'

As if she had heard, I saw Joséphine redden slightly, lowering her head against the breast of her coat. One hand was drawn up against her stomach in an odd, protective gesture. I could see her mouth, perpetually downturned, moving slightly, in the rhythms of prayer or cursing.

I served the ladies – a white box, gold ribbon, two paper *cornets*, a rose, a pink valentine bow – amidst exclamations and laughter. Outside Joséphine Muscat muttered and rocked and dug her large ungainly fists into her stomach. Then, just as I was serving the last customer she raised her head in a kind of defiance and walked in. This last order was a large and rather complicated one. Madame wanted *just* such a selection, in a round box, with ribbons and flowers and golden hearts and a calling card left blank – at this the ladies turned up their eyes in roguish ecstasy, *hihihihi!* – so that I almost missed the moment. The large hands are surprisingly nimble, rough quick hands reddened with housework. One stays lodged in the pit of the stomach, the other flutters briefly at her side like a gunslinger's swift draw, and the little silver packet with the rose – marked ten francs – has gone from the shelf and into the pocket of her coat.

Nice work. I pretended not to notice until the ladies had left the shop with their parcels. Joséphine, left alone in front of the counter, pretended to examine the display, turned over a couple of boxes with nervous, careful fingers. I closed my eyes. The thoughts she sent me were complex, troubling. A rapid series of images flickered through my mind: smoke, a handful of gleaming trinkets, a bloodied knuckle. Behind it all a jittering undercurrent of worry.

'Madame Muscat, may I help you?' My voice was soft and pleasant. 'Or would you just like to look around?'

She muttered something inaudible, turned as if to leave.

'I think I may have something you'll like.' I reached under the counter and brought out a silver packet similar to the one I had seen her take, though this one was larger. A white ribbon secured the package, sewn with tiny yellow flowers. She looked at me, her wide unhappy mouth drooping with a kind of panic. I pushed the packet across the counter towards her.

'On the house, Joséphine,' I told her gently. 'It's all right. They're your favourites.'

Joséphine Muscat turned and fled.

5

Saturday, February 15

I KNOW THIS ISN'T MY USUAL DAY, *MON PÈRE*. BUT I NEEDED to talk. The bakery opened yesterday. But it isn't a bakery. When I awoke yesterday morning at six the wrapping was off, the awning and the shutters were in place and the blind was raised in the display window. What was an ordinary, rather drab old house like all the others around it has become a red-and-gold confection on a dazzling white ground. Red geraniums in the window boxes. Crêpe-paper garlands twisted around the railings. And above the door a hand-lettered sign in black on oak:

La Céleste Praline
Chocolaterie Artisanale

Of course it's ridiculous. Such a shop might well be

popular in Marseille or Bordeaux – even in Agen where the tourist trade grows every year. But in Lansquenet-sous-Tannes? And at the beginning of Lent, the traditional season of self-denial? It seems perverse, perhaps deliberately so. I looked into the display window this morning. On a white marble shelf are aligned innumerable boxes, packages, *cornets* of silver and gold paper, rosettes, bells, flowers, hearts and long curls of multicoloured ribbon. In glass bells and dishes lie the chocolates, the pralines, Venus's nipples, truffles, *mendiants*, candied fruits, hazelnut clusters, chocolate seashells, candied rose-petals, sugared violets . . . Protected from the sun by the half-blind which shields them, they gleam darkly, like sunken treasure, Aladdin's cave of sweet clichés. And in the middle she has built a magnificent centrepiece. A gingerbread house, walls of chocolate-coated *pain d'épices* with the detail piped on in silver and gold icing, roof tiles of florentines studded with crystallized fruits, strange vines of icing and chocolate growing up the walls, marzipan birds singing in chocolate trees . . . And the witch herself, dark chocolate from the top of her pointed hat to the hem of her long cloak, half-astride a broomstick which is in reality a giant *guimauve*, the long twisted marshmallows that dangle from the stalls of sweet-vendors on carnival days. From my own window I can see hers, like an eye closing in a sly, conspiratorial wink. Caroline Clairmont broke her Lenten vow because of that shop and what it sells. She told me in the confessional yesterday, in that breathless girlish tone which goes so ill with her promises of repentance.

'Oh, *mon père*, I feel so dreadful about it! But what could I do when that *charming* woman was so sweet? I mean, I never even *thought* about it until it was too late, though if there's anyone who should give up chocolates ... I mean, the way my hips have absolutely *ballooned* in the last year or two, it makes me want to *die*—'

'Two *Avés*.' God, that woman. Through the grille I can feel her hungry, adoring eyes. She feigns chagrin at my abruptness.

'Of course, *mon père*.'

'And remember why we fast for Lent. Not for vanity. Not to impress our friends. Not so that we can fit into next summer's expensive fashions.' I am deliberately brutal. It is what she wants.

'Yes, I *am* vain, aren't I?' A tiny sob, a tear, blotted delicately with the corner of a lawn handkerchief. 'Just a vain, foolish woman.'

'Remember Our Lord. His sacrifice. His humility.' I can smell her perfume, something flowery, too strong in this enclosed darkness. I wonder whether this is temptation. If so, I am stone.

'Four *Avés*.'

It is a kind of despair. It frets at the soul, reduces it piece by piece, as a cathedral may be levelled over the years by the erosion of flying dust and fragments of sand. I can feel it chipping away at my resolve, my joy, my faith. I should like to lead them through tribulation, through wilderness. Instead, this. This languid procession of liars, cheats, gluttons and pathetic self-deceivers. The battle of good and evil reduced to a fat woman standing in front of a chocolate shop, saying, *'Will I? Won't I?'* in pitiful indecision. The devil is a coward; he will not show his face. He is without substance, breaking into a million pieces which worm their evil ways into the blood, into the soul. You and I were born too late, *mon père*. The harsh, clean world of the Old Testament calls to me. We knew then where we stood. Satan walked amongst us in flesh. We made difficult decisions; we sacrificed our children in the Lord's name. We loved God, but we feared Him more.

Don't think I blame Vianne Rocher. Indeed I hardly think of her at all. She is only one of the influences against which I must fight every day. But the thought of that shop with its carnival awning, a wink against denial, against faith . . . Turning from the doorway to receive the congregation I catch a movement from within. *Try me. Test me. Taste me.* In a lull between the verses of a hymn I hear the delivery-van's horn as it pulls up in front. During the sermon – the very sermon, *mon père!* – I stop mid-phrase, certain I hear the rustle of sweet-papers.

I preached with greater severity than usual this morning, though the congregation was small. Tomorrow I'll make them pay. Tomorrow, Sunday, when the shops are closed.

6

Saturday, February 15

SCHOOL FINISHED EARLY TODAY. BY TWELVE THE STREET was rampant with cowboys and Indians in bright anoraks and denim jeans, dragging their schoolbags – the older ones dragging on illicit cigarettes, with turned-up collars and half a nonchalant eye to the display window as they pass. I noticed one boy walking alone, very correct in grey overcoat and beret, his school *cartable* perfectly squared to his small shoulders. For a long moment he stared in at the window of La Céleste Praline, but the light was shining on the glass in such a way that I did not catch his expression. Then a group of four children of Anouk's age stopped outside, and he moved on. Two noses snubbed briefly against the window, then the children retreated into a cluster as the four emptied pockets and pooled resources. A moment of hesitation as they decided who to send in. I pretended to be occupied with something behind the counter.

'Madame?' A small, smudgy face peered suspiciously up at me. I recognized the wolf from the Mardi Gras parade.

'Now, I have you down as a peanut brittle man.' I kept my face serious, for this purchase of sweets is serious business. 'It's good value, easy to share, doesn't melt in your pockets and you can get' – I indicated with hands held apart – 'oh, this much at least for five francs. Am I right?'

No answering smile, but a nod, as of one businessman to another. The coin was warm and a little sticky. He took the packet with care.

'I like the little gingerbread house,' he said gravely. 'In the window.' In the doorway the three others nodded shyly, pressing together as if to give themselves courage. 'It's *cool*.' The American word was uttered with a kind of defiance, like smoke from a secret cigarette. I smiled.

'Very cool,' I agreed. 'If you like, you and your friends can come over and help me eat it when I take it down.'

Eyes widened.

'Cool!'

'*Hypercool!*'

'When?'

I shrugged. 'I'll tell Anouk to remind you,' I told them. 'That's my little girl.'

'We know. We saw her. She doesn't go to school.' This last was uttered with some envy.

'She will on Monday. It's a pity she doesn't have any friends yet, because I told her she could ask them over. You know, to help me with the displays.' Feet shuffled, sticky hands held out, shoving and pushing to be first in line.

'We can—'

'*I* can—'

'I'm Jeannot—'

'Claudine—'

'Lucie.'

I sent them out with a sugar mouse each and watched them fan across the square like dandelion seeds in the wind. A slice of sunlight glanced off their backs one after the other as they ran – red-orange-green-blue – then they were gone. From the shaded arch of St Jérôme's I saw the priest, Francis Reynaud, watching them with a look of curiosity and, I thought, disapproval. I felt a moment's surprise. Why should he disapprove? Since his duty visit on our first day he has not called again, though I have heard of him often from other people. Guillaume speaks of him with respect, Narcisse with temper, Caroline with that archness which I sense she adopts when speaking of any man under fifty. There is little warmth in their speech. He is not a local, I understand. A Paris seminarian, all his learning from books – he does not

33

know the land, its needs, its demands. This from Narcisse, who has had a running feud with the priest ever since he refused to attend Mass during the harvesting season. A man who does not suffer fools, says Guillaume, with that small gleam of humour from behind his round spectacles, that is to say so many of us, with our foolish little habits and our unbreakable routines. He pats Charly's head affectionately as he says it, and the dog gives his single, solemn bark.

'He thinks it's ridiculous to be so devoted to a dog,' said Guillaume ruefully. 'He's far too polite to say so, but he thinks it's – *inappropriate*. A man of my age . . .' Before his retirement Guillaume was a master at the local school. There are only two teachers there now to deal with the falling numbers, though many of the older people still refer to Guillaume as *le maître d'école*. I watch as he scratches Charly gently behind the ears, and I am sure I sense the sadness I saw in him at the carnival; a furtive look which is almost guilt.

'A man of any age can choose his friends where he likes,' I interrupted with some heat. 'Perhaps monsieur le curé could learn a few things from Charly himself.' Again that sweet, sad almost-smile.

'Monsieur le curé tries his best,' he told me gently. 'We should not expect more.'

I did not answer. In my profession it is a truth quickly learned that the process of giving is without limits.

Guillaume left La Praline with a small bag of florentines in his pocket; before he had turned the corner of Avenue des Francs Bourgeois I saw him stoop to offer one to the dog. A pat, a bark, a wagging of the short stubby tail. As I said, some people never have to think about giving.

The village is less strange to me now. Its inhabitants too. I am beginning to know faces, names; the first secret skeins of histories twisting together to form the umbilical which will eventually bind us. It is a more complex place than its geography at first suggests, the Rue Principale forking off into a hand-shaped branch of laterals – Rue des Poètes, Avenue des Francs Bourgeois, Ruelle des Frères de la Révolution – someone amongst the town planners had a fierce republican streak. My own square, Place Saint-Jérôme, is the culmination of these reaching fingers, the church standing white and proud in an oblong of linden trees, the square of red shingle where the old men play *pétanque* on fine evenings. Behind it, the hill falls away sharply towards that region of narrow streets collectively called Les Marauds. This is Lansquenet's tiny slum, close half-timbered houses staggering down the uneven cobbles towards the Tannes. Even there it is some distance before the houses give way to marshland; some are built on the river itself on platforms of rotting wood, dozens flank the stone embankment, long fingers of damp reaching towards their small high windows from the sluggish water. In a town like Agen, Les Marauds would attract tourists for its quaintness and rustic decay. But here there are no tourists. The people of Les Marauds are scavengers, living from what they can reclaim from the river. Many of their houses are derelict; elder trees grow from the sagging walls. I closed La Praline for two hours at lunch and Anouk and I went walking down towards the river. A couple of skinny children dabbled in the green mud by the waterside; even in February there was a mellow stink of sewage and rot. It was cold but sunny, and Anouk was wearing her red woollen coat and hat, racing along the stones and shouting to Pantoufle scampering in her wake. I have become so accustomed to Pantoufle – and to the rest of the strange menagerie which she trails in her bright wake – that at such times I can almost see him clearly; Pantoufle with his grey-whiskered face and wise eyes, the world suddenly brightening as if by a strange transference I have *become* Anouk, seeing with her eyes, following where she travels. At such times I feel I could die for love of her, my little stranger; my heart swelling dangerously so that the only release is to run too, my red coat flapping around my shoulders like wings, my hair a comet's tail in the patchy blue sky.

A black cat crossed my path and I stopped to dance around it widdershins and to sing the rhyme:

Où va-t-i, mistigri?

Passe sans faire de mal ici.

Anouk joined in and the cat purred, rolling over into the dust to be stroked. I bent down and saw a tiny old woman watching me curiously from the angle of a house. Black skirt, black coat, grey hair coiled and plaited into a neat, complex bun. Her eyes were sharp and black as a bird's. I nodded to her.

'You're from the *chocolaterie*,' she said. Despite her age – which I took to be eighty, maybe more – her voice was brisk and strongly accented with the rough lilt of the *Midi*.

'Yes, I am.' I gave my name.

'Armande Voizin,' she said. 'That's my house over there.' She nodded towards one of the river-houses, this one in better repair than the rest, freshly whitewashed and with scarlet geraniums in the window boxes. Then, with a smile which worked her apple-doll face into a million wrinkles, she said, 'I've seen your shop. Pretty enough, I'll grant you that, but no good to folks like us. Much too fancy.' There was no disapproval in her voice as she spoke, but a half-laughing fatalism. 'I hear our m'sieur le curé already has it in for you,' she added maliciously. 'I suppose he thinks a chocolate shop is *inappropriate* in his square.' She gave me another of those quizzical, mocking glances. 'Does he know you're a witch?' she asked.

Witch, witch. It's the wrong word, but I knew what she meant.

'What makes you think that?'

'Oh, it's obvious. Takes one to know one, I expect,' and she laughed, a sound like violins gone wild. 'M'sieur le Curé doesn't believe in magic,' she said. 'Tell you the truth, I wouldn't be so sure he even believes in God.' There was indulgent contempt in her voice. 'He has a lot to learn, that man, even if he has got a degree in theology. And my silly daughter too. You don't get degrees in *life*, do you?' I agreed that you didn't, and enquired whether I knew her daughter.

'I expect so. Caro Clairmont. The most empty-headed piece of foolishness in all of Lansquenet. Talk, talk, talk, and not a particle of sense.'

She saw my smile and nodded cheerily. 'Don't worry, dear, at my age nothing much offends me any more. And she takes after her father, you know. That's a great consolation.' She looked at me quizzically. 'You don't get much entertainment around here,' she observed. 'Especially if you're old.' She paused and peered at me again. 'But with you I think maybe we're in for a little amusement.' Her hand brushed mine like a cool breath. I tried to catch her thoughts, to see if she was making fun of me, but all I felt was humour and kindness.

'It's only a chocolate shop,' I said with a smile.

Armande Voizin chuckled. 'You really must think I was born yesterday,' she observed.

'Really, Madame Voizin—'

'Call me Armande.' The black eyes snapped with amusement. 'It makes me feel young.'

'All right. But I really don't see why—'

'I know what wind you blew in on,' said Armande keenly. 'I felt it. Mardi Gras, carnival day. Les Marauds was full of carnival people; gypsies, Spaniards, tinkers, *pieds-noirs* and undesirables. I knew you at once, you and your little girl – what are you calling yourselves this time?'

'Vianne Rocher.' I smiled. 'And this is Anouk.'

'Anouk,' repeated Armande softly. 'And the little grey friend – my eyes aren't as good as they used to be – what is it? A cat? A squirrel?'

Anouk shook her curly head. 'He's a *rabbit*,' she said with cheery scorn. 'Called Pantoufle.'

'Oh, a rabbit. Of course.' Armande gave me a sly wink. 'You see, I know what wind you blew in on. I've felt it myself once or twice. I may be old, but no-one can pull the wool over my eyes. No-one at all.'

I nodded. 'Maybe that's true,' I said. 'Come over to La Praline one day; I know everyone's favourite. I'll treat you to a big box of yours.'

Armande laughed. 'Oh, I'm not allowed *chocolate*. Caro and that idiot doctor won't allow it. Or anything else I might enjoy,' she added wryly. 'First smoking, then alcohol, now this . . . God knows, if I gave up breathing perhaps I might live for ever.' She gave a snort of laughter, but it had a tired sound, and I saw her raise a hand to her chest in a clutching gesture eerily reminiscent of Joséphine Muscat. 'I'm not blaming them, exactly,' she said. 'It's just their way. Protection – from everything. From life. From death.' She gave a grin which was suddenly very gamine in spite of the wrinkles.

'I might call in to see you anyway,' she said. 'If only to annoy the *curé*.'

I pondered her last remark for some time after she disappeared behind the angle of the whitewashed house. Some distance away Anouk was throwing stones onto the mud flats at the riverbank.

The *curé*. It seemed his name was never far from the lips. For a moment I considered Francis Reynaud.

In a place like Lansquenet it sometimes happens that one person – schoolteacher, café proprietor, or priest – forms the lynchpin of the community. That this single individual is the essential core of the machinery which turns lives, like the central pin of a clock mechanism, sending wheels to turn wheels, hammers to strike, needles to point the hour. If the pin slips or is damaged, the clock stops. Lansquenet is like that clock, needles perpetually frozen at a minute to midnight, wheels and cogs turning uselessly behind the bland blank face. Set a church clock wrong to fool the devil, my mother always told me. But in this case I suspect the devil is not fooled. Not for a minute.

7

Sunday, February 16

MY MOTHER WAS A WITCH. AT LEAST, THAT'S WHAT SHE called herself, falling so many times into the game of believing herself that at the end there was no telling fake from fact. Armande Voizin reminds me of her in some ways; the bright, wicked eyes, the long hair which must have been glossy black in her youth, the blend of wistfulness and cynicism. From her I learned what shaped me. The art of turning bad luck into good. The forking of the fingers to divert the path of malchance. The sewing of a sachet, brewing of a draught, the conviction that a spider brings good luck before midnight and bad luck after. Most of all she gave me her love of new places, the gypsy wanderlust which took us all over Europe and further; a year in Budapest, another in Prague, six months in Rome, four in Athens, then across the Alps to Monaco, along the coast, Cannes, Marseille, Barcelona ... By my eighteenth year I had lost count of the cities in which we had lived, the languages we had spoken. Jobs were as varied; waitressing, interpreting, car repair. Sometimes we escaped from the windows of cheap overnight hotels without paying the bill. We rode trains without tickets, forged work permits, crossed borders illicitly. We were deported countless times. Twice my mother was arrested, but released without charge. Our names changed as we moved, drifting from one regional variant to another; Yanne, Jeanne, Johanne, Giovanna, Anne, Anouchka. Like thieves we were perpetually on the run, converting the unwieldy ballast of life into francs, pounds, kroner, dollars, as we fled where the wind took us. Don't think I suffered; life was a fine adventure for those years. We had each other, my mother and I. I never felt the need for a father. My friends were countless. And yet it must have preyed upon her sometimes, the lack of permanence, the need always to contrive. Still we raced faster as the years wore on, staying a month, two at the most, then moving on like fugitives racing the sunset. It took me some years to understand that it was death we fled.

She was forty. It was cancer. She'd known for some time, she told me, but recently ... No, there was to be no hospital. No hospital, did I understand? There were months, years left in her and she wanted to see America: New York, the Florida Everglades. We were moving almost every day now, Mother reading the cards at night when she thought I was asleep. We boarded a cruiser from Lisbon, both of us working in the kitchens. Finishing at two or three every morning, we rose at dawn. Every night the cards, slippery to the touch with age and respectful handling, were laid out on the bunk beside her. She whispered their names to herself, sinking deeper every day into the mazy confusion which would eventually claim her altogether.

Ten of Swords, death. Three of Swords, death. Two of Swords, death. The Chariot. Death.

The Chariot turned out to be a New York cab one summer evening as we shopped for groceries in the busy Chinatown streets. It was better than cancer, in any case.

When my daughter was born nine months later I called her after both of us. It seemed appropriate. Her father never knew her – nor am I sure which one he was in the wilting daisy-chain of my brief encounters. It doesn't matter. I could have peeled an apple at midnight and thrown the rind over my shoulder to know his initial, but I never cared enough to do it. Too much ballast slows us down.

And yet . . . Since I left New York, haven't the winds blown less hard, less often? Hasn't there been a kind of wrench every time we leave a place, a kind of regret? I think there has. Twenty-five years, and at last the spring has begun to grow tired, just as my mother grew tired in the final years. I find myself looking at the sun and wondering what it would be like to see it rise above the same horizon for five – maybe ten, maybe twenty – years. The thought fills me with a strange dizziness, a feeling of fear and longing. And Anouk, my little stranger? I see the brave adventure we lived for so long in a different light now that I am the mother. I see myself as I was, the brown girl with the long uncombed hair, wearing cast-off charity-shop clothing, learning maths the hard way, geography the hard way – *How much bread for two francs? How far will a fifty-mark rail ticket take us?* – and I do not want it for her. Perhaps this is why we have stayed in France for the last five years. For the first time in my life, I have a bank account. I have a trade.

My mother would have despised all this. And yet perhaps she would have envied me too. *Forget yourself if you can*, she would have told me. *Forget who you are. For as long as you can bear it. But one day, my girl, one day it will catch you. I know.*

I opened as usual today. For the morning only – I'll allow myself a half-day with Anouk this afternoon – but it's Mass this morning and there will be people in the square. February has reasserted its drab self and now it is raining; a freezing, gritty rain which slicks the paving and colours the sky the shade of old pewter. Anouk reads a book of nursery rhymes behind the counter and keeps an eye on the door for me as I prepare a batch of *mendiants* in the kitchen. These are my own favourites – thus named because they were sold by beggars and gypsies years ago – biscuit-sized discs of dark, milk or white chocolate upon which have been scattered lemon-rind, almonds and plump Malaga raisins. Anouk likes the white ones, though I prefer the dark, made with the finest 70 per cent couverture ... Bitter-smooth on the tongue with the taste of the secret tropics. My mother would have despised this, too. And yet this is also a kind of magic.

Since Friday I have fitted a set of bar stools next to the counter of La Praline. Now it looks a little like the diners we used to visit in New York, red leather seats and chrome stems, cheerily kitsch. The walls are a bright daffodil colour. Poitou's old orange armchair lolls cheerily in one corner. A menu stands to the left, hand-lettered and coloured by Anouk in shades of orange and red:

chocolat chaud 10F
chocolat espresso 15F
chococcino 12F
mocha 12F

I baked a cake last night, and the hot chocolate is standing in a pot on the hob, awaiting my first customer. I make sure that a similar menu is visible from the window and I wait.

Mass comes and goes. I watch the passers-by, morose beneath the freezing drizzle. My door, slightly open, emits a hot scent of baking and sweetness. I catch a number of longing glances at the source of this, but a flick of the eye backwards, a shrugging of the shoulders, a twist of the mouth which may be resolve or simply temper, and they are gone, leaning into the wind with rounded, miserable shoulders, as if an angel with a flaming sword were standing at the door to bar their entry.

Time, I tell myself. This kind of thing takes time. But all the same, a kind of impatience, almost anger, penetrates me. What is wrong with these people? Why do they not come? Ten o'clock sounds, then eleven. I can see people going into the bakery opposite and coming out again with loaves tucked under their arms. The rain stops, though the sky remains grim. Eleven-thirty. The few people who still linger in the square turn homewards to prepare the Sunday meal. A boy with a dog skirts the corner of the church, carefully avoiding the dripping guttering. He walks past with barely a glance.

Damn them. Just when I thought I was beginning to get through. Why do they not come? Can they not see, not *smell*? What else do I have to do?

Anouk, always sensitive to my moods, comes to hug me. '*Maman*, don't cry.'

I am not crying. I never cry. Her hair tickles my face, and I feel suddenly dizzy with the fear that one day I might lose her.

'It isn't your fault. We tried. We did everything right.'

True enough. Even to the red ribbons around the door, the sachets of cedar and lavender to repel bad influences. I kiss her head. There is moisture on my face. Something, perhaps the bittersweet aroma of the chocolate vapour, stings my eyes.

'It's all right, *chérie*. What they do shouldn't affect us. We can at least have a drink to cheer ourselves up.'

We perch on our stools like New York barflies, a cup of chocolate each. Anouk has hers with *crème Chantilly* and chocolate curls; I drink mine hot and black, stronger than *espresso*. We close our eyes in the fragrant steam and *see* them coming – two, three, a dozen at a time, their faces lighting up, sitting beside us, their hard, indifferent faces melting into expressions of welcome and delight. I open my eyes quickly and Anouk is standing by the door. For a second I can see Pantoufle perched on her shoulder, whiskers twitching. The light behind her seems warmer somehow; altered. Alluring.

I jump to my feet.

'Please. Don't do that.'

She gives me one of her darkling glances. 'I was only trying to *help*—'

'Please.' For a second she faces me out, her face set stubbornly. Glamours swim between us like golden smoke. It would be so easy, she tells me with her eyes, so easy, like invisible fingers stroking, inaudible voices coaxing the people in . . .

'We can't. We shouldn't.' I try to explain to her. It sets us apart. It makes us different. If we are to stay we must be as like them as possible. Pantoufle looks up at me in appeal, a whiskery blur against the golden shadows. Deliberately I close my eyes against him, and when I open them again, he is gone.

'It's all right,' I tell Anouk firmly. 'We'll be all right. We can wait.'

And finally, at twelve-thirty, someone comes.

Anouk saw him first – '*Maman!*' – but I was on my feet at once. It was Reynaud, one hand shielding his face from the dripping canvas of the awning, the other hesitating at the door handle. His pale face was serene, but there was something in his eyes . . . a furtive satisfaction. I somehow understood he was not a customer. The bell jangled as he entered, but he did not walk up to the counter. Instead he remained in the doorway, the wind blowing the folds of his soutane into the shop like the wings of a black bird.

'Monsieur.' I saw him eye the red ribbons with mistrust. 'Can I help you? I'm sure I know your favourites.' I lapsed into my sales banter automatically, but it is untrue. I have no idea of this man's tastes. He is a complete blank to me, a man-shaped darkness cut into the air. I feel no point of contact with him, and my smile broke on him like a wave on a rock. Reynaud gave me a narrow look of contempt.

'I doubt that.' His voice was low and pleasant, but I sensed dislike behind the professional tones. I recalled Armande Voizin's words – *I hear our M'sieur le Curé already has it in for you.* Why? An instinctive mistrust of unbelievers? Or can there be more? Beneath the counter I forked my fingers at him in secret.

'I wasn't expecting you to be open today.'

He is more sure of himself now he thinks he knows us. His small, tight smile is like an oyster, milky-white at the edges and sharp as a razor.

'On a Sunday, you mean?' I was at my most innocent. 'I thought I might catch the rush at the end of Mass.'

The tiny jibe failed to sting him.

'On the first Sunday of Lent?' He sounded amused, but beneath the amusement, there was disdain. 'I shouldn't think so. Lansquenet folk are simple folk, Madame Rocher,' he told me. '*Devout* folk.' He stressed the word gently, politely.

'It's *Mademoiselle* Rocher.' Small victory, but enough to

49

break his stride. His eyes flicked towards Anouk who was still sitting at the counter with the tall chocolate-glass in one hand. Her mouth was smeared with frothy chocolate, and I felt it again like the sudden sting of a concealed nettle – the panic, the irrational terror of losing her. But to whom? I shook the thought with growing anger. To *him*? Let him try.

'Of course,' he replied smoothly. 'Mademoiselle Rocher. I do apologize.'

I smiled sweetly at his disapproval. Something in me continued to court it, perversely; my voice, a shade too loud, took on a ring of vulgar self-confidence to hide my fear.

'It's so nice to meet someone in these rural parts who understands.' I flashed him my hardest, brightest smile. 'I mean, in the city, where we used to live, no-one gave us a thought. But here . . .' I managed to look contrite and unrepentant at the same time. 'I mean, it's absolutely lovely here, and the people have been so helpful . . . so *quaint* . . . But it isn't Paris, is it?'

Reynaud agreed – with the tiniest of sneers – that it wasn't.

'It's *quite* true what they say about village communities,' I went on. '*Everyone* wants to know your business! I expect it comes of having so little entertainment,' I explained kindly. 'Three shops and a church. I mean—' I broke off with a giggle. 'But of course you know all that.'

Reynaud nodded gravely. 'Perhaps you could explain to me, Mademoiselle . . .'

'Oh, do call me Vianne,' I interrupted.

'. . . why you decided to move to Lansquenet?' His tone was silken with dislike, his thin mouth more like a closed oyster than ever. 'As you say, it's a little different to Paris.' His eyes made it clear that it was a difference entirely in Lansquenet's favour. 'A boutique like this' – an elegant hand indicated the shop and its contents with languid indifference – 'surely such a specialist shop would be more successful – more *appropriate* – in a city? I'm sure that in Toulouse or even Agen . . .' I knew now why no customers had dared to come this morning. That word – *appropriate* – held all the glacial condemnation of a prophet's curse.

I forked at him again, savagely, under the counter. Reynaud slapped at the back of his neck, as if an insect had stung him there.

'I don't think the cities have the franchise on enjoy-ment,' I snapped. 'Everyone needs a little luxury, a little self-indulgence from time to time.'

Reynaud did not reply. I suppose he disagreed. I said as much. 'I expect you preached exactly the opposite doctrine in your sermon this morning?' I ventured boldly. Then, as he still did not answer, 'Still, I'm sure there's room enough in this town for both of us. Free enterprise, isn't that right?'

Looking at his expression I could see he understood the

challenge. For a moment I held his gaze, making myself brazen, hateful. Reynaud flinched back from my smile as if I had spat in his face.

Softly, 'Of course.'

Oh, I know his type. We saw them enough, Mother and I, on our chase around Europe. The same polite smiles, the disdain, the indifference. A small coin dropped from the plump hand of a woman outside Rheims' crowded cathedral; admonishing looks from a group of nuns as a young Vianne leaps to grab it, bare knees scuffing the dusty floor. A black-frocked man in angry, earnest conversation with my mother; she running white-faced from the shadow of the church, squeezing my hand until it hurt . . . Later I learned she had tried to confess to him. What prompted her to do it? Loneliness, perhaps; the need to talk, to confide in someone who was not a lover. Someone with an understanding face. But didn't she *see*? His face, now not so understanding, contorted in angry frustration. It was sin, mortal *sin* . . . She should leave the child in the care of good people. If she loved little – what was her name? Anne? If she loved her she must – *must* – make this sacrifice. He knew a convent where she could be cared for. He took her hand, crushing her fingers. Didn't she love her child? Didn't she want to be saved? Didn't she? Didn't she?

That night my mother wept, rocking me to and fro in her arms. We left Rheims in the morning, more like thieves than ever, she carrying me close like stolen treasure, her eyes hot and furtive.

I understood he had almost convinced her to leave me behind. After that she often asked me if I was happy with her, whether I missed having friends, a home ... But however often I told her yes, no, no, however often I kissed her and said I regretted nothing, *nothing*, a little of the poison remained. For years we ran from the priest, the Black Man, and when his face returned time and again in the cards it would be time to run once more, time to hide from the darkness he had opened in her heart.

And here he is again, just as I thought we had found our place at last, Anouk and I. Standing at the door like the angel at the gate.

Well, this time, I swear I will not run. Whatever he does. However he turns the people of this place against me. His face is as smooth and certain as the turn of an evil card. And he has declared himself my enemy – and I his – as clearly as if we had both spoken aloud.

'I'm so glad we understand each other.' My voice is bright and cold.

'And I.'

Something in his eyes, some light where there was none before, alerts me. Amazingly, he is *enjoying* this, this closing of two enemies for battle; nowhere in his armoured certainty is there room for the thought that he might not win.

He turns to go, very correct, with just the right inclination of the head. Just so. Polite contempt. The barbed and poisonous weapon of the righteous.

'M'sieur le Curé!' For a second he turns back, and I press a small beribboned packet into his hands. 'For you. On the house.' My smile brooks no refusal, and he takes the packet with bemused embarrassment. 'My pleasure.'

He frowns slightly, as if the thought of my pleasure pains him. 'But I don't really like—'

'Nonsense.' The tone is brisk, unanswerable. 'I'm sure you'll like these. They just remind me so much of you.'

Behind his calm exterior I think he looks startled. Then he is gone, the little packet white in his hand, into the grey rain. I notice that he does not run for shelter but walks with the same measured tread, not indifferent but with the look of one who relishes even that small discomfort.

I like to think he will eat the chocolates. More probably he will give them away, but I like to think he will at least open them and look . . . Surely he can spare one glance for the sake of curiosity.

They remind me so much of you.

A dozen of my best *huîtres de Saint-Malo*, those small flat pralines shaped to look like tightly closed oysters.

8

Tuesday, February 18

FIFTEEN CUSTOMERS YESTERDAY. TODAY, THIRTY-FOUR. Guillaume was among them; he bought a *cornet* of florentines and a cup of chocolate. Charly was with him, curling obediently beneath a stool while, from time to time, Guillaume dropped a piece of brown sugar into his expectant, insatiable jaws.

It takes time, Guillaume tells me, for a newcomer to be accepted in Lansquenet. Last Sunday, he says, Curé Reynaud preached such a virulent sermon on the topic of abstinence that the opening of La Céleste Praline that very morning had seemed a direct affront against the Church. Caroline Clairmont – who is beginning another of her diets – was especially cutting, saying loudly to her friends in the congregation that it was *Quite shocking, just like stories of Roman decadence, my dears, and if that woman*

*thinks she can just shimmy into town like the Queen of Sheba –
disgusting the way she flaunts that illegitimate child of hers as if
– oh, the chocolates? Nothing special, my dears, and far too
pricey.* The general conclusion amongst the ladies was that
'it' – whatever it was – wouldn't last. I would be out of
town within a fortnight. And yet, the number of my
customers has doubled since yesterday, amongst them a
number of Madame Clairmont's cronies, bright-eyed if a
little shameful, telling each other it was curiosity, that was
all, that all they wanted was to see for themselves.

I know all their favourites. It's a knack, a professional
secret like a fortune-teller reading palms. My mother
would have laughed at this waste of my skills, but I have
no desire to probe further into their lives than this. I do
not want their secrets or their innermost thoughts. Nor do
I want their fears or gratitude. A tame alchemist, she
would have called me with kindly contempt, working
domestic magic when I could have wielded marvels. But I
like these people. I like their small and introverted
concerns. I can read their eyes, their mouths, so easily:
this one with its hint of bitterness will relish my zesty
orange twists; this sweet-smiling one the soft-centred
apricot hearts; this girl with the windblown hair will love
the *mendiants*; this brisk, cheery woman the chocolate
brazils. For Guillaume, the florentines, eaten neatly over a
saucer in his tidy bachelor's house. Narcisse's appetite for
double-chocolate truffles reveals the gentle heart beneath

the gruff exterior. Caroline Clairmont will dream of cinder toffee tonight and wake hungry and irritable. And the children ... Chocolate curls, white buttons with coloured vermicelli, *pains d'épices* with gilded edging, marzipan fruits in their nests of ruffled paper, peanut brittle, clusters, cracknels, assorted misshapes in half-kilo boxes ... I sell dreams, small comforts, sweet harmless temptations to bring down a multitude of saints crash-crash-crashing amongst the hazels and nougatines.

Is that so bad?

Curé Reynaud thinks so, apparently.

'Here, Charly. Here boy.' Guillaume's voice is warm when he speaks to his dog, but always a little sad. He bought the animal when his father died, he tells me. That was eighteen years ago. But a dog's life is shorter than a man's, and they grew old together.

'It's here.' He brings my attention to a growth under Charly's chin. It is about the size of a hen's egg, gnarled like an elm burr. 'It's growing.' A pause during which the dog stretches luxuriously, one leg pedalling as his master scratches his belly. 'The vet says there's nothing to be done.'

I begin to understand the look of guilt and love I see in Guillaume's eyes.

'You wouldn't put an old *man* to sleep,' he tells me earnestly. 'Not if he still had' – he struggles for words – 'some quality of life. Charly doesn't suffer. Not really.' I nod, aware he is trying to convince himself. 'The drugs keep it under control.'

For the moment. The words ring out unspoken.

'When the time comes, I'll know.' His eyes are soft and horrified. 'I'll know what to do. I won't be afraid.' I top up his chocolate-glass without a word and sprinkle the froth with cocoa powder, but Guillaume is too busy with his dog to see. Charly rolls onto his back, head lolling.

'M'sieur le Curé says animals don't have souls,' says Guillaume softly. 'He says I should put Charly out of his misery.'

'Everything has a soul,' I answer. 'That's what my mother used to tell me. Everything.'

He nods, alone in his circle of fear and guilt. 'What would I do without him?' he asks, face still turned towards the dog, and I understand he has forgotten my presence. 'What would I do without you?'

Behind the counter I clench my fist in silent rage. I know that look – fear, guilt, covetousness – I know it well. It is the look on my mother's face the night of the Black Man. His words – *What would I do without you?* – are the words she whispered to me all through that miserable night. As I glance into my mirror last thing in the evening, as I awake with the growing fear – knowledge, certainty – that my own daughter is slipping away from me, that I am losing her, that I *will* lose her if I do not find The Place . . . it is the look on my own.

I put my arms around Guillaume. For a second he tenses, unused to female contact. Then he relaxes. I can feel the strength of his distress coming from him in waves.

'Vianne,' he says softly. 'Vianne.'

'It's all right to feel this way,' I tell him firmly. 'It's allowed.'

Beneath us, Charly barks his indignation.

We made close to three hundred francs today. For the first time, enough to break even. I told Anouk when she came home from school, but she looked distracted, her bright face unusually still. Her eyes were heavy, dark as the cloud-line of an oncoming storm.

I asked her what was wrong.

'It's Jeannot.' Her voice was toneless. 'His mother says he can't play with me any more.'

I remembered Jeannot as Wolf Suit in the Mardi Gras carnival, a lanky seven-year-old with shaggy hair and a suspicious expression. He and Anouk played together in the square last night, running and shouting arcane war cries, until the light failed. His mother is Joline Drou, one of the two primary teachers, a crony of Caroline Clairmont.

'Oh?' Neutrally. 'What does she say?'

'She says I'm a bad influence.' She flicked a dark glance at me. 'Because we don't go to church. Because you opened on Sunday.'

You opened on Sunday.

I looked at her. I wanted to take her in my arms, but her rigid, hostile stance alarmed me. I made my voice very calm.

'And what does Jeannot think?' I asked gently.

'He can't do anything. She's always there. Watching.' Anouk's voice rose shrilly and I guessed she was close to tears. 'Why does this always have to happen?' she demanded. 'Why don't I *ever*—' She broke off with an effort, her thin chest hitching.

'You have other friends.' It was true; there had been four or five of them last night, the square ringing with their catcalls and laughter.

'*Jeannot*'s friends.' I saw what she meant. Louis Clairmont. Lise Poitou. *His* friends. Without Jeannot the group would soon disperse. I felt a sudden pang for my daughter, surrounding herself with invisible friends to people the spaces around her. Selfish, to imagine that a mother could fill that space completely. Selfish and blind.

'We could go to church, if that's what you want.' My voice was gentle. 'But you know it wouldn't change anything.'

Accusingly, 'Why not? *They* don't believe. They don't care about God. They just go.'

I smiled then, not without some bitterness. Six years old, and she still manages to surprise me with the depth of her occasional perception.

'That may be true,' I said. 'But do *you* want to be like that?'

A shrug, cynical and indifferent. She shifted her weight from one foot to the other, as if in fear of a lecture. I searched for the words to explain. But all I could think of was the image of my mother's stricken face as she rocked me and murmured, almost fiercely, *What would I do without you? What would I do?*

Oh, I taught her all of this long ago; the hypocrisy of the Church, the witch-hunts, the persecution of travellers and people of other faiths. She understands. But the knowledge does not transpose well to everyday life, to the reality of loneliness, to the loss of a friend.

'It's not fair.' Her voice was still rebellious, the hostility subdued but not entirely.

Neither was the sack of the Holy Land, nor the burning of Joan of Arc, nor the Spanish Inquisition. But I knew better than to say so. Her features were pinched, intense; any sign of weakness and she would have turned on me.

'You'll find other friends.' A weak and comfortless answer. Anouk looked at me with disdain.

'But I wanted this one.' Her tone was strangely adult, strangely weary as she turned away. Tears swelled her eyelids, but she made no move to come to me for comfort. With a sudden overwhelming clarity I saw her then, the child, the adolescent, the adult, the stranger she would one day become, and I almost cried out in loss and terror, as if our positions had somehow been reversed, she the adult, I the child.

Please! What would I do without you?

But I let her go without a word, aching to hold her but too aware of the wall of privacy slamming down between us. Children are born wild, I know. The best I can hope for is a little tenderness, a seeming docility. Beneath the surface the wildness remains, stark, savage and alien.

She remained virtually silent for the rest of the evening. When I put her to bed she refused her story but stayed awake for hours after I had put out my own light. I heard her from the darkness of my room, walking to and fro, occasionally talking to herself – or to Pantoufle – in fierce staccato bursts too low for me to hear. Much later, when I was sure she was asleep, I crept into her room to switch off the light and found her, curled at the end of her bed, one arm flung wide, head turned at an awkward but absurdly touching angle that tore at my heart. In one hand she clutched a small Plasticine figure. I removed it as I straightened the bedclothes, meaning to return it to Anouk's toybox. It was still warm from her hand, releasing an unmistakable scent of primary school, of secrets whispered, of poster paint and newsprint and half-forgotten friends.

Six inches long, a stick figure painstakingly rendered, eyes and mouth scratched on with a pin, red thread wound about the waist and something – twigs or dried grass – stuck into the scalp to suggest shaggy brown hair.

There was a letter scratched into the Plasticine-boy's body, just above the heart; a neat capital J. Beneath it and just close enough to overlap, a letter A.

I replaced the figure softly on the pillow beside her head and left, putting out the light. Some time before dawn she crept into bed with me as she often had when she was a child, and through soft layers of sleep I heard her whisper, 'It's all right, *Maman*. I'll never leave you.'

She smelt of salt and baby soap, her hug fierce and warm in the enclosing dark. I rocked her, rocked myself, in sweetness, hugged us both in relief so intense that it was almost pain.

'I love you, *Maman*. I'll always love you for ever. Don't cry.'

I wasn't crying. I never cry.

I slept poorly inside a kaleidoscope of dreams; awoke at dawn with Anouk's arm across my face and a dreadful, panicky urge to run, to take Anouk and keep on running. How can we live here, how could we have been foolish enough to think he wouldn't find us even here? The Black Man has many faces, all of them unforgiving, hard and strangely envious. *Run, Vianne. Run, Anouk. Forget your small sweet dream and run.*

But not this time. We have run too far already, Anouk and I, Mother and I, too far from ourselves.

This is one dream I mean to cling to.

9

Wednesday, February 19

THIS IS OUR REST DAY. SCHOOL IS CLOSED AND, WHILE Anouk plays by Les Marauds, I will receive deliveries and work on this week's batch of items.

This is an art I can enjoy. There is a kind of sorcery in all cooking: in the choosing of ingredients, the process of mixing, grating, melting, infusing and flavouring, the recipes taken from ancient books, the traditional utensils – the pestle and mortar with which my mother made her incense turned to a more homely purpose, her spices and aromatics giving up their subtleties to a baser, more sensual magic. And it is partly the transience of it that delights me; so much loving preparation, so much art and experience put into a pleasure which can last only a moment, and which only a few will ever fully appreciate. My mother always viewed my interest with indulgent contempt. To her, food was no pleasure but a tiresome necessity to be worried over, a tax on the price of our freedom. I stole menus from restaurants and looked longingly into *pâtisserie* windows. I must have been ten years old – maybe older – before I first tasted real chocolate. But still the fascination endured. I carried recipes in my head like maps. All kinds of recipes; torn from abandoned magazines in busy railway stations, wheedled from people on the road, strange marriages of my own confection. Mother with her cards, her divinations directed our mad course across Europe. Cookery cards anchored us, placed landmarks on the bleak borders. Paris smells of baking bread and *croissants*; Marseille of *bouillabaisse* and grilled garlic. Berlin was *Eisbrei* with *Sauerkraut* and *Kartoffelsalat*, Rome was the ice-cream I ate without paying in a tiny restaurant beside the river. Mother had no time for landmarks. All her maps were inside, all places the same. Even then we were different. Oh, she taught me what she could. How to see to the core of things, of people, to see their thoughts, their longings. The driver who stopped to give us a lift, who drove ten kilometres out of his way to take us to Lyon, the grocers who refused payment, the policemen who turned a blind eye. Not every time, of course. Sometimes it failed for no reason we could understand. Some people are unreadable, unreachable. Francis Reynaud is one of these. And even when it did not, the casual intrusion disturbed me. It was all too easy. Now making chocolate is a different matter. Oh, some skill is required. A certain lightness of touch, speed, a patience my mother would never have had. But the formula remains the same every time. It is safe. Harmless. And I do not have to look into their hearts and take what I need; these are wishes which can be granted simply, for the asking.

Guy, my confectioner, has known me for a long time. We worked together after Anouk was born and he helped me to start my first business, a tiny *pâtisserie-chocolaterie* in the outskirts of Nice. Now he is based in Marseille, importing the raw chocolate liquor direct from South America and converting it to chocolate of various grades in his factory.

I only use the best. The blocks of couverture are slightly larger than house bricks, one box of each per delivery, and I use all three types: the dark, the milk and the white. It has to be tempered to bring it to its crystalline state, ensuring a hard, brittle surface and a good shine. Some confectioners buy their supplies already tempered, but I like to do it myself. There is an endless fascination in handling the raw dullish blocks of couverture, in grating them by hand – I never use electrical mixers – into the large ceramic pans, then melting, stirring, testing each painstaking step with the sugar thermometer until just the right amount of heat has been applied to make the change.

There is a kind of alchemy in the transformation of

base chocolate into this wise fool's gold, a layman's magic which even my mother might have relished. As I work I clear my mind, breathing deeply. The windows are open, and the through draught would be cold if it were not for the heat of the stoves, the copper pans, the rising vapour from the melting couverture. The mingled scents of chocolate, vanilla, heated copper and cinnamon are intoxicating, powerfully suggestive; the raw and earthy tang of the Americas, the hot and resinous perfume of the rainforest. This is how I travel now, as the Aztecs did in their sacred rituals. Mexico, Venezuela, Colombia. The court of Montezuma. Cortez and Columbus. The food of the gods, bubbling and frothing in ceremonial goblets. The bitter elixir of life.

Perhaps this is what Reynaud senses in my little shop; a throwback to times when the world was a wider, wilder place. Before Christ – before Adonis was born in Bethlehem or Osiris sacrificed at Easter – the cocoa bean was revered. Magical properties were attributed to it. Its brew was sipped on the steps of sacrificial temples; its ecstasies were fierce and terrible. Is this what he fears? Corruption by pleasure, the subtle transubstantiation of the flesh into a vessel for debauch? Not for him the orgies of the Aztec priesthood. And yet, in the vapours of the melting chocolate something begins to coalesce – a vision, my mother would have said – a smoky finger of perception which points ... points ...

There. For a second I almost had it. Across the glossy surface a vaporous ripple forms. Then another, filmy and pale, half-hiding, half-revealing. For a moment I almost saw the answer, the secret which he hides – even from himself – with such fearful calculation, the key which will set all of us into motion.

Scrying with chocolate is a difficult business. The visions are unclear, troubled by rising perfumes which cloud the mind. And I am not my mother, who retained until the day of her death a power of augury so great that the two of us ran before it in wild and growing disarray. But before the vision dissipates I am sure I see something – a room, a bed, an old man lying on the bed, his eyes raw holes in his white face . . . And fire. Fire.

Is this what I was meant to see?

Is this the Black Man's secret?

I need to know his secret if we are to stay here. And I do need to stay. Whatever it takes.

10

Wednesday, February 19

A WEEK, *MON PÈRE*. THAT'S ALL IT'S BEEN. ONE WEEK. BUT it seems longer. Why she should disturb me so is beyond me; it's clear what she is. I went to see her the other day, to reason with her about her Sunday morning opening time. The place is transformed; the air perfumed with bewildering scents of ginger and spices. I tried not to look at the shelves of sweets: boxes, ribbons, bows in pastel colours, sugared almonds in gold-silver drifts, sugared violets and chocolate rose leaves. There is more than a suspicion of the boudoir about the place, an *intimate* look, a scent of rose and vanilla. My mother's room had just such a look; all crêpe and gauze and cut-glass twinkling in the muted light, the ranks of bottles and jars on her dressing-table an army of genies awaiting release. There is something unwholesome about such a concentration of sweetness. A promise, half-fulfilled, of the forbidden. I try not to look, not to smell.

She greeted me politely enough. I saw her more clearly now; long black hair twisted back into a knot, eyes so dark they seem pupilless. Her eyebrows are perfectly straight, giving her a stern look belied by the comic twist to her mouth. Hands square and functional; nails clipped short. She wears no make-up, and yet there is something slightly indecent about that face. Perhaps it is the directness of her look, the way her eyes linger appraisingly, that permanent crease of irony about the mouth. And she is tall, too tall for a woman, my own height. She stares at me eye to eye, with thrown-back shoulders and defiant chin. She wears a long, flared, flame-coloured skirt and a tight black sweater. This colouring looks dangerous, like a snake or a stinging insect, a warning to enemies.

And she *is* my enemy. I feel it immediately. I sense her hostility and suspicion though her voice remains low-pitched and pleasant throughout. I feel she has lured me here to taunt me, that she knows some secret that even I— But this is nonsense. What can she know? What can she *do*? It is merely my sense of order which is offended, as a conscientious gardener might take offence at a patch of seeding dandelions. The seed of discord is everywhere, *mon père*. And it spreads. It spreads.

I know. I am losing my perspective. But we must be vigilant all the same, you and I. Remember Les Marauds, and the gypsies we ousted from the banks of the Tannes. Remember how long it took, how many fruitless months of complaints and letter-writing until we took the matter into our own hands. Remember the sermons I preached! Door after door was closed against them. Some shopkeepers co-operated at once. They remembered the gypsies from the last time, and the sickness, the thieving and the whoring. They were on our side. I recall we had to pressure Narcisse, who, typically, would have offered them summer employment in his fields. But at last, we uprooted them all: the sullen men and their bold-eyed slatterns, their foul-mouthed barefooted children, their scrawny dogs. They left, and volunteers cleaned up the filth they left behind them. A single dandelion seed, *mon père*, would be enough to bring them back. You know that as well as I. And if she is that seed . . .

I spoke to Joline Drou yesterday. Anouk Rocher has joined the primary school. A pert child, black hair like her mother's and a bright, insolent smile. Apparently Joline found her son Jean, among others, playing some kind of game with the child in the schoolyard. A corrupting influence, I gather, divination or some such nonsense, bones and beads in a bag scattered in the dirt. I told you I knew their kind. Joline has forbidden Jean to play with her again, but the lad has a stubborn streak in him and turned sullen. At that age nothing answers but the strictest discipline. I offered to give the boy a talking-to myself, but the mother won't agree. That's what they're like, *mon père*. Weak. Weak. I wonder how many of them have already broken their Lenten vows. I wonder how many ever intended to keep them. For myself, I feel that fasting cleanses me. The sight of the butcher's window appals; scents are heightened to a point of intensity that makes my head reel. Suddenly the morning odour of baking from Poitou's is more than I can bear; the smell of hot fat from the *rôtisserie* in the Place des Beaux-Arts a shaft from hell. I myself have touched neither meat nor fish nor eggs for over a week, subsisting on bread, soups, salads and a single glass of wine on Sunday, and I am cleansed, *père*, cleansed. I only wish I could do more. *This* is not suffering. *This* is not penance. I sometimes feel that if I could only *show* them the right example, if it could be *me* on that cross bleeding, suffering . . . That witch Voizin mocks me as she goes by with her basket of groceries. Alone in that family of good churchgoers she scorns the Church, grinning at me as she hobbles past, her straw hat tied around her head with a red scarf and her stick rapping the flags at her feet. I bear with her only because of her age, *mon père*, and the pleas of her family. Stubbornly denying treatment, denying comfort, she thinks she'll live for ever. But she'll break one day. They always do. And I'll give her absolution in all humility; I'll grieve in spite of her many aberrations, her pride and her defiance. I'll have her in the end, *mon père*. In the end, won't I have them all?

11

Thursday, February 20

I WAS WAITING FOR HER. TARTAN COAT, HAIR SCRAPED
back in an unflattering style, hands deft and nervous as a
gunslinger's. Joséphine Muscat, the lady from the carnival.
She waited until my regulars – Guillaume, Georges and
Narcisse – had left before she came in, hands thrust
deeply into her pockets.

'Hot chocolate, please.' She sat down uncomfortably at
the counter, speaking down into the empty glasses I had
not yet had time to clear.

'Of course.' I did not ask her how she liked her drink
but brought it to her with chocolate curls and Chantilly,
decorated with two coffee creams at the side. For a
moment she looked at the glass with narrowed eyes, then
touched it tentatively.

'The other day,' she said, with forced casualness. 'I

forgot to pay for something.' She has long fingers, oddly delicate in spite of the calluses on the fingertips. In repose her face seems to lose some of its dismayed expression, becoming almost attractive. Her hair is a soft brown, her eyes golden. 'I'm sorry.' She threw the ten-franc piece onto the counter with a kind of defiance.

'That's OK.' I made my voice casual, disinterested. 'It happens all the time.' Joséphine looked at me for a second, suspiciously, then sensing no malice, relaxed a little. 'This is good.' Sipping the chocolate. 'Really good.'

'I make it myself,' I explained. 'From the chocolate liquor before the fat is added to make it solidify. This is exactly how the Aztecs drank chocolate, centuries ago.'

She shot me another quick, suspicious glance.

'Thank you for the present,' she said at last. 'Chocolate almonds. My favourite.' Then, quickly, the words rushing out of her in desperate, ungainly haste, 'I never took it on purpose. They'll have spoken about me, I know. But I don't steal. It's *them*' – contemptuous now, her mouth turned down in rage and self-hatred – 'the Clairmont bitch and her cronies. Liars.'

She looked at me again, almost defiantly. 'I heard you don't go to church.' Her voice was brittle, too loud for the small room and the two of us.

I smiled. 'That's right. I don't.'

'You won't last long here if you don't,' said Joséphine in the same high, glassy voice. 'They'll have you out of here the way they do everyone they don't approve of. You'll see. All this' – a vague, jerking gesture at the shelves, the boxes, the display window with its *pièces montées* – 'none of this will help you. I've heard them talking. I've heard the things they say.'

'So have I.' I poured myself a cup of chocolate from the silver pot. Small and black, like espresso, with a chocolate spoon to stir it. My voice was gentle. 'But I don't have to listen.' A pause while I sipped. 'And neither do you.'

Joséphine laughed.

The silence revolved between us. Five seconds. Ten.

'They say you're a witch.' That word again. She lifted her head defiantly. 'Are you?'

I shrugged, drank. 'Who says?'

'Joline Drou. Caroline Clairmont. Curé Reynaud's bible groupies. I heard them talking outside St Jérôme's. Your daughter was telling the other children. Something about spirits.' There was curiosity in her voice and an underlying, reluctant hostility I did not understand. 'Spirits!' she hooted.

I traced the dim outline of a spiral against the yellow mouth of my cup. 'I thought you didn't care what those people had to say.'

'I'm curious.' That defiance again, like a fear of being liked. 'And you were talking to Armande the other day. No-one talks to Armande. Except me.' Armande Voizin. The old lady from Les Marauds.

'I like her,' I said simply. 'Why shouldn't I talk to her?'

Joséphine clenched her fists against the counter. She seemed agitated, her voice cracking like frostbitten glass. 'Because she's mad, that's why!' She waved her fingers at her temple in a vague indicative gesture. 'Mad, mad, *mad*.' She lowered her voice for a moment. 'I'll tell you something,' she said. 'There's a line across Lansquenet' – demonstrating on the counter with a callused finger – 'and if you cross it, if you *don't* go to confession, if you *don't* respect your husband, if you *don't* cook three meals a day and sit by the fire thinking decent thoughts and waiting for him to come home, if you don't have *children* – and you don't bring flowers to your friends' funerals or vacuum the parlour or – *dig – the – flowerbeds!*' She was red-faced with the effort of speaking. Her rage was intense, enormous. *'Then you're crazy!'* she spat. 'You're crazy, you're abnormal and people – talk – about – you behind your back and – and – and—'

She broke off, the agonized expression slipping from her face. I could see her looking beyond me through the window, but the reflection against the glass was enough to obscure what she might be seeing. It was as if a shutter had descended over her features; blank and sly and hopeless.

'Sorry. I got a bit carried away for a moment.' She swallowed a last mouthful of chocolate. 'I shouldn't talk to you. You shouldn't talk to me. It's going to be bad enough already.'

'Is that what Armande says?' I asked gently.

'I have to go.' Her clenched fists dug into her breastbone again in the recriminatory gesture which seemed so characteristic of her. 'I have to go.' The look of dismay was back on her face, her mouth turning downwards in a panicked rictus so that she looked almost dull-witted. And yet the angry, tormented woman who had spoken to me a moment ago was far from that. What – *whom* – had she seen to make her react in that way? As she left La Praline, head pushed down into an imaginary blizzard, I moved to the window to watch her. No-one approached her. No-one seemed to be looking in her direction. It was then that I noticed Reynaud standing by the arch of the church door. Reynaud and a balding man I did not recognize. Both were staring fixedly at the window of La Praline.

Reynaud? Could he be the source of her fear? I felt a prick of annoyance at the thought that he might be the one who had warned Joséphine against me. And yet she had seemed scornful, not afraid, when she mentioned him earlier. The second man was short but powerful; checked shirt rolled up over shiny red forearms, small intellectual's glasses oddly at variance with the thick, fleshy features. A look of unfocused hostility hung about him, and at last I realized I had seen him before. In a white beard and red robe, flinging sweets into the crowd. At the carnival. Santa Claus, throwing bonbons to the crowd as if he hoped he might take out someone's eye. At that moment a group of children came up to the window and I was unable to see more, but I thought I knew now why Joséphine had fled in such haste.

'Lucie, do you see that man in the square? The one in the red shirt? Who is he?'

The child pulls a face. White chocolate mice are her special weakness; five for ten francs. I slip a couple of extra ones into the paper *cornet*. 'You know him, don't you?'

She nods. 'Monsieur Muscat. From the café.' I know it; a drab little place down at the end of the Avenue des Francs Bourgeois. Half-a-dozen metal tables on the pavement, a faded Orangina parasol. An ancient sign identifies it; Café de la République. Clutching her *cornet* of sweets the small girl turns to go, reconsiders, turns again. 'You won't ever guess *his* favourite,' she says. 'He hasn't got one.'

'I find that difficult to believe,' I smile. 'Everyone has a favourite. Even Monsieur Muscat.'

Lucie considers this for a moment. 'Maybe his favourite is the one he takes from someone else,' she tells me limpidly. Then she is gone, with a little wave through the display window.

'Tell Anouk we're off to Les Marauds after school!'

'I will.' Les Marauds. I wonder what they find there to

amuse them. The river with its brown, stinking banks. The narrow streets drifted with litter. An oasis for children. Dens, flat stones flick-flacking across the stagnant water. Secrets whispered, stick swords and shields made of rhubarb leaves. Warfare amongst the blackberry tangle, tunnels, explorers, stray dogs, rumours, purloined treasures . . . Anouk came from school yesterday with a new jauntiness in her step and a picture she had drawn to show me.

'That's me.' A figure in red overalls topped with a scribble of black hair. 'Pantoufle.' The rabbit is sitting on her shoulder like a parrot, ears cocked. 'And Jeannot.' A boy figure in green, one hand outstretched. Both children are smiling. It seems mothers – even schoolteacher mothers – are not allowed in Les Marauds. The Plasticine figure still sits beside Anouk's bed, and she has stuck the picture to the wall above it.

'Pantoufle told me what to do.' She scoops him up in a casual embrace. In this light I can see him quite clearly, like a whiskered child. I sometimes tell myself I should discourage this pretence of hers, but cannot bear to inflict such loneliness upon her. Maybe, if we can stay here, Pantoufle can give way to more substantial playmates.

'I'm glad you managed to stay friends,' I told her, kissing the top of her curly head. 'Ask Jeannot if he wants to come here some day soon, to help take down the display. You can bring your other friends too.'

'The gingerbread house?' Her eyes were sunlight-on-water. 'Oh *yes!*' Skipping across the room with sudden exuberance, almost knocking over a stool, skirting an imaginary obstacle with a giant leap, then up the stairs three at a time – 'Race you, Pantoufle!' A thump as she slammed the door against the wall – *bam-bam!* A sudden stabbing sweetness of love for her, taking me off guard as it always does. My little stranger. Never still, never silent.

I poured myself another cup of chocolate, turning as I heard the door-chimes jangle. For a second I saw his face unguarded, the appraising look, chin thrust out, shoulders squared, the veins popping out on the bare shiny forearms. Then he smiled, a thin smile without warmth.

'Monsieur Muscat, isn't it?' I wondered what he wanted. He looked out of place, glancing, head lowered, at the displays. His gaze fell short of my face, flicking casually to my breasts; once, twice.

'What did she want?' His voice was soft but heavily accented. He shook his head once, as if in disbelief. 'What the hell did she want in a place like this?' He indicated a tray of sugared almonds at fifty francs a packet. 'This sort of thing, *hé?*' He appealed to me, hands spread. 'Weddings and christenings. What's she want with wedding and christening stuff?' He smiled again. Wheedling now, trying for charm and failing. 'What did she buy?'

'I take it you mean Joséphine.'

'My wife.' He gave the words an odd intonation, a kind

of flat finality. 'That's women for you. Work yourself senseless to earn money to live on and what do they do, *hé*? Waste it all on—' Another gesture at the ranks of chocolate gems, marzipan fruit garlands, silver paper, silk flowers. 'What was it, a present?' There was suspicion in his voice. 'Who's she buying presents for? Herself?' He gave a short laugh, as if the thought was ludicrous.

I didn't see what business it was of his. But there was a kind of aggression in his manner, a nervousness around the eyes and the gesticulating hands, that made me careful. Not for myself – I learned enough ways to take care of myself in the long years with Mother – but for her. Before I could prevent it an image leaped out from him towards me; a bloodied knuckle etched in smoke. I closed my fists under the counter. There was nothing in this man I wanted to see.

'I think you may have misunderstood,' I told him. 'I asked Joséphine in for a cup of chocolate. As a friend.'

'Oh.' He seemed taken aback for a moment. Then he gave that barking laugh again. It was almost genuine now, real amusement touched with contempt. '*You* want to be friends with Joséphine?' Again the look of appraisal. I felt him comparing us, his hot eyes flicking to my breasts over the counter. When he spoke again it was with a caress in the voice, a crooning note of what he imagined to be seduction. 'You're new here, aren't you?'

I nodded.

'Perhaps we could get together some time. You know. Get to know each other.'

'Perhaps.' I was at my most casual. 'Maybe you could ask your wife to come too,' I added smoothly.

A beat of time. He looked at me again, this time a measuring glance of sly suspicion. 'She's not been saying anything, has she?'

Blankly: 'What kind of thing?'

A quick shake of the head. 'Nothing. Nothing. She talks, that's all. She's all talk. Doesn't do anything but, *hé*? Day in, day out.' Again, the short, mirthless laugh. 'You'll find that out soon enough,' he added with sour satisfaction.

I murmured something non-committal. Then, on impulse, I brought out a small packet of chocolate almonds from beneath the counter and handed them to him.

'Perhaps you could give these to Joséphine for me,' I said lightly. 'I was going to give them to her, but I forgot.'

He looked at me, but did not move. '*Give* them to her?' he repeated.

'Free. On the house.' I gave my most winning smile. 'A present.'

His smile broadened. He took the chocolates in their pretty silver sachet. 'I'll see she gets them,' he said, cramming the packet into his jeans' pocket.

'They're her favourites,' I told him.

'You won't go far in this job if you keep giving out freebies,' he said indulgently. 'You'll be out of business in a month.' Again the hard, greedy look, as if I too were a chocolate he couldn't wait to unwrap.

'We'll see,' I said blandly, and watched him leave the shop and begin the road home, shoulders slouched in a thickset James Dean swagger. He didn't even wait to be out of sight before I saw him take out Joséphine's chocolates and open the packet. Perhaps he guessed I might be watching. One, two, three, his hand went to his mouth with lazy regularity, and before he had crossed the square the silver wrapping was already balled in a square fist, the chocolates gone. I imagined him cramming them in like a greedy dog who wants to finish his own food before robbing another's plate. Passing the baker's he popped the silver ball at the bin outside but missed, bouncing it off the rim and onto the stones. Then he continued on his way past the church and down the Avenue des Francs Bourgeois without looking back, his engineer boots kicking sparks from the smooth cobbles underfoot.

12

Friday, February 21

THE WEATHER TURNED COLD AGAIN LAST NIGHT.
St Jérôme's weathervane turned and swung in anxious
indecision all night, scraping shrilly against its rusted
moorings as if to warn against intruders. The morning
began in fog so dense that even the church tower, twenty
paces from the shopfront, seemed remote and spectral; the
bell for Mass tolling thickly through wadded candyfloss as
the few comers approached, collars turned against the fog,
to collect absolution.

When she had finished her morning milk, I wrapped
Anouk into her red coat and, in spite of her protests,
pushed a fluffy cap onto her head.

'Don't you want any breakfast?'

She shook her head emphatically, grabbed an apple
from a dish by the counter.

'What about my kiss?' This has become a morning ritual.

Wrapping sly arms around my neck, she licks my face wetly, jumps away giggling, blows a kiss from the doorway, runs out into the square. I mime appalled horror, wiping my face. She laughs delightedly, pokes out a small sharp tongue in my direction, bugles, '*I love you!*' and is off like a scarlet streamer into the fog, her satchel dragging behind her. I know that in thirty seconds the fluffy hat will be relegated to the inside of the satchel, along with books, papers and other unwanted reminders of the adult world. For a second I see Pantoufle again, jumping in her wake, and banish the unwanted image in haste. A sudden loneliness of loss – how can I face an entire day without her? – and, with difficulty, I suppress an urge to call her back.

Six customers this morning. One is Guillaume, on his way back from the butcher's with a piece of *boudin* wrapped in paper.

'Charly likes *boudin*,' he tells me earnestly. 'He hasn't been eating very well recently, but I'm sure he'll love this.'

'Don't forget you have to eat too,' I remind him gently.

'Of course.' He gives his sweet, apologetic smile. 'I eat like a horse. Really I do.' He gives me a sudden, stricken look. 'Of course, it's Lent,' he says. 'You don't think animals should observe the Lenten fast, do you?'

I shake my head at his dismayed expression. His face is small, delicately featured. He is the kind of man who breaks biscuits in two and saves the other half for later.

'I think you should both look after yourselves better.' Guillaume scratches Charly's ear. The dog seems listless, barely interested in the contents of the butcher's package in the basket beside him.

'We manage.' His smile comes as automatically as the lie. 'Really we do.' He finishes his cup of *chocolat espresso*. 'That was excellent,' he says as he always does. 'My compliments, Madame Rocher.' I have long since stopped asking him to call me Vianne. His sense of propriety forbids it. He leaves the money on the counter, tips his old felt hat and opens the door. Charly scrambles to his feet and follows, lurching slightly to one side. Almost as soon as the door closes behind them, I see Guillaume stoop to pick him up and carry him.

At lunchtime I had another visitor. I recognized her at once in spite of the shapeless man's overcoat she affects; the clever winter-apple face beneath the black straw hat, the long black skirts over heavy workboots.

'Madame Voizin! You said you'd drop in, didn't you? Let me get you a drink.' Bright eyes flicked appreciatively from one side of the shop to another. I sensed her taking everything in. Her gaze came to rest on Anouk's menu:

chocolat chaud 10F
chocolat espresso 15F
chococcino 12F
mocha 12F

She nodded approvingly. 'It's been years since I had anything like this,' she said. 'I'd almost forgotten this sort of place existed.' There is an energy in her voice, a forcefulness to her movements, which belies her age. Her mouth has a humorous twist which reminds me of my mother. 'I used to love chocolate,' she declared.

As I poured her a tall glass of mocha and added a splash of kahlua to the froth she surveyed the bar stools with some suspicion.

'You don't expect me to climb all the way up there, do you?'

I laughed. 'If I'd known you were coming I would have brought a ladder. Wait a moment.' Stepping into the kitchen I brought out Poitou's old orange chair. 'Try this.'

Armande plumped into the chair and took her glass in both hands. She looked eager as a child, her eyes shining, her expression rapt.

'Mmmm.' It was more than appreciation. It was almost reverence. 'Mmmmmm.' She had closed her eyes as she tasted the drink. Her pleasure was almost frightening.

'This is the real thing, isn't it?' She paused for a moment, bright eyes speculatively half-closed. 'There's cream and – cinnamon, I think – and what else? Tia Maria?'

'Close enough,' I said.

'What's forbidden always tastes better anyway,' declared Armande, wiping froth from her mouth in satisfaction.

'But this' – she sipped again, greedily – 'is better than anything I remember, even from childhood. I bet there are ten thousand calories in here. More.'

'Why should it be forbidden?' I was curious. Small and round as a partridge, she seems as unlike her figure-conscious daughter as can be.

'Oh, doctors.' Armande was dismissive. 'You know what they're like. They'll say anything.' She paused to drink again through her straw. 'Oh, this is good. *Good.* Caro's been trying to make me go into some kind of a home for years. Doesn't like the idea of me living next door. Doesn't like to be reminded where she comes from.' She gave a rich chuckle. 'Says I'm sick. Can't look after myself. Sends that miserable doctor of hers to tell me what I can eat and what I can't. Anyone would think they *wanted* me to live for ever.'

I smiled. 'I'm sure Caroline cares very much about you,' I said.

Armande shot me a look of derision. 'Oh, you *are*?' She gave a vulgar cackle of laughter. 'Don't give me that, girl. You know perfectly well that my daughter doesn't care for anyone but herself. I'm not a fool.' A pause as she narrowed her bright, challenging gaze at me. 'It's the boy I feel for,' she said.

'Boy?'

'Luc, his name is. My grandson. He'll be fourteen in April. You may have seen him in the square.'

I remembered him vaguely; a colourless boy, too correct in his pressed flannel trousers and tweed jacket, cool green-grey eyes beneath a lank fringe. I nodded.

'I've made him the beneficiary of my will,' Armande told me. 'Half a million francs. In trust until his eighteenth birthday.' She shrugged. 'I never see him,' she added shortly. 'Caro won't allow it.'

I've seen them together. I remember now; the boy supporting his mother's arm as they passed on their way to church. Alone of all Lansquenet's children, he has never bought chocolates from La Praline, though I think I may have seen him looking in at the window once or twice.

'The last time he came to see me was when he was ten.' Armande's voice was unusually flat. 'A hundred years ago, as far as he's concerned.' She finished her chocolate and put the glass back onto the counter with a sharp final sound. 'It was his birthday, as I recall. I gave him a book of Rimbaud's poetry. He was very – polite.' There was bitterness in her tone. 'Of course I've seen him in the street a few times since,' she said. 'I can't complain.'

'Why don't you call?' I asked curiously. 'Take him out, talk, get to know him?'

Armande shook her head. 'We fell out, Caro and I.' Her voice was suddenly querulous. The illusion of youth had left with her smile, and she looked suddenly, shockingly old. 'She's ashamed of me. God knows what she's been telling the boy.' She shook her head. 'No. It's

too late. I can tell by the look on his face – that *polite* look
– the polite meaningless little messages in his Christmas
cards. Such a well-mannered boy.' Her laughter was bitter.
'Such a polite, well-mannered boy.'

She turned to me and gave me a bright, brave smile. 'If
I could know what he was doing,' she said. 'Know what he
reads, what teams he supports, who his friends are, how
well he does at school. If I could know that—'

'If?'

'I could *pretend* to myself—' For a second I saw her close
to tears. Then a pause, an effort, a gathering of the will.
'Do you know, I think I might manage another of those
chocolate specials of yours. How about another?' It was
bravado, but I admired it more than I could say. That she
can still play the rebel through her misery, the suspicion
of a swagger in her movements as she props her elbows on
the bar, slurping.

'Sodom and Gomorrah through a straw. *Mmmm.* I
think I just died and went to heaven. Close as I'm going
to get, anyway.'

'I could get news of Luc, if you wanted. I could pass it
on to you.'

Armande considered this in silence. Beneath the
lowered eyelids I could feel her watching me. Assessing.

At last she spoke. 'All boys like sweets, don't they?' Her
voice was casual. I agreed that most boys did. 'And his
friends come here too, I suppose?' I told her I wasn't sure

who his friends were, but that most of the children came and went regularly.

'I might come here again,' decided Armande. 'I like your chocolate, even if your chairs are terrible. I might even become a regular customer.'

'You'd be welcome,' I said.

Another pause. I understood that Armande Voizin does things in her own way, in her own time, refusing to be hurried or advised. I let her think it through.

'Here. Take this.' The decision was made. Briskly she slapped a hundred-franc note down on the counter.

'But I—'

'If you see him, buy him a box of whatever he likes. Don't tell him they're from me.'

I took the note.

'And don't let his mother get to you. She's at it already, more than likely, spreading her gossip and her condescension. My only child, and she had to turn into one of Reynaud's Salvation Sisters.' Her eyes narrowed mischievously, working webby dimples into her round cheeks. 'There are rumours already about you,' she said. 'You know the kind. Getting involved with me will only make things worse.'

I laughed. 'I think I can manage.'

'I think you can.' She looked at me, suddenly intent, the teasing note gone from her voice. 'There's something about you,' she said in a soft voice. 'Something familiar. I don't suppose we've met before that time in Les Marauds, have we?'

Lisbon, Paris, Florence, Rome. So many people. So many lives intersected, fleetingly criss-crossed, brushed by the mad weft-warp of our itinerary. But I didn't think so.

'And there's a smell. Something like burning, the smell of a summer lightning-strike ten seconds after. A scent of midsummer storms and cornfields in the rain.' Her face was rapt, her eyes searching out mine. 'It's true, isn't it? What I said? What you are?'

That word again.

She laughed delightedly and took my hand. Her skin was cool, foliage, not flesh. She turned my hand over to see the palm. 'I knew it!' Her finger traced lifeline, heartline. 'I knew it the minute I saw you!' To herself, head bent, voice so low it was no more than a breath against my hand, 'I knew it. I knew it. But I never thought to see you here, in this town.' A sharp, suspicious glance upwards.

'Does Reynaud know?'

'I'm not sure.' It was true; I had no idea what she was talking about. But I could smell it too; the scent of the changing winds, that air of revelation. A distant scent of fire and ozone. A squeal of gears left long unused, the infernal machine of synchronicity. Or maybe Joséphine was right and Armande was crazy. After all, she could see Pantoufle.

'Don't let Reynaud know,' she told me, her mad, earnest eyes gleaming. 'You know who *he* is, don't you?'

I stared at her. I must have imagined what she said then. Or maybe our dreams touched briefly once, on one of our nights on the run.

'He's the Black Man.'

Reynaud. Like a bad card. Again and again. Laughter in the wings.

Long after I had put Anouk to bed I read my mother's cards for the first time since her death. I keep them in a sandalwood box and they are mellow, perfumed with memories of her. For a moment I almost put them away unread, bewildered by the flood of associations that scent brings with it. New York, hotdog stands billowing steam. The Café de la Paix, with its immaculate waiters. A nun eating an ice-cream outside Notre-Dame cathedral. One-night hotel rooms, surly doormen, suspicious *gendarmes*, curious tourists. And over it all the shadow of *It*, the nameless implacable thing we fled.

I am not my mother. I am not a fugitive. And yet the need to see, to *know*, is so great that I find myself taking them from their box and spreading them, much as she did, by the side of the bed. A glance backwards to ensure Anouk is still asleep. I do not want her to sense my unease. Then I shuffle, cut, shuffle, cut until I have four cards.

Ten of Swords, death. Three of Swords, death. Two of Swords, death. The Chariot. Death. The Hermit. The Tower. The Chariot. Death.

The cards are my mother's. This has nothing to do with me, I tell myself, though the Hermit is easy enough to identify. But the Tower? The Chariot? Death?

The Death card, says my mother's voice within me, may not always portend the physical death of the self but the death of a way of life. A change. A turning of the winds. Could this be what it means?

I don't believe in divination. Not in the way she did, as a way of mapping out the random patterns of our trajectory. Not as an excuse for inaction, a crutch when things turn from bad to worse, a rationalization of the chaos within. I hear her voice now and it sounds the same to me as it did on the ship, her strength transformed to sheer stubbornness, her humour into a fey despair.

What about Disneyland? What do you think? The Florida Keys? The Everglades? There's so much to see in the New World, so much we haven't even begun to dream about. Is that it, do you think? Is that what the cards are saying?

By then Death was on every card, Death and the Black Man, who had begun to mean the same thing. We fled him, and he followed, packed in sandalwood.

As an antidote I read Jung and Herman Hesse, and learned about the collective unconscious. Divination is a means of telling ourselves what we already know. What we fear. There are no demons but a collection of archetypes every civilization has in common. The fear of loss – Death. The fear of displacement – the Tower. The fear of transience – the Chariot.

And yet Mother died.

I put the cards away tenderly into their scented box. Goodbye, Mother. This is where our journey stops. This is where we stay to face whatever the wind brings us. I shall not read the cards again.

13

Sunday, February 23

BLESS ME, FATHER, FOR I HAVE SINNED. I KNOW YOU CAN hear me, *mon père*, and there is no-one else to whom I would care to confess. Certainly not the bishop, secure in his distant diocese of Bordeaux. And the church seems so empty. I feel foolish at the foot of the altar, looking up at Our Lord in his gilt and agony – the gilding has tarnished with the smoke from the candles and the dark staining gives Him a sly and secretive look – and prayer, which came as such a blessing, such a source of joy in the early days, is a burden, a cry on the side of a bleak mountain which might at any time unleash the avalanche upon me.

Is this doubt, *mon père*? This silence within myself, this inability to pray, to be cleansed, humbled . . . is it my fault? I look about the church which is my life and I try to feel love for it. Love, as you loved, for the statues – St

Jérôme with the chipped nose, the smiling Virgin, Jeanne D'Arc with her banner, St Francis with his painted pigeons. I myself dislike birds. I feel this may be a sin against my namesake but I cannot help it. Their squawking, their filth – even at the doors of the church, the whitewashed walls streaked with the greenish daub of their leavings – their noise during sermons. I poison the rats which infest the sacristy and gnaw at the vestments there. Should I not also poison the pigeons which disrupt my service? I have tried, *mon père*, but to no avail. Perhaps St Francis protects them.

If only I could be more worthy. My unworthiness dismays me, my intelligence – which is far in excess of that of my flock – serving only to heighten the weakness, the cheapness of the vessel God has chosen to serve. Is this my destiny? I dreamed of greater things, of sacrifices, of martyrdoms. Instead I fritter away time in anxieties which are unworthy of me, unworthy of you.

My sin is that of pettiness, *mon père*. For this reason God is silent in His house. I know it, but I do not know how to cure the ill. I have increased the austerity of my Lenten fast, choosing to continue even on the days when a relaxation is permitted. Today, for instance, I poured my Sunday libation onto the hydrangeas and felt a definite lifting of the spirit. For now water and coffee will be the only accompaniment to my meals, the coffee to be taken black and sugarless to enhance the bitter taste. Today I had a carrot salad with olives – roots and berries in the wilderness. True, I feel a little light-headed now, but the sensation is not unpleasant. I feel a prick of guilt at the thought that even my deprivation gives me pleasure, and I resolve to place myself in the path of temptation. I shall stand for five minutes at the window of the *rôtisserie*, watching the chickens on the spit. If Arnauld taunts me, so much the better. In any case, he should be closed for Lent.

As for Vianne Rocher . . . I have hardly thought of her these past few days. I walk past her shop with my face averted. She has prospered in spite of the season and the disapproval of the right-thinking elements of Lansquenet, but this I attribute to the novelty of such a shop. That will wear off. Our parishioners have little enough money already for their everyday needs without subsidizing a place more suited to the big cities.

La Céleste Praline. Even the name is a calculated insult. I shall take the bus to Agen, to the housing rental agency, and complain. She should never have been allowed to take the lease in the first place. The central location of the shop ensures a kind of prosperity, encourages temptation. The bishop should be informed. Perhaps he may be able to exercise the influence I do not possess. I shall write to him today. I see her sometimes in the street. She wears a yellow raincoat with green daisies, a child's garment but for its length, slightly indecent on a grown woman. Her hair remains uncovered even in the rain, gleaming sleekly as a seal's pelt. She wrings it out like a long rope as she reaches the awning. There are often people waiting under that awning, sheltering from the interminable rain and watching the window display. She has installed an electric fire now, close enough to the counter to provide comfort though not close enough to damage her wares, and with the stools, the glass *cloches* filled with cakes and pies, the silver jugs of chocolate on the hob, the place looks more like a café than a shop. I often see ten or more people in there on some days; some standing, some leaning against the padded counter and talking. On Sunday and Wednesday afternoons the smell of baking fills the damp air and she leans in the doorway, floury to the elbows, throwing out pert remarks at the passers-by. I am amazed at how many people she now knows by name – it was six months before I knew all of my flock – and she always seems ready with a question or a comment about their lives, their problems. Poitou's arthritis. Lambert's soldier son. Narcisse and his prize orchids. She even knows the name of Duplessis's dog. Oh, she is wily. Impossible to fail to notice her. One must respond or seem churlish. Even I – even I must smile and nod though inside I am seething. Her daughter follows her lead, running wild in Les Marauds with a gang of older girls and boys. Eight or nine years old, most of them, and they treat her with affection, like a little sister, like a mascot. They are always together, running, shouting, making their arms into bomber planes and shooting each other, chanting, catcalling. Jean Drou is among them, in spite of his mother's concern. Once or twice she has tried to forbid him, but he grows more rebellious every day, climbing out of his bedroom window when she shuts him in. But I have more serious concerns, *mon père*, than the misbehaviour of a few unruly brats. Passing by Les Marauds before Mass today I saw, moored at the side of the Tannes, a houseboat of the type you and I both know well. A wretched thing, green-painted but peeling miserably, a tin chimney spouting black and noxious fumes, a corrugated roof, like the roofs of the cardboard shacks in Marseille's *bidonvilles*. You and I know what this means. What it will bring about. The first of spring's dandelions poking their heads from out of the sodden turf of the roadside. Every year they try it, coming upriver from the cities and the shanty-towns or worse, further afield from Algeria and Morocco. Looking for work. Looking for a place to settle, to breed . . . I preached a sermon against them this morning, but I know that in spite of this some of my parishioners – Narcisse amongst them – will make them welcome in defiance of me. They are vagrants. They have no respect and no values. They are the river-gypsies, spreaders of disease, thieves, liars, murderers when they can get away with it. Let them stay and they will spoil everything we have worked for, *père*. All our education.

Their children will run with ours until everything we have done for them is ruined. They will steal our children's minds away. Teach them hatred and disrespect for the Church. Teach them laziness and avoidance of responsibility. Teach them crime and the pleasures of drugs. Have they already forgotten what happened that summer? Are they fool enough to believe the same thing will not happen again?

I went to the houseboat this afternoon. Two more had already joined it, one red and one black. The rain had stopped and there was a line of washing strung between the two new arrivals, upon which children's clothes hung limply. On the deck of the black boat a man sat with his back to me, fishing. Long red hair tied with scrap of cloth, bare arms tattooed to the shoulder in henna. I stood watching the boats, marvelling at their wretchedness, their defiant poverty. What good are these people doing themselves? We are a prosperous country. A European power. There should be jobs for these people, useful jobs, good housing. Why do they then choose to live like this, in idleness and misery? Are they so lazy? The redhaired man on the deck of the black boat forked a protective sign at me and returned to his fishing.

'You can't stay here,' I called across the water. 'This is private property. You must move on.'

Laughter and jeering from the boats. I felt an angry throbbing at my temples, but remained calm. 'You can talk to me,' I called again. 'I am a priest. We can perhaps find a solution.'

Several faces had appeared at the windows and doorways of the three boats. I saw four children, a young woman with a baby and three or four older people, swathed in the grey no-colour which characterizes these people, their faces sharp and suspicious. I saw that they turned to Red Hair for their cue. I addressed him. 'Hey, you!'

His posture was all attentiveness and ironic deference.

'Why don't you come over here and talk? I can explain better if I'm not shouting at you across half the river,' I told him.

'Explain away,' he said. He spoke with such a thick Marseille accent I could hardly make out his words. 'I can hear you fine.' His people on the other boats nudged each other and sniggered. I waited patiently for silence.

'This is private property,' I repeated. 'You can't stay here, I'm afraid. There are people living along here.' I indicated the riverside houses along the Avenue des Marais. True, many of these are now deserted, having fallen into disrepair from damp and neglect, but some are still inhabited.

Red Hair gave me a scornful look. 'There are also people living here,' he said, indicating the boats.

'I understand that, but nevertheless—'

He cut me short. 'Don't worry. We're not staying long.'

His tone was final. 'We need to make repairs, collect supplies. We can't do that in the middle of the countryside. We'll be two weeks, maybe three. Think you can live with that, *hé?*'

'Perhaps a bigger village . . .' I felt myself bristling at his insolent air, but remained calm. 'A town like Agen, maybe—'

Shortly: 'That's no good. We came from there.'

I'm sure he did. They take a hard line with vagrants in Agen. If only we had our own police in Lansquenet.

'I've got a problem with my engine. I've been trailing oil for miles downriver. I've got to fix it before I can move on.'

I squared my shoulders. 'I don't think you'll find what you're looking for here,' I said.

'Well, everyone has an opinion.' He sounded dismissive, almost amused. One of the old women cackled. 'Even a priest is entitled to that.' More laughter. I kept my dignity. These people are not worth my anger.

I turned to leave.

'Well, well, it's M'sieur le Curé.' The voice came from just behind me, and in spite of myself I recoiled. Armande Voizin gave a small crow of laughter. 'Nervous, *hé?*' she said maliciously. 'You should be. You're out of your territory here, aren't you? What's the mission this time? Converting the pagans?'

'Madame.' In spite of her insolence I gave her a polite nod. 'I trust you are in good health.'

'Oh do you?' Her black eyes fizzed with laughter. 'I was under the impression that you couldn't wait to give me the last rites.'

'Not at all, Madame.' I was coldly dignified.

'Good. Because this old lamb's never going back into the fold,' she declared. 'Too tough for you, anyway. I remember your mother saying—'

I bit her off more sharply than I intended. 'I'm afraid I have no time for chit-chat today, Madame. These people' – a gesture in the direction of the river-gypsies – 'these people must be dealt with before the situation gets out of hand. I have the interests of my flock to protect.'

'What a windbag you are nowadays,' remarked Armande lazily. '*The interests of your flock.* I remember when you were just a little boy, playing Indians in Les Marauds. What did they teach you in the city, apart from pompousness and self-importance?'

I glared at her. Alone in all Lansquenet, she delights in reminding me of things best forgotten. It occurs to me that when she dies, that memory will die with her, and I am almost glad of it.

'*You* may relish the thought of vagrants taking over Les Marauds,' I told her sharply. 'But other people – your daughter among them – understand that if you allow them to get a foot in the door—'

Armande gave a snort of laughter. 'She even talks like you,' she said. 'Strings of pulpit clichés and nationalist platitudes. Seems to me these people are doing no harm. Why make a crusade of expelling them when they'll be leaving soon anyway?'

I shrugged. 'Clearly you don't want to understand the issue,' I said shortly.

'Well, I already told Roux over there' – a sly wave to the man on the black houseboat – 'I told him he and his friends would be welcome for as long as it takes to fix his engine and stock up on food.' She gave me a sly, triumphant look. 'So you can't say they're trespassing. They're here, in front of my house, with my blessing.' She gave the last word special emphasis, as if to taunt me.

'As are their friends, when they arrive.' She shot me another of her insolent glances. '*All* their friends.'

Well, I should have expected it. She would have done it only to spite me. She enjoys the notoriety it affords her, knowing that as the village's oldest resident a certain license is allowed her. There is no point in arguing with her, *mon père*. We know that already. She would enjoy the argument as much as she relishes contact with these people, their stories, their lives. Not surprising that she has already learned their names. I will not allow her the satisfaction of seeing me plead. No, I must go about the business in other ways.

I have learned one thing from Armande, at least. There

will be others. How many, we must wait and see. But it is as I feared. Three of them today. Tomorrow, how many more?

I called on Clairmont on the way here. He will spread the word. I expect some resistance – Armande still has friends – Narcisse may need some persuasion. But on the whole I expect co-operation. I am still someone in this village. My good opinion counts for something. I saw Muscat too. He sees most people in his café. Head of the Residents' Committee. A right-thinking man in spite of his faults, a good churchgoer. And if a strong hand were needed – of course we all deplore violence, but with these people we cannot rule out the possibility – well, I am certain that Muscat would oblige.

Armande called it a crusade. She meant it as an insult, I know, but even so . . . I feel a surge of excitement at the thought of this conflict. Could this be the task for which God has chosen me?

This is why I came to Lansquenet, *mon père*. To fight for my people. To save them from temptation. And when Vianne Rocher sees the power of the Church – *my* influence over every single soul in the community – then she will know she has lost. Whatever her hopes, her ambitions. She will understand that she cannot stay. Cannot fight and hope to win.

I will stand triumphant.

14

Monday, February 24

CAROLINE CLAIRMONT CALLED JUST AFTER MASS. HER SON was with her, satchel slung across his shoulders, a tall boy with a pale, impassive face. She was carrying a bundle of yellow hand-lettered cards.

I smiled at them both. The shop was almost empty – I expect the first of my regulars at about nine, and it was eight-thirty. Only Anouk was sitting at the counter, a half-finished bowl of milk and a *pain au chocolat* in front of her. She shot a bright glance at the boy, waved the pastry in a vague gesture of greeting, and returned to her breakfast.

'Can I help you?'

Caroline looked around her with an expression of envy and disapproval. The boy stared straight in front of him, but I saw his eyes wanting to slide towards Anouk. He looked polite and sullen, his eyes bright and unreadable beneath an overlong fringe.

'Yes.' Her voice is light and falsely cheery, her smile as sharp and sweet as icing, setting the teeth on edge. 'I'm distributing these' – she held up the stack of cards – 'and I wonder if you'd mind displaying one in your window.' She held it out. 'Everyone else is putting them up,' she added, as if that might sway my decision.

I took the card. Black on yellow, in neat, bold capitals:

NO HAWKERS, VAGRANTS OR PEDLARS.
THE MANAGEMENT RETAINS THE RIGHT
TO REFUSE TO SERVE AT ANY GIVEN TIME.

'Why do I need this?' I frowned, puzzled. 'Why should I want to refuse to serve anyone?'

Caroline sent me a look of pity and contempt. 'Of course, you *are* new here,' she said with a sugared smile. 'But we have had problems in the past. It's just a precaution, anyway. I very much doubt you'll get a visit from Those People. But you may as well be safe as sorry, don't you think?'

I still didn't understand. 'Sorry about what?'

'Well, the gypsies. The river people.' There was a note of impatience in her voice. 'They're back, and they'll be wanting to' – she made a small, elegant moue of disgust – 'do whatever it is they do.'

'And?' I prompted gently.

'Well, we'll have to show them we won't stand for it!' Caroline was becoming flustered. 'We're going to have an agreement not to serve these people. Make them go back to wherever it is they came from.'

'Oh.' I considered what she was saying. '*Can* we refuse to serve them?' I enquired curiously. 'If they have the money to spend, can we refuse?'

Impatiently: 'Of course we can. Who's to stop us?'

I thought for a moment, then handed back the yellow card. Caroline stared at me. 'You're not going to do it?' Her voice rose half an octave, losing much of its well-bred intonation in the process.

I shrugged. 'It seems to me that if someone wants to spend their money here, it isn't up to me to stop them,' I told her.

'But the community . . .' insisted Caroline. 'Surely you don't want people of that type – itinerants, thieves, *Arabs* for heaven's sake—'

Flutter-click snapshot of memory, scowling New York doormen, Paris ladies, Sacré-Coeur tourists, camera in hand, face averted to avoid seeing the beggar-girl with her too-short dress and too-long legs . . . Caroline Clairmont, for all her rural upbringing, knows the value of finding the right *modiste*. The discreet scarf she wears at her throat bears an Hermès label, and her perfume is Coco de Chanel. My reply was sharper than I intended.

'It strikes me that the community should mind its own business,' I said tartly. 'It isn't up to me – or *anybody* – to decide how these people should live their lives.'

Caroline gave me a venomous look. 'Oh, well, if that's how you feel' – turning superciliously towards the door – 'then I won't keep you from your business.' A slight emphasis upon the last word, a disdainful glance at the empty seats. 'I just hope you don't regret your decision, that's all.'

'Why should I?'

She shrugged petulantly. 'Well, if there's trouble, or anything.' From her tone I gathered the conversation was at an end. 'These people can cause all kinds of trouble, you know. Drugs, violence . . .' The sourness of her smile suggested that if there were any such trouble she would be pleased to see me the victim of it. The boy stared at me without comprehension. I smiled back.

'I saw your grandmother the other day,' I told him. 'She told me a lot about you.' The boy flushed and mumbled something unintelligible.

Caroline stiffened. 'I'd heard she was here,' she said. She forced a smile. 'You really shouldn't encourage my mother,' she added with counterfeit archness. 'She's quite bad enough already.'

'Oh, I found her most entertaining company,' I replied without taking my eyes off the boy. 'Quite refreshing. And *very* sharp.'

'For her age,' said Caroline.

'For any age,' I said.

'Well, I'm sure she seems so to a stranger,' said Caroline tightly. 'But to her family . . .' She flashed me another of her cold smiles. 'You have to understand that my mother is very old,' she explained. 'Her mind isn't what it used to be. Her grasp of reality—' She broke off with a nervous gesture. 'I'm sure I don't have to explain to you,' she said.

'No, you don't,' I answered pleasantly. 'It's none of my business, after all.' I saw her eyes narrow as she registered the barb. She may be bigoted, but she isn't stupid.

'I mean . . .' she floundered for a few moments. For a second I thought I saw a glint of humour in the boy's eyes, though that might have been my imagination. 'I mean my mother doesn't always know what's best for her.' She was back in control again, her smile as lacquered as her hair. 'This shop, for instance.'

I nodded encouragement. 'My mother is diabetic,' explained Caroline. 'The doctor has warned her repeatedly to avoid sugar in her diet. She refuses to listen. She won't accept treatment.' She glanced at her son with a kind of triumph. 'Tell me, Madame Rocher, is that *normal*? Is that a *normal* way to behave?' Her voice was rising again, becoming shrill and petulant. Her son looked vaguely embarrassed and glanced at his watch.

'*Maman*, I'll be l-late.' His voice was neutral and polite. To me: 'Excuse me, Madame, I have to get to s-school.'

'Here, have one of my special pralines. On the house.' I held it out to him in a twist of Cellophane.

'My son doesn't eat chocolate.' Caroline's voice was sharp. 'He's hyperactive. Sickly. He knows it's bad for him.'

I looked at the boy. He looked neither sickly nor hyperactive, merely bored and a little self-conscious.

'She thinks a great deal about you,' I told him. 'Your grandmother. Maybe you could drop in and say hello one of these days. She's one of my regulars.' The bright eyes flickered for a moment from beneath the lank brown hair.

'Maybe.' The voice was unenthusiastic.

'My son doesn't have time to hang about in sweet-shops,' said Caroline loftily. 'My son's a gifted boy. He knows what he owes his parents.' There was a kind of threat in what she said, a smug note of certainty. She turned to walk past Luc, who was already in the doorway, his satchel swinging.

'Luc.' My voice was low, persuasive. He turned again with some reluctance. I was reaching for him before I knew it, seeing past the polite blank face and seeing – seeing . . .

'Did you like Rimbaud?' I spoke without thinking, my head reeling with images.

For a moment the boy looked guilty. 'What?'

'Rimbaud. She gave you a book of his poems for your birthday, didn't she?'

'Y-yes.' The reply was almost inaudible. His eyes – they are a bright green-grey – lifted towards mine. I saw him give a tiny shake of his head, as if in warning. 'I d-didn't read them, though,' he said in a louder voice. 'I'm not a f-fan of p-poetry.' A dog-eared book, carefully hidden at the bottom of a clothes chest. A boy murmuring the lovely words to himself with a peculiar fierceness. Please come, I whispered silently. Please, for Armande's sake.

Something in his eyes flickered. 'I have to go now.'

Caroline was waiting impatiently at the door.

'Please. Take these.' I handed him the tiny packet of pralines. The boy has secrets. I could feel them itching to escape. Deftly, keeping out of his mother's line of vision he took the packet, smiled. I might almost have imagined the words he mouthed as he went.

'Tell her I'll be there,' he whispered, when M-*maman* goes to the h-hairdresser's.' Then he was gone.

I told Armande about their visit when she came later today. She shook her head and rocked with laughter when I recounted my conversation with Caroline.

'*Hé, hé, hé!*' Ensconced in her sagging armchair, a cup of mocha in her delicate claw, she looked more like an apple-doll than ever. 'My poor Caro. Doesn't like to be reminded, does she?' She sipped the drink gleefully. 'Where does she get off, *hé?*' she demanded with some testiness. 'Telling you what I can and can't have. Diabetic, am I? That's what her doctor would like us all to think.' She grunted. 'Well, I'm still alive, aren't I? I'm careful. But that isn't enough for *them*, no. They have to have control.' She shook her head. 'That poor boy. He stutters, did you notice that?' I nodded.

'That's his mother's doing.' Armande was scornful. 'If she'd left him alone – but no. Always correcting him. Always carrying on. Making him worse. Making out there's something wrong with him all the time.' She made a sound of derision. 'There's nothing wrong with him that a good dose of living wouldn't cure,' she declared stoutly. 'Let him run awhile without worrying what would happen if he fell over. Let him loose. Let him *breathe*.'

I said that it was normal for a mother to be protective of her children.

Armande gave me one of her satirical glances. 'Is *that* what you call it?' she said. 'The same way the mistletoe is *protective* of the apple tree?' She gave a cackle. 'I used to have apple trees in my garden,' she told me. 'Mistletoe got them all, one by one. Nasty little plant, doesn't look like much, pretty berries, no strength of its own, but lord! Invasive!' She sipped again at her drink. 'And poison to everything it touches.' She nodded to me knowingly. 'That's my Caro,' she said. 'That's her.'

I saw Guillaume again after lunch. He didn't stop except to say hello, saying he was on his way to the newsagent for his papers. Guillaume is addicted to film magazines, although he never goes to the cinema, and every week he receives an entire parcel of them; *Vidéo* and *Ciné-Club*, *Télérama* and *Film Express*. His is the only satellite dish in the village, and in his sparse little house there is a widescreen television and a Toshiba video recorder wall-mounted above an entire bookcase of video cassettes. I noticed that he was carrying Charly again, the dog looking dull-eyed and listless on his master's arm. Every few moments Guillaume stroked the dog's head with the familiar gesture of tenderness and finality.

'How is he?' I asked at last.

'Oh, he has his good days,' said Guillaume. 'There's plenty of life in him yet.' And they went on their way, the small dapper man clutching his sad brown dog as if his life depended upon it.

Joséphine Muscat went by but did not stop. I was a little disappointed that she did not come in, for I'd been hoping to talk to her again, but she simply shot me a wild-eyed look as she passed, hands jammed deeply into her pockets. I noticed her face looked puffy, the eyes slitted closed, though it might have been against the gritty rain, the mouth zipped shut. A thick no-colour scarf bound her head like a bandage. I called to her, but she did not answer, quickening her step as if at some impending danger.

I shrugged and let her go. These things take time. Sometimes for ever.

Still, later, when Anouk was playing in Les Marauds

and I had closed shop for the day, I found myself strolling down the Avenue des Francs Bourgeois in the direction of the Café de la République. It is a small, dingy place, soaped windows with an unchanging *spécialité du jour* scrawled across, and a scruffy awning which reduces the available light still further. Inside, a couple of silent slot machines flank the round tables at which the few customers sit, moodily discussing matters of no importance over interminable *demis* and *cafés-crème*. There is the bland oily smell of microwaved food, and a pall of greasy cigarette smoke hangs over the room, even though no-one seems to be smoking. I noticed one of Caroline Clairmont's hand-lettered yellow cards in a prominent position by the open door. A black crucifix hangs above it.

I looked in, hesitated, and entered.

Muscat was at the bar. He eyed me as I walked in, his mouth stretching. Almost imperceptibly I saw his eyes flick to my legs, my breasts – *whap-whap*, lighting up like the dials on a slot-machine. He laid a hand on the pump, flexing one heavy forearm. 'What can I give you?'

'*Café-cognac*, please.'

The coffee came in a small brown cup with two wrapped sugar lumps. I took it to a table by the window. A couple of old men – one with the *Légion d'honneur* clipped to one frayed lapel – eyed me with suspicion.

'D'you want some company?' smirked Muscat from

behind the bar. 'It's just that you look a little – *lonely*, sitting there on your own.'

'No, thank you,' I told him politely. 'In fact, I thought I might see Joséphine today. Is she here?'

Muscat looked at me sourly, his good humour gone. 'Oh yes, your bosom friend.' His voice was dry. 'Well, you missed her. She just went upstairs to lie down. One of her sick headaches.' He began to polish a glass with peculiar ferocity. 'Spends all afternoon shopping, then has to lie down in the bloody evening while I do the work.'

'Is she all right?'

He looked at me. 'Course she is.' His voice was sharp. 'Why shouldn't she be? If Her Bloody Ladyship could just get up off her fat arse once in a while we might even be able to keep this business afloat.' He dug his dishcloth-wrapped fist into the glass, grunting with the effort.

'I mean.' He made an expressive gesture. 'I mean, just look at this place.' He glanced at me as if about to say something else, then his gaze slid past me to the door.

'*Hé!*' I gathered he was addressing someone just out of my field of vision. 'Don't you people listen? I'm closed!'

I heard a man's voice say something indistinct in reply. Muscat gave his wide, cheerless grin. 'Can't you idiots read?' Behind the bar he indicated the yellow twin of the card I had seen at the door. 'Get lost, go on!'

I stood up to see what was happening. There were five people standing uncertainly at the café entrance, two men and three women. All five were strangers to me, unremarkable but for their air of indefinable otherness; the patched trousers, the workboots, the faded T-shirts which proclaimed them outsiders. I should know that look. I had it once. The man who had spoken had red hair and a green bandanna to keep it out of his face. His eyes were cautious, his tone carefully neutral.

'We're not selling anything,' he explained. 'We just want to get a couple of beers and some coffee. We're not going to be any trouble.'

Muscat looked at him in contempt. 'I said, we're closed.'

One of the women, a drab, thin girl with a pierced eyebrow, tugged at the redhead's sleeve. 'It's no good, Roux. We better—'

'Wait a minute.' Roux shook her off impatiently. 'I don't understand. The lady who was here a moment ago – your wife – she was going to—'

'*Screw* my wife!' exclaimed Muscat shrilly. 'My wife couldn't find her arse with both hands and a pocket torch! It's *my* name above the door, and I – say – we're – *closed*!' He had taken three steps from behind the bar, and now he stood barring the doorway, hands on hips, like an overweight gunslinger in a spaghetti western. I could see the yellowy gleam of his knuckles at his belt, hear the whistle of his breath. His face was congested with rage.

'Right.' Roux's face was expressionless. He flicked a

hostile, deliberate glance at the few customers scattered about the room. 'Closed.' Another glance around the room. For a moment our eyes met. 'Closed to *us*,' he said quietly.

'Not as stupid as you look, are you?' said Muscat with sour glee. 'We had enough of your lot last time. This time, we're not standing for it!'

'OK.' Roux turned to go. Muscat saw him off, strutting stiff-legged, like a dog scenting a fight.

I walked past him without a word, leaving my coffee half-finished on the table. I hope he wasn't expecting a tip.

I caught up with the river-gypsies halfway down the Avenue des Francs Bourgeois. It had begun to drizzle again, and the five of them looked drab and sullen. I could see their boats now, down in Les Marauds, a dozen of them – two dozen – a flotilla of green-yellow-blue-white-red, some flying flags of damp washing, others painted with Arabian nights and magic carpets and unicorn variations reflected in the dull green water.

'I'm sorry that happened,' I told them. 'They're not an especially welcoming lot in Lansquenet-sous-Tannes.'

Roux gave me a flat, measuring look.

'My name is Vianne,' I told him. 'I have the *chocolaterie* just opposite the church. La Céleste Praline.' He watched me, waiting. I recognized myself in his carefully expressionless face. I wanted to tell him – to tell all of

119

them – that I knew their rage and humiliation, that I'd known it too, that they weren't alone. But I also knew their pride, the useless defiance which remains after everything else has been scoured away. The last thing they wanted, I knew, was sympathy.

'Why don't you drop in tomorrow?' I asked lightly. 'I don't do beer, but I think you might enjoy my coffee.'

He looked at me sharply, as if he suspected me of mocking him.

'Please come,' I insisted. 'Have coffee and a slice of cake on the house. All of you.' The thin girl looked at her friends and shrugged. Roux returned the gesture. 'Maybe.' The voice was non-committal.

'We got a busy schedule,' chirped the girl pertly.

I smiled. 'Find a window,' I suggested.

Again that measuring, suspicious look. 'Maybe.'

I watched them go down into Les Marauds as Anouk came running up the hill towards me, the tails of her red raincoat flapping like the wings of an exotic bird. 'Maman, Maman! Look, the boats!'

We admired them for a while, the flat barges, the tall houseboats with the corrugated roofs, the stovepipe chimneys, the frescoes, the multicoloured flags, slogans, painted devices to ward against accident and shipwreck, the small barques, fishing lines, pots for crayfish hoisted up against the tidemark for the night, tattered umbrellas sheltering decks, the beginnings of campfires in steel drums on the riverside. There was a smell of burning wood and petrol and frying fish, a distant sound of music from across the water as a saxophone began its eerily human melodious wail. Halfway across the Tannes I could just make out the figure of a redheaded man standing alone on the deck of a plain black houseboat. As I watched he lifted his arm. I waved back. It was almost dark when we made our way home. Back in Les Marauds a drummer had joined the saxophone, and the sounds of his drumming slapped flatly off the water. I passed the Café de la République without looking in.

I had barely reached the top of the hill when I felt a presence at my elbow. I turned and saw Joséphine Muscat, coatless now but with a scarf around her head and half-covering her face. In the semi-darkness she looked pallid, nocturnal.

'Run home, Anouk. Wait for me there.'

Anouk gave me a curious glance, then turned and ran off obediently up the hill, her coat-tails flapping wildly.

'I heard what you did.' Joséphine's voice was hoarse and soft. 'You walked out because of that business with the river people.'

I nodded. 'Of course.'

'Paul-Marie was furious.' The stern note in her voice was almost admiration. 'You should have heard the things he was saying.'

I laughed. 'Fortunately *I* don't have to listen to anything Paul-Marie has to say,' I told her blandly.

'Now I'm not supposed to talk to you any more,' she went on. 'He thinks you're a bad influence.' A pause, as she looked at me with nervous curiosity. 'He doesn't want me to have friends,' she added.

'Seems to me I'm hearing rather too much about what Paul-Marie wants,' I said mildly. 'I'm not really all that interested in him. Now you—' I touched her arm fleetingly. 'I find *you* quite interesting.'

She flushed and looked away, as if expecting to find someone standing at her shoulder. 'You don't understand,' she muttered.

'I think I do.' With my fingertips I touched the scarf which hid her face.

'Why do you wear this?' I asked abruptly. 'Do you want to tell me?'

She looked at me in hope and panic. Shook her head. I pulled gently at the scarf. 'You're pretty,' I said as it came loose. 'You could be beautiful.'

There was a fresh bruise just beneath her lower lip, bluish in the failing light. She opened her mouth for the automatic lie. I interrupted her. 'That's not true,' I said.

'How can you know that?' Her voice was sharp. 'I hadn't even *said*—'

'You didn't have to.'

Silence. Across the water a flute scattered bright notes

among the drumbeats. When she spoke at last her voice was thick with self-loathing. 'It's stupid, isn't it?' Her eyes were tiny crescents. 'I never blame him. Not really. Sometimes I even forget what really happened.' She took a deep breath, like a diver going under. 'Walking into doors. Falling downstairs. St-stepping on rakes.' She sounded close to laughter. I could hear hysteria bubbling beneath the surface of her words. 'Accident-prone, that's what he says I am. Accident-prone.'

'Why was it this time?' I asked gently. 'Was it because of the river people?'

She nodded. 'They didn't mean any harm. I was going to serve them.' Her voice rose shrilly for a second. 'I don't see why I should have to do what that bitch Clairmont wants all the time! Oh we *must* stand together,' she mimicked savagely. 'For the sake of the community. For our *children*, Madame Muscat' – breaking back into her own voice with a stricken intake of breath – 'when in normal circumstances she wouldn't say *hello* to me in the *street* – wouldn't give me *steam* off her *shit!*' She took another deep breath, controlling the outburst with an effort.

'It's always Caro this, Caro that. I've seen the way he looks at her in church. "Why can't you be like Caro Clairmont?"' Now she was her husband, his voice thick with beery rage. She even managed his mannerisms, the thrust-out chin, the strutting, aggressive posture. '"She makes you look like a clumsy sow. She's got *style*. *Class*. She's got a fine son doing well at school. And what have *you* got, *hé?*" '

'Joséphine.'

She turned towards me with a stricken expression. 'I'm sorry. For a moment I almost forgot where—'

'I know.' I could feel rage pricking at my thumbs.

'You must think I'm stupid to have stayed with him all these years.' Her voice was dull, her eyes dark and resentful.

'No, I don't.'

She ignored my reply. 'Well I am,' she declared. 'Stupid and weak. I don't love him – can't remember a time when I *ever* loved him – but when I think of actually leaving him—' She broke off in confusion. 'Actually *leaving* him,' she repeated in a low, wondering voice.

'No. It's no use.' She looked up at me again and her face was closed, final. 'That's why I can't talk to you again,' she told me in calm desperation. 'I couldn't leave you guessing – you deserve better than that. But this is how it has to be.'

'No,' I told her. 'It doesn't.'

'But it does.' She defends herself bitterly, desperately, against the possibility of comfort. 'Can't you see? I'm no good. I steal. I lied to you before. I steal things. I do it all the time!'

Gently: 'Yes. I know.'

The clear realization turns quietly between us like a Christmas bauble.

'Things can be better,' I told her at last. 'Paul-Marie doesn't rule the world.'

'He might as well,' retorted Joséphine mulishly.

I smiled. If that stubbornness of hers could be turned out instead of in, what could she not achieve? I could do it, too. I could feel her thoughts, so close, welcoming me in. It would be so easy to take control . . . I turned the thought aside impatiently. I had no right to force her to any decision.

'Before, you had no-one to go to,' I said. 'Now you do.'

'Do I?' In her mouth, it was almost an admission of defeat.

I did not reply. Let her answer that for herself.

She looked at me in silence for a while. Her eyes were full of river lights from Les Marauds. Again it struck me, with what small a twist she might become beautiful.

'Goodnight, Joséphine.' I did not turn to look at her, but I know she watched me as I made my way up the hill, and I know she stood watching long after I had rounded the corner and disappeared from sight.

15

Tuesday, February 25

STILL MORE OF THIS INTERMINABLE RAIN. IT FALLS LIKE A piece of the sky upended to pour misery onto the aquarium life below. The children, bright plastic ducks in their waterproofs and boots, squawk and waddle across the square, their cries ricocheting off the low clouds. I work in the kitchen with half an eye to the children in the street. This morning I unmade the window display, the witch, the gingerbread house and all the chocolate animals sitting around watching with glossy expectant faces, and Anouk and her friends shared the pieces between excursions into the rainy backwaters of Les Marauds. Jeannot Drou watched me in the kitchen, a piece of gilded *pain d'épices* in each hand, eyes shining. Anouk stood behind him, the others behind her, a wall of eyes and whisperings.

'What next?' He has the voice of an older boy, an air of casual bravado and a smear of chocolate across the chin. 'What are you doing next? For the display?'

I shrugged. 'Secret,' I said, stirring *crème de cacao* into an enamel basin of melted couverture.

'No, really.' He insists. 'You ought to make something for Easter. You know. Eggs and stuff. Chocolate hens, rabbits, things like that. Like the shops in Agen.'

I remember them from my childhood; the Paris *chocolateries* with their baskets of foil-wrapped eggs, shelves of rabbits and hens, bells, marzipan fruits and *marrons glacés, amourettes* and filigree nests filled with *petits fours* and caramels and a thousand and one epiphanies of spun-sugar magic-carpet rides more suited to an Arabian harem than the solemnities of the Passion.

'I remember my mother telling me about the Easter chocolates.' There was never enough money to buy those exquisite things, but I always had my own *cornet surprise*, a paper cone containing my Easter gifts, coins, paper flowers, hard-boiled eggs painted in bright enamel colours, a box of coloured papier mâché – painted with chickens, bunnies, smiling children amongst the buttercups, the same every year and stored carefully for the next time – encasing a tiny packet of chocolate raisins wrapped in Cellophane, each one to be savoured, long and lingeringly, in the lost hours of those strange nights between cities, with the neon glow of hotel signs blink-blinking between the shutters and my mother's breathing, slow and some-how eternal, in the umbrous silence.

'She used to say that on the eve of Good Friday the bells leave their steeples and church towers in the secret of the night and fly with magical wings to Rome.' He nods, with that look of half-believing cynicism peculiar to the growing young.

'They line up in front of the Pope in his gold and white, his mitre and his gilded staff, big bells and tiny bells, *clochettes* and heavy *bourdons*, carillons and chimes and *do-si-do-mi-sols*, all waiting patiently to be blessed.'

She was filled with this solemn children's lore, my mother, eyes lighting up with delight at the absurdity. All stories delighted her – Jesus and Eostre and Ali Baba working the homespun of folklore into the bright fabric of belief again and again. Crystal healing and astral travel, abductions by aliens and spontaneous combustions, my mother believed them all, or pretended to believe.

'And the Pope blesses them, every one, far into the night, the thousands of France's steeples waiting empty for their return, silent until Easter morning.'

And I her daughter, listening wide-eyed to her charm-ing apocrypha, with tales of Mithras and Baldur the Beautiful and Osiris and Quetzalcoatl all interwoven with stories of flying chocolates and flying carpets and the Triple Goddess and Aladdin's crystal cave of wonders and the cave from which Jesus rose after three days, amen, abracadabra, amen.

'And the blessings turn into chocolates of all shapes and kinds, and the bells turn upside-down to carry them home. All through the night they fly, and when they reach their towers and steeples on Easter Sunday they turn over and begin swinging to peal out their joy.'

Bells of Paris, Rome, Cologne, Prague. Morning bells, mourning bells, ringing the changes across the years of our exile. Easter bells so loud in memory that it hurts to hear them.

'And the chocolates fly out across the fields and towns. They fall through the air as the bells sound. Some of them hit the ground and shatter. But the children make nests and place them high in the trees to catch the falling eggs and pralines and chocolate hens and rabbits and *guimauves* and almonds . . .'

Jeannot turns to me with vivid face and broadening grin. '*Cool!*'

'And that's the story of why you get chocolates at Easter.'

His voice is awed, sharp with sudden certainty. '*Do* it! Please, do it!'

I turn deftly to roll a truffle in cocoa powder. 'Do what?'

'Do *that*! The Easter story. It'd be so cool – with the bells and the Pope and everything – and you could have a chocolate festival – a whole week – and we could have

nests – and Easter-egg hunts – and—' He breaks off
excitedly, tugging at my sleeve imperiously. 'Madame
Rocher, *please*.'

Behind him Anouk watches me closely. A dozen
smudgy faces in the background mouth shy entreaties.

'A *Grand Festival du Chocolat*.' I consider the thought.
In a month's time the lilacs will be out. I always make a
nest for Anouk, with an egg and her name on it in silver
icing. It could be our own carnival, a celebration of our
acceptance in this place. The idea is not new to me, but
to hear it from this child is almost to touch its reality.

'We'd need some posters.' I pretend hesitation.

'*We'll* make those!' Anouk is the first to suggest it, her
face vivid with excitement.

'And flags – bunting—'

'Streamers—'

'And a chocolate Jesus on the cross with—'

'The Pope in *white* chocolate—'

'Chocolate lambs—'

'Egg-rolling competitions, treasure hunts—'

'We'll invite everyone, it'll be—'

'*Cool!*'

'So cool—'

I waved my arms at them for silence, laughing. An
arabesque of acrid chocolate powder followed my gesture.

'You make the posters,' I told them. 'Leave the rest to
me.'

Anouk leaped at me, arms outflung. She smells of salt and rainwater, a cuprous scent of soil and water-logged vegetation. Her tangled hair is barbed with droplets.

'Come up to my room!' she shrieked in my ear. 'They can, can't they, *Maman*, say they can! We can start right now, I've got paper, crayons—'

'They can,' I said.

An hour later the display window was embellished by a large poster – Anouk's design executed by Jeannot. The text, in large shaky green letters, read:

GRAND FESTIVAL DU CHOCOLAT
AT LA CELESTE PRALINE
BEGINS EASTER SUNDAY
EVERYONE WELCOME
!!!BUY NOW WHILE STOCKS LAST!!!

Around the text capered various creatures of fanciful design. A figure in a robe and a tall crown I took to be the Pope. Cutout shapes of bells had been pasted thickly at his feet. All the bells were smiling.

I spent most of the afternoon tempering the new batch of couverture and working on the window display. A thick covering of green tissue-paper for the grass. Paper flowers – daffodils and daisies, Anouk's contribution – pinned to the window-frame. Green-covered tins which once contained cocoa powder, stacked up against each other to make a craggy mountainside. Crinkly Cellophane paper wraps it like a covering of ice. Running past and winding into the valley, a river of blue silk ribbon, upon which a cluster of houseboats sit quiet and unreflecting. And below a procession of chocolate figures, cats, dogs, rabbits, some with raisin eyes, pink marzipan ears, tails made of licorice-whips with sugar flowers between their teeth . . . And mice. On every available surface, mice. Running up the sides of the hill, nestling in corners, even on the riverboats. Pink and white sugar coconut mice, chocolate mice of all colours, variegated mice marbled through with truffle and maraschino cream, delicately tinted mice, sugar-dappled frosted mice. And standing above them, the Pied Piper resplendent in his red and yellow, a barley-sugar flute in one hand, his hat in the other. I have hundreds of moulds in my kitchen, thin plastic ones for the eggs and the figures, ceramic ones for the cameos and liqueur chocolates. With them I can recreate any facial expression and superimpose it upon a hollow shell, adding hair and detail with a narrow-gauge pipe, building up torso and limbs in separate pieces and fixing them in place with wires and melted chocolate. A little camouflage – a red cloak, rolled from marzipan. A tunic, a hat of the same material, a long feather brushing the ground at his booted feet. My Pied Piper looks a little like Roux with his red hair and motley garb.

I cannot help myself; the window is inviting enough, but I cannot resist the temptation to gild it a little, closing my eyes, to light the whole with a golden glow of welcome. An imaginary sign which flashes like a beacon – COME TO ME. I want to give, to make people happy; surely that can do no harm. I realize that this welcome may be in response to Caroline's hostility to the travellers, but in the joy of the moment I can see no harm in that. I *want* them to come. Since we last spoke I have glimpsed them occasionally, but they seem suspicious and furtive, like urban foxes, ready to scavenge but not to be approached. Mostly I see Roux, their ambassador – carrying boxes or plastic bags of groceries – sometimes Zézette, the thin girl with the pierced eyebrow. Last night two children tried to sell lavender outside the church, but Reynaud moved them on. I tried to call them back, but they were too wary, watching me with slant-eyed hostility before pelting off down the hill into Les Marauds.

I was so absorbed in my plans and the layout of my window that I lost track of the time. Anouk made her friends sandwiches in the kitchen, then they disappeared again in the direction of the river. I put on the radio and sang to myself as I worked, carefully placing the choc-olates into pyramids. The magic mountain opens to reveal a bewildering, half-glimpsed, array of riches: multi-coloured piles of sugar crystals, glacé fruits and sweets which glitter like gems. Behind this, and shielded from the light by the concealed shelving, lie the saleable wares. I will have to begin work on the Easter goods almost straight away, anticipating extra custom. It is a good thing there is storage space in the cool basement of the house. I must order gift boxes, ribbons, Cellophane paper and trimmings. I was so absorbed that I barely heard Armande as she came in through the half-open door.

'Well, hello,' she said in her brusque manner. 'I came for another one of your chocolate specials, but I can see you're busy.'

I manoeuvred carefully out of the window. 'No, of course not,' I told her. 'I was expecting you. Besides, I've nearly finished, and my back is killing me.'

'Well, if it's no trouble . . .' Her manner was different today. There was a kind of crispness in her voice, a studied casualness which masked a high level of tension. She was wearing a black straw hat trimmed with ribbon and a coat – also black – which looked new.

'You're very chic today,' I observed.

She gave a sharp crack of laughter. 'No-one's said *that* to me for a while, I'll tell you,' she said, poking a finger at one of the stools. 'Could I climb up there without breaking a leg, d'you think?'

'I'll get you a chair from the kitchen,' I suggested, but the old lady stopped me with an imperious gesture.

'Rubbish!' She eyed the stool. 'I used to be quite a climber in my youth.' She drew up her long skirts, revealing stout boots and lumpy grey stockings. 'Trees, mostly. I used to climb up them and throw twigs onto the heads of passers-by. Hah!' A grunt of satisfaction as she swung herself onto the stool, grabbing hold of the counter-top for support. I caught a sudden, alarming swirl of scarlet from under her black skirt.

Armande perched on the stool, looking absurdly pleased with herself. Carefully she smoothed her skirts back over the shimmer of scarlet petticoat. 'Red silk undies,' she grinned, seeing my look. 'You probably think I'm an old fool but I like them. I've been in mourning for so many years – seems every time I can decently wear colours someone else drops dead – that I've pretty much given up wearing anything but black.' She gave me a look fizzing with laughter. 'But *underwear* – now that's a different thing.' She lowered her voice conspiratorially. 'Mail order from Paris,' she said. 'Costs me a fortune.' She rocked with silent laughter on her perch. 'Now, how about that chocolate?'

I made it strong and black, and, with her diabetic condition in mind, added as little sugar as I dared.

Armande saw my hesitancy and stabbed an accusing

finger at her cup. 'No rationing!' she ordered. 'Give me the works. Chocolate chips, one of those sugar stirrer-things, everything. Don't you start getting like the others, treating me as if I didn't have the wit to look after myself. Do I look senile to you?'

I admitted she didn't.

'Well, then.' She sipped the strong, sweetened mixture with visible satisfaction. 'Good. Hmm. Very good. Supposed to give you energy, isn't it? It's a, what do you call it, a stimulant?'

I nodded.

'An *aphrodisiac* too, so I heard,' added Armande roguishly, peeping at me from above the rim of her cup. 'Those old men down at the café had better watch out. You're never too old to have a good time!' She cawed laughter. She sounded shrill and keyed-up, her crabbed hands unsteady. Several times she put her hand to the brim of her hat, as if to adjust it.

I looked at my watch under cover of the counter, but she saw my movement.

'Don't expect he'll turn up,' she said shortly. 'That grandson of mine. I'm not expecting him, anyway.' Her every gesture belied her words. The tendons in her throat stood out like an ancient dancer's.

We talked for a while of trifling matters: the children's idea of the chocolate festival – Armande squawking with laughter when I told her about Jesus and the white-chocolate Pope – and the river-gypsies. It seems that Armande has ordered their food supplies herself, in her name, much to Reynaud's indignation. Roux offered to pay her in cash, but she prefers to have him fix her leaky roof instead. This will infuriate Georges Clairmont, she revealed with an impish grin.

'He'd like to think he's the only one who can help me out,' she said with satisfaction. 'Bad as each other, both of them, clucking about subsidence and damp. They want me out of that house, there's the truth of it. Out of my nice house and into some lousy old folks' home where you have to ask permission to go to the bathroom!' She was indignant, her black eyes snapping.

'Well, I'll show them,' she declared. 'Roux used to be a builder, before he went on the river. He and his friends will make a good enough job of it. And I'd rather pay them to do the work honestly than to have that *imbécile* do it for free.'

She adjusted the brim of her hat with unsteady hands. 'I'm not expecting him, you know.'

I knew it was not the same person to whom she referred. I looked at my watch. Four-twenty. Night was already falling. And yet I'd been so *sure* . . . That was what came of interfering, I told myself savagely. So easy to inflict pain on others, on myself.

'I never imagined he would come,' continued Armande in that crisp, determined voice '*She*'s seen to that all right.

Taught him well, she has.' She began to struggle off her perch. 'I've been taking up too much of your time already,' she said shortly. 'I must be—'

'M-mémée.'

She twists around so abruptly that I am sure she must fall. The boy is standing quietly by the door. He is wearing jeans and a navy sweatshirt. He has a wet baseball cap on his head. In his hand he carries a small, scuffed hardback book. His voice is soft and self-conscious.

'I had to w-wait until my m-mother went out. She's at the h-hairdresser's. She won't be back till s-six.'

Amande looks at him. They do not touch, but I feel something pass between them like a jolt of electricity. Too complex for me to analyse, but there is warmth and anger, embarrassment, guilt – and behind it all a promise of softness.

'You look soaked. I'll make you a drink,' I suggest, going into the kitchen. As I leave the room I hear the boy's voice again, low and hesitant.

'Thanks for the b-book,' he says. 'I've got it here with me.' He holds it out like a white flag. It is no longer new, but worn like a book which has been read and reread, lovingly and often. Armande registers this, and the fixed look disappears from her face.

'Read me your favourite poem,' she says.

From the kitchen, as I pour chocolate into two tall glasses, as I stir in cream and kahlua, as I make enough noise with pots and bottles to give the illusion of privacy, I hear his voice raised, stilted at first, then gaining rhythm and confidence. I cannot make out the words, but from a distance it sounds like prayer or invective. I notice that when he reads, the boy does not stutter.

I set the two glasses carefully onto the counter. As I entered the boy stopped speaking mid-sentence and eyed me with polite suspicion, his hair falling into his eyes like the mane of a shy pony. He thanked me with scrupulous courtesy, sipped his drink with more mistrust than pleasure.

'I'm not s-supposed to have this,' he said doubtfully. 'My mother s-says ch-chocolate makes me c-come out in z-zits.'

'And it could make me drop dead on the spot,' said Armande smartly. She laughed at his expression. 'Come on, boy, don't you *ever* doubt what your mother says? Or has she brainwashed what little sense you might have inherited from me right out of you?'

Luc looked nonplussed. 'I-it's just what sh-she s-says,' he repeated lamely.

Armande shook her head. 'Well, if I want to hear what Caro says I can make an appointment,' she said. 'What have *you* got to say? You're a smart lad, or used to be. What do you think?'

Luc sipped again. 'I think she might have been

exaggerating,' he said with a tiny smile. 'You look p-pretty good to me.'

'No zits, either,' said Armande.

He was surprised into laughter. I liked him better this way, his eyes flaring a brighter green, his impish smile oddly like his grandmother's. He remained guarded, but behind his deep reserve I began to glimpse a ready intelligence and sharp sense of humour.

He finished his chocolate but refused a slice of cake, though Armande took two. For the next half-hour they talked while I pretended to go about my business. Once or twice I caught him looking at me with a wary curiosity, the flickering contact between us broken as soon as it was made. I left them to it.

It was half-past five when they both said goodbye. There was no talk of another meeting, but the casual fashion with which they parted suggested that both had the same thought in mind. It surprised me a little to see them so alike, circling each other with the caution of friends reunited after long years of separation. They both have the same mannerisms, the same direct way of looking, the slanting cheekbones, sharp chin. When his features are in repose this similarity is partially obscured, but animation makes him more like her, erasing from them that look of bland politeness which she deplores. Armande's eyes are shining beneath the brim of her hat. Luc seems almost relaxed, his stutter receding to a slight hesitancy, barely noticeable. I see him pause at the door, wondering perhaps whether he should kiss her. On this occasion his adolescent's dislike of contact is still too strong. He lifts a hand in a shy gesture of farewell, then is gone.

Armande turns towards me, flushed with triumph. For a second her face is naked in its love, hope, pride. Then the reserve which she shares with her grandson returns, a look of enforced casualness, a gruff note in her voice as she says, 'I enjoyed that, Vianne. Perhaps I'll come again.' Then she gives me one of her direct looks, reaching out a hand to touch my arm. 'You're the one who brought him here,' she said. 'I wouldn't have known how to do it myself.'

I shrugged. 'It would have happened at some time or another,' I said. 'Luc isn't a child any more. He has to learn to do things his own way.'

Armande shook her head. 'No, it's you,' she told me stubbornly. She was close enough for me to smell her lily-of-the-valley perfume. 'The wind's changed since you've been here. I can still feel it. Everyone feels it. Everything's on the move. *Whee!*' She gave a little crow of amusement.

'But I'm not doing anything,' I protested, half-laughing with her. 'I'm just minding my own business. Running my shop. Being me.' In spite of my own laughter I felt uneasy.

'It doesn't matter,' replied Armande. 'It's still you that's doing it. Look at all the changes; me, Luc, Caro, the folks out on the river' – she jerked her head sharply in the direction of Les Marauds – 'even him in his ivory tower across the square. All of us changing. Speeding up. Like an old clock being wound up after years of telling the same time.'

It was too close to my own thoughts of the week before. I shook my head emphatically. 'That isn't me,' I protested. 'It's him. Reynaud. Not me.'

A sudden image at the back of my mind, like the turn of a card. The Black Man in his clock tower, turning the machinery faster and faster, ringing the changes, ringing the alarum, ringing us out of town ... And with that unsettling image came one of an old man on a bed, tubes in his nose and arms, and the Black Man standing over him in grief or triumph, while at his back, fire burned.

'Is it his father?' I said the first words which came into my head. 'I mean – the old man he visits. In the hospital. Who is it?'

Armande gave me a sharp look of surprise. 'How do you know about that?'

'Sometimes I have – feelings – about people.' For some reason I was reluctant to admit to scrying with the chocolate, reluctant to use the terminology with which my mother had made me so familiar.

'Feelings.' Armande looked curious, but did not question me further.

'So there *is* an old man, then?' I could not shake off the

thought that I had stumbled upon something important. Some weapon, perhaps, in my secret struggle against Reynaud. 'Who is he?' I insisted.

Armande gave a shrug. 'Another priest,' she said, with dismissive contempt, and would say no more.

16

Wednesday, February 26

WHEN I OPENED THIS MORNING ROUX WAS WAITING AT THE door. He was wearing denim overalls, and his hair was tied back with string. He looked to have been waiting for some time, because his hair and shoulders were furred with droplets from the morning mist. He gave me something that was not quite a smile, then looked behind me into the shop where Anouk was playing.

'Hello, little stranger,' he said to her. This time the smile was real enough, lighting his wary face briefly.

'Do come in.' I beckoned him inside. 'You should have knocked. I didn't see you out there.'

Roux muttered something in his thick Marseille accent and crossed the threshold rather self-consciously. He moves with an odd combination of grace and clumsiness, as if he feels uncomfortable indoors.

I poured him a tall glass of black chocolate laced with kahlua. 'You should have brought your friends,' I told him lightly.

He gave a shrug in reply. I could see him looking around, taking in his surroundings with keen, if suspicious, interest.

'Why don't you sit down?' I asked, pointing to the stools at the counter.

Roux shook his head. 'Thanks.' He took a mouthful of the chocolate. 'Actually, I wondered if you'd be able to help me. Us.' He sounded embarrassed and angry at the same time. 'It isn't money,' he added quickly, as if to prevent me from speaking. 'We'd pay for it all right. It's just the – *organization* – we're having difficulty with.'

He shot me a look of unfocused resentment. 'Armande – Madame Voizin – said you'd help,' he said.

He explained the situation as I listened quietly, nodding encouragement on occasion. I began to understand that what I had taken for inarticulacy was simply a deep dislike of having to ask for help. Through the thick accent Roux spoke like an intelligent man. He had promised Armande that he would repair her roof, he explained. It was a relatively easy job which would take only a couple of days. Unfortunately the only local supplier of wood, paint and the other materials needed to complete the task was Georges Clairmont, who flatly refused to supply them to either Armande or Roux. If

Mother wanted repairs to her roof, he told her reasonably, then she should ask him, not a bunch of swindling vagrants. It wasn't as if he hadn't been asking – *begging* – her to let him do the work free of charge for years. Let the gypsies into her house and God only knew what might happen. Valuables looted, money stolen ... It wasn't unknown for an old woman to be beaten or killed for the sake of her few poor possessions. No. It was an absurd scheme, and in all conscience he couldn't—

'Sanctimonious bastard,' said Roux viciously. 'Knows nothing about us – nothing! The way he talks, we're all thieves and murderers. I've always paid my way. I've never begged from anyone, I've always worked—'

'Have some more chocolate,' I suggested mildly, pouring another glassful. 'Not everybody thinks like Georges and Caroline Clairmont.'

'I know that.' His posture was defensive, arms crossed over his body.

'I've used Clairmont to do repairs for me before,' I continued. 'I'll tell him I want to do some more work on the house. If you give me a list of what you need, I'll get it.'

'I'll pay for it all,' said Roux again, as if this issue of payment were something he could not stress enough. 'The money really isn't a problem.'

'Of course.'

He relaxed a little and drank more chocolate. For the

first time he seemed to register how good it was, and gave me a smile of sudden and peculiar sweetness. 'She's been good to us, Armande,' he said. 'She's been ordering food supplies for us, and medicine for Zézette's baby. She stood up for us when that poker-faced priest of yours turned up again.'

'He's no priest of mine,' I interrupted quickly. 'In his mind, I'm as much of an interloper in Lansquenet as you are.' Roux looked at me in surprise. 'No, really,' I told him. 'I think he sees me as a corrupting influence. Chocolate orgies every night. Fleshly excesses when decent people should be in bed, alone.'

His eyes are the hazy no-colour of a city skyline in the rain. When he laughs they gleam with malice. Anouk, who had been sitting in uncharacteristic silence while he spoke, responded to it and laughed too.

'Don't you want any breakfast?' piped Anouk. 'We've got *pain au chocolat*. We've got croissants too, but the *pain au chocolat* is better.'

He shook his head. 'I don't think so,' he said. 'Thanks.'

I put one of the pastries on a plate and set it beside him. 'On the house,' I told him. 'Try one, I make them myself.'

Somehow it was the wrong thing to say. I saw his face close again, the flicker of humour replaced by the now familiar look of careful blankness.

'I can pay,' he said with a kind of defiance. 'I've got

money.' He struggled to pull out a handful of coins from his overall pocket. Coins rolled across the counter.

'Put that away,' I told him.

'I told you, I can pay.' Stubborn now, igniting into rage. 'I don't need—'

I put my hand on his. I felt resistance for a moment, then his eyes met mine. 'Nobody *needs* to do anything,' I said gently. I realized I had hurt his pride with my show of friendship. 'I invited you.' The look of hostility remained unchanged. 'I did the same with everyone else,' I persisted. 'Caro Clairmont. Guillaume Duplessis. Even Paul-Marie Muscat, the man who ran you out of the café.' A second's pause for him to register that. 'What makes you so special, that you can refuse when none of them did?'

He looked ashamed then, mumbling something under his breath in his thick dialect. Then his eyes met mine again and he smiled. 'Sorry,' he said. 'I didn't understand.' He paused awkwardly for a few moments before picking up the pastry. 'But next time *you're* the ones invited to *my* place,' he said firmly. 'And I shall be most offended if you refuse.'

He was all right after that, losing much of his constraint. We talked of neutral topics for a while, but soon progressed to other things. I learned that Roux had been on the river for six years, alone at first then travelling with a group of companions. He had been a builder once, and still earned money doing repair jobs and harvesting crops in summer and autumn. I gathered that there had been problems which forced him into the itinerant life, but knew better than to press for details.

He left immediately as soon as the first of my regulars arrived. Guillaume greeted him politely and Narcisse gave his brief nod of welcome, but I could not persuade Roux to stay to talk with them. Instead he crammed what remained of his *pain au chocolat* into his mouth and walked out of the shop with that look of insolence and aloofness he feels he has to affect with strangers.

As he reached the door he turned abruptly. 'Don't forget your invitation,' he told me, as if on an afterthought. 'Saturday night, seven o'clock. Bring the little stranger.'

Then he was gone, before I could thank him.

Guillaume lingered longer than usual over his chocolate. Narcisse gave his place to Georges, then Arnauld came over to buy three champagne truffles – always the same, three champagne truffles and a look of guilty anticipation – and Guillaume was still sitting in his usual place, a troubled look on his small-featured face. Several times I tried to draw him out, but he responded in polite monosyllables, his thoughts elsewhere. Beneath his seat Charly was limp and immobile.

'I spoke to Curé Reynaud yesterday,' he said at last, so abruptly that I gave a start. 'I asked him what I ought to do about Charly.'

I looked at him enquiringly.

'It's hard to explain to him,' continued Guillaume in his soft, precise voice. 'He thinks I'm being stubborn, refusing to hear what the vet has to say. Worse still, he thinks I'm being foolish. It isn't as if Charly were a person, after all.' A pause during which I could hear the effort he was making to retain his control.

'Is it really that bad?'

I already knew the answer.

Guillaume looked at me with sad eyes. 'I think so.'

'I see.'

Automatically he stooped to scratch Charly's ear. The dog's tail thumped in a perfunctory way, and he whined softly.

'There's a good dog.' Guillaume gave me his small, bewildered smile. 'Curé Reynaud isn't a bad man. He doesn't mean to sound cruel. But to say that – in such a way—'

'What did he say?'

Guillaume shrugged. 'He told me I'd been making a fool of myself over that dog for years now. That it was all the same to him what I did, but that it was ridiculous to coddle the animal as if it were a human being, or to waste my money on useless treatments for it.'

I felt a prick of anger. 'That was a spiteful thing to say.'

Guillaume shook his head. 'He doesn't understand,' he said again. 'He doesn't really care for animals. But Charly and I have been together for so long—' Tears stood in his eyes and he moved his head sharply to hide them.

'I'm on my way to the vet's now, just as soon as I've finished my drink.' His glass had been standing empty on the counter for over twenty minutes. 'It might not be today, might it?' There was a note almost of desperation in his voice. 'He's still cheerful. He's been eating better recently, I know he has. No-one can *make* me do it.' Now he sounded like a fractious child. 'I'll know when the time really comes. I'll know.'

There was nothing I could say that would make him feel better. I tried, though. I bent to stroke Charly, feeling the closeness of bone to skin beneath my moving fingers. Some things can be healed. I made my fingers warm, probing gently, trying to *see*. The burr already seemed larger. I knew it was hopeless.

'He's your dog, Guillaume,' I said. 'You know best.'

'That's right.' He seemed to brighten for a moment. 'His medicine keeps the pain away. He doesn't whine any more in the night.'

I thought of my mother in those last months. Her pallor, the way the flesh melted from her, revealing a delicate beauty of stripped bone, bleached skin. Her bright and feverish eyes – *Florida, sweetheart, New York, Chicago, the Grand Canyon, so much to see!* – and her furtive cries in the night.

'After a while you just have to stop,' I said. 'It's pointless. Hiding behind justifications, setting short-term goals to see out the week. After a while it's the lack of dignity that hurts more than anything else. You need to rest.'

Cremated in New York; ashes scattered across the harbour. Funny, how you always imagine dying in bed, surrounded by your loved ones. Instead, too often, the brief bewildering encounter, the sudden realization, the slow-motion panic ride with the sun coming up behind you like a swinging pendulum however much you try to outrun it.

'If I had a choice I'd take this one. The painless needle. The friendly hand. Better that than alone in the night, or under the wheels of a cab in a street where no-one stops to look twice.' I realized that without meaning to, I had spoken aloud. 'I'm sorry, Guillaume,' I said, seeing his stricken look. 'I was thinking about something else.'

'That's all right,' he said quietly, putting the coins down onto the counter in front of him. 'I was just going anyway.'

And picking up his hat with one hand and Charly with the other, he went out, stooping a little more than usual, a small drab figure carrying what might have been a sack of groceries or an old raincoat or something else altogether.

17

Saturday, March 1

I HAVE BEEN WATCHING HER SHOP. I REALIZE THAT I HAVE done so since her arrival, its comings and goings, its furtive gatherings. I watch it much as I used to watch wasps' nests in my youth, with loathing and fascination. They began slyly at first, calling in the secret hours of dusk and early morning. They took the guise of genuine clients. A cup of coffee here, a packet of chocolate raisins for their children. But now they have abandoned the pretence. The gypsies call openly now, casting defiant looks at my shuttered window; the redhead with the insolent eyes, the skinny girl and the bleached-haired girl and the shaven-headed Arab. She calls them by name; Roux and Zézette and Blanche and Ahmed. Yesterday at ten Clairmont's van came by with a load of building supplies; wood and paint and roofing pitch. The lad who was driving it set the goods down on her doorstep without a word. She wrote him a cheque. Then I had to watch while her grinning friends lifted the boxes and joists and cartons onto their shoulders and bore them down, laughing, into Les Marauds. A ruse, that was all. A lying ruse: For some reason she wants to abet them. Of course it is to spite me that she acts in this way. I can do nothing but maintain a dignified silence and pray for her downfall. But she makes my task so much harder! Already I have to deal with Armande Voizin, who puts their food on her own shopping bill. I have already dealt with this, but too late. The river-gypsies have enough supplies now to last them a fortnight. They bring their daily supplies – bread, milk – from Agen upriver. The thought that they might stay any longer fills me with bile. But what can be done, whilst such people befriend them? You would know what to do, *père*, if only you could tell me. And I know you would not flinch from your duty, however unpleasant. If only you could tell me what to do. The slightest pressure of the fingers would be enough. A flicker of an eyelash. Anything. Anything to show that I am forgiven. No? You do not move. Only the ponderous noise – *hissh-thump!* – of the machine as it breathes for you, sending the air through your atrophied lungs. I know that one day soon you will awake, healed and purified, and that mine will be the first name you speak. You see, I do believe in miracles. I, who have passed through fire. I do believe.

I decided to talk to her today. Rationally, without recrimination, as father to daughter. Surely she would understand. We began on the wrong footing, she and I. Perhaps we could begin again. You see, *père*, I was ready to be generous. Ready to understand. But as I approached the shop I saw through the window that the man Roux was in there with her, his hard, light eyes fixed on me with that mocking look of disdain which all his kind affects. There was a drink of some sort in his hand. He looked dangerous, violent in his filthy overalls and long, loose hair, and for a second I felt a thin stab of anxiety for the woman. Doesn't she realize what dangers she is courting, just by being with these people? Does she not care for herself, for her child? I was about to turn away when a poster in the shop window caught my eye. I pretended to study it for a minute whilst secretly watching her – watching them – from outside. She was wearing a dress of some rich wine-coloured material, and her hair was loose. From inside the shop I heard her laughter.

My eyes skimmed over the poster again. The writing was childish, unformed.

GRAND FESTIVAL DU CHOCOLAT
AT LA CELESTE PRALINE
BEGINS EASTER SUNDAY
EVERYONE WELCOME
!!!BUY NOW WHILE STOCKS LAST!!!

I read it again, slow indignation dawning. Inside the shop I could still hear the sound of her voice above the clinking of glasses. Too absorbed in her conversation, she had still not noticed me, but stood with her back to the door, one foot turned out like a dancer. She wore flat pumps with little bows on them, and no stockings.

BEGINS EASTER SUNDAY

I see it all now. Her malice, her damnable malice. She must have planned this from the start, this chocolate festival, planned it to coincide with the most holy of the Church's ceremonies. From her arrival on carnival day she must have had this in mind, to undermine my authority, to make a mockery of my teachings. She and her friends from the river.

Too angry now to withdraw, as I should have, I pushed the door and went into the shop. A brightly mocking carillon heralded my entrance, and she turned to look at me, smiling. If I had not that moment received irrefutable proof of her vindictiveness, I could have sworn that smile was genuine.

'Monsieur Reynaud.'

The air is hot and rich with the scent of chocolate. Quite unlike the light powdery chocolate I knew as a boy, this has a throaty richness like the perfumed beans from the coffee-stall on the market, a redolence of amaretto and tiramisu, a smoky, burnt flavour which enters my mouth somehow and makes it water. There is a silver jug of the stuff on the counter, from which a vapour rises. I recall that I have not breakfasted this morning.

'Mademoiselle.' I wish my voice were more commanding. Rage has tightened my throat and instead of the righteous bellow which I intended I release nothing but a croak of indignation, like a polite frog. 'Mademoiselle Rocher.' She looks at me enquiringly. 'I have seen your poster!'

'Thank you,' she says. 'Would you join us in a drink?'

'No!'

Coaxingly: 'My *chococcino* is wonderful if you have a delicate throat.'

'I do not have a delicate throat!'

'Don't you?' Her voice is falsely solicitous. 'I thought you sounded rather hoarse. A *grand crème*, then? Or a mocha?'

With an effort I regained my composure. 'I won't trouble you, thank you.'

At her side the redhaired man gives a low laugh and says something in his gutter patois. I notice his hands are streaked with paint, a pale tint which fills the creases in his palms and his knuckles. Has he been working? I ask myself uneasily. And if so, for whom? If this were Marseille the police would arrest him for working illegally. A search of his boat might reveal enough

evidence – drugs, stolen property, pornography, weapons –
to put him away for good. But this is Lansquenet. Nothing
short of serious violence would bring the police here.

'I saw your poster.' I begin again, with all the dignity I
can muster. She watches me with that look of polite
concern, her eyes dancing. 'I have to say' – at this point I
clear my throat, which has filled again with bile – 'I have
to say that I find your timing – the timing of your – *event* –
deplorable.'

'My timing?' She looks innocent. 'You mean the Easter
festival?' She gives a small, mischievous smile. 'I rather
thought your people were responsible for that. You ought
to take it up with the Pope.'

I fix her with a cold stare. 'I think you know exactly
what I'm talking about.'

Again, that look of polite enquiry.

'Chocolate festival. All welcome.' My anger is rising
like boiling milk, uncontrollable. For the instant I feel
empowered, energized by its heat. I stab an accusing finger
at her. 'Don't think I haven't guessed what this is all
about.'

'Let me guess.' Her voice is mild, interested. 'It's a
personal attack on you. A deliberate attempt to undermine the foundations of the Catholic Church.' She gives
a laugh which betrays itself in sudden shrillness. 'God
forbid that a chocolate shop should sell Easter eggs at
Easter.' Her voice is unsteady, almost afraid, though of

what I am unsure. The redhaired man glares at me. With an effort she recovers, and the glimpse of fear I thought I saw in her is swallowed by her composure.

'I'm sure there's room here for both of us,' she says evenly. 'Are you sure you don't want a drink of chocolate? I could explain what I—'

I shake my head furiously, like a dog tormented by wasps. Her very calm infuriates me, and I can hear a kind of buzzing in my head, an unsteadiness which sends the room spinning about me. The creamy smell of chocolate is maddening. For a moment my senses are unnaturally enhanced; I can smell her perfume, a caress of lavender, the warm spicy scent of her skin. Beyond her, a whiff of the marshes, a musky tang of engine-oil and sweat and paint from her redhaired friend.

'I – no – I . . .' Nightmarishly, I have forgotten what I intended to say. Something about respect, I think, about the community. About pulling together in the same direction, about righteousness, decency, about morality. Instead I gulp air, my head swimming. 'I – I . . .' I cannot shake the thought that *she* is doing this, pulling the threads of my senses apart, reaching into my mind. She leans forward, pretending solicitude, and her scent assails me once more.

'Are you all right?' I hear her voice from a great distance. 'Monsieur Reynaud, are you all right?'

I push her away with trembling hands. 'Nothing.' At

last I manage to speak. 'An – indisposition. Nothing. I'll bid you good—' Blindly I stumble towards the door. A red sachet suspended from the door-jamb brushes my face – more of her superstition – and I cannot shake off the absurd impression that the ridiculous thing is responsible for my malaise; herbs and bones sewn together and hung there to trouble my mind. I stagger out into the street, gasping for breath. My head clears as soon as the rain touches it, but I keep walking. Walking.

I did not stop until I reached you, *mon père*. My heart was pounding, my face running with sweat, but at last I feel purged of her presence. Was this what you felt, *mon père*, that day in the old chancery? Did temptation wear this face?

The dandelions are spreading, their bitter leaves pushing up the black earth, their white roots forking deep, biting hard. Soon they will be in bloom. I will walk home via the river, *père*, to observe the small floating city which even now grows, spreads across the swollen Tannes. More boats have arrived since last we spoke so that the river is paved with them. A man might walk across.

EVERYONE WELCOME.

Is this what she intends? A gathering of these people, a celebration of excess? How we fought to eradicate those remaining pagan traditions, *père*, how we preached and cajoled. The egg, the hare, still-living symbols of the tenacious root of paganism, exposed for what they are. For a time we were pure. But with her the purge must begin anew. This is a stronger strain, defying us once again. And my flock, my stupid, trustful flock, turning to her, *listening* to her ... Armande Voizin. Julien Narcisse. Guillaume Duplessis. Joséphine Muscat. Georges Clairmont. They will hear their names spoken in tomorrow's sermon along with all those who have listened to her. The chocolate festival is only a part of the sickening whole, I will tell them. The befriending of the river-gypsies. Her deliberate defiance of our customs and observances. The influence she brings to bear on our children. All signs, I will tell them, all signs of the insidious effect of her presence here.

This festival of hers will fail. Ridiculous to imagine that with such strength of opposition it could succeed. I will preach against it every Sunday. I will read out the names of her collaborators and pray for their deliverance. Already the gypsies have brought unrest. Muscat complains that their presence deters his customers. The noise from their camp, the music, the fires, have made Les Marauds into a floating shanty town, the river gleaming with spilled oil, drifts of litter sailing downstream. And his wife would have welcomed them, so I heard. Fortunately Muscat is not intimidated by these people. Clairmont tells me he ousted them easily last week when they dared to set foot in his café. You see, *père*, in spite of their bravado they are cowards. Muscat has blocked off the path from Les Marauds to discourage them from passing. The possibility of violence should appal me, *père*, but in a way I would welcome it. It might give me the excuse I need to call the police from Agen. I should talk to Muscat again. He would know what to do.

18

Saturday, March 1

ROUX'S BOAT IS ONE OF THE NEAREST TO THE SHORE, moored some distance from the rest, opposite Armande's house. Tonight paper lanterns were strung across its bows like glowing fruit, and, as we made our way into Les Marauds, we caught the sharp scent of grilling food from the river bank. Armande's windows had been flung open to overlook the river, and the light from the house made irregular patterns on the water. I was struck by the absence of litter, the care with which every scrap of waste had been placed in the steel drums for burning. From one of the boats further downriver came the sound of a guitar playing. Roux was sitting on the little jetty, looking into the water. A small group of people had already joined him, and I recognized Zézette, another girl called Blanche and the North African, Mahmed. Beside them something was cooking on a portable brazier filled with coals.

Anouk ran to the fire at once. I heard Zézette warn her in a soft voice, 'Careful, sweetheart, it's hot.'

Blanche held out a mug containing warm spiced wine and I took it with a smile. 'See what you think of this.'

The drink was sweet and sharp with lemon and nutmeg, the spirit so strong that it caught at the throat. For the first time in weeks the night was clear, and our breath made pale dragons in the still air. A thin mist hung over the river, lit here and there by the lights from the boats.

'Pantoufle wants some too,' said Anouk, pointing at the pan of spiced wine.

Roux grinned. 'Pantoufle?'

'Anouk's rabbit,' I told him quickly. 'Her – imaginary friend.'

'I'm not sure Pantoufle would like this very much,' he told her. 'Perhaps he'd like a little apple juice instead?'

'I'll ask him,' said Anouk.

Roux seemed different here, more relaxed, outlined in fire as he supervised his cooking. I remember river crayfish, split and grilled over the embers, sardines, early sweetcorn, sweet potatoes, caramelized apples rolled in sugar and flash-fried in butter, thick pancakes, honey. We ate with our fingers from tin plates and drank cider and more of the spiced wine. A few children joined Anouk in a game by the river bank. Armande came down to join us too, holding out her hands to warm them by the brazier.

'If only I were younger,' she sighed. 'I wouldn't mind this every night.' She took a hot potato from its nest of coals and juggled it deftly to cool it. 'This is the life I used to dream about as a child. A houseboat, lots of friends, parties every night . . .' She gave Roux a malicious look. 'I think I'll run away with you,' she declared. 'I always had a soft spot for a redheaded man. I may be old, but I bet I could still teach you a thing or two.'

Roux grinned. There was no trace of self-consciousness in him tonight. He was good-humoured, filling and refilling the mugs with wine and cider, touchingly pleased to be the host. He flirted with Armande, paying her extravagant compliments, making her caw with laughter. He taught Anouk how to skim flat stones across the water. Finally he showed us his boat, carefully maintained and clean, the tiny kitchen, the storage hold with its water tank and food stores, the sleeping area with its plexiglass roof.

'It was nothing but a wreck when I bought it,' he told us. 'I fixed it up so that now it's as good as any house on land.' His smile was a little rueful, like that of a man confessing to a childish pastime. 'All that work, just so I can lie on my bed at night and listen to the water and watch the stars.'

Anouk was exuberant in her approval. 'I like it,' she

declared. 'I like it a lot! And it isn't a mid – mid – whatever Jeannot's mother says it is.'

'A midden,' suggested Roux gently. I looked at him quickly, but he was laughing. 'No, we're not as bad as some people think we are.'

'We don't think you're bad at all!' Anouk was indignant.

Roux shrugged.

Later there was music, a flute and a fiddle and some drums improvised from cans and dustbins. Anouk joined in with her toy trumpet, and the children danced so wildly and so close to the river bank that they had to be sent away to a safe distance. It was well past eleven when we finally left, Anouk drooping with fatigue but protesting fiercely.

'It's OK,' Roux told her. 'You can come back any time you like.'

I thanked him as I picked up Anouk in my arms.

'You're welcome.' For a second his smile faltered as he looked beyond me to the top of the hill. A faint crease appeared between his eyes.

'What's wrong?'

'I'm not sure. Probably nothing.'

There are few streetlights in Les Marauds. The only illumination comes from a single yellow lantern outside the Café de la République, shining greasily on the narrow causeway. Beyond that is the Avenue des Francs Bourgeois, broadening to a well-lit avenue of trees. He watched for a moment longer, eyes narrowed.

'I just thought I saw someone coming down the hill, that's all. Must have been a trick of the light. There's no-one there now.'

I carried Anouk up the hill. Behind us, soft calliope music from the floating carnival. On the jetty Zézette was dancing, outlined against the dying fire, her frenzied shadow leaping below her. As we passed the Café de la République I saw that the door was ajar, though all the lights were out. From inside the building I heard a door close softly, as if someone had been watching, but that might have been the wind.

19

Sunday, March 2

MARCH HAS BROUGHT AN END TO THE RAIN. THE SKY IS
raw now, a screeching blue between fast-moving clouds,
and a sharpening wind has risen during the night, gusting
in corners, rattling windows. The church bells ring wildly
as if they too have caught a little of this sudden change.
The weathervane turn-turns against the wheeling sky, its
rusty voice rising shrilly. Anouk sings a wind-song to
herself as she plays in her room:

> V'là l'bon vent, v'là l'joli vent
> V'là l'bon vent, ma vie m'appelle
> V'là l'bon vent, v'là l'joli vent
> V'là l'bon vent, ma mie m'attend.

March wind's an ill wind, my mother used to say. But in

spite of that it feels good, smelling of sap and ozone and the salt of the distant sea. A good month, March, with February blowing out of the back door and spring waiting at the front. A good month for change.

For five minutes I stand alone in the square with my arms held out, feeling the wind in my hair. I have forgotten to bring a coat and my red skirt billows out around me. I am a kite, feeling the wind, rising in an instant above the church tower, rising above myself. For a moment I am disorientated, seeing the scarlet figure below in the square, at once *here* and *there* – falling back into myself, breathless, I see Reynaud's face staring out from a high window, his eyes dark with resentment. He looks pale, the bright sunlight barely grazing his skin with colour. His hands are clenched on the sill before him and his knuckles are the bleached whiteness of his face.

The wind has gone to my head. I send him a cheery wave as I turn to go back into the shop. He will see this as defiance, I know, but this morning I do not care. The wind has blown my fears away. I wave to the Black Man in his tower, and the wind plucks gleefully at my skirts. I feel delirious, expectant.

Some of this new courage seems to have infused the people of Lansquenet. I watch them as they walk to church – the children running into the wind with arms spread like kites, the dogs barking wildly at nothing, even the adults bright-faced, eyes streaming from the cold.

Caroline Clairmont in a new spring coat and hat, her son holding her by the arm. For a moment Luc glances at me, gives me a smile hidden by his hand. Joséphine and Paul-Marie Muscat, arms entwined like lovers, though her face is twisted and defiant beneath her brown beret. Her husband glares at me through the glass and quickens his step, his mouth working. I see Guillaume, without Charly today, though he still carries the bright plastic lead dangling from one wrist, a forlorn figure oddly bereft without his dog. Arnauld looks my way and nods. Narcisse stops to inspect a tub of geraniums by the door, rubs a leaf between his thick fingers, sniffs the green sap. He is sweet-toothed in spite of his gruffness, and I know he will be in later for his mocha and chocolate truffles.

The bell slows to an insistent drone – *domm! domm!* – as the people make their way through the open doors. I catch another glimpse of Reynaud – white-cassocked now, hands folded, solicitous – as he welcomes them in. I think he looks at me again, a brief flicker of the eyes across the square, a subtle stiffening of the spine beneath the robe – but I cannot be sure.

I settle at the counter, a cup of chocolate in my hand, to await the end of Mass.

The service was longer than usual. I suppose that as Easter approaches Reynaud's demands will become greater. It was over ninety minutes before the first people emerged furtively, heads bowed, the wind tugging impudently at headscarves and Sunday jackets, ballooning under skirts in sudden salaciousness, hurrying the flock across the square. Arnauld gave me a sheepish smile as he passed; no champagne truffles this morning. Narcisse came in as usual, but was even less communicative, pulling a paper out of his tweed coat and reading it in silence as he drank. Fifteen minutes later half the members of the congregation were still inside, and I guessed they must be awaiting confession. I poured more chocolate and drank. Sunday is a slow day. Better to be patient.

Suddenly I saw a familiar figure in a tartan coat slip through the half-open church door. Joséphine glanced across the square, and, seeing it empty, ran across towards the shop. She noticed Narcisse and hesitated for a moment before deciding to come in. Her fists were clenched protectively in the pit of her stomach.

'I can't stay,' she said at once. 'Paul's in confession. I've got two minutes.' Her voice was sharp and urgent, the hurried words falling over themselves like dominoes in a line.

'You have to stay away from those people,' she blurted. 'The travellers. You have to tell them to move on. *Warn* them.' Her face worked with the effort of speaking. Her hands opened and closed.

I looked at her. 'Please, Joséphine. Sit down. Have a drink.'

'I can't!' She shook her head emphatically. Her wind-tangled hair blurred wildly around her face. 'I told you I don't have time. Just do as I say. Please.' She sounded strained and exhausted, looking towards the church door as if afraid of being seen with me.

'He's been preaching against them,' she told me in a fast, low tone. 'And against you. Talking about you. Saying things.'

I shrugged indifferently. 'So? What do I care?'

Joséphine put her fists to her temples in a gesture of frustration. 'You have to warn them,' she repeated. 'Tell them to go. Warn Armande too. Tell her he read her name out this morning. And yours. He'll read mine out as well if he sees me here, and Paul—'

'I don't understand, Joséphine. What can he do? And why should I care, anyway?'

'Just tell them, all right?' Her eyes flicked warily to the church again, from which a few people were drifting. 'I can't stay,' she said. 'I have to go.' She turned towards the door.

'Wait, Joséphine—'

Her face as she turned back was a blur of misery. I could see that she was close to tears. 'This always happens,' she said in a harsh, unhappy voice. 'Whenever I find a friend *he* manages to ruin it for me. It'll happen the way it always does. You'll be well out of it by then, but *me*—'

I took a step forward, meaning to steady her. Joséphine pulled back with a clumsy gesture of warding.

'No! I can't! I know you mean well, but I just – *can't*!' She recovered with an effort. 'You have to understand. I live here. I *have* to live here. You're free, you can go where you like, you—'

'So can you,' I replied gently.

She looked at me then, touching my shoulder very briefly with the tips of her fingers.

'You don't understand,' she said without resentment. 'You're different. For a while I thought maybe I could learn to be different too.'

She turned, her agitation leaving her, to be replaced by a look of distant, almost sweet, abstraction. She dug her hands into her pockets once more.

'I'm sorry, Vianne,' she said. 'I really tried. I know it isn't your fault.' For a moment I saw a brief return of animation to her features. 'Tell the river people,' she urged. 'Tell them they have to go. It isn't their fault either – I just don't want anyone to be hurt,' finished Joséphine softly. 'All right?'

I shrugged. 'No-one is going to be hurt,' I told her.

'Good.' She gave a smile painful in its transparency. 'And don't worry about me. I'm fine. I really am.' Again that stretched, painful smile. As she edged past me through the door I caught a glimpse of something shiny in her hand, and saw that her coat pockets were stuffed with costume jewellery. Lipsticks, compacts, necklaces and rings spilled from between her fingers.

'Here. This is for you,' she said brightly, pushing a handful of looted treasure at me. 'It's OK. I've got lots more.' Then with a smile of dazzling sweetness she was off, leaving me with chains and earrings and pieces of bright plastic set in gilt weeping from my fingers onto the floor.

Later in the afternoon I took Anouk for a walk into Les Marauds. The travellers' camp looked cheery in the new sunlight, with washing flapping on lines drawn between the boats, and all the glass and paint gleaming. Armande was sitting in a rocking-chair in her sheltered front garden, watching the river. Roux and Mahmed were perched on the roof's steep incline, resetting the loose slates. I noticed that the rotten facia and the gable-ends had been replaced and repainted a bright yellow. I waved at the two men and sat on the garden wall next to Armande while Anouk raced off to the river bank to find her friends of last night.

The old lady looked tired and puffy-faced beneath the brim of a wide straw hat. The piece of tapestry in her lap looked listless, untouched. She nodded to me briefly, but did not speak. Her chair rocked almost imperceptibly, *tick-tick-tick-tick*, on the path. Her cat slept curled beneath it.

'Caro came over this morning,' she said at last. 'I suppose I should feel honoured.' A movement of irritation.

Rocking; *tick-tick-tick-tick*.

'Who *does* she think she is?' snapped Armande abruptly. 'Marie Bloody Antoinette?' She brooded fiercely for a moment, her rocking gaining momentum. 'Trying to tell me what I can and can't do. Bringing her *doctor*—' She broke off to fix me with her piercing, birdlike gaze. 'Interfering little busybody. She always was, you know. Always telling tales to her father.' She gave a short bark of laughter. 'She doesn't get these airs from me, in any case. Not on your life. I never needed any doctor – or any priest – to tell me what to think.' Armande pushed out her chin defiantly and rocked even harder.

'Was Luc there?' I asked.

'No.' She shook her head. 'Gone to Agen for a chess tournament.' Her fixed expression softened. 'She doesn't know he came over the other day,' she declared with satisfaction. 'And she won't get to know, either.' She smiled. 'He's a good lad, my grandson. Knows how to hold his tongue.'

'I hear we were both mentioned in church this morning,' I told her. 'Consorting with undesirables, so I'm told.'

Armande snorted. 'What I do in my own house is my own business,' she said shortly. 'I've told Reynaud, and I

175

told Père Antoine before him. They never learn, though. Always peddling the same old rubbish. Community spirit. Traditional values. Always the same tired old morality play.'

'So it's happened before?' I was curious.

'Oh yes.' She nodded emphatically. 'Years ago. Reynaud must have been Luc's age in those days. Course, we've had travellers since then, but they never stayed. Not till now.' She glanced upwards at her half-painted house. 'It's going to look good, isn't it?' she said with satisfaction. 'Roux says he'll have it finished by tonight.' She gave a sudden frown. 'I can have him work for me all I choose,' she declared irritably. 'He's an honest man and a good worker. Georges has no right to tell me otherwise. No right at all.'

She picked up her unfinished tapestry, but put it down again without setting a stitch. 'I can't concentrate,' she said crossly. 'It's bad enough being woken up by those bells at the crack of dawn without having to look at Caro's simpering face first thing in the morning. "*We pray for you every day, Mother*," ' she mimicked. ' "*We want you to understand why we worry so much about you.*" Worry about their own standing with the neighbours, more like. It's just too embarrassing to have a mother like me, reminding you all the time of how you began.'

She gave a small, hard smile of satisfaction. 'While I'm alive they know there's someone who remembers everything,' she declared. 'The trouble she got into with that boy. Who paid for that, eh? And him – Reynaud, Mr Whiter-than-White.' Her eyes were bright and malicious. 'I bet I'm the only one still alive who remembers *that* old business. Not many knew in any case. Could have been the biggest scandal in the county if I'd not known how to hold my tongue.' She shot me a look of pure mischief. 'And don't go looking at me like that, girl. I can still keep a secret. Why d'you think he leaves me alone? Plenty of things he could do, if he put his mind to it. Caro knows. She tried already.' Armande chuckled gleefully – *heh-heh-heh*.

'I'd rather understood Reynaud wasn't a local,' I said curiously.

Armande shook her head. 'Not many people remember,' she said. 'Left Lansquenet when he was a boy. Easier for everyone that way.' For a moment she paused, reminiscing. 'But he'd better not try anything this time. Not against Roux or any of his friends.' The humour had gone from her face and she sounded older, querulous, ill. 'I *like* them being here. They make me feel young.' The small crabby hands plucked meaninglessly at the tapestry in her lap. The cat, sensing the movement, uncurled from beneath the rocking-chair and jumped onto her knees, purring. Armande scratched its head and it buzzed and butted at her chin with small playful gestures.

'Lariflete,' said Armande. After a moment I realized that was the cat's name. 'I've had her nineteen years. That

177

makes her nearly my age, in cat time.' She made a small clucking sound at the cat, which purred louder. 'I'm supposed to be allergic,' said Armande. 'Asthma or something. I told them that I'd rather choke than get rid of my cats. Though there are some *humans* I could give up without a second thought.' Lariflete whisker-twitched lazily. I looked across at the water and saw Anouk playing under the jetty with two black-haired river children. From what I could hear Anouk, the youngest of the three, seemed to be directing operations.

'Stay and have some coffee,' suggested Armande. 'I was going to make some when you came along, anyway. I've got some lemonade for Anouk, too.'

I made the coffee myself in Armande's curious, small kitchen with its cast-iron range and low ceiling. Everything is clean there, but the one tiny window looks onto the river, giving the light a greenish underwater look. Hanging from the dark unpainted beams are bunches of dry herbs in their muslin sachets. On the whitewashed walls, copper pans hang from hooks. The door – like all the doors in the house – has a hole cut into the base to allow free passage to her cats. Another cat watched me curiously from a high ledge as I made the coffee in an enamelled tin pot. The lemonade, I noticed, was sugar-free, and the sweetener in the basin was some kind of sugar substitute. In spite of her bravado, it seems as if she does take some precautions after all.

'Foul stuff,' she commented without rancour, sipping the drink from one of her hand-painted cups. 'They say you can't taste the difference. But you can.' She made a wry face. 'Caro brings it when she comes. Goes through my cupboards. I suppose she means well. Can't help being a ninny.'

I told her she ought to take more care.

Armande snorted. 'When you get to my age,' she told me, 'things start to break down. If it isn't one thing, then it's another. It's a fact of life.' She took another sip of the bitter coffee. 'When he was sixteen Rimbaud said he wanted to experience as much as possible with the greatest possible intensity. Well, I'm going on eighty now, and I'm beginning to think he was right.' She grinned, and I was again struck by the youthfulness of her face, a quality that has less to do with colouring or bone structure than with a kind of inner brightness and anticipation, the look of someone who has hardly begun to discover what life has to offer.

'I think you're probably too old to join the Foreign Legion,' I told her with a smile. 'And didn't Rimbaud's experiences run rather to excess at times?'

Armande shot me an impish look. 'That's right,' she replied. 'I could do with a bit more excess. From now on I'm going to be immoderate – and volatile – I shall enjoy loud music and lurid poetry. I shall be *rampant*,' she declared with satisfaction.

I laughed. 'You are quite absurd,' I said with mock severity. 'No wonder your family despairs of you.'

But even though she laughed with me, rocking with merriment in her chair, what I recall now is not her laughter but what I glimpsed *behind* the laughter; that look of giddy abandon, desperate glee.

And it was only later, late into the night when I awoke sweating from some dark half-forgotten nightmare, that I remembered where I had seen that look before.

How about Florida, sweetheart? The Everglades? The Keys? How about Disneyland, chérie, or New York, Chicago, the Grand Canyon, Chinatown, New Mexico, the Rocky Mountains?

But with Armande there was none of my mother's fear, none of her delicate parrying and wrangling with death, none of her mad hit-and-run flights of fantasy into the unknown. With Armande there was only the hunger, the desire, the terrible awareness of time.

I wonder what the doctor said to her this morning, and how much she really understands. I lay awake for a long time wondering, and when I finally slept, I dreamed of myself and Armande walking through Disneyland with Reynaud and Caro hand-in-hand as the Red Queen and the White Rabbit from *Alice's Adventures in Wonderland*, with big, white, cartoon gloves on their hands. Caro had a red crown on her giant head, and Armande had a stick of candyfloss in each fist.

Somewhere in the distance I could hear the sounds of New York traffic, the blaring of horns getting closer.

'*Oh my, oh don't eat that, it's poison,*' squeaked Reynaud shrilly, but Armande went on gobbling candyfloss with both hands, her face glossy and self-possessed. I tried to warn her about the cab, but she looked at me and said in my mother's voice, 'Life's a carnival, *chérie*, more people die every year crossing the road, it's a statistical fact,' and went on eating in that terrible voracious way, and Reynaud turned towards me and squeaked, in a voice made all the more menacing for its lack of resonance, '*This is all your fault, you and your chocolate festival, everything was all right until you came along and now everyone's dying DYING DYING DYING—*'

I held my hands out protectively. 'It isn't me,' I whispered. 'It's *you*, it's supposed to be you, you're the Black Man, you're—' Then I was falling backwards through the looking glass with cards spraying out in all directions around me – *nine of Swords, DEATH. Three of Swords, DEATH. The Tower, DEATH. The Chariot, DEATH.*

I awoke screaming, with Anouk standing above me, her dark face blurry with sleep and anxiety. '*Maman,* what is it?'

Her arms are warm around my neck. She smells of chocolate and vanilla and peaceful untroubled sleep.

'Nothing. A dream. Nothing.'

She croons to me in her small soft voice, and I have an unnerving impression of the world reversed, of myself melting into her like a nautilus into its spiral, round-around-around, of her hand cool on my forehead, her mouth against my hair.

'Out-out-out,' she murmurs automatically. '*Evil spirits, get thee hence.* It's OK now, *Maman*. All gone.' I don't know where she picks these things up from. My mother used to say that, but I don't remember ever teaching Anouk. And yet she uses it like an old familiar formula. I cling to her for a moment, paralysed by love.

'It's going to be OK, isn't it, Anouk?'

'Of course.' Her voice is clear and adult and self-assured. 'Of course it is.' She puts her head on my shoulder and curls sleepily into the circle of my arms. 'I love you too, *Maman*.'

Outside the dawn is a moonshimmer away on the greying horizon. I hold my daughter tightly as she drifts back again into sleep, her curls tickling my face. Is this what my mother feared? I wonder as I listen to the birds – a single *craw-craw* at first then a full congregation of them – was this what she fled? Not her own death, but the thousands of tiny intersections of her life with others, the broken connections, the links in spite of themselves, the *responsibilities*? Did we spend all those years running from our loves, our friendships, the casual words uttered in passing that can alter the course of a lifetime?

I try to recall my dream, the face of Reynaud – his lost expression of dismay, *I'm late, I'm late* – he, too, running from or into some unimaginable fate of which I am an unwitting part. But the dream has fragmented, its pieces scattered like cards in a high wind. Difficult to remember whether the Black Man pursues or is pursued. Difficult now to be sure whether he *is* the Black Man. Instead the face of the White Rabbit returns, like that of a frightened child on a carnival-wheel, desperate to get off.

'Who rings the changes?'

In my confusion I take the voice for someone else's; a second later I understand I have spoken aloud. But as I sink back towards sleep I am almost sure I hear another voice reply, a voice which sounds something like Armande's, something like my mother's.

You do, Vianne, it tells me softly. *You do.*

20

Tuesday, March 4

THE FIRST GREEN OF THE SPRING CORN GIVES THE LAND A mellower look than you and I are used to. At a distance it seems lush – a few early drones stitch the air above its swaying, giving the fields a somnolent appearance. But we know that in two months' time all this will be burnt to stubble by the sun, the earth bared and cracked to a red glaze through which even the thistles are reluctant to grow. A hot wind scours what is left of the country, bringing with it drought, and in its wake, a stinking stillness which breeds disease. I remember the summer of '75, *mon père*, the dead heat and the hot white sky. We had plague after plague that summer. First the river-gypsies, crawling up what was left of the river in their filthy floating hovels, staying stranded in Les Marauds on the baking mudflats. Then the sickness which struck first their animals and then our own; a kind of madness, a rolling of the eyes, feeble jerking of the legs, bloating of the body though the animals refused to take water, then sweating, shivering and death amongst a heaving of purple-black flies; oh God, the air was ripe with them, ripe and sweet like the juice of a foul fruit. Do you remember? So hot that the desperate wild animals came off the dried *marais* to the water. Foxes, polecats, weasels, dogs. Many of them rabid, flushed from their habitat by hunger and the drought. We would shoot them as they stumbled onto the river banks, shoot them or kill them with stones. The children stoned the gypsies too, but they were as trapped and desperate as their animals and they kept coming back. The air was blue with flies and the stench of their burning as they tried to halt the disease. Horses succumbed first, then cows, oxen, goats, dogs. We kept them at bay, refusing to sell goods or water, refusing medicine. Stranded on the flats of the dwindling Tannes, they drank bottled beer and river water. I remember watching them from Les Marauds, the silent slouching figures over their campfires at night, hearing the sobbing of someone – a woman or a child, I think – across the dark water.

Some people, weaklings – Narcisse amongst them – began to talk about charity. About pity. But you stayed strong. You knew what to do.

At Mass you read out the names of those who refused to co-operate. Muscat – old Muscat, Paul's father – barred them from the café until they saw reason. Fights broke out at night between the gypsies and the villagers. The church was desecrated. But you stood fast.

One day we saw them trying to hoist their boats across the flats to the open river. The mud was still soft and they slid thigh-deep in places, scrabbling for purchase against the slimy stones. Some pulled, harnessed to their barques by ropes, others pushed from behind. Seeing us watching, some cursed us in their harsh, hoarse voices. But it was another two weeks before they left at last, leaving their wrecked boats behind them. A fire, you said, *mon père*, a fire left untended by the drunkard and his slattern who owned that boat, the flames spreading in the dry electric air until the river was dancing with it. An accident.

Some people talked; some always do. Said you had encouraged it with your sermons; nodded wisely at old Muscat and his young son, so nicely placed to see and hear, but who, on that night, had seen and heard nothing. Mostly, though, there was relief. And when the winter rain came and the Tannes swelled once more, even the hulks were covered over.

I went round there again this morning, *Père*. The place haunts me. Barely different to the way it was twenty years ago, there is a sly stillness to the place, an air of anticipation. Curtains twitch at grimy windows as I walk by. I seem to hear a low, continuous laughter coming at me across the quiet spaces. Will I be strong enough, *père*? In spite of all my good intentions, will I fail?

Three weeks. Already I have spent three weeks in the wilderness. I should be purged of uncertainties and weaknesses. But the fear remains. I dreamed of her last night. Oh, not a voluptuous dream, but one of incomprehensible menace. It is the sense of disorder which she brings, *père*, which so unnerves me. That wildness.

Joline Drou tells me the daughter is as bad. Running wild in Les Marauds, talk of ritual and superstition. Joline tells me the child has never attended church, never learnt to pray. She talks to her of Easter and the Resurrection; the child gabbles a farrago of pagan nonsense in return. And this festival; there is one of her posters in every shop window. The children are crazed with excitement.

'Leave them alone, *père*, you're only young once,' says Georges Clairmont indulgently. His wife looks at me archly from beneath her plucked eyebrows. 'Well, I don't see what actual *harm* it could do,' she says simperingly. The truth is, I suspect, that their son has shown an interest. 'And anything which reinforces the Easter message—'

I do not attempt to make them understand. To rail against a children's celebration is to court ridicule. Already Narcisse has been heard to refer to my *brigade anti-chocolat*, amidst disloyal sniggering. But it rankles.

That she should use the Church's celebration to undermine the Church – to undermine *me*. Already I have jeopardized my dignity. I dare not go further than this. And with every day her influence spreads. Part of it is the shop itself. Half-café, half-*confiserie*, it projects an air of cosiness, of confidences. Children love the chocolate shapes at pocket-money prices. Adults enjoy the atmosphere of subtle naughtiness, of secrets whispered, grievances aired. Several families have begun to order a chocolate cake for lunch every Sunday; I watch them as they collect the beribboned boxes after Mass. The inhabitants of Lansquenet-sous-Tannes have never eaten as much chocolate. Yesterday Denise Arnauld was eating – *eating!* – in the confessional. I could smell the sweetness on her breath, but I had to pretend to maintain anonymity.

'*Blesh me*, mon père, *I have shinned.*' I could hear her chewing, hear the flat little sucking sounds she made against her teeth. I listened in growing rage as she confessed to a list of trifling sins which I barely even heard, the smell of chocolate growing more pungent in the enclosed space by the second. Her voice was thick with it, and I felt my own mouth moisten in sympathy. Finally I could not bear it any longer.

'Are you eating something?' I snapped.

'No, *père*.' Her voice was almost indignant. 'Eating? Why should I—'

'I'm *sure* I can hear you eating.' I did not bother to

lower my voice but half-stood in the darkness of the cubicle, my hands gripping the ledge. 'What do you take me for, an idiot?' Once again I heard the sucking sound of saliva against the tongue, and my rage flared. 'I can *hear* you, Madame,' I said harshly. 'Or do you imagine you are inaudible, as well as invisible?'

'*Mon père*, I assure you—'

'Quiet, Madame Arnauld, before you perjure yourself still further!' I roared, and suddenly there *was* no smell of chocolate, no lapping sound, simply a gasp of tearful outrage and a panicked scuffling as she fled from the cubicle, her high heels skidding on the parquet as she ran.

Alone in the cubicle I tried to recapture the scent, the sound, the certainty I had felt, the indignation – the rightness – of my anger. But as the dark closed around me, scented with incense and candle smoke and not a trace of chocolate, I faltered, doubting. Then the absurdity of it all struck me and I doubled up in a paroxysm of mirth as unexpected as it was alarming. I was left shaken and drenched with sweat, my stomach churning. The unexpected thought that *she* would be the only person to fully appreciate the humour of the situation was enough to provoke another convulsion, and I was obliged to cut short confession, pleading a slight malaise. My walk was unsteady as I made my way back to the vestry, and I caught a number of people looking at me strangely. I must be more careful. Gossip abounds in Lansquenet.

Since then things have been quiet. I attribute my outburst in the confessional to a slight fever which passed during the night. Certainly there has been no repetition of the incident. As a precaution I have reduced my evening meal still further, to prevent the digestive troubles which may be responsible for this. Still, I feel a sense of uncertainty – almost of expectation – around me. The wind has made the children giddy, sailing about the square with outstretched arms, calling to each other in birdlike voices. The adults too seem volatile, shifting uneasily from one extreme to the next. Women speak too loudly, self-consciously falling silent when I pass; some are close to tears; some aggressive. I spoke to Joséphine Muscat this morning as she sat outside the Café de la République and that dull, monosyllabic woman spat abuse in return, her eyes flaring and her voice trembling with fury.

'Don't talk to me,' she hissed. 'Haven't you already done enough?'

I kept my dignity and did not deign to answer, for fear of being caught in a shouting match. But she has changed; harder somehow, the slackness in her face gone, to be replaced by a kind of hateful *focus*. Another convert for the enemy camp.

Why can't they see, *mon père*? Why can't they see what the woman is doing to us? Breaking down our community spirit, our sense of purpose. Playing on what is worst and weakest in the secret heart. Earning for herself a kind of affection, of loyalty which – God help me! – I am weak enough to covet. Preaching a travesty of goodwill, of tolerance, of pity for the poor homeless outcasts on the river while all the time the corruption grows deeper entrenched. The devil works not through evil but through weakness, *père*. You of all people know that. Without the strength and purity of our convictions, where are we? How secure are we? How soon will it be before the disease spreads even to the Church itself? We have seen how quickly the rot has spread. Soon they will be campaigning for *non-denominational services to include alternative belief systems*, abolishing the confessional as *unnecessarily punitive*, celebrating the *inner self*, and before they know it all their seemingly forward-thinking, harmless liberal attitudes will have set their feet securely and irrevocably on the well-intentioned road to hell.

Ironic, isn't it? A week ago I was still questioning my own faith. Too self-absorbed to see the signs. Too feeble to play my part. And yet the Bible tells us quite clearly what we must do. Weeds and wheat cannot grow peacefully together. Any gardener could tell you the same thing.

21

Wednesday, March 5

LUC CAME AGAIN TODAY TO TALK WITH ARMANDE. HE seems more assured now, though he still stutters quite badly, relaxing enough to make the occasional discreet joke, at which he smirks with an air of faint surprise, as if the role of humorist is an unfamiliar one. Armande was in excellent form, having exchanged her black straw hat for a watered-silk headscarf. Her cheeks were rosy-apple red – though I suspected that this, like the unusual brightness of her lips, was due to artifice rather than mere high spirits. In such a short time she and her grandson have discovered that they have more in common than either had previously imagined; free of Caro's inhibiting presence, both seem remarkably at ease with each other. It is difficult to remember that until last week they were barely nodding acquaintances. There is a kind of intensity with them now, a lowered tone, a suggestion of intimacy. Politics, music, chess, religion, rugby, poetry – they swoop and segue from one topic to another, like gourmets at a buffet who cannot bear to leave any dish untasted. Armande directs the full laser intensity of her charm upon him – vulgar by turns, then erudite, winsome, gamine, solemn, wise.

No doubt about it; this is seduction.

This time it was Armande who noticed the hour. 'It's getting late, boy,' she said brusquely. 'Time for you to be getting back.'

Luc stopped in mid-sentence, looking absurdly chagrined. 'I – didn't realize it was g-getting so late.' He paused aimlessly, as if reluctant to leave. 'I suppose I ought,' he said without enthusiasm. 'If I'm late, M-mother'll have kittens. Or s-something. You know what she's l-like.'

Wisely, Armande has refrained from testing the boy's loyalty to Caro, keeping any disparaging comments about her to a minimum. At this implicit criticism she gave one of her malicious smiles. 'Don't I just,' she said. 'Tell me, Luc, don't you ever feel like rebelling – just a little?' Her eyes were summery with laughter. 'At your age you *ought* to be rebelling – growing your hair long and listening to rock music, seducing girls, or something. Otherwise there'll be hell to pay when you're eighty.'

Luc shook his head. 'Too risky,' he said shortly. 'I'd rather l-live.'

Armande laughed delightedly.

'Next week, then?' This time he kissed her lightly on the cheek. 'Same day?'

'I think I can manage it.' She smiled. 'I'm having a housewarming tomorrow night,' she told him abruptly. 'To thank everyone for the work they did on my roof. You can come too, if you like.'

For a moment Luc looked doubtful.

'Of course, if Caro would object . . .' She let the sentence trail ironically, fixing him with her bright, challenging stare.

'I'm sure I c-could think of some excuse,' said Luc, rallying beneath her look of amusement. 'It might be good f-fun.'

'Of course it will,' said Armande briskly. 'Everyone will be there. Except of course Reynaud and his bible groupies.' She gave him a sly little smile. 'Which in my book is a big bonus, in any case.'

A look of guilty amusement crosses his face and he smirks. 'B-bible groupies,' he repeats. '*Mémée*, that's actually p-pretty c-cool.'

'I'm *always* cool,' replies Armande with dignity.

'I'll see what I c-can do.'

*

Armande was finishing her drink, and I was about to close the shop when Guillaume came in. I've hardly seen him this week, and he looks rumpled somehow, colourless and sad-eyed beneath the rim of his felt hat. Always punctilious, he greeted us with his usual grave courtesy, but I could see he was troubled. His clothes seemed to hang vertically from his stooping shoulders, as if there were no body beneath. His small features were wide-eyed and anguished, like a capuchin's. No Charly accompanied him, though I noticed once more that he carried the dog's lead wrapped around his wrist. Anouk peeped at him curiously from the kitchen.

'I know you're closing.' His voice was clipped and precise, like that of a brave war bride in one of his beloved British movies. 'I shan't keep you long.' I poured him a demitasse of my blackest *choc. espresso*, and added a couple of his favourite florentines on the side. Anouk perched on a stool and eyed them enviously.

'I'm in no hurry,' I told him.

'Neither am I,' declared Armande in her blunt fashion, 'but I can be on my way if you'd rather.'

Guillaume shook his head. 'No, of course not.' He gave a smile of little conviction. 'It isn't a great matter.'

I waited for him to explain, already half-knowing. Guillaume took a florentine and bit into it automatically, cupping one hand beneath to avoid dropping crumbs.

'I've just buried old Charly,' he said in that brittle

voice. 'Under a rosebush in my bit of garden. He'd have liked that.'

I nodded. 'I'm sure he would.'

Now I could smell the grief on him, a sour tang like earth and mildew. There was soil beneath his fingernails as he held the florentine.

Anouk watched him solemnly. 'Poor Charly,' she said.

Guillaume seemed hardly to hear her. 'I had to take him in the end,' he continued. 'He couldn't walk, and he whined when I carried him. Last night he wouldn't stop whining. I sat with him all night, but I knew.' Guillaume looked almost apologetic, caught in a grief too complex to articulate. 'I know it's stupid,' he said. 'Only a dog, as the *curé* said. Stupid to make a song and dance about it.'

'Not so,' broke in Armande unexpectedly. 'A friend is a friend. And Charly was a good one. Don't expect Reynaud to understand about that kind of thing.'

Guillaume gave her a grateful look. 'It's kind of you to say so.' He turned towards me. 'And you too, Madame Rocher. You tried to warn me last week, but I wasn't ready to listen. I suppose I imagined that by ignoring all the signs I could somehow make Charly survive indefinitely.'

Armande watched him with an odd expression in her black eyes. 'Sometimes survival is the worst alternative there is,' she observed mildly.

Guillaume nodded. 'I should have taken him earlier,' he said. 'Given him a bit of dignity.' His smile was painful in its nakedness. 'At least I should have spared us both that last night.'

I was unsure what to say to him. In a way I don't think he needed me to say anything. He just wanted to talk. I avoided the usual clichés and said nothing. Guillaume finished his florentine and gave another of his terrible, wan smiles.

'It's dreadful,' he said, 'but I have *such* an appetite. I feel as if I haven't eaten for a month. I've just buried my dog and I could eat a—' He broke off in confusion. 'It feels terribly wrong somehow,' he said. 'Like eating meat on Good Friday.'

Armande gave a cackle of laughter and laid a hand on Guillaume's shoulder. Beside him she looked very solid, very capable. 'You come with me,' she ordered. 'I've got bread and *rillettes*, and a nice Camembert just about ready for eating. Oh, and, Vianne' – turning to me with an imperious gesture – 'I'll have a box of those chocolate things, what are they? Florentines? A nice big box.'

That at least I can provide. Small comfort, perhaps, to a man who has lost his best friend. Secretly, with my fingertip, I traced a little sign on the lid of the box for luck and protection.

Guillaume began to protest, but Armande cut him short. 'Rubbish!' She was unanswerable, her energy infusing the wan little man in spite of himself. 'What are you going to do otherwise? Sit in your house and mope?'

She shook her head emphatically. 'No. It's been a long time since I entertained a gentleman friend. I'll enjoy it. Besides,' she added reflectively, 'there's something I want to talk to you about.'

Armande gets her way. It's virtually a maxim. I watched them both as I wrapped the box of florentines and tied it with long silver ribbons. Guillaume was already responding to her warmth, confused but gratified. 'Madame Voizin—'

Firmly: 'Armande. Madame makes me feel so old.'

'Armande.'

It is a small victory.

'And you can leave *that* behind, too.' Gently she disentangles the dog's lead from around Guillaume's wrist. Her sympathy is robust but unpatronizing. 'No point carrying useless ballast. It won't change a thing.'

I watch as she manoeuvres Guillaume out of the doorway. Pausing halfway, she gives me a wink. A wave of sudden affection for them both submerges me. Then out into the night.

Lying in bed hours later, watching the sky's slow wheeling from our attic window, Anouk and I are still awake. Anouk has been very solemn since Guillaume's visit, showing none of her usual exuberance. She has left the door between us open, and I wait for the inevitable question with a feeling of dread; I asked it myself often enough in those nights after Mother died, and I am still none the wiser. But the question does not come. Instead, long after I am sure she is asleep, she creeps into my bed and tucks a cold hand into mine.

'Maman?' She knows I am awake. 'You won't die, will you?'

I give a soft laugh in the dark. 'No-one can promise that,' I tell her gently.

'Not for a long time, anyway,' she insists. 'Not for years and *years.*'

'I hope not.'

'Oh.' She digests this for a moment, turning her body comfortably into the curve of mine. 'We live longer than dogs, don't we?'

I agree that we do. Another silence.

'Where do you think Charly is now, *Maman?*'

There are lies I could tell her; comforting lies. But I find I cannot. 'I don't know, Nanou. I like to think – we start again. In a new body that isn't old or sick. Or in a bird, or a tree. But no-one really knows.'

'Oh.' The little voice is doubtful. 'Even dogs?'

'I don't see why not.'

It is a fine fantasy. Sometimes I find myself caught up in it, like a child in her own invention; find myself seeing my mother's vivid face in that of my little stranger.

Brightly: 'We should find Guillaume's dog for him,

then. We could do it tomorrow. Wouldn't that make him feel better?'

I try to explain that it isn't as easy as that, but she is determined. 'We could go to all the farms and find out which dogs have had puppies. D'you think we'd be able to recognize Charly?'

I sigh. I should be used to this tortuous track by now. Her conviction reminds me so much of my mother that I am close to tears. 'I don't know.'

Stubbornly: '*Pantoufle* would recognize him.'

'Go to sleep, Anouk. School tomorrow.'

'He would. I *know* he would. Pantoufle sees *everything*.'

'Shh.'

I hear her breathing slow at last. Her sleeping face is turned to the window, and I can see starlight on her wet eyelashes. If I could only be *certain*, for her sake. But there are no certainties. The magic in which my mother believed so implicitly did not save her in the end; none of the things we did together could not have been explained by simple coincidence. Nothing is so easy, I tell myself; the cards, candles, incense, incantations merely a child's trick to keep away the dark. And yet it hurts me to think of Anouk's disappointment. In sleep her face is serene, trustful. I imagine us on tomorrow's fool's errand, inspecting puppies, and my heart gives a wrench of protest. I should not have told her what I couldn't *prove* . . .

Carefully, so as not to wake her, I slip out of bed. The

boards are smooth and cold beneath my bare feet. The door creaks a little as I open it, but though she murmurs something in her sleep, she does not wake. I have a responsibility, I tell myself. Without wanting to, I have made a promise.

My mother's things are still there in her box, packed in sandalwood and lavender. Her cards, herbs, books, oils, the scented ink she used for scrying, runes, charms, crystals, candles of many colours. But for the candles I would rarely open the box. It smells too strongly of wasted hope. But for Anouk's sake – Anouk who reminds me so much of her – I suppose I must try. I feel a little ridiculous. I should be sleeping, regaining my strength for a busy day tomorrow. But Guillaume's face haunts me. Anouk's words make sleep impossible. There is danger in all of this, I tell myself desperately; in using these almost forgotten skills I enhance my otherness and make it all the more difficult for us to stay.

The habit of ritual, so long abandoned, returns with unexpected ease. Casting the circle – water in a glass, a dish of salt and a lit candle on the floor – is almost a comfort, a return to days when everything had a simple explanation. I sit cross-legged on the floor, closing my eyes, and let my breathing slow.

My mother delighted in rituals and incantations. I was less willing. I was inhibited, she would tell me with a chuckle. I feel very close to her now, eyes shut and with the scent of her in the dust on my fingers. Perhaps that is why tonight I find this so easy. People who know nothing of real magic imagine it to be a flamboyant process. I suspect this is why my mother, who loved theatrics, made such a show of it. And yet the real business is very undramatic; simply the focusing of the mind towards a desired objective. There are no miracles, no sudden apparitions. I can see Guillaume's dog perfectly clearly in my mind's eye, gilded with that glow of welcome, but no dog appears in the circle. Perhaps tomorrow, or the day after, a seeming coincidence, like the orange chair or the red bar-stools we imagined on our first day. Perhaps nothing will come.

Looking at the watch which I have left on the floor I realize it is almost three-thirty. I must have remained here for longer than I thought, for the candle is burning low and my limbs are cold and stiff. And yet my unease has vanished, leaving me oddly rested, satisfied for no reason that I can quite understand.

I climb back into bed – Anouk has expanded her empire, flinging arms wide across the pillows – and curl into the warmth. My demanding little stranger will be placated. As I sink softly into sleep, for a moment I think I hear my mother's voice, very close, whispering.

22

Friday, March 7

THE GYPSIES ARE LEAVING. I WALKED BY LES MARAUDS early this morning and they were making ready, stacking their fishing-pots and taking in their interminable lines of washing. Some left last night, in darkness – I heard the sounds of their whistles and airhorns, like a final defiance – most superstitiously awaiting first light. It was just after seven when I passed. In the pale grey-green of the dawn they looked like war refugees, white-faced, sullenly tying the last remains of their floating circus into bundles. What was garish and magical-tawdry last night is now merely drab, scorched of its glamour. A smell of burning and oil hangs in the mist. A sound of flapping canvas, the hacking of early-morning engines. Few even bother to look at me, going about their business with tight mouths and narrowed eyes. No-one speaks. I do not see Roux among these stragglers. Perhaps he left with the early crowd. There are maybe thirty boats still left on the river, their bows sagging with the weight of the accumulated baggage. The girl Zézette works alongside the wrecked hulk, transferring unidentifiable pieces of blackened something onto her own boat. A crate of chickens rests precariously on top of a charred mattress and a box of magazines. She flings me a look of hatred, but says nothing.

Don't think I feel nothing for these people. There is no personal grudge, *mon père*, but I have my own congregation to think of. I cannot waste time in unsolicited preaching to strangers, to be jeered at and insulted. And yet I am not unapproachable. Any one of them would be welcome in my church, if their contrition were sincere. If they need guidance, they know they can come to me.

I slept badly last night. Since the beginning of Lent I have suffered troubled nights. I often leave my bed in the early hours, hoping to find sleep in the pages of a book, or in the dark silent streets of Lansquenet, or on the banks of the Tannes. Last night I was more restless than usual, and, knowing I would not sleep, left the house at eleven for an hour's walk along the river. I skirted Les Marauds and the gypsies' camp and made my way across the fields and upriver, though the sounds of their activity remained clearly audible behind me. Looking back downriver I could see campfires on the river bank, dancing figures outlined in the orange glow. Looking at my watch I realized I had been walking for almost an hour, and I turned to retrace my footsteps. I had not intended to pass through Les Marauds, but to walk across the fields once more would add half an hour onto my journey home, and I was feeling dull and dizzy with fatigue. Worse, the combination of cold air and sleeplessness had awoken in me an acute feeling of hunger which I already knew would be inadequately broken by my early morning collation of coffee and bread. It was for this reason that I made my way to Les Marauds, *père*, my thick boots sinking deep into the clay of the banking and my breath glowing with the light of their fires. I was soon close enough to distinguish what was going on. A kind of party was under way. I saw lanterns, candles stuck onto the sides of the barques, giving the carnival scene a strangely devotional look. A scent of woodsmoke and something tantalizing which might be grilling sardines; beneath that the sharp, bitter scent of Vianne Rocher's chocolate wafted across the river. I should have known she would be there. But for her the gypsies would have left long ago. I could see her on the jetty below Armande Voizin's house, her long red coat and loose hair giving her an oddly pagan look among the flames. For a second she turned towards me and I saw a flare of bluish fire rise from her outstretched hands, a burning something between her fingers lighting the surrounding faces purple . . .

For a moment I was frozen with terror. Irrational

thoughts – arcane sacrifice, devil worship, live burnt-offerings to some savage ancient god – leaped within my mind and I almost fled, stumbling in the thick mud, hands held out to prevent a fall into the tangle of blackthorn bushes which hid me. Then relief. Relief, understanding and a searing embarrassment at my own absurdity as she turned back towards me, the flames dying down even as I watched.

'*Mother of God!*' My knees almost gave way beneath me with the intensity of my reaction. 'Pancakes. Flambéed pancakes. That was all.'

I was half-laughing now, breathless with hysteria. My stomach ached and I dug my fists into my guts to stop the laughter spilling out. As I watched she lit another mountain of pancakes and served them deftly from the frying pan, liquid flame running from plate to plate like St Elmo's fire.

Pancakes. This is what they have done to me, *père*. Hearing things – seeing things – which are not there. This is what she has done to me, she and her friends from the river. And yet she looks so innocent. Her face is open, delighted. The sound of her voice across the water – her laughter mingling with that of the others – is alluring, vibrant with humour and affection. I find myself wondering what my own voice would sound like amongst those others, my own laughter meshed with hers, and the night is suddenly very lonely, very cold, very empty.

If only I could, I thought. Walk out from my hiding

place and join them. Eat, drink – suddenly the thought of food was a delirious imperative, my mouth filling enviously. To gorge myself on pancakes, to warm myself by the brazier and the light from her golden skin.

Is this temptation, *père*? I tell myself that I resisted it, that my inner strength defeated it, that my prayer – *please oh please oh please oh please* – was one of deliverance, not of desire.

Did you feel this too? Did you pray? And when you succumbed that day in the chancery, was the pleasure bright and warm as a gypsies' campfire, or was it with a brittle sob of exhaustion, a final unheard cry in the darkness?

I should not have blamed you. One man – even a priest – cannot hold back the tide for ever. And I was too young to know the loneliness of temptation, the sour taste of envy. I was very young, *père*. I looked up to you. It was less the nature of the act – or even with whom you performed it – than the simple fact that you were *capable* of sin. Even you, *père*. And knowing that, I realized that nothing was safe. No-one. Not even myself.

I do not know how long I watched, *père*. Too long, for when I moved at last my hands and feet were without sensation. I saw Roux among the gathering, and his friends Blanche and Zézette, Armande Voizin, Luc Clairmont, Narcisse, the Arab, Guillaume Duplessis, the tattooed girl, the fat woman with the green headscarf.

Even the children – mainly river children, but some like Jeannot Drou and, of course, Anouk Rocher – were there, some almost asleep, some dancing by the river's edge or eating sausages wrapped in thick barley pancakes, or drinking hot lemonade laced with ginger. My sense of smell seemed preternaturally enhanced so that I could almost taste every dish – the fish grilled in the ashes of the brazier, the roasted goat's cheese, the dark pancakes and the light, hot chocolate cake, the *confit de canard* and the spiced *merguez*. I could hear Armande's voice above the rest; her laughter was like that of an overtired child. Sprinkled across the water's edge, the lanterns and candles looked like Christmas lights.

At first I took the cry of alarm for one of amusement. A bright spike of sound, laughter, perhaps, or hysteria. For a moment I thought one of the children had fallen into the water. Then I saw the fire.

It was on one of the boats closest to the bank, a little distance away from the revellers. A fallen lantern, maybe, a careless cigarette, a candle dripping burning wax onto a roll of dry canvas. Whatever it was, it spread fast. One second it was on the roof of the boat, the next it had spilled onto the deck. The flames began the same gauzy blue as the flambéed pancakes, but warmed as they spread, becoming the vivid orange of a burning haystack on a hot August night. The redhaired man, Roux, was the first to react. I supposed it was his boat. The flames had barely time to change colour and he was on his feet, jumping from one boat to another to reach the fire. One of the women called after him in distress. But he paid no attention. He is surprisingly light on his feet. He crossed two other boats in a matter of thirty seconds, yanking at the ropes which bound them together to free them, kicking one untethered barque away from the next and moving on. I saw Vianne Rocher watching with her hands outstretched; the others stood in a silent circle at the jetty. The barques which had been freed from their moorings drifted slowly downriver, and the water itself was choppy with their rocking motion. Roux's boat was already beyond salvation, black pieces of airborne *debris* drifting on a column of heat across the water. In spite of this I saw him grab a roll of half-charred tarpaulin and try to beat at the flames, but the heat was too intense. A speck of fire adhered to his jeans, another to his shirt; dropping the tarpaulin he beat them out with his hands. Another attempt to reach the cabin, one arm shielding his face; I heard him cry out some angry profanity in his thick dialect. Armande was calling to him now, her voice sharp with worry. I caught something about petrol, and tanks.

Fear and elation, clawing so sweetly, nostalgically, at my viscera. It was so like that other time, the smell of burning rubber, the full-throated roar of the fire, the reflections . . . I could almost have believed that I was a boy again, that you were the *curé*, both of us absolved by some miracle of all responsibility.

209

Ten seconds later Roux jumped off the burning boat into the water. I saw him swimming back, though the petrol tank did not rupture until several minutes later, and then it was with a dull thumping sound and not the gaudy fireworks which I had expected. For a few minutes he disappeared from sight, hidden by the strings of flame skating effortlessly across the water. I stood up, no longer afraid of being seen, craning my neck to catch sight of him. I think I prayed.

You see, *père*. I am not without compassion. I *feared* for him.

Vianne Rocher was already in the water, hip-deep in the sluggish Tannes with her red coat soaked to the armpits, one hand over her eyes, scanning the river. Beside her, Armande, sounding anxious and old. And when they pulled him dripping onto the jetty I felt relief so great that my knees buckled and I fell into the mud at the river bank in an attitude of prayer. But the elation of seeing their camp burning – that was glorious, like a memory of childhood, the joy of secretly watching, of *knowing* . . . In my darkness I felt power, *père*, I felt that somehow I had caused it – the fire, the confusion, the man's escape – that somehow by my proximity I had brought about a re-enactment of that distant summer. Not a miracle. Nothing so gauche as that. But a sign. Surely, a sign.

I crept home in silence, keeping to the shadows. In the crowd of onlookers, of crying children, angry adults, silent stragglers holding hands before the blazing river like dazed children in some evil fairy tale, one man could easily pass unnoticed. One man – or two.

I saw him as I reached the top of the hill. Sweating and grinning, he was red-faced from his exertions, his glasses smeared. The sleeves of his checked shirt were rolled above the elbow, and in the lurid afterglow of the fire his skin looked hard and red as polished cedar. He showed no surprise at my presence but simply grinned. A foolish, sly grin, like that of a child caught out by an indulgent parent. I noticed that he smelt strongly of petrol.

'Evening, *mon père*.'

I dared not acknowledge him, as if by so doing I should be obliged to admit a responsibility of which silence might absolve me. Instead I lowered my head, a reluctant conspirator, and hurried on. Behind me I sensed Muscat watching me, face slickered with sweat and reflections, but when I finally looked back, he had gone.

A candle, dripping wax. A cigarette flicked across the water, bouncing into a pile of stovewood. One of their lanterns, the bright paper catching, powdering the deck with embers. Anything could have started it.

Anything at all.

2 3

Saturday, March 8

I CALLED ON ARMANDE AGAIN THIS MORNING. SHE WAS
sitting in her rocking-chair in her low-ceilinged living
room, one of her cats lying sprawled across her knees.
Since the fire at Les Marauds she has looked frail and
determined, her round apple-face sinking slowly in upon
itself, eyes and mouth swallowed by wrinkles. She was
wearing a grey housedress over lumpy black stockings, and
her hair was lank and unplaited.

'They've gone, you noticed.' Her voice was flat, almost
indifferent. 'Not a single boat left on the river.'

'I know.'

Walking down the hill into Les Marauds I find their
absence is still a shock, like the ugly patch of yellowed
grass where a circus tent once stood. Only the hulk
of Roux's boat remains, a waterlogged carcass a few

feet below the surface, blackly visible against the river mud.

'Blanche and Zézette have moved a little way down-river. They said they'd be back sometime today, to see how things were doing.'

She began to work her long grey hair into her customary plait. Her fingers were stiff and awkward, like sticks.

'What about Roux? How is he?'

'Angry.'

As well he might be. He knows the fire was no accident, knows he has no proof, knows that even if he had, it wouldn't help him. Blanche and Zézette offered him a place on their cramped houseboat, but he refused. The work on Armande's house is still unfinished, he says flatly. He needs to see to that first. I myself have not spoken to him since the night of the fire. I saw him once, briefly on the river bank, burning litter left by the travellers. He looked dour and unresponsive, eyes red-dened by the smoke, refusing to answer when I addressed him. Some of his hair was burnt away in the fire and he has chopped the rest spikily short, so that now he looks like a newly struck match.

'What is he going to do now?'

Armande shrugged. 'I'm not sure. I think he's been sleeping in one of the derelict houses down the road. Last night I left him some food on the doorstep, and this morning it had gone. I already offered him money, but he won't take it.' She pulled irritably at her finished plait. 'Stubborn young fool. What good's all that money to me, at my age? Might as well give some of it to him as to the Clairmont clan. Knowing them, it'll probably end up in Reynaud's collection-box anyway.'

She made a sound of derision. 'Pigheaded, that's what it is. Redhaired men, God save us. You can't tell them anything.' She shook her head peevishly. 'He stalked off in a temper yesterday, and I haven't seen him since.'

I smiled in spite of myself. 'You're a pair,' I told her. 'Each as stubborn as the other.'

Armande shot me a look of indignation. '*Me?*' she exclaimed. 'You're comparing me with that carrot-topped, obstreperous—'

Laughing, I recanted. 'I'll see if I can find him,' I told her.

I did not find him, though I spent an hour on the banks of the Tannes looking. Even my mother's methods failed to reveal him. I did find where he was sleeping, however. A house not far from Armande's, one of the least run-down of the derelicts. The walls are slick with damp, but the top floor seems sound enough and there is glass in several of the windows. Passing by I noticed that the door had been forced open, and that a fire had been lit recently in the living-room grate. Other signs of occupancy; a roll of charred tarpaulin salvaged from the fire, a stack of driftwood, a few pieces of furniture, presumably left in the house as being of no value. I called Roux's name, but there was no answer.

By eight-thirty I had to open La Praline, so I abandoned the search. Roux would emerge when he wanted to. Guillaume was waiting outside the shop when I arrived, although the door was unlocked.

'You should have gone inside to wait for me,' I told him.

'Oh no.' His face was gravely mocking. 'That would have been taking a liberty.'

'Live dangerously,' I advised him, laughing. 'Come in and try some of my new *religieuses*.'

He still seems diminished since Charly's death, shrunken to less than his size, his young-old face impish and wizened with grief. But he has retained his humour, a wistful, mocking quality which saves him from self-pity. This morning he was full of what had happened to the river-gypsies.

'Not a word from Curé Reynaud at Mass this morning,' he declared as he poured chocolate from the silver pot. 'Not yesterday or today. Not a single word.' I admitted that, given Reynaud's interest in the travelling community, this silence was unusual.

'Perhaps he knows something he can't tell,' Guillaume suggested. 'You know. The secret of the confessional.'

He has seen Roux, he tells me, talking to Narcisse outside his nurseries. Perhaps he can offer Roux a job. I hope so.

'He often takes on occasional labourers, you know,' said Guillaume. 'He's a widower. He never had children. There's no-one to manage the farm except a nephew in Marseille. And he doesn't mind who he takes on in the summer when it gets busy. As long as they're reliable it doesn't matter whether they go to church or not.' Guillaume gave a little smile, as he does when he is about to say something he considers daring. 'I sometimes wonder,' he said reflectively, 'whether Narcisse isn't a better Christian, in the purest sense, than me or Georges Clairmont – or even Curé Reynaud.' He took a mouthful of his chocolate. 'I mean, at least Narcisse *helps*,' he said seriously. 'He gives work to people who need the money. He lets gypsies camp on his land. Everyone knows he was sleeping with his housekeeper for all those years, and he never bothers with church except as a means of seeing his customers, but at least he helps.'

I uncovered the dish of *religieuses* and put one on his plate. 'I don't think there is such a thing as a good or bad Christian,' I told him. 'Only good or bad people.'

He nodded and took the little round pastry between finger and thumb. 'Maybe.'

A long pause. I poured a glass for myself, with *noisette* liqueur and hazelnut chips. The smell is warm and intoxicating, like that of a woodpile in the late autumn sun. Guillaume ate his *religieuse* with careful enjoyment, dabbling the crumbs from the plate with a moistened forefinger.

'In that case, the things I've believed all my life – about sin and redemption and the mortification of the body – you'd say none of those things mean anything, wouldn't you?'

I smiled at his seriousness. 'I'd say you've been talking to Armande,' I said gently. 'And I'd also say that you and she are entitled to your beliefs. As long as they make you happy.'

'Oh.' He watched me warily, as if I were about to sprout horns. 'And what – if it isn't an impertinent question – what do *you* believe?'

Magic-carpet rides, rune magic, Ali Baba and visions of the Holy Mother, astral travel and the future in the dregs of a glass of red wine . . .

Florida? Disneyland? The Everglades? What about it, chérie? *What about it,* hein?

Buddha. Frodo's journey into Mordor. The transubstantiation of the sacrament. Dorothy and Toto. The Easter Bunny. Space aliens. The Thing in the closet. The Resurrection and the Life at the turn of a card . . . I've believed them all at one time or another. Or pretended to.

Or pretended not to.

Whatever you like, Mother. Whatever makes you happy.

And now? What do I believe right now?

'I believe that being happy is the only important thing,' I told him at last.

Happiness. Simple as a glass of chocolate or tortuous as the heart. Bitter. Sweet. Alive.

In the afternoon Joséphine came. Anouk was back from school, and ran off almost at once to play in Les Marauds, wrapped tightly in her red anorak and with strict instructions to run back if it began to rain. The air smells sharp as new-cut wood, slicing low and sly round the angles of buildings. Joséphine was wearing her coat buttoned to the neck, her red beret and a new red scarf which fluttered wildly in her face. She walked into the shop with a defiant look of assurance, and for a moment she was a radiant, striking woman, cheeks flushed and eyes sparkling with the wind. Then the illusion dispersed and she was herself once more, hands digging fiercely into her pockets and head lowered as if to headbutt some unknown aggressor. She pulled off her beret revealing wildly tousled hair and a new, fresh welt across her forehead. She looked both terrified and euphoric.

'I've done it,' she declared recklessly. 'Vianne, I've done it.'

For a dreadful instant I was sure she was going to

confess to murdering her husband. She had that look –
a wild and lovely look of abandon – her lips drawn
back over her teeth as if she had bitten into a sour
fruit. Fear came from her in alternating hot and cold
waves.

'I've left Paul,' she said. 'I've done it at last.'

Her eyes were knives. For the first time since we met I
saw Joséphine as she was before ten years of Paul-Marie
Muscat made her wan and ungainly. Half-mad with fear,
but underneath the madness, a sanity which chills the
heart.

'Does he know yet?' I asked, taking her coat. The
pockets were heavy, though not, I thought, with jewellery.

Joséphine shook her head. 'He thinks I'm at the
grocer's,' she said breathlessly. 'We ran out of microwave
pizzas. He sent me out to stock up.' She gave a smile of
almost childish mischief. 'And I took some of the
housekeeping money,' she told me. 'He keeps it in a
biscuit tin under the bar. Nine hundred francs.' Beneath
the coat she was wearing a red jumper and a black pleated
skirt. It was the first time I could remember her wearing
anything but jeans. She glanced at her watch.

'I want a *chocolat espresso*, please,' she said. 'And a big
bag of almonds.' She put the money on the table. 'I'll have
just enough time before my bus leaves.'

'Your bus?' I was puzzled. 'To where?'

'Agen.' Her look was mulish, defensive. 'Then I don't

know. Marseille, maybe. As far away from *him* as I can get.' She gave me a look of suspicion and surprise. 'Don't start saying I shouldn't do it, Vianne. You were the one who encouraged me. I'd never have thought of it if you hadn't given me the idea.'

'I know, but—'

Her words sounded like an accusation. 'You told me I was free.'

True enough. Free to run, free to take off on a word from a virtual stranger, cut loose like an untethered balloon to drift on the changing winds. The fear was suddenly chill certainty in my heart. Was this the price of my remaining? To send her out in my place? And what choice had I really given her?

'But you were safe.' I choked out the words with difficulty, seeing my mother's face in hers. To give up her safety in exchange for a little knowledge, a glimpse of an ocean . . . and what then? The wind always brings us back to the foot of the same wall. A New York cab. A dark alley. A hard frost.

'You can't just run away from it all,' I said. 'I know. I've tried it.'

'Well, I can't stay in Lansquenet,' she snapped, and I could see she was close to tears. 'Not with him. Not now.'

'I remember when we lived like that. Always moving. Always running away.'

She has her own Black Man. I can see him in her eyes.

He has the unanswerable voice of authority, a specious logic which keeps you frozen, obedient, fearful. To break free from that fear, to run in hope and despair, to run and to find that all the time you were carrying him inside yourself like a malignant child. At the end, Mother knew it. Saw him at every street corner, in the dregs of every cup. Smiling from a billboard, watching from behind the wheel of a fast car. Getting closer with every beat of the heart.

'Start running away and you'll be on the run for ever,' I told her fiercely. 'Stay with me instead. Stay and fight with me.'

Joséphine looked at me. 'With you?' Her astonishment was almost comic.

'Why not? I have a spare room, a camp bed—' She was already shaking her head and I subdued an urge to clutch at her, to *force* her to stay. I knew I could do it. 'Just for a while, till you find somewhere else, till you find a job—'

She laughed in a voice tight with hysteria. 'A job? What can I do? Apart from clean – and cook – and wipe ashtrays and – pull pints and dig the garden and screw my h-husband every Fri-Friday night—' She was laughing harder now, grabbing at her stomach.

I tried to take her arm. 'Joséphine. I'm serious. You'll find something. You don't have to—'

'You should see him sometimes.' She was still laughing, each word a bitter bullet, her voice metallic with self-loathing. 'The pig in heat. The fat, hairy porker.' Then she was crying with the same hard rattling sounds as her laughter, eyes squeezed shut and hands pressing against her cheeks as if to prevent some inner explosion. I waited.

'And when it was over he'd turn away, and I'd hear him snoring. And in the morning I'd try' – her face contorted, her mouth twisting to form the words – 'I'd try – to *shake* – his *stink* – out of the sheets, and all the time I'd be thinking: *what happened to me?* To Joséphine Bonnet, who was so bright at s-school and who used to dream of being a d-dancer—'

She turned to me abruptly, her hot face flaring, but calm. 'It sounds stupid, but I used to think that there must have been a mistake somewhere, that one day someone was going to come and tell me that it wasn't happening, that this was all some other woman's dream and that none of it could ever have happened to *me*—'

I took her hand. It was cold and trembling. One of her nails was torn down to the quick, and there was blood grimed into the palm.

'The funny thing is, I try to remember what it must have been like loving him, but there's nothing there. It's all a blank. Nothing there at all. I remember everything else – the first time he hit me, oh I remember *that* – but you'd think that even with Paul-Marie there'd be *some-thing* to remember. Something to excuse it all. All that wasted time.'

She stopped abruptly and looked at her watch. 'I've talked too much,' she said in surprise. 'I won't have time for any chocolate if I'm going to catch my bus.'

I looked at her. 'Have the chocolate *instead* of the bus,' I told her. 'On the house. I only wish it could have been champagne.'

'I have to go,' she said fractiously. Her fists dug repeatedly into her stomach. Her head dropped like a charging bull's.

'No.' I looked at her. 'You have to stay here. You have to fight him face to face. Otherwise you may as well never have left him.'

She returned my look for a moment, half-defiant. 'I can't.' There was a desperate note in her voice. 'I won't be able to. He'll say things, he'll twist everything—'

'You have friends here,' I said gently. 'And even if you don't realize it yet, you're strong.'

Then Joséphine sat down, very deliberately, on one of my red stools, put her face against the counter and cried silently.

I let her. I didn't say it would be OK. I made no effort to comfort her. Sometimes it's better to leave things as they are, to let grief take its course. Instead I went into the kitchen and very slowly prepared the *chocolat espresso*. By the time I'd poured it, added cognac and chocolate chips, put the cups onto a yellow tray with a wrapped sugar lump in each saucer, she was calm again. It's a small kind of magic, I know, but it sometimes works.

'Why did you change your mind?' I asked when the cup was half-finished. 'Last time we talked about this you seemed very sure you weren't going to leave Paul.'

She shrugged, deliberately avoiding meeting my eyes. 'Was it because he hit you again?'

This time she looked surprised. Her hand went to her forehead where the broken skin looked angry, inflamed. 'No.'

'Then why?'

Her eyes slid from mine again. With her fingertips she touched the *espresso* cup, as if to test its reality. 'Nothing. I don't know. Nothing.'

It is a lie, and a visible one. Automatically I reach for her thoughts, so open a moment ago. I need to know if I *made* her do it, if I forced her in spite of my good intentions. But for the moment her thoughts are formless, smoky. I can see nothing there but darkness.

To press her would have been useless. There is a stubborn streak in Joséphine which refuses to be hurried. She will tell me in time. If she wants to.

It was evening before Muscat came looking for her. By then we had made up her bed in Anouk's room – for the moment Anouk will sleep on the camp bed beside me. She takes Joséphine's arrival in her stride, as she accepts so many other things. I knew a momentary pang for my daughter, for the first room of her own she had ever had, but promised it would not be for long.

'I have an idea,' I told her. 'Perhaps we could have the attic space beneath the roof made into a room just for you, with a ladder to climb up, and a trapdoor above it, and little round windows cut into the roof. Would you like that?'

It is a dangerous, beguiling notion. It suggests we are going to stay here a long time.

'Could I see the stars from up there?' asked Anouk eagerly.

'Of course.'

'Good!' said Anouk, and bounced upstairs to tell Pantoufle.

We sat down to table in the cramped kitchen. The table was left from the shop's bakery days, a massive piece of rough-cut pine cross-hatched with knife scars into which veins of ancient dough, dried to the consistency of cement, have worked to produce a smooth marbly finish. The plates are mismatched: one green, one white, Anouk's flowered. The glasses, too, are all different: one tall, one short, one which still bears the label *Moutarde Amora*. And yet this is the first time we have really *owned* such things. We used hotel crockery, plastic knives and forks. Even in Nice, where we lived for over a year, the furnishings were borrowed, leased with the shop. The novelty of possession is still an exotic thing to us, a precious thing, intoxicating. I envy the table its scars, the scorch marks caused by the hot bread tins. I envy its calm sense of time and I wish I could say: I did this five years ago. I made this mark, this ring caused by a wet coffee cup, this cigarette burn, this ladder of cuts against the wood's coarse grain. This is where Anouk carved her initials, the year she was six years old, this secret place behind the table leg. I did this on a warm day seven summers ago with the carving knife. Do you remember? Do you remember the summer the river ran dry? Do you remember?

I envy the table's calm sense of place. It has been here a long time. It belongs.

Joséphine helped me prepare dinner: a salad of green beans and tomatoes in spiced oil, red and black olives from the Thursday market stall, walnut bread, fresh basil from Narcisse, goat's cheese, red wine from Bordeaux. We talked as we ate, but not about Paul-Marie Muscat. Instead I told her about us, Anouk and I, of the places we had seen, of the *chocolaterie* in Nice, of our time in New York just after Anouk was born and of the times before, of Paris, of Naples, of all the stopping-places Mother and I had made into temporary homes in our long flight across the world. Tonight I want to recall only the bright things, the funny, the good things. There are too many sad thoughts in the air already. I put a white candle on the table to clear bad influences, and its scent is nostalgic, comforting. I remembered for Joséphine the little canal at Ourcq, the Pantheon, the Place des Artistes, the lovely avenue of Unter den Linden, the Jersey ferry, Viennese pastries eaten in their hot papers on the street, the seafront at Juan-les Pins, dancing in the streets in San Pedro. I watched her face lose a little of its set expression. I remembered how Mother sold a donkey to a farmer in a village near Rivoli, and how the creature kept finding us again, time after time, almost as far as Milan. Then the story of the flower-sellers in Lisbon, and how we left that city in a refrigerated florist's van which delivered us half-frozen four hours later by the hot white docks at Porto. She began to smile, then to laugh. There were times when we had money, Mother and I, and Europe was sunny and full of promise. I remembered them tonight; the Arab gentleman in the white limousine who serenaded Mother that day in San Remo, how we laughed and how happy she was, and how long we lived afterwards on the money he gave us.

'You've seen so much.' Her voice was envious and a little awed. 'And you're still so young.'

'I'm nearly the same age as you.'

She shook her head. 'I'm a thousand years old.' She gave a smile which was both sweet and wistful. 'I'd like to be an adventurer,' she said. 'To follow the sun with

227

nothing but a single suitcase, to have no idea at all of where I might be tomorrow.'

'Believe me,' I told her gently, 'you get tired. And after a while everywhere starts to look the same.'

She looked doubtful.

'Trust me,' I said. 'I mean it.'

It isn't quite true. Places all have their own characters, and returning to a city where you have lived before is like coming home to an old friend. But the *people* begin to look the same; the same faces recurring in cities a thousand miles apart, the same expressions. The flat, hostile stare of the official. The curious look of the peasant. The dull unsurprised faces of the tourists. The same lovers, mothers, beggars, cripples, vendors, joggers, children, policemen, taxi-drivers, pimps. After a while one begins to feel slightly paranoid, as if these people were secretly following from one town to another, changing clothes and faces but remaining essentially unchanged, going about their dull business with half an eye slyly cocked at us, the intruders. At first one feels a kind of superiority. We are a race apart, we the travellers. We have seen, experienced, so much more than they. Content to run out their sad lives in an endless round of sleep-work-sleep, to tend their neat gardens, their identical suburban houses, their small dreams; we hold them in a little contempt. Then, after a while, comes envy. The first time it is almost funny; a sharp sudden sting which subsides nearly straight away. A woman in a park, bending over a child in a pushchair, both faces lit by something which is not the sun. Then comes the second time, the third; two young people on the seafront, arms intertwined; a group of office-girls on their lunchbreak, giggling over coffee and croissants ... before long it is an almost constant ache. No, *places* do not lose their identity, however far one travels. It is the heart which begins to erode after a time. The face in the hotel mirror seems blurred some mornings, as if by too many casual looks. By ten the sheets will be laundered, the carpet swept. The names on the hotel registers change as we pass. We leave no trace as we pass on. Ghostlike, we cast no shadow.

I was roused from my thoughts by the imperious knocking at the front door. Joséphine half-stood, fear starting in her eyes, both fists clenched against her ribs. It was what we had been waiting for; the meal, the conversation, merely a pretence at normality. I stood up.

'It's OK,' I told her. 'I won't let him in.'

Her eyes were glazed with fear. 'I'm not talking to him,' she said in a low voice. 'I can't.'

'You may have to,' I answered. 'But it's all right. He can't walk through walls.'

She gave a shaky smile. 'I don't even want to hear his voice,' she said. 'You don't know what he's like. He'll say—'

I began to move towards the unlit shop area. 'I know exactly what he's like,' I said firmly. 'And whatever you might think, he isn't unique. The advantage of travel is that after a while you begin to realize that wherever you go most people aren't really all that much different.'

'I just hate *scenes*,' murmured Joséphine quietly as I put on the shop lights. 'And I hate *shouting*.'

'Soon be over,' I said as the hammering began again. 'Anouk can make you some chocolate.'

The door is on a safety-chain. I put it on when we arrived, being used to city security, though there was never a need for it until now. In the slice of light from the shop, Muscat's face is congested with rage.

'Is my wife here?' His voice is thick and beery, his breath foul.

'Yes.' There is no reason for subterfuge. Better have it out now and show him where he stands. 'I'm afraid she has left you, Monsieur Muscat. I offered to let her sleep here for a few nights, until things are sorted out. It seemed the best thing to do.' I try to make my voice neutral, polite. I know his type. We met it a thousand times, Mother and I, in a thousand places. He gapes at me in stupefaction. Then the mean intelligence in his eyes takes over, his gaze narrows, his hands open to show that he is harmless, bewildered, ready to be amused. For a moment he seems almost charming. Then he takes a step closer towards the door. I can smell the rankness of his breath, like beer and smoke and sour anger.

'Madame Rocher.' His voice is soft, almost appealing. 'I want you to tell that fat cow of mine to get her arse out of there right now, or I'll be in to get her. And if *you* get in my way, you bra-burning bitch—' He rattles at the door.

'Take the chain off.' He is smiling, wheedling, his rage burning from him with a faint chemical stink. 'I said take the fucking chain off before I *kick* it off!' His voice is womanish in anger. His squeal sounds like that of an angry pig.

Very slowly I explain the situation to him. He swears and shrieks his frustration. He kicks at the door several times, making the hinges wince.

'If you break into my house, Monsieur Muscat,' I tell him evenly, 'I'll assume you're a dangerous intruder. I keep a can of *Contre-Attaq*' in my kitchen drawer, which I used to carry when I lived in Paris. I've tried it once or twice. It's very effective.'

The threat calms him. I suspect he believes he alone has the right to make threats. 'You don't understand,' he whines. 'She's my wife. I care for her. I don't know what she's been telling you, but—'

'What she's been telling me doesn't matter, Monsieur. The decision is hers. If I were you I'd stop making an exhibition of myself, and go home.'

'Fuck that!' His mouth is so close to the door that his

spittle peppers me with hot, foul shrapnel. 'This is your fault, you bitch. *You* started filling her head with all this emancipation bullshit.' He mimics Joséphine's voice in a savage falsetto. 'Oh, it was all *Vianne says this*, and *Vianne thinks that*. Let me talk to her for just one minute and we'll see what *she* says for a change.'

'I don't think that's—'

'It's all right.' Joséphine has come up behind me, softly, a cup of chocolate held between her folded hands as if to warm them. 'I'll have to talk to him, or he'll never go away.'

I look at her. She is calmer, her eyes clear. I nod. 'OK.'

I step aside and Joséphine goes to the door. Muscat begins to talk but she cuts him short, her voice surprisingly sharp and even. 'Paul. Just listen to me.'

Her tone slices through his blustering, silencing him mid-phrase. 'Go away. I've nothing more to say to you. All right?'

She is shaking, but her voice is calm and level. I feel a sudden rush of pride for her, and give her arm a reassuring squeeze. Muscat is silent for a moment. Then the wheedling tone returns to his voice, though I can still hear the rage behind it, like the buzz of interference on a distant radio signal.

'José,' he says softly, 'this is stupid. Just come out and we can talk about it properly. You're my *wife*, José. Doesn't that deserve at least another try?'

She shakes her head. 'Too late, Paul,' she tells him in a tone of finality. 'I'm sorry.'

Then she shut the door very gently, very firmly, and though he hammered on it for several minutes longer, swearing and cajoling and threatening by turns, even weeping as he became maudlin and began to believe his own fiction, we did not answer it again.

At midnight I heard him shouting outside, and a clod of earth hit the window with a dull thumping sound, leaving a smear of clay across the clear glass. I stood up to see what was happening and saw Muscat like a squat, malevolent goblin in the square below, his hands thrust deep into his pockets so that I could see the soft roll of his stomach above the waistband of his trousers. He looked drunk.

'You can't stay in there for ever!' I saw a light go on in one of the windows behind him. 'You'll have to come out some time! And then, you bitches! And *then*!' Automatically I forked his ill-wishing back at him with a quick flick of the fingers.

Avert. Evil spirit, get thee hence.

Another one of Mother's ingrained reflexes. And yet it is surprising how much more secure I feel now. I lay calm and awake for a long time after that, listening to my daughter's soft breathing and watching the random shifting shapes of moonlight through the leaves. I think I tried scrying again, looking in the moving patterns for a sign, a word of reassurance ... At night such things are easier to believe, with the Black Man standing watch outside and the weathervane shrilling *cri-criii* at the top of the church tower. But I saw nothing, felt nothing, and finally fell asleep once more and dreamed of Reynaud standing at the foot of an old man's hospital bed with a cross in one hand and a box of matches in the other.

2 4

Sunday, March 9

ARMANDE CAME IN EARLY THIS MORNING FOR GOSSIP AND chocolate. Wearing a new blonde-straw hat decorated with a red ribbon she looked fresher and more vital than she appeared yesterday. The cane which she has taken to carrying is an affectation; tied with a bright red bow it looks like a little flag of defiance. She ordered *chocolat viennois* and a slice of my black-and-white layer cake and sat down comfortably on a stool. Joséphine, who is helping me in the shop for a few days until she decides what to do next, watched with a little apprehension from the kitchen.

'I heard there was some fuss last night,' said Armande in her brusque way. The kindness in her bright black eyes redeems her forwardness. 'That lout Muscat, I heard, out here yelling and carrying on.'

I explained as blandly as I could. Armande listened appreciatively.

'I only wonder why she didn't leave him years ago,' she said when I had finished. 'His father was just as bad. Too free with their opinions, both of them. *And* with their hands.' She nodded cheerily at Joséphine, standing in the doorway with a pot of hot milk in one hand. 'Always knew you'd see sense one day, girl,' she said. 'Don't you let anyone talk you out of it now.'

Joséphine smiled. 'Don't worry,' she said. 'I won't.'

We had more customers this morning in La Praline than we have had on any Sunday since Anouk and I moved in. Our regulars – Guillaume, Narcisse, Arnauld and a few others – said little, nodding kindly at Joséphine and going on much as normal.

Guillaume turned up at lunchtime, with Anouk. In the excitement of the past couple of days I had only spoken to him a couple of times, but as he walked in I was struck by the abrupt change in him. Gone was his shrunken, diminished look. Now he walked with a jaunty step, and he was wearing a bright red scarf around his neck which gave him an almost dashing air. From the corner of my eye I saw a darkish blur at his feet. Pantoufle. Anouk ran past Guillaume, her satchel swinging carelessly, ducking under the counter to give me a kiss.

'*Maman!*' she bugled in my ear. 'Guillaume's found a *dog*!'

I turned to look, my arms still full of Anouk. Guillaume was standing beside the door, his face flushed. At his feet, a small brown-and-white mongrel, no more than a puppy, lolled adoringly.

'Shh, Anouk. It isn't my dog.' Guillaume's expression was a complex of pleasure and embarrassment. 'He was by Les Marauds. I think maybe someone wanted to get rid of him.'

Anouk was feeding sugar lumps to the dog. 'Roux found him,' she piped. 'Heard him crying down by the river. He told me so.'

'Oh? You saw Roux?'

Anouk nodded absently and tickled the dog, who rolled over with a happy snarl. 'He's so cute,' she said. 'Are you going to keep him?'

Guillaume smiled, a little sadly. 'I don't think so, sweetheart. You know, after Charly—'

'But he's *lost*, he hasn't anywhere else—'

'I'm sure there are plenty of people willing to give a nice little dog like this a good home.' Guillaume bent down and gently pulled the dog's ears. 'He's a friendly little chap, full of life.'

Insistently: 'What are you going to call him?'

Guillaume shook his head. 'I don't think I'll be keeping him for long enough for that, *ma mie*.'

Anouk gave me one of her comical looks, and I shook my head at her in silent warning.

'I thought perhaps you could put a card in the shop window,' said Guillaume, sitting down at the counter. 'To see if anyone claims him, you know.'

I poured him a cup of mocha and set it down in front of him, with a couple of florentines on the side.

'Of course.' I smiled.

When I looked back a moment later, the dog was sitting on Guillaume's knee, eating the florentines. Anouk looked at me and winked.

Narcisse had brought me a basket of endives from his nursery, and seeing Joséphine, handed her a little bunch of scarlet anemones which he took from his coat pocket, muttering that they would cheer the place up a bit.

Joséphine blushed, but looked pleased and tried to thank him. Narcisse shuffled off, embarrassed, gruffly disclaiming.

After the kind came the curious. Word had spread during the sermon that Joséphine Muscat had moved into La Praline, and there was a steady flow of visitors throughout the morning. Joline Drou and Caro Clairmont arrived in their spring twinsets and silk headscarves with an invitation to a fund-raising tea on Palm Sunday.

Armande gave a delighted cackle on seeing them. 'My

my, it's the Sunday morning fashion parade!' she exclaimed.

Caro looked annoyed. 'You really shouldn't be here, *maman*,' she said reproachfully. 'You know what the doctor said, don't you?'

'I do indeed!' replied Armande. 'What's wrong, aren't I dying fast enough for you? Is that why you have to send that death's-head on a stick to spoil my morning?'

Caro's powdered cheeks reddened. 'Really, *maman*, you shouldn't say things like—'

'I'll mind my mouth if you mind your business!' snapped Armande smartly, and Caro almost chipped the tiles with her high heels in her haste to leave.

Then, Denise Arnauld came to see if we needed any extra bread.

'Just in case,' she said, eyes gleaming with curiosity. 'Seeing as now you have a guest, and everything.' I assured her that if we needed bread, we knew where to come.

Then Charlotte Edouard, Lydie Perrin, Georges Dumoulin: one wanting an early birthday present; another details of the chocolate festival – *such* an original idea, *madame*; another had dropped a purse outside St Jérôme's and wondered whether I might have seen it. I kept Joséphine behind the counter with one of my clean yellow aprons to protect her clothes from chocolate spillages, and she managed surprisingly well. She has taken pains with her appearance today. The red jumper and black skirt are neat and businesslike, the dark hair carefully secured with ribbon. Her smile is professional, her head high, and though her eyes occasionally drift towards the open door in anxious expectation there is little in her bearing to suggest a woman in fear for herself or for her reputation.

'Brazen, that's what she is,' hissed Joline Drou to Caro Clairmont as they passed the door in haste. 'Quite brazen. When I think of what that poor man had to bear with—'

Joséphine's back was turned, but I saw her stiffen. A lull in conversation made Joline's words very audible, and though Guillaume faked a coughing fit in order to cover them, I knew she had heard.

There was a small, embarrassed silence.

Then Armande spoke. 'Well, girl, you know you've made it when those two disapprove,' she said briskly. 'Welcome to the wrong side of the tracks!'

Joséphine gave her a sharp glance of suspicion, then, as if reassured that the joke was not against her, she laughed. The sound was open, carefree; surprised, she brought her hand to her mouth as if to check that the laughter belonged to her. That made her laugh all the more, and the others laughed with her. We were still laughing when the doorbell chimed and Francis Reynaud came quietly into the shop.

'Monsieur le Curé.' I saw her face change even before I saw him, becoming hostile and stupid, her hands returning to their accustomed position at the pit of her stomach.

Reynaud nodded gravely. 'Madame Muscat.' He placed special emphasis on the first word. 'I was sorry not to see you in church this morning.'

Joséphine muttered something graceless and inaudible. Reynaud took a step towards the counter and she half-turned as if to bolt into the kitchen, then thought better of it and turned to face him.

'That's right, girl,' said Armande approvingly. 'Don't let him give you any of his jabber.' She faced Reynaud and gestured sternly with a piece of cake. 'You let that girl alone, Francis. If anything, you should be giving her your blessing.'

Reynaud ignored her. 'Listen to me, *ma fille*,' he said earnestly. 'We need to talk.' His eyes went with some distaste to the red good-luck sachet hanging by the door. 'Not in here.'

Joséphine shook her head. 'I'm sorry. There's work to do. And I don't want to listen to anything you have to say.'

Reynaud's mouth set stubbornly. 'You have never needed the Church as much as you need it now.' A cold, rapid glance in my direction. 'You have weakened. You have allowed others to lead you astray. The sanctity of the marriage vow—'

Armande interrupted him again with a crow of derision.

'The sanctity of the marriage vow? Where did you dig

that one up? I would have thought that you of all people—'

'Please, Madame Voizin.' At last a trace of expression in his flat voice. His eyes are wintry. 'I would be most appreciative if you would—'

'Speak as you were raised to,' snapped Armande. 'That mother of yours never taught you to talk with a potato in your mouth, did she?' She gave a chuckle. 'Pretending we're better than the rest of us, are we? Forgot all about us at that fancy school?'

Reynaud stiffened. I could feel the tension coming from him. He has definitely lost weight in the past few weeks, his skin stretched like a tambourine's across the dark hollows of his temples, the articulation of his jaw clearly visible beneath the meagre flesh. A lank diagonal of hair across his forehead gives him a slyly artless look; the rest is crisp-creased efficiency.

'Joséphine.' His voice was gentle, compelling, excluding the rest of us as effectively as if they had been alone. 'I know you want me to help you. I've talked to Paul-Marie. He says you've been under a lot of strain. He says—'

Joséphine shook her head. 'Mon père.' The blank expression had left her face and she was serene. 'I know you mean well. But I'm not going to change my mind.'

'But the sacrament of marriage . . .' he looked agitated now, leaning forward against the counter with his face twisted in distress. His hands clutched at the padded surface as if for support. Another surreptitious glance at the bright sachet at the door. 'I know you have been confused. Others have influenced you.' Meaningfully: 'If only we could speak in *private*—'

'No.' Her voice was firm. 'I'm staying here with Vianne.'

'For how long?' His voice registered dismay whilst trying for incredulity. 'Madame Rocher may be your friend, Joséphine, but she's a businesswoman, she has a shop to run, a child to care for. How long will she tolerate a stranger in the house?' This shot was more successful. I saw Joséphine hesitate, the look of uncertainty back in her eyes. I'd seen it too often in my mother's face to mistake it; that look of disbelief, of fear.

We don't need anyone but each other. A fierce, remembered whisper in the hot dark of some anonymous hotel room. *What the hell would we want anyone else for?* Brave words, and if there were tears the darkness hid them. But I felt her shaking, almost imperceptibly, as she held me beneath the covers, like a woman in the throes of a hidden fever. Perhaps that was why she fled them, those kind men, kind women who wanted to befriend, to love, to understand her. We were contagious, fevered with mistrust, the pride we carried with us the last refuge of the unwanted.

'I'm offering Joséphine a job here with me.' I made my voice sweet and brittle. 'I'm going to need a lot of extra help if I'm to have time to prepare the chocolate festival for Easter.'

His look, finally unveiled, was stark with hatred.

'I'll train her in the basics of chocolate-making,' I continued. 'She can cover for me in the shop while I work in the back.' Joséphine was looking at me with an expression of hazy astonishment. I winked at her.

'She'll be doing me a favour, and I'm sure the money will come in useful for her too,' I said smoothly. 'And as for staying' – I spoke to her directly, fixing her eyes with mine – 'Joséphine, you're welcome to stay for as long as you like. It's a pleasure to have you here.'

Armande cackled. 'So you see, *mon père*,' she said gleefully. 'You needn't waste any more of your time. Everything seems to be going just fine without you.' She sipped chocolate with an air of concentrated naughtiness. 'A drink of this might do you good,' she suggested. 'You're looking peaky, Francis. Been hitting the communion wine again, have you?'

He gave her a smile like a clenched fist. 'Very droll, Madame. It's good that you haven't lost your sense of humour.'

Then he turned smartly on his heels, and with a nod and a curt 'Messieurs-Dames' to the customers he was gone, like the polite Nazi in a bad war film.

25

Monday, March 10

THEIR LAUGHTER FOLLOWED ME OUT OF THE SHOP AND into the street like a volley of birds. The scent of chocolate, like that of my anger, made me light-headed, almost euphoric with rage. We were right, *père*. This vindicates us completely. By striking at the three areas closest to us – the community, the Church's festivals and now one of its holiest sacraments – she reveals herself at last. Her influence is pernicious and fast-growing, seeding already into a dozen, two dozen fertile minds. I saw the season's first dandelion in the churchyard this morning, wedged in the space behind a gravestone. It has already grown far deeper than I can reach, thick as a finger, searching out the darkness beneath the stone. In a week's time the whole plant will have grown again, stronger than before.

I saw Muscat for communion this morning, though he was not present for confession. He looks drawn and angry, uncomfortable in his Sunday clothes. He has taken his wife's departure badly.

When I left the *chocolaterie* he was waiting for me, smoking, leaning against the small arch beside the main entrance.

'Well, *père?*'

'I have spoken to your wife.'

'When is she coming home?'

I shook my head. 'I would not like to give you false hope,' I said gently.

'She's a stubborn cow,' he said, dropping his cigarette and crunching it with his heel. 'Pardon my language, *père*, but that's how it is. When I think of the things I gave up for that crazy bitch – the *money* she's cost me—'

'She too has had much to bear,' I told him meaningfully, thinking of our many sessions in the confessional.

Muscat shrugged. 'Oh, I'm not an angel,' he said. 'I know my weaknesses. But tell me, *père*' – he spread his hands appealingly – 'didn't I have some reason? Waking up to her stupid face every morning? Catching her time and again with her pockets full of stolen stuff from the market, lipsticks and bottles of perfume and jewellery? Having everyone looking at me in church and laughing? *Hé?*' He looked at me winningly. '*Hé, père?* Haven't I had my own cross to bear?'

I'd heard much of this before. Her sluttishness, her stupidity, her thieving, her laziness about the house. I am not required to have an opinion on such things. My role is to offer advice and comfort. Still, he disgusts me with his excuses, his conviction that had it not been for her he might have achieved great, brave things.

'We are not here to allocate blame,' I said with a note of rebuke. 'We should be trying to find ways to save your marriage.'

He was instantly subdued. 'I'm sorry, *père*. I – I shouldn't have said those things.' He tried for sincerity, showing teeth like ancient ivory. 'Don't think I'm not fond of her, *père*. I mean, I want her back, don't I?'

Oh yes. To cook his meals. To iron his clothes. To run his café. And to prove to his friends that no-one makes a fool of Paul-Marie Muscat, no-one. I despise this hypocrisy. He must indeed win her back. I agree with that at least. But not for those reasons.

'If you want her back, Muscat,' I told him with some tartness, 'then you have been about it in a remarkably idiotic way so far.'

He bridled. 'I don't see that necessarily—'

'Don't be a fool.'

Lord, *père*, how can you ever have had such patience with these people?

'Threats, profanities, last night's shameful drunken display? How do you think *that* would help your case?'

Sullenly: 'I couldn't let her get away with what she did, *père*. Everyone's saying my wife walked out on me. And that interfering bitch Rocher . . .' His mean eyes narrowed behind his wire glasses. 'Serve her right if something happened to that fancy shop of hers,' he said flatly. 'Get rid of the bitch for good.'

I looked at him sharply. 'Oh?'

It was too close to what I have thought myself, *mon père*. God help me, when I saw that boat burning . . . It is a primitive delight, unworthy of my calling, a pagan thing which by right I should not feel. I have wrestled with it myself, *père*, in the small hours of the mornings. I have subdued it in myself, but like the dandelions it grows back, sending out insidious small rootlets. It was perhaps because of this – because I *understood* – that my voice was harsher than I intended as I replied. 'What kind of thing did you have in mind, Muscat?'

He muttered something barely audible.

'A fire, perhaps? A convenient fire?' I could feel the pressure of my rage growing against my ribs. Its taste, which is both metallic and sweetly rotten, filled my mouth. 'Like the fire which got rid of the gypsies?'

He smirked. 'Perhaps. Dreadful fire risk, some of these old houses.'

'Listen to me.' Suddenly I was appalled at the thought that he might have mistaken my silence that night for complicity. 'If I thought – even *suspected* – outside of the confessional that you were involved in such a thing – if anything happens to that shop—' I had him by the shoulder now, my fingers digging into the pulpy flesh.

Muscat looked aggrieved. 'But *père* – you said yourself that—'

'*I said nothing!*' I heard my voice ricochet flatly across the square – *tat-tat-tat!* – and I lowered it in haste. 'I certainly never meant for you—' I cleared my throat, which suddenly felt wedged full. 'This is not the Middle Ages, Muscat,' I said crisply. 'We do not – *interpret* – God's laws to suit ourselves. Or the laws of our country,' I added heavily, looking him in the eye. His corneas were as yellow as his teeth. 'Do we understand each other?'

Resentfully: 'Yes, *mon père.*'

'Because if anything happens, Muscat, *anything*, a broken window, a little fire, anything at all . . .' I overtop him by a head. I am younger, fitter than he. He responds instinctively to the physical threat. I give him a little push which sends him against the stone wall at his back. I can barely contain my rage. That he should dare – that he should *dare!* – to take my role, *père*. That it should be he, this miserable self-deluding sot. That he should place me in this situation; to be obliged officially to *protect* the woman who is my enemy. I contain myself with an effort.

'Keep well away from that shop, Muscat. If there's anything to be done, *I'll* do it. Do you understand?'

Humbler now, his bluster evaporating: 'Yes, *père.*'

'Leave the situation entirely to me.'

Three weeks until her grand festival. That's all I have left. Three weeks to find some way of curbing her influence. I have preached against her in church to no effect but my own ridicule. Chocolate, I am told, is not a moral issue. Even the Clairmonts see my obduracy as slightly irregular, she simpering with mock concern that I seem over-wrought, he grinning outright. Vianne Rocher herself takes no notice. Far from trying to blend in she flaunts her alien status, calling impertinent greetings to me across the square, encouraging the antics of such as Armande, perpetually dogged by the children whose growing wild-ness she invites. Even in a crowd she is instantly recognizable. Where others walk up a street, she runs down it. Her hair, her clothes; perpetually wind-torn, wildflower colours, orange and yellow and polka-dotted and floral-patterned. In the wild, a parakeet amongst sparrows would soon be torn apart for its bright plumage. Here she is accepted with affection, even amusement. What might raise eyebrows elsewhere is tolerated because it is only Vianne. Even Clairmont is not impervious to her charm, and his wife's dislike has nothing to do with moral superiority and everything to do with a kind of envy which does Caro little credit. At least Vianne Rocher is no hypocrite, using God's words to elevate her social standing. And yet the thought – suggesting as it does a sympathy, even a liking, that a man in my position can ill afford – is another danger. I can have no sympathies. Rage and liking are equally inappropriate. I must be impartial, for the sake of the community and the Church. Those are my first loyalties.

26

Wednesday, March 12

WE HAVE NOT SPOKEN TO MUSCAT FOR DAYS. JOSÉPHINE, who for some time would not leave La Praline, can now be persuaded to walk down the street to the bakery, or across the square to the florist's, without me to accompany her. As she refuses to return to the Café de la République I have lent her some of my own clothes. Today she is wearing a blue jumper and a flowered sarong, and she looks fresh and pretty. In only a few days she has changed; the look of vapid hostility has gone, as have the defensive mannerisms. She seems taller, sleeker, abandoning her permanently hunched posture and the multiple layers of clothing which gave her such a dumpy look. She keeps the shop for me while I work in the kitchen, and I have already taught her how to temper and blend chocolate types as well as how to make some of the simpler types of praline. She has good, quick hands. Laughingly I remind her of her gunslinger's deftness on that first day and she flushes.

'I'd never take anything from you!' Her indignation is touching, sincere. 'Vianne, you don't think I'd—'

'Of course not.'

'You know I—'

'Of course.'

She and Armande, who barely knew each other in the old days, have become good friends. The old lady calls every day now, sometimes to talk, sometimes for a *cornet* of her favourite apricot truffles. Often she comes in with Guillaume, who has become a regular visitor. Today Luc was here too, and the three of them sat together in the corner with a pot of chocolate and some éclairs. I could hear occasional laughter and exclamations from the small group.

Just before closing-time Roux walked in, looking cautious and diffident. It was the first time I had seen him close to since the fire, and I was struck by the changes in him. He looks thinner, his hair pasted back from a blank, sullen face. There is a dirty bandage on one hand. One side of his face still shows a hectic splash of marks which resembles bad sunburn.

He looked taken-aback when he saw Joséphine.

'I'm sorry. I thought Vianne was—' He turned abruptly as if to go.

'No. Please. She's in the back.' Her manner has become more relaxed since she begun working in the shop, but she sounded awkward, intimidated, perhaps, by his appearance.

Roux hesitated. 'You're from the café,' he said at last. 'You're—'

'Joséphine Bonnet,' she interrupted. 'I'm living here now.'

'Oh.'

I came out of the kitchen and saw him watching her with a speculative look in his light eyes. But he did not pursue the matter any further, and Joséphine withdrew gratefully into the kitchen.

'It's good to see you again, Roux,' I told him directly. 'I wanted to ask you a favour.'

'Oh?'

He can make a single syllable sound very meaningful. This was polite incredulity, suspicion. He looked like a nervous cat about to strike.

'I need some work doing on the house, and I wonder if you might—' It is difficult to phrase this correctly. I know he will not accept what he considers to be charity.

'This wouldn't be anything to do with our friend Armande, would it?' His tone was light but hard. He turned to where Armande and the others were sitting. 'Doing good by stealth again, were we?' he called caustically.

Turning back to me again, his face was careful and expressionless. 'I didn't come here to ask for a job. I wanted to ask you if you saw anyone hanging round my boat that night.'

I shook my head. 'I'm sorry, Roux. I didn't see anyone.'

'OK.' He turned again as if to leave. 'Thanks.'

'Look, wait.' I called out after him. 'Can't you at least stay for a drink?'

'Some other time.' His tone was brusque to the point of rudeness. I could feel his anger reaching out for something to strike at.

'We're still your friends,' I said as he reached the door. 'Armande and Luc and I. Don't be so defensive. We're trying to help you.'

Roux turned abruptly. His face was bleak. His eyes were crescents. 'Get this, all of you.' He spoke in a low, hateful voice, the accent so thick that his words were barely distinguishable. 'I don't need any help. I should never have got involved with you in the first place. I only hung around this long because I thought I might find out who fired my boat.'

Then he was gone, stumbling bearishly through the doorway in a bright angry carillon of chimes.

When he had gone we all looked at each other.

'Redhaired men,' said Armande with feeling. 'Stubborn as mules.'

Joséphine looked shaken. 'What a horrible man,' she

255

said at last. '*You* didn't set fire to his boat. What right has he to take it out on you?'

I shrugged. 'He feels helpless and angry, and he doesn't know who to blame,' I told her gently. 'It's a natural reaction. And he thinks we're offering help because we feel sorry for him.'

'I just hate scenes,' said Joséphine, and I knew she was thinking of her husband. 'I'm glad he's gone. Do you think he'll leave Lansquenet now?'

I shook my head. 'I don't think so,' I said. 'After all, where would he go?'

27

Thursday, March 13

I WENT DOWN TO LES MARAUDS YESTERDAY AFTERNOON to talk to Roux, with no more success than last time. The derelict house has been padlocked from the inside and the shutters closed. I can imagine him holed up in the dark with his rage like a wary animal. I called his name, and knew he heard me, but he did not answer. I considered leaving a message for him on the door, but decided against it. If he wants to come, it must be on his own terms. Anouk came with me, carrying a paper boat I had made for her out of the cover of a magazine. As I was standing outside Roux's door she went down the banking to launch it, keeping it from drifting too far with the aid of a long flexible branch. When Roux would not make an appearance I returned to La Praline, where Joséphine had already begun the week's batch of couverture, and left

Anouk to her own devices.

'Watch out for crocodiles,' I told her seriously.

Anouk grinned at me from under her yellow beret. With her toy trumpet in one hand and the guiding-stick in the other, she proceeded to sound a loud and tuneless alarm, jumping from one foot to the other in mounting excitement.

'Crocodiles! Crocodile attack!' she crowed. 'Man the cannons!'

'Steady,' I warned. 'Don't fall in.'

Anouk blew me an extravagant kiss and returned to the game. When I turned back at the top of the hill she was bombarding the crocodiles with pieces of turf, and I could still hear the thin blare of the trumpet – *paar-paa-raar!* – interspersed with sound effects – *prussh! proom!* – as battle continued.

Surprising that it should still surprise, the fierce onrush of tenderness. If I squint hard enough against the low sunlight I can almost see the crocodiles, the long brown snapping shapes in the water, the flash of the cannon. As she moves between the houses, the red and yellow of her coat and beret shooting out sudden flares from the shadows, I can almost make out the half-visible menagerie which surrounds her. As I watch she turns and waves at me, screeches *I love you!* and returns to the serious business of play.

*

We were closed in the afternoon, and Joséphine and I worked hard to make enough pralines and truffles to last for the rest of the week. I have already begun to make the Easter chocolates, and Joséphine has become skilled at decorating the animal shapes and packing them into boxes tied with multicoloured ribbon. The cellar is an ideal place to store them: cool, though not so cold that the chocolate takes on the whitish bloom which refrigeration encourages; dark and dry, so we can store all of our special stock there, packed into cartons, and still have room for our household supplies. The floor is made of old flagstones, polished brown as oak, cool and smooth underfoot. A single lightbulb overhead. The door to the cellar is bare pine, with a hole cut into the base for a long-departed cat. Even Anouk likes the cellar, which smells of stone and ancient wine, and she has drawn coloured chalk figures on the flags and the whitewashed walls; animals and castles and birds and stars. In the shop Armande and Luc stayed to talk for a while, then they left together. They meet more often now, though not always at La Praline; Luc tells me that he went to her house twice last week, and did an hour's work in the garden each time.

'She needs some w-work doing in the flowerbeds, now the h-house is fixed,' he told me earnestly. 'She can't manage the digging the way she used to, but she says she wants some f-flowers this year instead of just weeds.'

Yesterday he brought a tray of plants from Narcisse's nursery and planted them in the newly dug soil at the foot of Armande's wall.

'I've got l-lavenders and primroses and tulips and daffodils,' he explained. 'She likes the bright, scented ones best. She doesn't see all that well, so I got lilac and wallflowers and broom, and things she'll notice.' He smiled shyly. 'I want them settled before her b-birthday,' he explained.

I asked him when Armande's birthday was.

'March the twenty-eighth,' he explained. 'She'll be eighty-one. I've already thought of a p-present.'

'Oh?'

He nodded. 'I thought I'd buy her a s-silk slip.' His tone was faintly defensive. 'She likes underwear.'

Suppressing a smile, I told him that sounded like a fine idea.

'I'll have to go to Agen,' he said seriously. 'And I'll have to hide it from my m-mother, or she'll have a bird.' He gave a sudden grin. 'Perhaps we could throw a party for her. You know, to welcome her into the next d-decade.'

'We could ask her what she thinks,' I suggested.

At four Anouk came home tired and cheerful and muddy to the armpits, and Joséphine made lemon tea while I ran the bathwater. Stripping off her dirty clothes I tipped

Anouk into hot honey-scented water, then afterwards we all sat down to *pains au chocolat* and *brioche* with raspberry jam and plump sweet apricots from Narcisse's greenhouse. Joséphine seemed preoccupied, turning her apricot softly over and over in one palm.

'I keep thinking about that man,' she said at last. 'You know, the one who was in this morning.'

'Roux.'

She nodded. 'His boat catching fire . . .' she said tentatively. 'You don't think it could have been an accident, do you?'

'He doesn't think so. He said he smelt petrol.'

'What do you think he would do if he found out' – with an effort – 'who did it?'

I shrugged. 'I really don't know. Why, Joséphine, have you any idea who it was?'

Quickly: 'No. But if someone did know – and didn't tell . . .' She let the phrase falter miserably. 'Would he – I mean – what would . . .'

I looked at her. She refused to meet my gaze, rolling the apricot absently, over and over across her hand. I caught a sudden glimpse of smoke from her thoughts.

'You know who it was, don't you?'

'No.'

'Look, Joséphine, if you know something—'

'I don't know anything.' Her voice was flat. 'I wish I did.'

'It's all right. No-one's blaming you.' I made my voice gentle, coaxing.

'I don't know anything!' she repeated shrilly. 'I really don't. Besides, he's leaving, he said so, he isn't from here and he should never have been here and—' She bit off the phrase with an audible click of her teeth.

'I saw him this afternoon,' said Anouk, through a mouthful of *brioche*. 'I saw his house.'

I turned to her in some curiosity. 'He talked to you?'

She nodded emphatically. 'Course he did. He said he'd make me a boat next time, a proper wooden one that won't sink. That is, if the bussteds don't set that one afire as well.' She manages his accent very well. In her mouth the ghosts of his words snarl and prance. I turned away to hide a smile.

'His house is cool,' continued Anouk. 'There's a fire in the middle of the carpet. He said I could come whenever I liked. Oh.' She put a guilty hand to her mouth. 'He said as long as I don't tell you.' She sighed theatrically. 'And I did, *Maman*. Didn't I?'

I hugged her, laughing. 'You did.'

I could see Joséphine looking alarmed.

'I don't think you ought to go into that house,' she told her anxiously. 'You don't really know that man, Anouk. He could be violent.'

'I think she's all right,' I winked at Anouk. 'As long as she *does* tell me.' Anouk winked back.

*

Today there was a funeral – one of the old people from
Les Mimosas down the river – and business was slow, out
of fear or respect. The deceased was a woman of ninety-
four, says Clothilde at the florist's, a relative of Narcisse's
dead mother. I saw Narcisse, his one concession to the
occasion being a black tie with his old tweed jacket, and
Reynaud, standing starkly in the doorway in his black and
white, his silver cross in one hand and the other extended
benevolently to welcome the mourners. These were few.
Maybe a dozen old women, none of whom I recognized,
one in a wheelchair pushed by a blonde nurse, some round
and birdy like Armande, some with the almost translucent
thinness of the very old, all in black, black stockings and
bonnets and headscarves, some in gloves, others with
their pale twisted hands clasped to their flattened breasts
like Grünewald virgins. I saw mainly their heads as they
made their way to St Jérôme's in a tight softly clucking
group; among the lowered heads the occasional grey-faced
glance, bright black eyes flicking suspiciously at me from
the safety of the enclave whilst the nurse, competent and
resolutely cheery, pushed from the back. They seemed to
feel no distress. The wheelchair-bound one held a small
black missal in one hand and sang in a high mewing voice
as they entered the church. The rest remained silent for
the most part, bobbing their heads at Reynaud as they
passed into the darkness, some handing him a black-
bordered note to read out during the service. The village's

only hearse arrived late. Inside, a black-draped coffin with a lone spray of flowers. A single bell sounded flatly. As I waited in the empty shop I heard the organ play a few listless, fugitive notes, like pebbles dropping into a well.

Joséphine, who was in the kitchen taking out a batch of chocolate-cream meringues, came in quietly and shuddered. 'It's gruesome,' she said.

I remember the city crematorium, the piped organ music – a Bach toccata – the cheap shiny casket, the smell of polish and flowers. The minister pronounced Mother's name wrong – *Jean Roacher*. It was all over within ten minutes.

Death should be a celebration, she told me. *Like a birthday. I want to go up like a rocket when my time comes, and fall down in a cloud of stars, and hear everyone go: Ahhhh!*

I scattered her ashes across the harbour on the night of the Fourth of July. There were fireworks and candyfloss and cherry-bombs blatting off the pier and the sharp burn of cordite in the air and the smell of hotdogs and frying onions and the faint whiff of garbage from the water. It was all the America she had ever dreamed of, a giant amusement-park, neons flaring, music playing, crowds of people singing and jostling, all the slick and sentimental tawdriness she loved. I waited for the brightest part of the display, when the sky was a trembling eruption of light and colour, and I let them drift softly into the slipstream, turning blue-white-red as they fell. I would have said something, but nothing seemed to be left to say.

'Gruesome,' repeated Joséphine. 'I hate funerals. I never go to them.' I said nothing, but watched the silent square and listened to the organ. At least it wasn't the same toccata. Undertakers' assistants carried the coffin into the church. It looked very light, and their steps were brisk and barely reverent on the cobbles.

'I wish we weren't so close to the church,' said Joséphine restlessly. 'I can't think with that going on right next door.'

'In China, people wear white at funerals,' I told her. 'They give out presents in bright red packages, for luck. They light firecrackers. They talk and laugh and dance and cry. And at the end, everyone jumps over the embers of the funeral pyre, one by one, to bless the smoke as it rises.'

She looked at me curiously. 'Did you live there too?'

I shook my head. 'No. But we knew plenty of Chinese people in New York. For them death was a celebration of the dead person's life.'

Joséphine looked doubtful. 'I don't see how anyone can *celebrate* dying,' she said at last.

'You don't,' I told her. '*Life* is what you celebrate. All of it. Even its end.' I took the pot of chocolate from the hot plate and poured two glasses.

After a while I went into the kitchen for two

meringues, which were still warm and treacly inside their chocolate envelopes and served with thick *crème Chantilly* and chopped hazelnuts.

'It doesn't seem right, doing this, at this moment,' said Joséphine, but I noticed she ate anyway.

It was almost noon when the mourners left, dazed and blinking in the bright sunshine. The chocolate and meringues were all finished, the dark kept at bay for a little longer. I saw Reynaud at the doorway again, then the old women went away in their minibus – Les Mimosas lettered on the side in bright yellow – and the square was back to normal again. Narcisse came in when he had seen off the mourners, sweating heavily in his tight collar. When I gave him my condolences he gave a shrug.

'Never really knew her,' he said indifferently. 'Great-aunt of my wife's. Went off to Le Mortoir twenty years ago. Her mind was gone.'

Le Mortoir. I saw Joséphine grimace at the name. Behind all its mimosa sweetness, that's all it is, after all. A place in which to die. Narcisse is merely following convention. The woman was long dead already.

I poured chocolate, black and bittersweet. 'Would you like a slice of cake?' I offered.

He deliberated for a moment. 'Better not while I'm in mourning,' he declared obscurely. 'What kind is it?'

'*Bavaroise*, with caramel icing.'

'Perhaps a little slice.'

Joséphine was looking out of the window into the empty square. 'That man's hanging about again,' she observed. 'The one from Les Marauds. He's going into the church.'

I looked out of the door. Roux was standing just in the side doorway of St Jérôme's. He looked agitated, shifting uneasily from one foot to the other, his arms clasped tightly around his body as if he were cold.

Something was wrong. I felt a sudden, panicky certainty. Something was very wrong. As I watched Roux turned abruptly towards La Praline. He half-ran into the doorway and remained there, head lowered, rigid with guilt and misery.

'It's Armande,' he said. 'I think I've killed her.'

For a moment we stared at him. He made a helpless awkward little gesture with his hands, as if to ward off bad thoughts.

'I was going to get the priest. She doesn't have a phone, and I thought perhaps he—' He broke off. Distress had thickened his accent so that his words were exotic and incomprehensible, a language of strange gutturals and ululations which might have been Arabic, Spanish or *verlan*, or an arcane melding of all three.

'I could see she – she told me to go to the fridge and – there was medicine in there—' He broke off again in increasing agitation. 'I didn't touch her. I never touched her. I *wouldn't*—' He spat the words out with an effort, like broken teeth. 'They'll say I attacked her. I wanted to take her money. It isn't true. I gave her some brandy and she just—'

He stopped. I could see him struggling to maintain control.

'It's all right,' I told him calmly. 'You can tell me on the way down. Joséphine can stay with the shop. Narcisse can phone the doctor from the florist's.'

Stubbornly: 'I'm not going back there. I've done what I could. I don't want—'

I grabbed him by the arm and pulled him after me. 'We haven't got time for this. I need you with me.'

'They'll say it was my fault. The police—'

'*Armande* needs you. Now come *on*!'

On the way to Les Marauds I heard the rest of the disjointed tale. Roux, feeling ashamed of his outburst in La Praline the previous day, and seeing Armande's door open, decided to call on her and found her sitting half-conscious in her rocking-chair. He managed to rouse her enough for her to speak a few words. *Medicine . . . fridge . . .* On top of the refrigerator was a bottle of brandy. He poured a glassful, forced some of the liquid between her lips.

'She just – slumped. I couldn't get her to come round.' Distress ebbed from him. 'Then I remembered she was a diabetic. I probably killed her trying to help.'

'You didn't kill her.' I was out of breath with running, a stitch cramping my left side. 'She'll be all right. You got help in time.'

'What if she dies? Who do you think'll believe me?' His voice was harsh.

'Save your breath. The doctor will be here soon.'

Armande's door is still open, a cat wound halfway around the frame. Beyond it the house is still. A piece of loosened guttering spouts rainwater from the roof. I see Roux's eyes flick to it in sudden, professional appraisal: *I'll have to fix that.* He pauses at the door as if waiting to be invited in.

Armande is lying on the hearthrug, her face a dull mushroom colour, her lips bluish. At least he has put her in the recovery position, and one arm pillows the head, neck at an angle to free the airways. She is motionless, but a tremor of stale air between her lips tells me she is breathing. Her discarded tapestry lies beside her, a cup of spilled coffee forming a comma-shaped stain on the rug. The scene is strangely flat, like a still from a silent film. Her skin beneath my fingers is cold and fishy, her dark irises clearly visible beneath eyelids as thin as wet crêpe. Her black skirt has ridden up a little over her knees, revealing a crimson ruffle. I feel a sudden flare of sorrow for her arthritic old knees in their black stockings and the bright silk petticoats beneath the drab housedress.

'Well?' Anxiety makes Roux snarl.

'I think she'll be all right.'

His eyes are dark with disbelief and suspicion.

'She must have some insulin in the fridge,' I tell him. 'That must have been what she meant. Get it quickly.'

She keeps it with the eggs. A tupperware box contains six ampoules of insulin and some disposable needles. On the other side a box of truffles with La Céleste Praline lettered on the lid. Otherwise there is hardly anything to eat in the house; an open tin of sardines, a piece of paper with a smear of *rillettes*, some tomatoes. I inject her in the crook of her elbow. It is a technique I know well. During the final stages of the disease for which my mother tried so many alternative therapies – acupuncture, homoeopathy, creative visualization – we eventually fell back on good old morphine, black-market morphine when we couldn't get it on prescription, and though my mother loathed drugs she was happy to get it, with her body sweltering and the towers of New York swimming before her eyes like a mirage. Armande weighs almost nothing in my arms, her head rolling loosely. A trace of rouge on one cheek gives her a desperate, clownish look. I press her cold, rigid hands between my own, loosening the joints, working at the fingers.

'Armande. Wake up. *Armande.*'

Roux stands watching, uncertain, his expression a blur of confusion and hope. Her fingers feel like a bunch of keys in my hands.

'Armande.' I make my voice sharp, commanding. 'You can't sleep now. You have to wake up.'

There it is. The smallest of tremors, a leaf fluttering against another.

'*Vianne.*'

In a second, Roux was on his knees beside us. He looked ashen, but his eyes were very bright.

'Oh, say it again, you stubborn old woman!' His relief was so intense it hurt. 'I know you're in there, Armande, I know you can hear me!' He looked at me, eager, almost laughing. 'She spoke, didn't she? I didn't imagine it?'

I shook my head. 'She's strong,' I said. 'And you found her in time, before she lapsed into coma. Give the injection time to act. Keep talking to her.'

'OK.' He began to talk, a little wildly, breathlessly, looking into her face for signs of consciousness. I continued to rub her hands, feeling the warmth returning little by little.

'You're not fooling anyone, Armande, you old witch. You're as strong as a horse. You could live for ever. Besides, I've just fixed your roof. You don't think I did all that work just so that daughter of yours could inherit the lot, do you? I know you're listening, Armande. I know you can hear me. What are you waiting for? D'you want me to apologize? OK, I apologize.' Tears marbled his face. 'D'you hear that? I've apologized. I'm an ungrateful bastard and I'm sorry. Now wake up and—'

'. . . *loud bastard* . . .'

He stopped mid-sentence. Armande gave a tiny chuckle. Her lips moved soundlessly. Her eyes were bright and aware. Roux cupped her face gently in his hands.

'*Scared you, did I?*' Her voice was lace-thin.

'No.'

'*I did, though.*' With a trace of satisfaction and mischief.

Roux wiped his eyes with the back of his hand. 'You still owe me money for the work I did,' he said in a shaky voice. 'I was only scared you'd never get round to paying me.'

Armande chuckled again. She was gaining strength now, and between us we managed to lift her into her chair. She was still very pale, her face half-collapsed into itself like a rotten apple, but her eyes were clear and lucid. Roux turned towards me, his expression unguarded for the first time since the fire. Our hands touched. For a second, I caught a glimpse of his face in moonlight, the rounded curve of a bare shoulder against grass, a lingering ghost-scent of lilac . . . I felt my eyes widen in stupid surprise. Roux must have felt something too, because he stepped back, abashed. Behind us I heard a soft chuckle from Armande.

'I told Narcisse to phone the doctor,' I told her with a pretence at lightness. 'He'll be here any minute.'

Armande looked at me. Knowledge passed between us,

and not for the first time, I wondered just how clearly *she* saw things.

'I'm not having that death's-head in my house,' she said. 'You can send him right back where he came from. I don't need him telling me what to do.'

'But you're ill,' I protested. 'If Roux hadn't come along you might have died.'

She gave me one of her mocking looks. 'Vianne,' she said patiently. 'That's what old people do. They die. It's a fact of life. Happens all the time.'

'Yes, but—'

'And I'm not going to Le Mortoir,' she continued. 'You can tell them that from me. They can't force me to go. I've lived in this house for sixty years and when I die, it's going to be here.'

'No-one's going to force you to go anywhere,' said Roux sharply. 'You were careless with your medication, that's all. You'll know better next time.'

Armande smiled. 'It isn't quite that simple,' she said. Stubbornly: 'Why not?'

She shrugged. 'Guillaume knows,' she told him. 'I've been talking to him quite a lot. He understands.' She sounded almost normal now, though she was still weak. 'I don't *want* to take this medicine every day,' she said calmly. 'I don't want to follow endless diet-sheets. I don't want to be waited on by kind nurses who talk to me as if I were in kindergarten. I'm eighty years old, for crying out loud, and if I can't be trusted to know what I want at my age—' She broke off abruptly. 'Who's that?'

There is nothing wrong with her hearing. I heard it too, the faint sound of a car drawing up on the uneven pathway outside. The doctor.

'If it's that sanctimonious quack, tell him he's wasting his time,' snapped Armande. 'Tell him I'm fine. Tell him to go find someone else to diagnose. I don't want him.'

I glanced outside. 'He seems to have brought half of Lansquenet with him,' I remarked mildly. The car, a blue Citroën, was packed with people. As well as the doctor, a pallid man in a charcoal suit, I could see Caroline Clairmont, her friend Joline and Reynaud crammed together on the back seat. The front was occupied by Georges Clairmont, looking sheepish and uncomfortable, silently remonstrating. I heard the car door slam, and the peewit-shrill of Caroline's voice soaring above the sudden clamour.

'*I told her! Didn't I tell her, Georges? No-one can accuse me of neglecting my filial duty, I gave my all for that woman, and look how she—*'

A quick *crunch-criss* of steps across the stones, then the voices flared into cacophony as the unwanted visitors opened the front door.

'*Maman? Maman?* Hold on, darling, it's me! I'm coming! This way, Monsieur Cussonnet, this way into the

– oh yes, you know your way around, don't you? Oh dear, the times I've told her – positively *knew* something like this would happen—'

Georges, feebly protesting: 'Do you really think we ought to interfere, Caro darling? I mean, let the doctor get on with it, you know?'

Joline in her cool, supercilious tone: 'One does wonder what *he* was doing in her house in any case.'

Reynaud, barely audible: 'Should have come to me . . .'

I felt Roux stiffen even before they came into the room, looking quickly round for a way out. Even as he did it was too late. First Caroline and Joline with their immaculate chignons, their twin-sets and Hermès scarves, closely followed by Clairmont – dark suit and tie, unusual for a day at the lumber yard, or did she make him change for the occasion? – the doctor, the priest, like a scene from melodrama, all frozen in the doorway, faces shocked, bland, guilty, aggrieved, furious. Roux staring them out with that look of insolence, one hand bandaged, damp hair in his eyes, myself by the door, orange skirt mud-splashed from my run down to Les Marauds, and Armande, white but composed, rocking cheerily in her old chair with her black eyes snapping with malice and one finger crooked, witchlike.

'So the vultures are here.' She sounded affable, danger-ous. 'Didn't take you long to get here, did it?' A sharp glance at Reynaud, standing at the rear of the group.

'Thought you'd got your chance at last, did you?' she said acidly. 'Thought you'd slip in a quick blessing or two while I wasn't compos mentis?' She gave her vulgar chuckle. 'Too bad, Francis. I'm not quite ready for last rites yet.'

Reynaud looked sour. 'So it would appear,' he said. A quick glance in my direction. 'It was fortunate that Mademoiselle Rocher is so – competent – in the use of needles.' There was an implicit sneer in the words.

Caroline was rigid, her face a smiling mask of chagrin. 'Maman, chérie, you see what happens when we leave you on your own. Frightening everyone like this.'

Armande looked bored.

'Taking up all this time, putting people out—' Lariflete jumped up onto her knee as Caro was talking, and the old lady stroked the cat absently. 'Now do you understand why we tell you—'

'That I'd be better off in Le Mortoir?' finished Armande flatly. 'Really, Caro. You don't give up, do you? That's your father all over, you know. Stupid, but persistent. It was one of his most endearing characteristics.'

Caro looked petulant. 'It isn't Le Mortoir, it's Les Mimosas, and if you'd only have a look round—'

'Food through a tube, someone to take you to the toilet in case you fall over—'

'Don't be absurd.'

Armande laughed. 'My dear girl, at my age I can be anything I please. I can be absurd if I feel like it. I'm old enough to get away with *anything.*'

'Now you're behaving like a child.' Caro's voice was sulky. 'Les Mimosas is a *very* fine, very *exclusive* residential home, you'd be able to talk to people your own age, go on outings, have everything organized for you—'

'It sounds quite wonderful.' Armande continued to rock lazily in her chair. Caro turned to the doctor, who had been standing awkwardly at her side. A thin, nervy man, he looked embarrassed to be there at all, like a shy man at an orgy. 'Simon, *tell* her!'

'Well, I'm not sure it's really my place to—'

'Simon agrees with me,' interrupted Caro doggedly. 'In your condition and at your age, you simply *can't* go on living here on your own. Why, at any time, you might—'

'Yes, Madame Voizin.' Joline's voice was warm and reasonable. 'Perhaps you should *consider* what Caro – I mean, of *course* you don't want to lose your independence, but for your own *good* . . .'

Armande's eyes are quick and bright and abrasive. She stared at Joline for a few moments in silence. Joline bridled, then looked away, blushing. 'I want you out of here,' said Armande gently. '*All* of you.'

'But, *Maman*—'

'All of you,' repeated Armande flatly. 'I'll give the

quack here two minutes in private – seems I need to remind you of your Hippocratic oath, Monsieur Cusson-net – and by the time I've finished with him I expect the rest of you buzzards to be gone.' She tried to stand, pushing herself up from her chair with difficulty. I took her arm to steady her, and she gave me a wry, mischievous smile.

'Thanks, Vianne,' she said gently. 'You, too.' This was to Roux, still standing at the far side of the room looking drab and indifferent. 'I want to talk to you when I've seen the doctor. Don't go away.'

'Who, me?' Roux was uneasy. Caro glanced at him with undisguised contempt.

'I think that at a time like this, *Maman*, your family should be the—'

'If I need you, I know where to call,' said Armande tartly. 'For the moment, I want to make arrangements.'

Caro looked at Roux. 'O-oh?' The syllable was silky with dislike. 'Arrangements?' She flicked her eyes up and down him, and I saw him flinch slightly. It was the same reflex I had seen previously with Joséphine; a stiffening, a slight hunching of the shoulders, a drilling of the hands into the pockets as if to present a smaller target. Beneath that knowing scrutiny every flaw is revealed. For a second he sees himself as she sees him: filthy, uncouth.

Perversely he acts out the role she has handed him, snarling: 'What the fuck d'you think you're looking at?'

She gives him a startled look and backs away.

Armande grins. 'I'll see you later,' she tells me. 'And thank you.'

Caro followed me with visible chagrin. Caught between curiosity and her reluctance to talk to me, she is brisk and condescending. I gave her the facts with no elaboration. Reynaud listened, expressionless as one of his statues. Georges tried for diplomacy, smiling sheepishly, delivered platitudes. No-one offered me a lift back home.

28

Saturday, March 15

I WENT TO SPEAK TO ARMANDE VOIZIN ONCE AGAIN THIS morning. Once again she refused to see me. Her redhaired watchdog opened the door and growled at me in his uncouth patois, wedging his shoulders against the frame to prevent me from entering. Armande is quite well, he tells me. A little rest will bring about a complete recovery. Her grandson is with her, and her friends visit every day – this with a sarcasm which makes me bite my tongue. She is not to be disturbed. It galls me to plead with this man, *père*, but I know my duty. Whatever low company she has fallen into, whatever taunts she flings at me, my duty remains clear. To comfort – even where comfort is refused – and to guide. But it is impossible to speak to this man about the soul – his eyes are blank and indifferent as an animal's. I try to explain. Armande is old, I tell him. Old and stubborn. There is so little time for both of us. Doesn't he see that? Will he allow her to kill herself with neglect and arrogance?

He shrugs. 'She's fine,' he tells me, his face bland with dislike. 'No-one's neglecting her. She'll be just fine now.'

'That isn't true.' My voice is deliberately harsh. 'She's playing Russian roulette with her medication. Refusing to listen to what the doctor tells her. Eating *chocolates*, for God's sake! Have you only thought what that might do to her, in her condition?'

His face closes, becomes hostile and aloof. Flatly: 'She doesn't want to see you.'

'Don't you care? Don't you care that she's killing herself with gluttony?'

He shrugs. I can feel his rage through the thin pretence of indifference. Impossible to appeal to his better nature – he simply stands guard, as he has been instructed. Muscat tells me Armande has offered him money. Perhaps he has an interest in seeing her die. I know her perversity. To disinherit her family for the sake of this stranger would appeal to that part of her.

'I'll wait,' I told him. 'All day, if I have to.'

I waited for two hours outside in the garden. After that time it began to rain. I had no umbrella, and my soutane was heavy with moisture. I began to feel dizzy and numb. After a while a window opened and I caught the maddening smell of coffee and hot bread from the kitchen. I saw the watchdog looking at me with that look of surly disdain and knew that I might fall unconscious to the ground without his making a move to help me. I felt his eyes on my back as I returned slowly up the hill towards St Jérôme's. Somewhere across the water I thought I heard a sound of laughter.

I have failed too with Joséphine Muscat. Though she refuses to go to church, I have spoken with her several times, but to no avail. There is a deep core of some stubborn metal in her now, a kind of defiance, though she remains respectful and soft-spoken throughout our conversation. She never ventures far from La Céleste Praline, and it was outside the shop that I saw her today. She was sweeping the cobbles by the doorway, her hair tied with a yellow scarf. As I made my way towards her I could hear her singing to herself.

'Good morning, Madame Muscat.' I greeted her politely. I know that if she is to be won back it must be by gentleness and reason. She may be made to repent later, when our work is done.

She gave me a narrow smile. She looks more confident now, back straight, head high, mannerisms she has copied from Vianne Rocher.

'I'm Joséphine Bonnet now, *père*.'

'Not under the law, Madame.'

'*Bof*, the law.' She shrugged.

'*God*'s law,' I told her with emphasis, fixing her with

282

reproach. 'I have prayed for you, *ma fille*. I have prayed for your deliverance.'

She laughed at that, not unkindly. 'Then your prayers have been answered, *père*. I've never been so happy.'

She seems impregnable. Barely a week of that woman's influence and already I can hear that other's voice through hers. Their laughter is unendurable. Their mockery, like Armande's, a goad which makes me stupid and enraged. Already I feel something in me respond, *père*, something weak to which I thought I was immune. Looking across the square at the *chocolaterie*, its bright window, the boxes of pink and red and orange geraniums at the balconies and at either side of the door, I feel the insidious creeping of doubt in my mind, and my mouth fills at the memory of its perfume, like cream and marshmallow and burnt sugar and the heady mingling of cognac and fresh-ground cocoa beans. It is the scent of a woman's hair, just where the nape joins the skull's tender hollow, the scent of ripe apricots in the sun, of warm *brioche* and cinnamon rolls, lemon tea and lily-of-the-valley. It is an incense diffused on the wind and unfurling softly like a banner of revolt, this devil's spoor, not sulphurous as we were taught as children but this lightest, most evocative of perfumes, combined essence of a thousand spices, making the head ring and the spirit soar. I find myself standing outside St Jérôme's with my head lifted into the wind, straining to catch a trace of that perfume. It suffuses my dreams, and I awake sweating and famished. In my dreams I gorge on chocolates, I roll in chocolates, and their texture is not brittle but soft as flesh, like a thousand mouths on my body, devouring me in fluttering small bites. To die beneath their tender gluttony seems the culmination of every temptation I have ever known, and in such moments I can almost understand Armande Voizin, risking her life with every rapturous mouthful.

I said *almost*.

I know my duty. I sleep very little now, having extended my penance to include these stray moments of abandon. My joints ache, but I welcome the distraction. Physical pleasure is the crack into which the devil sends his roots. I avoid sweet scents. I eat a single meal a day, and then only the plainest and most flavourless of foods. When I am not going about my duties in the parish I work in the churchyard, digging the beds and weeding around the graves. There has been neglect there for the past two years, and I am conscious of a feeling of unease when I see what riot there is now in that hitherto orderly garden. Lavender, marjoram, goldenrod and purple sage have shot up in lavish abandon amongst the grasses and blue thistles. So many scents disturb me. I would like orderly rows of shrubs and flowers, perhaps with a box hedge around the whole. This profusion seems somehow wrong, irreverent, a savage thrusting of life, one plant choking another in a vain attempt at dominance. We were given mastery over these things, the Bible tells us. And yet I feel no mastery. What I feel is a kind of helplessness, for as I dig and prune and cut, the serried green armies simply fill the spaces at my back, pushing out long green tongues of derision at my efforts. Narcisse looks at me in amused contempt.

'Better get some planting done, *père*,' he tells me. 'Fill those spaces with something worthwhile. Otherwise the weeds will always get in.'

He is right, of course. I have ordered a hundred plants from his nursery, docile plants which I will put in by rows. I like the white begonias and the dwarf iris and the pale yellow dahlias and the Easter lilies, scentless but so lovely in their prim whorls of leaf. Lovely, but not invasive, promises Narcisse. Nature tamed by man.

Vianne Rocher comes over to look at my work. I ignore her. She is wearing a turquoise pullover and jeans with small purple suede boots. Her hair is a pirate flag in the wind.

'You've got a lovely garden,' she remarks. She lets one hand trail across a swathe of vegetation; she clenches her fist and brings it to her face full of scent.

'So many herbs,' she says. 'Lemon balm and eau-de-cologne mint and pineapple sage—'

'I don't know their names.' My voice is abrupt. 'I'm no gardener. Besides, they're just weeds.'

'I like weeds.'

She would. I felt my heart swell with anger – or was it the scent? I stood up hip-deep in rippling grasses and felt my lower vertebrae crackle under the sudden pressure. 'Tell me something, Mademoiselle.'

She looked at me obediently, smiling.

'Tell me what you think to achieve by encouraging my parishioners to uproot their lives, to give up their security—'

She gave me a blank look. 'Uproot?' She glanced uncertainly at the heap of weeds on the path at my side.

'I refer to Joséphine Muscat,' I snapped.

'Oh.' She tweaked at a stem of green lavender. 'She was unhappy.' She seemed to think that explained everything.

'And now, having broken her marriage vows, left everything she had, given up her old life, you think she will be happier?'

'Of course.'

'A fine philosophy,' I sneered, '*if* you're the kind of person who doesn't believe in sin.'

She laughed. 'But I don't,' she said. 'I don't believe in it at all.'

'Then I pity your poor child,' I said tartly. 'Brought up without God and without morality.'

She gave me a narrow unamused look. 'Anouk knows what's right and wrong,' she said, and I knew that at last I

had reached her. One small point scored. 'As for God—'
She bit off the phrase. 'I don't think that white collar
gives you sole right of access to the Divine,' she finished
more gently. 'I think there may be room somewhere for
both of us, don't you?'

I did not deign to answer. I can see through her
pretended tolerance. 'If you really want to do good,' I told
her with dignity, 'you will persuade Madame Muscat to
reconsider her rash decision. And you will make Armande
Voizin see sense.'

'Sense?' She pretended ignorance, but she knew what I
meant.

I repeated much of what I had told the watchdog.
Armande was old, I told her. Self-willed and stubborn.
But her generation is ill-equipped to understand medical
matters. The importance of diet and medication – the
stubborn refusal to listen to the facts.

'But Armande is quite happy where she is.' Her voice is
almost reasonable. 'She doesn't want to leave her house
and go into a nursing-home. She wants to die where she
is.'

'She has no right!' I heard my voice crack whiplike
across the square. 'It isn't her decision to make. She could
live a long time, another ten years perhaps—'

'She still may.' Her tone was reproachful. 'She is still
mobile, lucid, independent—'

'*Independent!*' I could barely conceal my disdain. 'When

she'll be stone blind in six months? What is she going to do then?'

For the first time she looked confused. 'I don't understand,' she said at last. 'Armande's eyes are all right, aren't they? I mean, she doesn't even wear glasses.'

I looked at her sharply. She didn't know. 'You haven't spoken to the doctor, have you?'

'Why should I? Armande—'

I cut her short. 'Armande has a problem,' I told her. 'One which she has systematically been denying. You see the extent of her stubbornness. She refuses to admit, even to herself, even to her family—'

'Tell me. Please.' Her eyes were hard as agates.

I told her.

29

Sunday, March 16

AT FIRST ARMANDE PRETENDED SHE DIDN'T KNOW WHAT I was talking about. Then switching to a high-handed tone, demanded to know who had blabbed, while at the same time declaring that I was an interfering busybody, and that I had no idea what I was talking about.

'Armande,' I said as soon as she paused for breath. 'Talk to me. Tell me what it means. Diabetic retinopathy—'

She shrugged. 'I might as well, if that damn doctor's going to blab it all over the village.' She sounded petulant. 'Treating me as if I wasn't fit to make my own decisions any more.' She gave me a stern look. 'And you're no better, madam,' she said. 'Clucking over me, fussing – I'm not a child, Vianne.'

'I know you're not.'

'Well, then.' She reached for the teacup at her elbow. I

289

saw the care with which she secured it between her
fingers, testing its position before she picked it up. It is not
she, but I, who have been blind. The red-ribboned
walking-stick, the tentative gestures, the unfinished tapestry, the eyes shadowed beneath a succession of hats . . .

'It isn't as if you could do anything to help,' continued
Armande in a gentler tone. 'From what I understood it's
incurable, so it's nobody's business but my own.' She took
a sip of the tea and grimaced. 'Camomile,' she said
without enthusiasm. 'Supposed to eliminate toxins. Tastes
like cat's piss.' She put the cup down again with the same
careful gesture.

'I miss reading,' she said. 'It's getting too hard to see
print nowadays, but Luc reads to me sometimes. Remember how I got him to read Rimbaud to me at that first
meeting?'

I nodded. 'You make it sound as if it was years ago,' I
told her.

'It was.' Her voice was light, almost uninflected. 'I've
had what I thought I'd never be able to have, Vianne. My
grandson visits me every day. We talk like adults. He's a
good lad, kind enough to grieve for me a little—'

'He loves you, Armande,' I interrupted. 'We all do.'

She chuckled. 'Maybe not all,' she said. 'Still, that
doesn't matter. I have everything I've ever wanted right
here and now. My house, my friends, Luc . . .' She gave

me a stubborn look. 'I'm not going to have any of that taken away from me,' she declared mutinously.

'I don't understand. No-one can force you to—'

'I'm not talking about any *one*,' she interrupted sharply. 'Cussonnet can talk as much as he likes about his retinal implants and his scans and laser therapies and what he likes' – her contempt for such things was apparent – 'but that doesn't change the plain facts. The truth is I'm going blind, and there's not a lot anyone can do to stop it.' She folded her arms with a gesture of finality.

'I should have gone to him sooner,' she said without bitterness. 'Now it's irreversible, and worsening. Six months of partial sight is the most he can give me, then Le Mortoir, like it or not, till the day I die.' She paused. 'I could live another ten years,' she said reflectively, echoing my words to Reynaud.

I opened my mouth to argue, to tell her it might not be all that bad, then closed it again.

'Don't look like that, girl.' Armande gave me a rallying nudge. 'After a five-course banquet you'd want coffee and liqueurs, wouldn't you? You wouldn't suddenly decide to round it all off with a bowl of pap, would you? Just so you could have an extra course?'

'Armande—'

'Don't interrupt.' Her eyes were bright. 'I'm saying you need to know when to stop, Vianne. You need to know

when to push away your plate and call for those liqueurs.
I'll be eighty-one in a fortnight—'

'That's not so old,' I wailed in spite of myself. 'I can't
believe you're giving up like this!'

She looked at me. 'And yet you were the one, weren't
you, who told Guillaume to leave Charly some dignity.'

'You're not a dog!' I retorted, angry now.

'No,' replied Armande softly, 'and I have a choice.'

A bitter place, New York, with its gaudy mysteries; cold in
winter and flashing with heat in summer. After three
months even the noise becomes familiar, unremarkable,
the sounds of cars-voices-cabs melting into a single sheet
of sound which covers the place like rain. Crossing the
road from the deli with our lunch in a brown sack
between her folded arms, I meeting her halfway, catching
her eye across a busy street, a billboard advertising
Marlboro cigarettes at her back; a man standing
against a vista of red mountains. I saw it coming. Opened
my mouth to shout, to warn her . . . Froze. For a second,
that was all, a single second. Was it fear which stapled my
tongue to the roof of my mouth? Was it simply the
slowness of the body's reaction when faced with the
imminence of danger, the thought reaching the brain an
aching eternity from the dull flesh's response? Or was it
hope, the kind of hope which comes when all dreams have

been stripped away and what remains is the long slow agony of pretence?

Of course, Maman, of course we'll make it to Florida. Of course we will.

Her face, rigid with smiling, her eyes far too bright, bright as Fourth-of-July fireworks.

What would I do, what would I do without you?

It's OK, Maman. We'll make it. I promise. Trust me.

The Black Man stands by with a flickering smile on his face and for that interminable second I know that there are worse things, *much* worse things, than dying. Then the paralysis breaks and I scream, but the cry of warning comes too late. She turns her face vaguely towards me, a smile forming on her pale lips – *Why, what is it, dear?* – and the cry which should have been her name is lost in the squealing of brakes.

'*Florida!*' It sounds like a woman's name, shrilling across the street, the young woman running through the traffic dropping her purchases as she runs – an armful of groceries, a carton of milk – her face contorting. It sounds like a name, as if the older woman dying in the street is actually *called* Florida, and she is dead before I reach her, quietly and without drama, so that I feel almost embarrassed to make so much fuss, and a large woman in a pink tracksuit puts her meaty arms around me, but what I feel most is *relief*, like a lanced boil, and my tears are relief, bitter burning relief that I have reached the end at last. Reached the end intact, or almost.

'You shouldn't cry,' said Armande gently. 'Aren't you the one who always says happiness is the only thing that matters?'

I was surprised to find my face wet.

'Besides, I need your help.' Pragmatic as always, she passed me a handkerchief from her pocket. It smelt of lavender. 'I'm having a party for my birthday,' she declared. 'Luc's idea. Expense no object. I want you to do the catering.'

'What?' I was confused, passing from death to feasting then back again.

'My last course,' explained Armande. 'I'll take my medicine till then, like a good girl. I'll even drink that filthy tea. I want to see my eighty-first birthday, Vianne, with all my friends around me. God knows, I might even invite that idiot daughter of mine. We'll bring in your chocolate festival in style. And then . . .' A quick shrug of indifference. 'Not everyone gets this lucky,' she observed. 'Getting the chance to plan everything, to tidy all the corners. And something else' – she gave me a look of laser intensity – 'not a word to anyone,' she said. 'Not *anyone*. I'm not having any interference. It's my choice, Vianne. My party. I don't want anyone crying and carrying on at my party. Understand?'

I nodded.

'Promise?' It was like talking to a fierce child.

'I promise.'

Her face took on the look of contentment it always wears when she speaks of good food. She rubbed her hands together. 'Now for the menu.'

30

Tuesday, March 18

JOSÉPHINE COMMENTED ON MY SILENCE AS WE WORKED together. We have made three hundred of the Easter boxes since we began, stacked neatly in the cellar and tied with ribbons, but I plan for twice that many. If I can sell them all we will make a substantial profit, perhaps enough to settle here for good. If not – I do not think of that possibility, though the weathervane creaks laughter at me from its perch. Roux has already started work on Anouk's room in the loft. The festival is a risk, but our lives have always been determined by such things. And we have made every effort to make the festival a success. Posters have been sent as far as Agen and the neighbouring towns. Local radio will mention it every day of Easter week. There will be music – a few of Narcisse's old friends have formed a band – flowers, games. I spoke to some of the Thursday traders and there will be stalls in the square selling trinkets and souvenirs. An Easter-egg hunt for the children, led by Anouk and her friends, *cornets-surprise* for every entrant. And in La Céleste Praline, a giant chocolate statue of Eostre with a corn sheaf in one hand and a basket of eggs in the other, to be shared between the celebrants. Less than two weeks left. We make the delicate liqueur chocolates, the rose-petal clusters, the gold-wrapped coins, the violet creams, the chocolate cherries and almond rolls in batches of fifty at a time, laying them out onto greased tins to cool. Hollow eggs and animal figures are carefully split open and filled with these. Nests of spun caramel with hard-shelled sugar eggs, each topped with a triumphantly plump chocolate hen; piebald rabbits heavy with gilded almonds stand in rows, ready to be wrapped and boxed; marzipan creatures march across the shelves. The smells of vanilla essence and cognac and caramelized apple and bitter chocolate fill the house.

And now there is Armande's party to prepare, too. I have a list of what she wants on order from Agen – foie gras, champagne, truffles and fresh *chantrelles* from Bordeaux, *plateaux de fruits de mer* from the *traiteur* in Agen. I will bring the cakes and chocolates myself.

'It sounds fun,' calls Joséphine brightly from the kitchen, as I tell her about the party. I have to remind myself of my promise to Armande.

'You're invited,' I told her. 'She said so.'

Joséphine flushes with pleasure at the thought. 'That's kind,' she says. 'Everyone's been so kind.'

She is remarkably unembittered, I tell myself, ready to see kindness in everyone. Even Paul-Marie has not destroyed this optimism in her. His behaviour, she says, is partly her own fault. He is essentially weak; she should have stood up to him long ago. Caro Clairmont and her cronies she dismisses with a smile. 'They're just foolish,' she tells me wisely.

Such a simple soul. She is serene now, at peace with the world. I find myself becoming less and less so, in a perverse spirit of contradiction. And yet I envy her. It has taken so little to bring her to this state. A little warmth, a few borrowed clothes and the security of a spare room . . . Like a flower she grows towards the light, without thinking or examining the process which moves her to do so. I wish I could do the same.

I find myself returning to Sunday's conversation with Reynaud. What moves him is still as much of a mystery to me as it ever was. There is a look of desperation about him nowadays as he works in his churchyard, digging and hoeing furiously – sometimes bringing out great clumps of shrubs and flowers along with the weeds – the sweat running down his back and making a dark triangle against his soutane. He does not enjoy the exercise. I see his face as he works, features crunching with the effort. He seems to hate the soil he digs, to hate the plants with which he struggles. He looks like a miser forced to shovel banknotes into a furnace: hunger, disgust and reluctant fascination. And yet he never gives up. Watching him I feel a familiar pang of fear, though for what I am not sure. He is like a machine, this man, my enemy. Looking at him I feel strangely exposed by his scrutiny. It takes all my courage to meet his eyes, to smile, to pretend nonchalance ... inside me something screams and struggles frantically to escape. It is not simply the issue of the chocolate festival which enrages him. I know this as keenly as if I had picked it out of his bleak thoughts. It is my very existence which does so. To him I am a living outrage. He is watching me now, covertly from his unfinished garden, his eyes sliding sideways to my window then back to his work in sly satisfaction. We have not spoken since Sunday, and he thinks he has scored a point against me. Armande has not returned to La Praline, and I can see in his eyes that he believes himself to have been the cause of this. Let him think it if it makes him happy.

Anouk tells me he went to the school yesterday. He spoke about the meaning of Easter – harmless stuff, though it chills me somehow to think of my daughter in his care – read a story, promised to come again. I asked Anouk if he had spoken to her.

'Oh yes,' she said blithely. 'He's nice. He said I could come and see his church if I wanted. See St Francis and all the little animals.'

'And do you want to?'

Anouk shrugged. 'Maybe,' she said.

I tell myself – in the small hours when everything seems possible and my nerves shriek like the unoiled hinges of the weathervane – that my fear is irrational. What could he do to us? How could he hurt us, even if that is his intention? He knows nothing. He can know nothing about us. He has no power.

Of course he has, says my mother's voice in me. *He's the Black Man.*

Anouk turns over restlessly in her sleep. Sensitive to my moods, she knows when I am awake and struggles towards wakefulness herself through a morass of dreams. I breathe deeply until she is under again.

The Black Man is a fiction, I tell myself firmly. An embodiment of fears underneath a carnival head. A tale for dark nights. Shadows in a strange room.

In lieu of an answer I see that picture again, bright as a transparency: Reynaud at an old man's bedside, waiting, his lips moving as if in prayer, fire at his back like sunlight through stained glass. It is not a comforting picture. There is something predatory in the priest's stance, a likeness between the two reddened faces, the glow of flame between them darkly menacing. I try to apply my studies in psychology. It is an image of the Black Man as Death, an archetype which reflects my fear of the unknown. The thought is unconvincing. The part of me that still belongs to my mother speaks with more eloquence.

You're my daughter, Vianne, she tells me inexorably. *You know what that means.*

It means moving on when the wind changes, seeing futures in the turn of a card, our lives a permanent fugue.

'I'm nothing special.' I am barely aware that I have spoken aloud.

'*Maman?*' Anouk's voice, doughy with sleep.

'Shh,' I tell her. 'It isn't morning yet. Sleep some more.'

'Sing me a song, *Maman,*' she murmurs, reaching out her hand to me in the darkness. 'Sing me the song about the wind again.'

And so I sing, listening to my own voice against the small sounds of the weathervane:

> *V'là l'bon vent, v'là l'joli vent*
> *V'là l'bon vent, ma mie m'appelle*
> *V'là l'bon vent, v'là l'joli vent*
> *V'là l'bon vent, ma mie m'attend.*

After a while I begin to hear Anouk's breathing steady again, and I know she is sleeping. Her hand still rests in mine, soft with sleep. When Roux has finished the work on the house she will have a room of her own again and

we will both sleep more easily. Tonight feels too close to
those hotel rooms which we shared, my mother and I,
bathed in the moisture of our own breathing, with
condensation running down the windows and the sounds
of the traffic, interminable, outside.

V'là l'bon vent, v'là l'joli vent . . .

Not this time, I promise myself silently. This time we
stay. Whatever happens. But even as I slide back into
sleep I find myself considering the thought, not only with
longing, but with disbelief.

31

Wednesday, March 19

THERE SEEMS TO BE LESS ACTIVITY AT THE ROCHER woman's shop these days. Armande Voizin has stopped visiting, though I have seen her a few times since her recovery, walking with a determined stride and with only a little help from her stick. Guillaume Duplessis is often with her, trailing that skinny puppy of his, and Luc Clairmont goes down to Les Marauds every day. On learning that her son has been seeing Armande in secret, Caroline Clairmont gives a smirk of chagrin.

'I can't do a thing with him these days, *père*,' she complains. 'Such a *good* boy, such an *obedient* boy one moment, and the next—' She raised her manicured hands to her bosom in a theatrical gesture.

'I only told him – in the *mildest* possible way – that perhaps he should have *told* me he was going to visit his grandmother.' She sighed. 'As if he thought I would *disapprove*, silly boy. Of course I don't, I told him. It's *wonderful* that you get on with her as well as you do – after all, you're going to inherit everything one day – and suddenly he's shouting at me and saying he doesn't *care* about the money, that the reason he didn't want me to know was that he knew I'd spoil everything, that I was an interfering bible groupie – *her* words, *père*, I'd stake my life on that.' She brushed her eyes with the back of her hand, taking care not to smudge her impeccable make-up.

'What have I done, *père*?' she pleaded. 'I've done *everything* for that boy, given him everything. And to see him turn away from me, to throw it all in my face because of *that woman* . . .' Her voice was hard beneath the tears. 'Sharper than a serpent's tooth,' she moaned. 'You can't imagine what it's like for a mother, *père*.'

'Oh, you're not the only person to have suffered from Madame Rocher's well-intentioned meddling,' I told her. 'Look around you at the changes she's made in just a few weeks.'

Caroline sniffed. 'Well-intentioned! You're too kind, *père*,' she sneered. 'She's malicious, that's what she is. She nearly killed my mother, turned my son against me . . .'

I nodded encouragingly.

'Not to mention what she's done to the Muscats' marriage,' continued Caroline. 'It amazes me that you've had so much patience, *père*. It really does.' Her eyes glittered with spite. 'I'm surprised you haven't used your influence, *père*,' she said.

I shrugged. 'Oh, I'm just a country priest,' I said. 'I don't have any influence as such. I can disapprove, but—'

'You can do a sight more than disapprove,' snapped Caroline tautly. 'We should have listened to you in the first place, *père*. We should never have tolerated her here.'

I shrugged. 'Anyone can say that with hindsight,' I reminded her. 'Even you patronized her shop, if I remember.'

She flushed. 'Well, we could help you now,' she said. 'Paul Muscat, Georges, the Arnaulds, the Drous, the Prudhommes ... We could pull together. Spread the word. We could turn the tide against her, even now.'

'For what reason? The woman hasn't broken the law. They'd call it malicious gossip, and you'd be no better off than before.'

Caroline gave a narrow smile. 'We could wreck her precious festival, that's for sure,' she said.

'Oh?

'Of course.' Intensity of feeling makes her ugly. 'Georges sees a lot of people. He's a wealthy man. Muscat, too, has influence. He sees people. He's persuasive; the Residents' Committee ...'

Of course he is. I remember his father, the summer of the river-gypsies.

'If she makes a loss on the festival – and I hear she's put

quite a sum into preparing it already – then she might be pressured—'

'She might,' I replied mildly. 'Of course I couldn't be seen to have any part of it. It might look – uncharitable.'

I could tell from her expression that she understood perfectly.

'Of course, *mon père*.' Her voice is eager and spiteful. For a second I feel utter contempt for her, panting and fawning like a bitch in heat, but it is with such contemptible tools, *père*, that our work is often done.

After all, *père*, you should know.

32

Friday, March 21

THE LOFT IS ALMOST FINISHED, THE PLASTER STILL WET IN patches but the new window, round and brass-bound like a ship's porthole, complete. Tomorrow Roux will lay the floorboards, and when they are finally polished and varnished, we will move Anouk's bed into her new room. There is no door. A trapdoor is the only entrance, with a dozen steps leading upwards. Already Anouk is very excited. She spends much of her time with her head through the trapdoor, watching and giving precise instructions on what needs to be done. The rest she spends with me in the kitchen, watching the preparations for Easter. Jeannot is often with her. They sit together by the kitchen door, both talking at once. I have to bribe them to go away. Roux seems more like his old self since Armande's illness, whistling as he puts the final touches to

Anouk's walls. He has done an excellent job, though he regrets the loss of his tools. The ones he is using, hired from Clairmont's yard, are inferior, he says. As soon as he can, he will buy more.

'There's a place in Agen selling old river-boats,' he told me today over chocolate and éclairs. 'I could get an old hulk and fix it up over the winter. I could make it nice and comfortable.'

'How much money would you need?'

He shrugged. 'Maybe five thousand francs to begin with, maybe four. It depends.'

'Armande would lend it to you.'

'No.' He is immovable on this issue. 'She's done enough already.' He traced a circle around the rim of his cup with his forefinger. 'Besides, Narcisse has offered me a job,' he told me. 'At the nursery, then helping with the *vendanges* in the grape season, then there's the potatoes, beans, cucumbers, aubergines . . . Enough work to keep me busy till November.'

'That's good.' A sudden wave of warmth for his enthusiasm, for the return of his good spirits. He looks better too, more relaxed and without that dreadful look of hostility and suspicion which shuttered his face like a haunted house. He has spent the last few nights at Armande's house, at her request.

'In case I have another one of my turns,' she says seriously, with a comic look at me behind his back. Deception or not, I am glad of his presence there.

Not so Caro Clairmont: she came into La Praline on Wednesday morning with Joline Drou, ostensibly to discuss Anouk. Roux was sitting at the counter, drinking mocha. Joséphine, who still seems afraid of Roux, was in the kitchen, packaging chocolates. Anouk was still finishing her breakfast, her yellow bowl of *chocolat au lait* and half a croissant on the counter in front of her. The two women gave sugary smiles to Anouk, and looked at Roux with wary disdain. Roux gave them one of his insolent stares.

'I hope I'm not coming at an inconvenient moment?' Joline has a smooth, practised voice, all concern and sympathy. Beneath it, however, nothing but indifference.

'Not at all. We were just having breakfast. Can I offer you a drink?'

'No, no. I never have breakfast.'

A coy glance at Anouk, which she, head in her breakfast-bowl, failed to notice.

'I wonder if I might talk to you,' said Joline sweetly. 'In *private*.'

'Well, you could,' I told her. 'But I'm sure you don't need to. Can't you say whatever it is here? I'm sure Roux won't mind.'

Roux grinned, and Joline looked sour. 'Well, it's a little *delicate*,' she said.

'Then are you sure I'm the person you should be talking to? I would have thought Curé Reynaud far more appropriate—'

'No, I definitely wish to speak to you,' said Joline, between compressed lips.

'Oh.' Politely: 'What about?'

'It concerns your daughter.' She gave me a brittle smile. 'As you know, I am in charge of her class at school.'

'I do know.' I poured another mocha for Roux. 'What's wrong? Is she backward? Is she having problems?'

I know perfectly well that Anouk has no problems. She has read voraciously since she was four and a half. She speaks English almost as well as French, a legacy from our New York days.

'No, no,' Joline assures me. 'She's a very bright little girl.' A quick glance flutters in Anouk's direction, but my daughter seems too much absorbed in finishing her croissant. Slyly, because she thinks I am not watching, she sneaks a chocolate mouse from the display and pushes it into the middle of the pastry to approximate a *pain au chocolat*.

'Her behaviour, then?' I ask with exaggerated concern. 'Is she disruptive? Disobedient? Impolite?'

'No, no. Of *course* not. Nothing like that.'

'What then?'

Caro looks at me with a vinegary expression. 'Curé

310

Reynaud has visited the school several times this week,'
she informs me. 'To talk to the children about Easter, and
the meaning of the Church's festival, and so on.'

I nodded encouragingly. Joline gave me another of her
compassionate smiles.

'Well, Anouk seems to be' – a coy glance in Anouk's
direction – 'well, not exactly *disruptive*, but she's been
asking him some very strange questions.' Her smile
narrowed between twin brackets of disapproval.

'*Very* strange questions,' she repeated.

'Oh well,' I said lightly. 'She's always been curious. I'm
sure you wouldn't like to discourage the spirit of enquiry
in any of your pupils. And besides,' I added mischievously,
'don't tell me there's any subject that Monsieur Reynaud
isn't equipped to answer questions on.'

Joline simpered, protesting. 'It upsets the other children, Madame,' she said tightly.

'Oh?'

'It seems Anouk has been telling them that Easter isn't
really a Christian festival at all, and that Our Lord is' –
she paused, embarrassed – 'that Our Lord's resurrection is
a kind of *throwback* to some corn god or other. Some
fertility deity from pagan times.' She gave a forced laugh,
but her voice was chilly.

'Yes.' I touched Anouk's curls briefly. 'She's a well-read
little thing, aren't you, Nanou?'

'I was only asking about Eostre,' said Anouk stoutly. 'Curé Reynaud says nobody celebrates it any more, and I told him *we* did.'

I hid my smile behind my hand. 'I don't suppose he understands, sweetheart,' I told her. 'Perhaps you shouldn't ask so many questions, if it upsets him.'

'It upsets the children, Madame,' said Joline.

'No, it doesn't,' retorted Anouk. 'Jeannot says we should have a bonfire when it comes, and have red and white candles, and everything. Jeannot says—'

Caroline interrupted her. 'Jeannot seems to have said a great deal,' she observed.

'He must take after his mother,' I said.

Joline looked affronted. 'You don't seem to be taking this very seriously,' she said, the smile slipping a little.

I shrugged. 'I don't see a problem,' I told her mildly. 'My daughter participates in class discussion. Isn't that what you're telling me?'

'Some subjects shouldn't be *open* to discussion,' snapped Caro, and for a moment, beneath that pastel-sweetness I saw her mother in her, imperious and overbearing. I liked her better for showing a little spirit. 'Some things should be accepted on *faith*, and if the child had any proper moral *grounding*—' She bit off the sentence in confusion. 'Far be it from me to tell *you* how to raise your child,' she finished in a flat voice.

'Good,' I said with a smile. 'I should have hated to quarrel with you.' Both women looked at me with the same expression of baffled dislike.

'Are you sure you won't have a drink of chocolate?'

Caro's eyes slid longingly over the display, the pralines, truffles, amandines and nougats, the éclairs, florentines, liqueur cherries, frosted almonds.

'I'm surprised the child's teeth aren't rotten,' she said tautly.

Anouk grinned, displaying the offending teeth. Their whiteness seemed to add to Caro's displeasure. 'We're wasting our time here,' she remarked coolly to Joline.

I said nothing, and Roux sniggered. In the kitchen I could hear Joséphine's little radio playing. For a few seconds there was no sound but the tinny squeak of the speaker against the tiles.

'Come *on*,' said Caro to her friend. Joline looked uncertain, hesitant.

'I said *come on*!' With a gesture of irritation she swept out of the shop with Joline in her wake. 'Don't think I don't know what you're playing at,' she spat in lieu of goodbye, then they were both gone, their high heels clacking against the stones as they crossed the square to St Jérôme's.

The next day we found the first of the leaflets. Scrunched up into a ball and tossed into the street, Joséphine picked it up as she was sweeping the pavement and brought it into the shop. A single page of typescript, photocopied onto pink paper then folded into two. It was unsigned, but something about the style suggested its possible author.

The title: 'Easter and the Return to Faith'. I scanned the sheet quickly. Much of the text was predictable. Rejoicing and self-purification, sin and the joys of absolution and prayer. But halfway down the page, in bolder text than the rest, was a sub-heading which caught my eye.

The New Revivalists: Corrupting the Spirit of Easter.
There will always be a small minority of people who attempt to use our Holy traditions for personal gain. The greetings card industry. The supermarket chains. Even more sinister are those people who claim to revive ancient traditions, involving our children in pagan practices in the guise of amusement. Too many of us see these as harmless, and view them with tolerance. Why else should our community have allowed a so-called Chocolate Festival to take place outside our church on the very morning of Easter Sunday? This makes a mockery of everything Easter stands for. We urge you to boycott this so-called Festival and all similar events, for the sake of your innocent children.
CHURCH, not CHOCOLATE, is the TRUE MESSAGE of EASTER!

'Church, not chocolate.' I laughed. 'Actually, that's a pretty good slogan. Don't you think?'

Joséphine was looking anxious. 'I don't understand you,' she said. 'You don't seem worried at all.'

'Why should I worry?' I shrugged. 'It's only a leaflet. And I'm certain I know who produced it.'

She nodded. 'Caro.' Her tone was emphatic. 'Caro and Joline. It's exactly their style. All that stuff about their innocent children.' She gave a snort of derision. 'But people listen to them, Vianne. It might make people think twice about coming. Joline's our schoolteacher. And Caro's a member of the Residents' Committee.'

'Oh?' I didn't know there even was a Residents' Committee. Self-important bigots with a taste for gossip. 'So what can they do? Arrest everybody?'

Joséphine shook her head. 'Paul's on that committee, too,' she said in a low voice.

'So?'

'So you know what he can do,' said Joséphine desperately. I have noticed that in times of stress she reverts to her old mannerisms, digging her thumbs into her breastbone. 'He's crazy, you know he is. He's just—'

She broke off miserably, fists clenched. Again I had the impression that she wanted to tell me something, that she *knew* something. I touched her hand, reaching gently for her thoughts, but saw nothing more than before: smoke, grey and greasy, against a purple sky.

Smoke! My hand tightened around hers. Smoke! Now that I knew what I was seeing I could make out details: his face a pale blur in the dark, his slicing, triumphant grin. She looked at me in silence, her eyes dark with knowledge.

'Why didn't you tell me?' I said at last.

'You can't prove it,' said Joséphine. 'I didn't tell you anything.'

'You didn't need to. Is that why you're afraid of Roux? Because of what Paul did?'

She put up her chin stubbornly. 'I'm not *afraid* of him.'

'But you won't talk to him. You won't even stay in the same room with him. You can't look him in the eye.'

Joséphine folded her arms with the look of a woman who has nothing more to say.

'Joséphine?' I turned her face towards mine, forced her to look at me. '*Joséphine?*'

'All right.' Her voice was harsh and sullen. 'I knew, all right? I knew what Paul was going to do. I told him I'd tell if he tried anything, I'd warn them. That was when he hit me.' She gave me a venomous look, her mouth half-broken with unshed tears. 'So I'm a coward,' she said in a loud, shapeless voice. 'Now you know what I am; I'm not brave like you, I'm a liar and a coward. I let him do it, someone could have been killed, Roux could have been killed or Zézette or her baby and it would all have been *my fault!*' She took a long grating breath.

'Don't tell him,' she said. 'I couldn't stand it.'

'*I* won't tell Roux,' I told her gently. '*You're* going to do that.'

She shook her head wildly. 'I'm not. I'm not. I couldn't.'

'It's all right, Joséphine,' I coaxed. 'It wasn't your fault. And no-one *was* killed, were they?'

Stubbornly: 'I couldn't. I can't.'

'Roux isn't like Paul,' I said. 'He's more like you than you imagine.'

'I wouldn't know what to say.' Her hands twisted. 'I wish he'd just leave,' she said fiercely. 'I wish he could just take his money and go somewhere else.'

'No you don't,' I told her. 'Besides, he isn't going to.' I told her what he had said to me about his job with Narcisse, and about the boat in Agen. 'He deserves at least to know who's responsible,' I insisted. 'That way he'll understand that only Muscat is to blame for what happened, and that no-one else hates him here. You should understand that, Joséphine. You know what it's like to feel the way he feels.' Joséphine sighed.

'Not today,' she said. 'I'll tell him, but some other time. OK?'

'It won't ever be any easier than it is today,' I warned. 'Do you want me to come with you?'

She stared at me. 'Well, he'll be due a break soon,' I explained. 'You could take him a cup of chocolate.'

A pause. Her face was blank and pale. Her gunslinger's hands were trembling at her sides. I took a *rocher noir* from a pile at my side and popped it into her half-open mouth before she had time to speak.

'Give you courage,' I explained, turning to pour the chocolate into a large cup. 'Go on then. Chew.' I heard her make a tiny sound, half-laughter. I gave her the cup. 'Ready?'

'I suppose.' Voice thick with chocolate. 'I'll try.'

I left them alone. I reread the leaflet Joséphine had found in the street. *Church, not Chocolate*. It's really quite funny. The Black Man finds a sense of humour at last.

It was warm outside in spite of the wind. Les Marauds glittered in the sunlight. I walked slowly down towards the Tannes, relishing the heat of the sun on my back. Spring has come with little prelude, like turning a rocky corner into a valley, and gardens and borders have blossomed suddenly, lush with daffodils, irises, tulips. Even the derelict houses of Les Marauds are touched with colour, but here the ordered gardens have run to rampant eccentricity: a flowering elder growing from the balcony of a house overlooking the water; a roof carpeted with dandelions; violets poking out of a crumbling façade. Once-cultivated plants have reverted to their wild state, small leggy geraniums thrusting between hemlock-umbels, self-seeded poppies scattered at random and bastardized from their original red to orange to palest mauve. A few days' sunshine is enough to coax them from sleep; after the rain they stretch and raise their heads towards the light. Pull out a handful of these supposed weeds and there are sages and irises, pinks and lavenders under the docks and ragwort. I wandered by the river for long enough for Joséphine and Roux to make up their differences, then I made my way gently home through the back streets, up the Ruelle des Frères de la Révolution and Rue des Poètes with its close, dark, almost windowless walls, broken only by the washing-lines slung casually from balcony to balcony or by a single window box trailing green festoons of convolvulus.

I found them in the shop together, a half-empty pot of chocolate on the counter between them. Joséphine looked pink-eyed but relieved, almost happy. Roux was laughing at some comment of hers, a strange, unfamiliar sound, exotic because it is so rarely heard. For a second I felt something almost like envy, thinking: *They belong together*.

I spoke to Roux about it later, when she had gone out to collect some shopping. He is careful to give nothing away when he speaks of her, but there is always a bright look in his eyes like a smile waiting to happen. It seems he suspected Muscat already.

'She did well to get away from the bastard,' he says with casual venom. 'The things he did—' For a moment he looks embarrassed, turns, moves a cup on the counter for no reason, moves it back. 'A man like that doesn't deserve a wife,' he mutters.

'What will you do?' I ask him.

He shrugs. 'Nothing to do,' he tells me prosaically. 'He'll deny it. The police aren't interested. Besides, I'd rather they didn't get involved.'

He does not elaborate. I take it that there are things in his past which may not bear scrutiny.

Since then, however, Joséphine and he have spoken many times. She brings him chocolate and biscuits when he breaks from work, and I often hear them laughing. She has lost her scared abstracted look. I notice that she has begun to dress with greater care. This morning she even announced that she wanted to go back to the café to collect some things.

'I'll go with you,' I suggested.

Joséphine shook her head.

'I'll be all right on my own.' She looked happy, almost elated with her decision. 'Besides, if I don't face Paul—' She broke off, looking vaguely embarrassed. 'I just thought I'd go, that's all,' she said. Her face was flushed, stubborn. 'I've got books, clothes . . . I want to collect them before Paul decides to throw them away.'

I nodded. 'When were you planning to go?'

Without hesitation: 'Sunday. He'll be going to church then. With a little luck I'll be able to get in and out of the café without even meeting him. It won't take long.'

I looked at her. 'You're sure you don't want company?'

She shook her head. 'It wouldn't be right, somehow.'

Her prim expression made me smile, but all the same I knew what she meant. It was his territory – *their* territory – indelibly marked with the traces of their life together. I didn't belong there.

'I'll be all right.' She smiled. 'I know how to handle him, Vianne. I've managed before.'

'I hope it won't come to that.'

'It won't.' Absurdly, she reached out and took my hand, as if to reassure me. 'I promise it won't.'

33

Sunday, March 23
Palm Sunday

THE BELL PEALS OUT FLATLY AGAINST THE WHITEWASHED walls of the houses and shops. Even the cobbles resonate with the sound; I can feel its dull buzz through the soles of my shoes. Narcisse has provided the *rameaux*, the palm crosses which I distribute at the end of the service and which will be kept in lapels, on mantelpieces, at bedsides, for the rest of Holy Week. I will bring you one too, *père*, and a candle to burn by your bedside; I see no reason why you should be denied. The attendants look at me with thinly veiled amusement. Only fear and respect for my habit prevents them from laughing aloud. Their rosy nursery-nurse faces glow with secret laughter. In the corridor, their girlish voices rise and fall in phrases made unintelligible by distance and the hospital acoustics:

He thinks he can hear him – oh yes – thinks he's going to

wake up – No, really? – No! – Talks to him, darling – heard him once – praying— Then schoolgirl laughter – *hihihihihi!* – like scattered beads on the tiles.

Of course they dare not laugh at me to my face. They might be nuns in their clean white uniforms, their hair tied back beneath starched caps, their eyes lowered. Convent children, mouthing the formulae of respect – *oui, mon père, non, mon père* – with a heart full of secret mirth. My congregation too has this truant spirit – a pert glance during the sermon, unseemly haste towards the *chocolaterie* afterwards – but today everything is orderly. They greet me with respect, almost with fear. Narcisse apologizes that the *rameaux* are not real palms, but cedar twisted and plaited to approximate the more traditional leaf.

'It's not an indigenous tree, *père*,' he explains in his gruff voice. 'It won't grow properly here. The frost scorches it.'

I pat his shoulder in a fatherly gesture. 'Not to worry, *mon fils*.' Their return to the fold has mellowed my mood so that I am avuncular, indulgent. 'Not to worry.'

Caroline Clairmont takes my hand between her gloved fingers. 'A lovely service.' Her voice is warm. '*Such* a lovely service.' Georges echoes her words. Luc stands at her shoulder, looking sullen. Behind him, the Drous, with their son, sheepish in his sailor collar. I cannot see Muscat amongst the departing congregation, but I suppose he must be there.

Caroline Clairmont gives me an arch smile. 'It looks as if we did it,' she says with satisfaction. 'We've got a petition with over a hundred signatures on it—'

'The chocolate festival.' I interrupt her in a low voice, displeased. It is too public a place to discuss this. She fails to take the hint.

'Of course!' Her voice is high and excited. 'We distributed two hundred leaflets. Collected signatures from half the people in Lansquenet. Visited every house' – she pauses, correcting herself scrupulously – 'well, *almost* every house.' She smirks. 'With a few obvious exceptions.'

'I see.' I make my voice frigid. 'Well, perhaps we could discuss this at some other time.'

I see her register the snub. She reddens. 'Of course, *père*.'

She is right, of course. There has been a measurable effect. The chocolate shop has been almost deserted for the past few days. The disapproval of the Residents' Committee is no small matter, after all, in such a closed community, as is the tacit disapproval of the Church. To buy, to cavort, to *gorge* beneath the very eye of that disapproval ... That takes a greater courage, a greater spirit of revolt than the Rocher woman gives them credit for. After all, how long has she lived here? The erring lamb returns to the fold, *père*. By instinct. She is a brief diversion for them, that's all. But in the end they always revert to type. I do not fool myself that they do it out of any great feeling of contrition or spirituality – sheep are no great thinkers – but their instincts, bred in them from the cradle, are sound. Their feet bring them home, even when their minds have wandered. I feel a sudden burst of love for them today, for my flock, my people. I want to feel their hands in mine, to touch their warm, stupid flesh, to revel in their awe and their trust.

Is this what I have been praying for, *père*? Is this the lesson I was meant to learn? I scan the crowd again for Muscat. He always comes to church on Sunday, and today, this special Sunday, he cannot have missed . . . And yet as the church empties I can still not see him. I do not recall him taking Communion. And surely he would not have left without exchanging a few words with me. Maybe he is still waiting in St Jérôme's, I tell myself. The situation with his wife has troubled him greatly. Perhaps he needs further guidance.

The pile of palm crosses at my side diminishes. Each one dipped in holy water, a murmured blessing, a touch of the hand. Luc Clairmont pulls away from my touch with an angry mutter. His mother remonstrates weakly, sending me a feeble smile across the bowed heads. There is still no sign of Muscat. I check the church's interior: but for a few old people still kneeling at the altar it is empty. St Francis stands at the door, absurdly jolly for a saint, surrounded by plaster pigeons, his beaming face more like that of a madman or a drunkard than that of a holy man. I feel a twitch of annoyance at whoever placed the statue there, so close to the entrance. My namesake, I feel, should have more weight, more dignity. Instead this lumbering, grinning fool seems to mock me, one hand held out in a vague gesture of benediction, the other cradling the plaster bird to his round belly, as if dreaming of pigeon pie. I try to recall whether the saint was in the same position when we left Lansquenet, *père*. Do you remember, or has it been moved since, perhaps by envious people who seek to mock me? St Jérôme, in whose name the place was built, has less prominence: in his dark alcove with the blackened oil-painting behind him he is shady, barely visible, the old marble from which he was hewn stained a nicotine-yellow by the smoke of a thousand candles. St Francis, on the other hand, remains mushroom-white in spite of the plaster's dampness, crumbling away in happy insouciance of his colleague's tacit disapproval. I remind myself to have him moved to a more appropriate spot as soon as possible.

Muscat is not in the church. I check the grounds, still half-believing that he may be waiting for me there, but there is no sign. Maybe he is ill, I tell myself. Only serious illness would prevent such an assiduous churchgoer from attending service on Palm Sunday. I change my clean cassock for my workaday soutane, leaving the ceremonial vestments in the vestry. The chalice and sacramental plate I lock away for safekeeping. In your day, *père*, there would have been no reason to do so, but in these uncertain times nothing can be taken on trust. Vagrants and gypsies – not to mention some of our own villagers – might take the prospect of hard cash more seriously than that of eternal damnation.

I make my way towards Les Marauds with a quick step. Muscat has been uncommunicative since last week, and I have only seen him in passing, though he looks doughy and ill, hunched like a sullen penitent, his eyes half-hidden beneath the puffy folds of his eyelids. Few people visit the café now, afraid perhaps of Muscat's haggard looks and quick temper. I went there myself on Friday; the bar was almost deserted. The floor had not been swept since Joséphine's departure. Cigarette-butts and sweet-wrappers slid underfoot. Empty glasses cluttered every surface. A few sandwiches and a reddish, curling thing which might have been a slice of pizza stood forlornly beneath the glass counter. Next to them, a pile of Caroline's leaflets, held down with a dirty beer glass. There was a low under-stench of vomit and mould beneath the rankness of Gauloises.

Muscat was drunk. 'So it's you.' His tone was morose, just this side of belligerent. 'Come to tell me to turn the other cheek again, have you?' He took a long drag of the cigarette clamped wetly between his teeth. 'You should be pleased. Haven't gone near the bitch in days.'

I shook my head. 'You mustn't be bitter,' I told him.

'I can be what I like in my own bar,' said Muscat in his slurred, aggressive way. 'It *is* my bar, isn't it, *père*? I mean, you're not going to give *that* to her on a plate as well, are you?'

I told him I understood what he must be feeling. He took another drag on his cigarette and coughed laughter and stale beer into my face.

'That's good, *père*.' His breath was foul and hot, like an animal's. 'That's very good. *Course* you understand. Course you do. The church took *your* balls when you took your vows. Stands to reason you shouldn't want *me* to keep *mine*.'

'You're drunk, Muscat,' I snapped.

'Well spotted, *père*,' he snarled. 'Not much gets past you, does it?' He made a sweeping gesture with the hand which held the cigarette. 'All she needs is to see the place like this,' he said harshly. 'That's all she needs to make her happy now. Knowing that she's ruined me' – he was close to tears now, his eyes filling with the drunkard's easy self-pity – 'knowing she's thrown our marriage wide open for people to laugh at—' He made a filthy sound, half-sob, half-belch. 'Knowing she's broken my fucking *heart*!' He wiped his nose wetly on the back of his hand.

'Don't think I don't know what's going on there,' he

said in a lower voice. 'The bitch and her queer friends. I know what they're doing.' His voice was getting louder again, and I looked around awkwardly to see his three or four remaining customers gaping at him curiously. I pressed his arm in warning.

'Don't lose hope, Muscat,' I urged, fighting my disgust at finding myself so close to him. 'This is no way to win her back. Remember that many married couples have moments of doubt, but—'

He sniggered. 'Doubt, is it?' He sniggered again. 'Tell you what, *père*. Give me five minutes alone with her, and I'll solve *that* problem for her for good. *I'll* fucking win her back, no doubt about that.'

He sounded vicious and stupid, his words barely formed around his shark's grin. I took him by the shoulders and articulated clearly, hoping that at least some of my meaning might penetrate. 'You will *not*,' I said into his face, ignoring the gaping drinkers at the bar. 'You will conduct yourself with *decency*, Muscat, you will follow the correct *procedure* if you wish to take action, and you will *keep away* from both of them! Understood?'

My hands were gripping his shoulders. Muscat protested, whining obscenities. 'I'm warning you, Muscat,' I told him. 'I've tolerated a great deal from you, but this kind of – *bullying* – behaviour I will *not* tolerate. Do you understand?'

He muttered something, apology or threat I could not

tell. At the time I thought it was *I'm sorry*, but thinking back it might just as easily have been *You'll be sorry*, his eyes glittering meanly behind his half-shed drunkard's tears.

Sorry. But *who* would be made to be sorry? And for what?

Hurrying down the hill towards Les Marauds, I wondered again if I had misread the signs. Could he be capable of violence towards himself? Might I, in my eagerness to prevent further disturbance, have overlooked the truth of the matter, the fact that the fellow was on the far edge of despair? When I reached the Café de la République it was shut, but a small circle of people were standing outside, apparently looking up at one of the first-floor windows. I recognized Caro Clairmont and Joline Drou amongst them. Duplessis was there too, a small dignified figure with his felt hat and his dog cavorting at his feet. Above the sound of voices I thought I could hear a higher, shriller sound which rose and fell in varying cadences, occasionally almost resolving itself into words, phrases, a scream . . .

'*Père*.' Caro's voice was breathless, her face flushed. Her expression was like that of the wide-eyed and eternally gasping beauties of certain glossy top-shelf magazines, and I found myself flushing at the thought.

'What is it?' My voice was crisp. 'Muscat?'

'It's Joséphine,' said Caro in excitement. 'He's got her up there in the top room, *père*, and she's *screaming.*'

Even as she spoke another volley of noise – combining screams, shouted abuse and the sound of projectiles smashing – came from the window, and a shower of debris scattered onto the cobbles. A woman's voice, high enough to shatter glass, screeched – though not, I thought, in terror but in wild and simple rage – followed almost at once by another explosion of household shrapnel. Books, rags, records, mantel ornaments . . . the mundane artillery of domestic strife.

I called up towards the window. 'Muscat? Can you hear me? *Muscat!*'

An empty canary-cage came hurtling through the air. '*Muscat!*'

From inside the house, no answer. The two adversaries sound inhuman – a troll and a harpy – and for a moment I feel almost uneasy, as if the world has turned a little further into the shadows, broadening the crescent of darkness which separates us from the light. Open the door and what might I see?

For a dreadful second the old memory hits home and I am sixteen again, opening the door of that old church annexe still referred to by some as the chancery, passing from the church's murky half-light into a deeper gloom, my feet almost soundless on the smooth parquet, with the strange thudding and groaning of an unseen monster in my ears. Opening the door, heart triphammering in my throat, fists clenched, eyes wide ... and seeing on the floor in front of me the pallid arching beast, its proportions half-familiar but bizarrely doubled, two faces raised towards me in frozen expressions of rage-horror-dismay.

Maman! Père!

Ludicrous, I know. There can be no connection. And yet looking at Caro Clairmont's moist and feverish countenance I wonder if perhaps she feels it too, the erotic belly-thrill of violence, the moment of power when the match strikes, the blow falls, the petrol ignites ...

It was not simply your betrayal, *père*, that made my blood freeze and the skin of my temples tauten like drumskins. I knew about sin – the sins of the flesh – only as a kind of disgusting abstraction, like lying down with animals. That there might be *pleasure* in it was almost incomprehensible. And yet you and my mother – hot, flushed, *working* at it in that mechanical way, oiled with and against each other like pistons, not quite naked, no, but *more* lewd for the vestiges of clothing – blouse, crumpled skirt, soutane drawn up ... No, it was not the flesh which so disgusted me, for I looked at the scene with a distant, disgusted disinterest. It was because I had *compromised* myself for you, *père*, only two weeks before, had compromised my soul for you – the bottle of oil slick against the palm of my hand, the thrill of righteous power, the sigh of rapture as the bottle flies into the air and ignites, splashing across the deck of the pitiful houseboat in a bright wave of hungry *flick-flick*ing flames, *flick-flick-flick* against the dry tarpaulin, *crisss* against the cracked dry wood, licking with salacious glee. They suspected arson, *père*, but never Reynaud's good, quiet boy, not Francis, who sang in the church choir and sat so pale and good during your sermons. Not pale young Francis, who had never so much as broken a window. Muscat, perhaps. Old Muscat and his tearaway son might have done it. For a time there was coldness towards them, unfriendly speculation. This time, things had gone too far. But they denied it steadfastly, and after all, there was no proof. The victims were none of ours. No-one made the connexion between the burning and the changes in the Reynaud fortunes, the parents' separation, the boy's departure for a select school in the North . . . I did it for you, *père*. For love of you. The burning boat on the dry flats lights up the brown night, people running out, screaming, scrabbling at the baked-earth banks of the arid Tannes, some trying hopelessly to drag out the few remaining bucketfuls of mud from the riverbed to throw over the burning boat, I waiting in the bushes, mouth dry, belly full of hot joy.

I could not have known of the sleepers in the houseboat, I tell myself. Wrapped so tight in their drunken darkness that even the fire failed to waken them. I dreamed of them later, charred one into the other, melded like perfect lovers. For months I screamed in the night, seeing those arms reaching longingly towards me, hearing their voices – a breath of ash – mouthing my name from whitened lips.

But you absolved me, *père*. Only a drunkard and his slattern, you told me. Worthless flotsam on the filthy river. Twenty *Paters* and as many *Avés* paid for their lives. Thieves who had desecrated our church, insulted our priest, deserved nothing more. I was a young boy with a bright future ahead, with loving parents who would grieve, who would be terribly unhappy if they knew. Besides, you said persuasively, it *might* have been an accident. You could never know, you said. God might have *meant* it this way.

I believed it. Or pretended to. And I am still grateful.

A touch on my arm. I start, alarmed. Looking into the pit of my memories I am momentarily dizzied by time. Armande Voizin stands behind me, her clever black eyes fixing me. Duplessis is at her side.

'Are you going to do something, Francis, or are you going to let that bear Muscat commit murder?' Her voice is crisp and cold. One claw grasps her stick, the other beckons witchlike at the closed door.

'It isn't . . .' My voice is high and childish, not my own at all. 'It isn't my business to interv—'

'Rubbish!' She raps my knuckles with her stick. 'I'm going to put a stop to this, Francis. Are you going to come with me, or are you going to stand there all day gawping?'

She does not wait for my answer, but pushes at the café door.

'It's locked,' I say feebly.

She shrugs. A single tap with the handle of her stick breaks one of the panes of the glass door.

'The key's in the lock,' she says sharply. 'Reach it for me, Guillaume.'

The door swings open as the key turns. I follow her up the stairs. The sounds of screaming and breaking glass are louder here, amplified by the hollow shell of the stairway. Muscat stands in the doorway of the upper room, his thick body half-blocking the landing. The room is barricaded shut; a small gap shows between the door and its frame, throwing a narrow edge of light onto the stairs. As I watch Muscat throws himself again at the blocked door; there is a crashing sound as something overturns, and grunting in satisfaction he thrusts his way into the room.

A woman screams. She is backed against the far wall of the room. Furniture – a dressing-table, a wardrobe, chairs – have been stacked against the door, but Muscat has managed to push his way through at last. She could not move the bed, a heavy wrought-iron thing, but the mattress still shields her as she crouches, a small pile of missiles to hand. She held out through the entire service, I tell myself with some wonder. I can see the signs of her flight; broken glass on the stairs, the marks of leverage against the locked bedroom door, the coffee-table he used as a battering-ram. On his face too, as he turns it towards me, I can see the marks of her desperate fingernails, a crescent of blood on his temple, nose swollen, shirt torn. There is blood on the stairs, a drop, a skid-mark, a dribble. Bloody hand-prints against the door.

'Muscat!' My voice is high, shaking. '*Muscat!*'

He turns towards me blankly. His eyes are needle-marks in dough.

Armande is at my side, her stick held out like a sword. She looks like the world's oldest swashbuckler. She calls to Joséphine. 'Are you all right, dear?'

'Get him *out* of here! Tell him to go *away*!'

Muscat shows me his bloody hands. He looks enraged but at the same time confused, exhausted, like a small child caught in a fight between much older boys. 'See what I mean, *père?*' he whines. 'What did I tell you? See what I *mean?*'

Armande pushes past me. 'You can't win, Muscat.' She sounds younger and stronger than I, and I have to remind myself that she is old and sick. 'You can't put things back to what they were. Back off and let her go.'

Muscat spits at her, looks astonished when Armande spits back with cobra speed and accuracy. He wipes his face, blustering. 'Why, you old—'

Guillaume steps in front of her, an absurdly protective gesture. His dog yaps shrilly, but she steps past them laughing. 'Don't try to bully me, Paul-Marie Muscat,' snaps Armande. 'I remember when you were still a snot-nosed brat, hiding in Les Marauds to get away from that drunken father of yours. Haven't changed that much, 'cept you got bigger and uglier. Now *back off*!'

Looking dazed, he stands back. For a moment he seems ready to appeal to me.

'*Père*. Tell her.' His eyes looked as if he'd rubbed them with salt. 'You know what I mean. Don't you?'

I pretend not to hear. There is nothing between us, this man and I. No point of comparison. I can smell him, the rank unwashed odour of his filthy shirt, the stale beery breath. He takes my arm. 'You understand, *père*,' he repeats desperately. 'I helped you out, with the gypsies. Remember? I helped you.'

She may be half-blind but she sees everything, damn her. *Everything*. I see her eyes flick to my face. 'Oh, you did?' She gives her vulgar chuckle. 'Two of a kind, eh, Curé?'

'I don't know what you're talking about, man.' I make my voice crisp. 'You're drunk as a pig.'

'But *père*' – struggling for words, his face contorting, purple – '*père*, you yourself said—'

Stonily: 'I said nothing.'

He opens his mouth again like a poor landed fish on the mud-flats of the summer Tannes.

'*Nothing!*'

Armande and Guillaume lead Joséphine away, one old

337

arm tucked around her shoulders. The woman throws me a strange, bright glance which almost frightens me. Dirt streaks her face, and her hands are bloody, but in that moment she is beautiful, disturbing. She looks at me as if for a second she is able to see straight through. I try to tell her not to blame me. I'm not like him; not a *man*, but a *priest*, a different species ... but the thought is absurd, almost a heresy.

Then Armande leads her away and I am alone with Muscat, his tears staining my neck, his hot arms around me. For a moment I am disoriented, drowning with him in the soup of my memories. Then I pull away, trying for gentleness but in the end with increasing violence, pushing at his flabby belly with palms, fists, elbows. And all the time shouting above his pleading, in a voice not my own, a high, bitter voice: 'Get away from me, you bastard, you've spoiled everything, you've—'

Francis, I'm sorry, I—

'*Père*—'

'Spoiled everything – *everything* – get *away!*' Grunting with the effort and finally breaking his thick hot grasp, pulling loose with sudden, desperate joy – free at last! – then running down the stairs, turning one ankle over on the loose carpet, his tears, his stupid wailing following me like an unwanted child.

Later there was time to talk to Caro and Georges. I will

not speak to Muscat. Besides, rumour has it that he has already left, has packed what he could into his old car and driven off. The café is closed, only the broken pane to show for what happened this morning. I went down there when night fell, stood for a long time in front of the window. The sky across Les Marauds was cool and sepia-green with a single milky filament on the horizon. The river was dark and silent.

I told Caro the Church would not back her campaign against the chocolate festival. *I* would not back it. Can't she see? The Committee can have no credibility after what he has done. It was too public this time, too brutal. They must have seen his face as I did, flushed with hatred and madness. To know a man beats his wife – to know in secret – is one thing. But to see it in all its ugliness . . . No. He will never survive it. Already Caro is telling the others that *she* saw through him, that she always knew. She disassociates herself as best she can – *Was ever a poor woman so deceived!* – as do I. We have been too close, I tell her. We used him when it was expedient. We must not be seen to do so now. For our own protection we must stand back. I do not tell her about the other business, that of the river people, but that too is in my mind. Armande suspects. Out of malice she might talk. And that *other* matter, forgotten for so long but still alight in her old head. No. I am helpless. Worse, I must even be seen to look upon the festival with indulgence. Otherwise the gossip will start, and who knows where it might end? Tomorrow I must preach tolerance, turn the tide which I have begun and change their minds. The remaining leaflets I will burn. The posters, due for display from Lansquenet to Montauban, must also be destroyed. It breaks my heart, *père*, but what else can I do? The scandal would kill me.

It is Holy Week. A single week before her festival. And she has won, *père*. She has won. Only a miracle could save us now.

34

Wednesday, March 26

STILL NO SIGN OF MUSCAT. JOSÉPHINE STAYED AT La Praline for most of Monday, but yesterday morning decided to return to the café. Roux went with her this time, but all they found was the mess. It seems the rumours are right. Muscat has gone. Roux, who has finished Anouk's new bedroom in the attic, has already begun work on the café. New locks on the door, the old linoleum pulled up and the grimy curtains stripped from the windows. He thinks that with a little effort – a coat of whitewash on the rough walls, a lick of paint on the battered old furniture, a lot of soap and water – the bar could be made into a bright and welcoming place. He offered to do the work for free, but Joséphine will not hear of it. Muscat has of course cleaned out their joint account, but she has a little money of her own, and she is sure the new café will be a success. The faded sign which has read Café de la République for the last thirty-five years has at last been pulled down. In its place, a bright red-and-white awning – the twin of my own – and a hand-painted sign from Clairmont's yard which reads Café des Marauds. Narcisse has planted geraniums in the wrought-iron window boxes and they trail down the walls, their scarlet buds opening in the sudden warmth. Armande watches with approval from her garden just down the hill.

'She's a good girl,' she tells me in her brusque way. 'She'll manage now she's got rid of the sot she married.'

Roux is living temporarily in one of the café's spare rooms, and Luc has taken his place with Armande, much to the annoyance of his mother.

'It's not a fit place for you to stay,' she snaps shrilly. I am standing in the square as they come out of the church, he in his Sunday suit, she in another of her innumerable pastel outfits, a silk scarf knotted over her hair.

His reply is polite, immovable. 'Just until the p-party,' he says. 'There's no-one there to look after her. Sh-she might h-have another f-fit.'

'Rubbish!' Her tone is dismissive. 'I'll tell you what she's doing. She's trying to drive a wedge between us. I forbid you, I absolutely forbid you to stay with her this week. And as for that ridiculous party—'

'I don't think you should f-forbid me, M-maman.'

'And why not? You're my *son*, damn it, you can't just

stand there and tell me you'd rather obey that crazy old woman than me!' Her eyes fill with angry tears. Her voice wavers.

'It's all right, *Maman*.' He is unmoved by the display, but puts an arm around her shoulder. 'It won't be for long. Just until the party. I p-promise. You're invited too, you know. It would make her happy if you c-came.'

'I don't *want* to go!' Her voice is spiteful and teary, like a tired child's.

He shrugs. 'Don't go, then. But d-don't expect her to listen to what *you* want, afterwards.'

She looks at him. 'What do you mean?'

'I mean, I could t-talk to her. P-persuade her.' He knows his mother, this clever boy. Understands her better than she knows. 'I c-could bring her round,' he says. 'But if you don't want to t-try—'

'I didn't *say* that.' On a sudden impulse she puts her arms around him. 'You're my clever boy,' she says, her poise regained. 'You *could* do it, couldn't you?' She plants a ringing kiss on his cheek and he submits patiently. 'My *good, clever* boy,' she repeats caressingly, and they walk off together, arm-in-arm, the boy already taller than his mother and looking across at her with the attentive look of a tolerant parent to a volatile infant.

Oh, he knows.

With Joséphine busy with her own affairs I have had little help with my Easter preparations; fortunately most of the work is done now, with only a few dozen remaining boxes to make. I work in the evenings to make the cakes and truffles, the gingerbread bells and the gilded *pains d'épices*. I miss Joséphine's light touch with the wrapping and the decoration, but Anouk helps me as best she can, fluffing out frills of Cellophane and pinning silk roses onto innumerable sachets.

I have hidden the front window as I work on Sunday's display, and the face of the shop looks much as it did when we arrived, with a screen of silver paper covering the glass. Anouk has decorated the screen with cut-outs of eggs and animals in coloured paper, and there is a large poster in the centre announcing:

GRAND FESTIVAL DU CHOCOLAT
Sunday, Place St Jérôme

Now that the school holidays have begun the square is abuzz with children, pressing their noses to the glass in the hope of catching a glimpse of the preparations. I have already taken more than eight thousand francs in orders – some from as far as Montauban and even Agen – and still they come, so that the shop is rarely empty. Caro's leaflet campaign seems to have ground to a halt. Guillaume tells me that Reynaud has assured his congregation that the chocolate festival has his absolute support, despite rumours spread by malicious gossips. Even so I sometimes see him watching me from his small window, and his eyes are hungry and hateful. I know he means me harm, but somehow his poison has been drawn. I try to ask Armande, who knows far more than she is telling, but she simply shakes her head.

'All that was a long time ago,' she tells me, deliberately vague. 'My memory isn't what it was.' Instead she wants to know every detail of the menu I have planned for her party, relishing everything in advance. She is brimming with suggestions. *Brandade truffée*, *vol-au-vents aux trois champignons*, cooked in wine and cream with wild *chantrelles* as a garnish, grilled *langoustines* with rocket salad, five different types of chocolate cake, all her favourites, home-made chocolate ice-cream . . . Her eyes are bright with delight and mischief.

'Never had parties when I was a girl,' she explains. 'Not a single one. Went to a dance once, over in Montauban, with a boy from the coast. *Whee!*' She made an expressive, lewd gesture. 'Dark as treacle, he was, and as sweet. We had champagne and strawberry sorbet, and we danced . . .' She sighed. 'You should have seen me then, Vianne. You wouldn't believe it now. He said I looked like Greta Garbo, the flatterer, and we both pretended he meant it.' She gave a low chuckle. 'Course, he wasn't the marrying kind,' she said philosophically. 'They never are.'

I lie awake almost every night now, sugarplums dancing before my eyes. Anouk sleeps in her new attic bedroom

and I dream, awake, doze, wake, dream, doze until my
eyelids glitter with sleeplessness and the room pitches
around me like a rolling ship. One more day, I tell myself.
One more day.

Last night I got up and took my cards from the box
where I promised they would stay. They felt cool between
my fingers, cool and smooth as ivory, the colours fanning
across my palms – blue-purple-green-black – the familiar
pictures sliding in and out of my line of vision like flowers
pressed between black sheets of glass. The Tower. Death.
The Lovers. Death. The Six of Swords. Death. The
Hermit. Death. I tell myself it doesn't mean anything.
Mother believed it, but where did that get her? Running,
running. The weathervane above St Jérôme's is silent
now, eerily calm. The wind has stopped. The lull disturbs
me more than the screeching of the old iron. The air is
warm and sweet with the new scents of approaching
summer. Summer comes quickly to Lansquenet in the
wake of the March winds, and it smells of the circus; of
sawdust and frying batter and cut green wood and animal
shit. My mother inside me whispers: *Time for a change.*
Armande's house is lit; I can see the small yellow square
in the window from here, throwing out chequered light
across the Tannes. I wonder what she is doing. She has
not spoken to me directly about her plan since that one
time. Instead she talks about recipes, the best way to
lighten a sponge cake, the sugar-to-spirit ratio for the best

cherries in brandy. I looked up her condition in my medical dictionary. The jargon is another kind of escape, obscure and hypothetical as the images on the cards. Inconceivable that these words could apply to real flesh. Her sight is diminishing, islands of darkness floating across her vision so that what she sees is pied, dappled, finally all but obscured. Then the dark.

I understand her situation. Why should she struggle to preserve for any longer a condition doomed to this inevitability? The thought of *waste* – my mother's thought, born from years of saving and uncertainty – is surely inappropriate here, I tell myself. Better the extravagant gesture, the blowout, bright lights and sudden darkness after. And yet something in me childishly wails *unfair!* Still hoping perhaps for the miracle. Again, my mother's thought. Armande knows better.

In the last weeks – the morphine was beginning to take over every moment and her eyes were a perpetual glaze – she would lose touch with reality for hours, drifting between fantasies like a butterfly between flowers. Some were sweet, dreams of floating, of lights, out-of-the-body meetings with dead movie stars and beings from ethereal planes. Some were back-shot with paranoia. The Black Man was never far in these, lurking at street corners, sitting at the window of a diner, behind the counter of a notion's store. Sometimes he was a cab driver, his cab a black hearse like the ones you find in London, a baseball cap drawn down over his eyes. The word DODGERS was written on his cap, she said, and that was because he was on the lookout for her, for us, for all the ones who had dodged him in the past, but not for ever, she said, shaking her head wisely, never for ever. During one of these black spells she brought out a yellow plastic wallet and showed it to me. It was stuffed with newspaper-cuttings, mostly dated from the late sixties and early seventies. Most were in French, but some were in Italian, German, Greek. All dealt with kidnappings, disappearances, attacks on children.

'So easily done,' she told me, her eyes huge and vague. 'Big places. So easy to lose a child. So easy to *lose* a child like you.' She winked at me blearily. I patted her hand in reassurance.

'It's OK, *Maman*,' I said. 'You were always careful. You looked out for me. I never did get lost.'

She winked again. 'Oh, you were *lost*,' she said, grinning. 'You were *lo-ost*.' She stared into space for a while after that, smiling-grimacing, her hand like a bunch of dry twigs in mine. '*L-ooo-ssstt*,' she repeated forlornly, and began to cry. I comforted her as best I could, stuffing the clippings back into the file. As I did I noticed that several dealt with the same case, the disappearance of eighteen-month-old Sylviane Caillou in Paris. Her mother left her strapped in her car-seat for two minutes while she stopped at a chemist's, and when she returned the baby had gone.

Gone too were the changing-bag and the child's toys, a red plush elephant and a brown teddy bear.

My mother saw me looking at the article and smiled again. 'I think you were two then,' she said in a sly voice. 'Or nearly two. And she was much fairer than you were. *Couldn't* have been you, could it? And anyway, I was a better mother than she was.'

'Of course not,' I said. 'You were a good mother, a wonderful mother. Don't worry. You wouldn't have done anything to put me at risk.'

Mother just rocked and smiled. 'Careless,' she crooned. 'Just careless. Didn't deserve a nice little girl like that, did she?'

I shook my head, feeling suddenly cold.

Childishly: 'I wasn't bad, was I, Vianne?'

I shivered. The pages felt scaly beneath my fingers. 'No,' I assured her. 'You weren't bad.'

'I looked after you all right, didn't I? Never gave you up. Not even when that priest said – said what he said. I never.'

'No, *Maman*. You never did.'

The cold was paralysing now, making thought difficult. All I could think of was the *name*, so similar to mine, the *dates* . . . And didn't I remember that bear, that elephant, its plush worn down to the red sailcloth, carried indefatigably from Paris to Rome, Rome to Vienna?

Of course it might have been one of her delusions.

There were others, like the snake under the bedclothes and the woman in the mirrors. It could have been make-believe. So much of my mother's life was just that. And besides . . . after so long, what did it matter?

At three I got up. The bed was hot and lumpy; sleep a million miles away. I lit a candle and took it into Joséphine's empty bedroom. The cards were back in their old place in Mother's box, shifting eagerly beneath my grasp. *The Lovers. The Tower. The Hermit. Death.* Sitting cross-legged on the bare floor I shuffled them with something more than mere idleness. The Tower with its falling people, its walls crumbling, I could understand. It is my constant fear of displacement, the fear of the road, of loss. The Hermit with his hood and lantern looks very like Reynaud, his sly pale face half-hidden in shadows. Death I know very well, and I forked my fingers at the card – *avert!* – with the old automatic gesture. But the Lovers? I thought of Roux and Joséphine, so alike without knowing it, and could not suppress a prick of envy. And yet behind it I felt a sudden conviction that the card had not yet given up all its secrets. A scent of lilac spilled across the room. Maybe one of Mother's bottles had a broken seal. I felt warm even in spite of the night chill, fingers of heat reaching into the pit of my stomach. *Roux?* Roux?

I turned the card over, in haste, with trembling fingers. One more day. Whatever it is can wait one more day. I shuffled the cards again, but I do not have my mother's deft touch and they slipped out of my hands onto the wood. The Hermit fell face-up. He looked more like Reynaud than ever in the flickering candlelight. His face seemed to grin viciously in the shadows. *I'll find a way*, he promised slyly. *You think you've won, but I'll still find a way.* I could feel his malevolence at my fingertips.

Mother would have called it a sign.

Suddenly, on an impulse I only half understood, I picked up the Hermit and held him up to the candle flame. For a moment the flame flirted with the stiff card, then the surface began to bubble. The pallid face grimaced and blackened.

'I'll show you,' I whispered. 'Try to interfere and I'll—'

A gout of flame flared alarmingly and I dropped the card onto the boards. The flame extinguished, spraying sparks and ash onto the wood.

I felt jubilant. *Who rings the changes now, Mother?*

And yet tonight I cannot rid myself of the feeling that I have somehow been manipulated, pushed into revealing what would have been better left alone. I did nothing, I tell myself. I intended no malice.

Still, tonight, I can't get the idea out of my mind. I feel light, insubstantial as milkweed fluff. Ready for any wind to blow away.

35

Friday, March 28
Good Friday

I SHOULD BE WITH MY FLOCK, *PÈRE*. I KNOW IT. THE church is thick with incense, funereal with purple and black, not a single piece of silver, a single wreath of flowers. I should be there. Today is my greatest day, *père*, the solemnity, the piety, the organ ringing like a giant underwater bell – the bells themselves silent, of course, in mourning for the crucified Christ. Myself in black and purple, my voice the middle note of the organ intoning the words. They watch me with wide, dark eyes. Even the renegades are here today, black-clad and hair greased. Their *need*, their *expectation* fills the hollow in me. For the briefest moment I really feel love, love for their sins, for their ultimate redemption, for their petty concerns, their insignificance. I know you understand, for you were their father too. In a very real sense you died for them as much as did Our Lord. To protect them from your sins and from their own. They never knew, did they, *père*? Never found out from me. But when I found you with my mother in the chancery ... A massive stroke, the doctor said. The shock must have been too great. You retreated. Went away into yourself though I know you can hear me, know that you see better than you ever did before. And I know that one day you will come back to us. I have fasted and prayed, *père*. I have humbled myself. And yet I feel unworthy. There is still one thing I have not done.

After the service a child – Mathilde Arnauld – came up to me. Putting her hand in mine she whispered, smiling: 'Will they bring chocolates for you too, Monsieur le Curé?'

'Will who bring chocolates?' I asked, puzzled.

Impatiently: 'But the *bells*, of course!' She gave a chuckle. 'The flying bells!'

'Oh, the bells. Of course.'

I was taken aback and for a moment did not know how to answer. She tugged at my soutane, insisting. 'You know, the *bells*. Flying to Rome to see the Pope and bringing back *chocolates*.'

It has become an obsession. A one-word refrain, a whispered-shouted-chorus to every thought. I could not prevent my voice from rising in anger, crumpling her eager face into dismay and terror. I roared: '*Why can no-one here think of anything but chocolates?*' and the child ran wailing across the square, the little shop with its gift-wrapping window grinning at me in triumph as I called after her too late.

Tonight there will be the ceremonial burial of the Host in the sepulchre, the acting-out of the last moments of Our Lord by children of the parish, the lighting of the candles as the light fails. This is usually one of the most intense moments of the year for me, the moment at which they belong to me, *my* children, black-swathed and grave. But this year, will they be thinking of the Passion, of the solemnity of the Eucharist, or will their mouths be watering in anticipation? Her stories – flying bells and feasting – are pervasive, seductive. I try to infuse the sermon with our own seductions, but the dark glories of the Church cannot compare with her magic carpet rides.

I called on Armande Voizin this afternoon. It's her birthday, and the house was in commotion. Of course, I knew there was to be a kind of party, but never suspected anything like this. Caro mentioned it to me once or twice – she is reluctant to go, but hopes to use it as an opportunity to make peace with her mother once and for all – though I suspect even she does not anticipate the scale of the event. Vianne Rocher was in the kitchen, having spent most of the day preparing food. Joséphine Muscat volunteered the café's kitchen as a supplementary cooking area, for Armande's house is too small to cope with such lavish preparations, and when I arrived a whole phalanx of helpers were bringing dishes, pans and tureens from the café to Armande's house. A rich, winey smell came from the open window, and in spite of myself I found my mouth watering. Narcisse was working in the garden, fixing flowers onto a kind of trellis constructed between the house and the gate. The effect is startling: clematis, morning glory, lilac and seringa seem to trail down the wooden structure, forming a thatch of colour above, through which the sun filters gently. Armande was nowhere to be seen.

I turned away, unsettled by this excessive display. Typical of her to have chosen Good Friday for this celebration. The lavishness of it all – flowers, food, crates of champagne delivered at the door and packed with ice to keep it cool – is almost blasphemous, a mocking cry in the face of the sacrificed god. I must speak to her about it tomorrow. I was about to leave when I caught sight of Guillaume Duplessis standing beside the wall, stroking one of Armande's cats. He raised his hat politely.

'Helping, are you?' I demanded.

Guillaume nodded. 'I said I might give a hand,' he admitted. 'There's still a lot of work to do before tonight.'

'I'm amazed you want to have anything to do with this,' I told him sharply. 'Today of all days, too! Really, I think Armande's taking it too far this time. The *expense*, quite apart from the disrespect to the Church . . .'

Guillaume shrugged. 'She's entitled to her little celebration,' he said mildly.

'She's more likely to kill herself with overeating,' I snapped tartly.

'I think she's old enough to do what she likes,' said Guillaume.

I eyed him disapprovingly. He has changed since he began his association with the Rocher woman. The look of mournful humility has gone from his face and there is something wilful, almost defiant, in its place.

'I don't like the way her family tries to run Armande's life for her,' he continued stubbornly.

I shrugged. 'I'm surprised that you, of all people, can take her side in this,' I told him.

'Life's full of surprises,' said Guillaume.

I wish it were.

36

Friday, March 28
Good Friday

AT SOME POINT QUITE EARLY ON I FORGOT WHAT THE
party was all about and began to enjoy myself. While
Anouk played in Les Marauds, I orchestrated preparations
for the largest and most lavish meal I had ever cooked,
and became lost in succulent detail. I had three kitchens:
my own large ovens at La Praline where I baked the cakes,
the Café des Marauds up the road for the shellfish, and
Armande's tiny kitchen for the soup, vegetables, sauces
and garnishes. Joséphine offered to lend Armande the
extra cutlery and plates she might need, but Armande
shook her head, smiling.

'That's all dealt with,' she replied. And so it was; early
on Thursday morning a van arrived bearing the name of a
large firm in Limoges and delivered two boxes of glass and
silverware and one of fine china, all wrapped in shredded

paper. The delivery man smiled as Armande signed the goods receipt.

'One of your granddaughters getting married, *hein?*' he asked cheerily.

Armande gave a bright chuckle. 'Could be,' she replied. 'Could be.'

She spent Friday in high spirits, supposedly overseeing things but mostly getting underfoot. Like a mischievous child she had her fingers in sauces, peeped under dish covers and the lids of hot pans until finally I begged Guillaume to take her to the hairdresser in Agen for a couple of hours, if only to get her out of the way. When she returned she was transformed: hair smartly cropped and set under a rakish new hat, new gloves, new shoes. Shoes, gloves and hat were all the same shade of cherry-red, Armande's favourite colour.

'I'm working upwards,' she informed me with satisfaction as she settled into her rocker to watch the proceedings. 'By the end of the week I might have the courage to buy a whole red dress. Imagine me walking into church with it on. *Wheee!*'

'Get some rest,' I told her sternly. 'You've a party to go to tonight. I don't want you falling asleep in the middle of dessert.'

'I won't,' she said, but accepted to doze for an hour in the late sun while I dressed the table and the others went home to rest and change for the evening. The dinner-table is large, absurdly so for Armande's little room, and with a little care would seat us all. A heavy piece of black oak, it took four people to manoeuvre it out into Narcisse's newly built arbour where it stood beneath a canopy of foliage and flowers. The tablecloth is damask, with a fine lace border, and smells of the lavender in which she laid it after her marriage – a gift, never yet used, from her own grandmother. The plates from Limoges are white with a tiny border of yellow flowers running around the rim; glasses – three different kinds – are crystal, nests of sunlight flicking rainbow flecks across the white cloth. A centrepiece of spring flowers from Narcisse, napkins folded neatly beside each plate. On each napkin, inscribed cards with the name of the guest: *Armande Voizin, Vianne Rocher, Anouk Rocher, Caroline Clairmont, Georges Clairmont, Luc Clairmont, Guillaume Duplessis, Joséphine Bonnet, Julien Narcisse, Michel Roux, Blanche Dumand, Cerisette Plançon.*

For a moment I did not recognize the last two names, then I remembered Blanche and Zézette, still moored upriver and waiting. I realized that until now I had not known Roux's name, had assumed it to be a nickname, perhaps, for his red hair.

The guests began to arrive at eight. I left my kitchen at seven for a quick change and a shower, and when I returned the boat was already moored under the house, and the river people were arriving. Blanche in her red dirndl and a lace shirt, Zézette in an old black evening dress with her arms tattooed in henna and a ruby in her eyebrow, Roux in clean jeans and a white T-shirt, all of them bringing presents with them, wrapped in scraps of gift paper or wallpaper or pieces of cloth. Then came Narcisse in his Sunday suit, then Guillaume, a yellow flower in his buttonhole, then the Clairmonts, resolutely cheery, Caro watching the river people with a wary eye but nevertheless prepared to enjoy herself if such a sacrifice was demanded. Over apéritifs, salted pinenuts and tiny biscuits we watched as Armande opened her presents: from Anouk a picture of a cat in a red envelope, from Blanche a jar of honey, Zézette sachets of lavender embroidered with the letter B – 'I didn't have time to do one with your initial,' she explained with cheery uncon-cern, 'but I promise I will next year' – from Roux a carved oak leaf, delicate as the real thing, with a cluster of acorns clinging to the stem, from Narcisse a big basket of fruit and flowers. More lavish gifts came from the Clairmonts; a scarf from Caro – *not* Hermès, I noticed, but silk nevertheless – and a silver flower vase, from Luc something shiny and red in an envelope of crinkly paper, which he hides from his mother as best he can beneath a pile of discarded wrapping-papers. Armande smirks and mouths at me – *Wheeee!* – behind her cupped hand. Joséphine brings a small gold locket, smiles apologetically. 'It's not new,' she says.

Armande puts it around her neck, hugs Joséphine roughly, pours St Raphaël with a reckless hand. I can hear the conversation from the kitchen; preparing so much food is a tricky business and much of my attention is given to it, but I catch some of what is going on. Caro is gracious, ready to be pleased; Joséphine silent; Roux and Narcisse have found a common interest in exotic fruit trees. Zézette sings part of a folk song in her piping voice, her baby crooked casually into her arm. I notice that even the baby has been ceremonially daubed with henna, so that it looks like a plump little *gris nantais* melon with its mottled golden skin and grey-green eyes.

They move to the table. Armande, in high spirits, supplies much of the conversation. I hear Luc's low, pleasant accents, talking about some book he has read. Caro's voice sharpens a little – I suspect Armande has poured herself another glass of St Raphaël.

'*Maman*, you know you shouldn't—' I hear her say, but Armande simply laughs.

'It's my party,' she declares merrily. 'I won't have anyone being miserable at my party. Least of all me.'

For the time being, nothing more is said on the subject. I hear Zézette flirting with Georges. Roux and Narcisse are discussing plums.

'*Belle du Languedoc*,' declares the latter earnestly. 'That's the best for me. Sweet and small, with a bloom on her like a butterfly's wing.'

But Roux is adamant. '*Mirabelle*,' he says firmly. 'The only yellow plum worth growing. *Mirabelle*.'

I turn back to my stove and for a while I hear nothing more. It is a self-taught skill, born of obsession. No-one taught me how to cook. My mother brewed spells and philtres, I sublimated the whole into a sweeter alchemy. We were never much alike, she and I. She dreamed of floating, of astral encounters and secret essences: I pored over recipes and menus filched from restaurants where we never could afford to dine. Gently she jeered at my fleshly preoccupations.

'It's a good thing we don't have the money,' she would say to me. 'Otherwise you'd get fat as a pig.' Poor Mother. When cancer had eaten away the best of her she was still vain enough to rejoice at the lost weight. And while she read her cards and muttered to herself, I would leaf through my collection of cookery cards, incanting the names of never-tasted dishes like mantras, like the secret formulae of eternal life. *Boeuf en Daube. Champignons farcis à la grèque. Escalopes à la Reine. Crème Caramel. Schokoladentorte. Tiramisu.* In the secret kitchen of my imagination I made them all, tested, tasted them, added to my collection of recipes wherever we went, pasted them into my scrapbook like photographs of old friends. They gave weight to my wanderings, the glossy clippings shining out from between the smeary pages like signposts along our erratic path.

I bring them out now like long-lost friends. *Soupe de tomates à la gasconne*, served with fresh basil and a slice of *tartelette méridonale*, made on biscuit-thin *pâte brisée* and lush with the flavours of olive oil and anchovy and the rich local tomatoes, garnished with olives and roasted slowly to produce a concentration of flavours which seems almost impossible. I pour the '85 Chablis into tall glasses. Anouk drinks lemonade from hers with an air of exaggerated sophistication. Narcisse expresses interest in the tartlet's ingredients, praises the virtues of the misshapen *Roussette* tomato as opposed to the tasteless uniformity of the European *Moneyspinner*. Roux lights the braziers at either side of the table and sprinkles them with citronella to keep away the insects. I catch Caro watching Armande with a look of disapproval. I eat little. Steeped in the scents of the cooking food for most of the day I feel light-headed this evening, keyed-up and unusually sensitive, so that when Joséphine's hand brushes against my leg during the meal I start and almost cry out. The Chablis is cool and tart, and I drink more of it than I should. Colours begin to seem brighter, sounds take on a cut-glass crispness. I hear Armande praising the cooking. I bring a herb salad to clear the palate, then foie gras on warm toast. I notice that Guillaume has brought his dog with him, surreptitiously feeding him with titbits under the crisp tablecloth. We pass from the political situation, to the Basque separatists, to ladies' fashions via the best way to grow rocket and the superiority of wild over cultivated lettuce. The Chablis runs smooth throughout. Then the *vol-au-vents*, light as a puff of summer air, then elder-flower sorbet followed by *plateau de fruits de mer* with grilled *langoustines*, grey shrimps, prawns, oysters, *berniques*, spider-crabs and the bigger *tourteaux* which can nip off a man's fingers as easily as I could nip a stem of rosemary, winkles, *palourdes* and atop it all a giant black lobster, regal on its bed of seaweed. The huge platter gleams with reds and pinks and sea-greens and pearly-whites and purples, a mermaid's cache of delicacies which gives off a nostalgic salt smell, like childhood days at the seaside. We distribute crackers for the crab claws, tiny forks for the shellfish, dishes of lemon wedges and mayonnaise. Impossible to remain aloof with such a dish; it demands attention, informality. The glasses and silver-ware glitter in the light of the lanterns hanging from the trellis above our heads. The night smells of flowers and the river. Armande's fingers are nimble as lacemakers'; the plate of discarded shells in front of her grows almost effortlessly. I bring more of the Chablis; eyes brighten, faces made rosy with the effort of extracting the shellfish's elusive flesh. This is food which must be worked at, food which demands time. Joséphine begins to relax a little, even to talk to Caro, struggling with a crab claw. Caro's hand slips, a jet of salt water from the crab hits her in the eye. Joséphine laughs. After a moment Caro joins in. I find myself talking too. The wine is pale and deceptive, its intoxication hidden beneath its smoothness. Caro is already slightly drunk, her face flushed, her hair coming down in tendrils. Georges squeezes my leg beneath the tablecloth, winks salaciously. Blanche talks of travelling; we have places in common, she and I. Nice, Vienna, Turin. Zézette's baby begins to wail; she dips a finger in Chablis for it to suck. Armande discusses de Musset with Luc, who stammers less the more he drinks. At last I remove the dismantled *plateau*, now reduced to pearly rubble on a dozen plates. Bowls of lemon-water and mint salad for the fingers and palate. I clear the glasses, replace them with the *coupes à champagne*. Caro is looking alarmed again. As I move into the kitchen once more I hear her talking to Armande in a low, urgent voice.

Armande shushes her. 'Talk to me about it later. Tonight I want to *celebrate*.'

She greets the champagne with a squawk of satisfaction.

The dessert is a chocolate fondue. Make it on a clear day – cloudy weather dims the gloss on the melted chocolate – with 70 per cent dark chocolate, butter, a little almond oil, double cream added at the very last minute and heated gently over a burner. Skewer pieces of cake or fruit and dip into the chocolate mixture. I have all their favourites here tonight, though only the *gâteau de savoie* is meant for dipping. Caro claims she cannot eat another thing, but takes two slices of the dark-and-white chocolate *roulade bicolore*. Armande samples everything, flushed now and growing more expansive by the minute. Joséphine is explaining to Blanche why she left her husband. Georges smiles lecherously at me from behind chocolate-smeared fingers. Luc teases Anouk who is half-asleep in her chair. The dog bites playfully at the tableleg. Zézette, quite unselfconsciously, begins to breastfeed her baby. Caro appears to be on the verge of comment, but shrugs and says nothing. I open another bottle of champagne.

'You're sure you're OK?' says Luc quietly to Armande. 'I mean, you don't feel ill or anything? You've been taking your medicine?'

Armande laughs. 'You worry too much for a boy of your age,' she tells him. 'You should be raising hell, making your mother anxious. Not teaching your grandmother how to suck eggs.' She is still good-humoured, but looks a little tired now. We have been at table almost four hours. It is ten to midnight.

'I know,' he says with a smile. 'But I'm in no hurry to i-inherit just yet.'

She pats his hand and pours him another glass. Her hand is not quite steady, and a little wine spills on the tablecloth. 'Not to worry,' she says brightly. 'Plenty more left.'

We round off the meal with my own chocolate ice-cream, truffles and coffee in tiny demi-tasses, with a calvados chaser, drunk from the hot cup like an explosion of flowers. Anouk demands her *canard*, a sugar-lump moistened with a few drops of the liqueur, then wants another for Pantoufle. Cups are drained, plates cleared. The braziers are burning lower. I watch Armande, still talking and laughing, but less animated than before, her eyes half-closed, holding Luc's hand under the table.

'What time is it?' she asks, some time later.

'Almost one,' says Guillaume.

She sighs. 'Time for me to go to bed,' she declares. 'Not as young as I was, you know.'

She fumbles to her feet, picking up an armful of presents from under her chair as she does so. I can see Guillaume watching her attentively. He knows. She throws him a smile of peculiar, quizzical sweetness.

'Don't think I'm going to make a speech,' she says with comical brusqueness. 'Can't bear speeches. Just wanted to thank you all – *all* of you – and to say what a good time I had. Can't remember a better. Don't think there's ever *been* a better. People always think the fun has to stop when you get old. Well it doesn't.' Cheers from Roux, Georges and Zézette. Armande nods wisely. 'Don't call on me too early tomorrow, though,' she advises with a little grimace. 'I don't think I've drunk so much since I was

367

twenty, and I need my sleep.' She gives me a quick glance, almost of warning. 'Need my sleep,' she repeats vaguely, beginning to make her way from the table.

Caro stood up to steady her, but she waved her away with a peremptory gesture. 'Don't fuss, girl,' she said. 'That was always your way. Always fussing.' She gave me one of her bright looks. 'Vianne can help me,' she declared. 'The rest can wait till the morning.'

I took her to her room while the guests left slowly, still laughing and talking. Caro was holding on to Georges's arm; Luc supported her from the other side. Her hair had come entirely undone now, making her look young and softer-featured. As I opened the door of Armande's room I heard her say: '. . . virtually *promised* she'd go to Les Mimosas – what a weight off my mind . . .' Armande heard it too and gave a sleepy chuckle. 'Can't be easy, having a delinquent mother,' she said. 'Put me to bed, Vianne. Before I drop.' I helped her undress. There was a linen nightdress laid out in readiness by the pillow. I folded her clothes while she pulled it over her head.

'Presents,' said Armande. 'Put them there, where I can see them.' A vague gesture in the direction of the dresser. 'Hmm. That's good.'

I carried out her instructions in a kind of daze. Perhaps I, too, had drunk more than I intended, for I felt quite calm. I knew from the number of insulin ampoules in the fridge that she had stopped taking it a couple of days ago. I wanted to ask her if she was sure, if she really knew what she was doing. Instead I draped Luc's present – a silk slip of lavish, brazen, indisputable redness – on the chair-back for her to see. She chuckled again, stretched out her hand to touch the fabric.

'You can go now, Vianne.' Her voice was gentle but firm. 'It was lovely.'

I hesitated. For a second I caught a glimpse of us both in the dressing-table mirror. With her newly cut hair she looked like the old man of my vision, but her hands were a splash of crimson and she was smiling. She had closed her eyes.

'Leave the light on, Vianne.' It was a final dismissal. 'Goodnight.'

I kissed her gently on the cheek. She smelt of lavender and chocolate. I went into the kitchen to finish the washing-up.

Roux had stayed behind to help me. The other guests had gone. Anouk was asleep on the sofa, a thumb corked into her mouth. We washed up in silence and I put the new plates and glasses into Armande's cupboards. Once or twice Roux tried to begin a conversation, but I could not talk to him; only the small percussive sounds of china and glass punctuated our silence.

'Are you all right?' he said at last. His hand was gentle on my shoulder. His hair was marigolds.

I said the first thing which came into my head. 'I was

thinking about my mother.' Strangely enough I realized it was true. 'She would have loved this. She loved – fireworks.'

He looked at me. His strange skyline eyes had darkened almost to purple in the dim yellow kitchen lighting. I wished I could tell him about Armande.

'I didn't know you were called Michel,' I said at last.

He shrugged. 'Names don't matter.'

'You're losing your accent,' I realized in surprise. 'You used to have such a strong Marseille accent, but now . . .'

He gave his rare, sweet smile. 'Accents don't matter, either.'

His hands cupped my face. Soft, for a labourer's, pale and soft as a woman's. I wondered if anything he had told me was true. For the time, it didn't seem to matter. I kissed him. He smelt of paint and soap and chocolate. I tasted chocolate in his mouth and thought of Armande. I'd always thought he cared for Joséphine. Even as I kissed him I knew it, but this was the only magic we had between us to combat the night. The simplest magic, the wildfire we bring down the mountainside at Beltane, this year a little early. Small comforts in defiance of the dark. His hands sought my breasts under my jumper.

For a second I hesitated. There have already been too many men along the road, men like this one, good men about whom I cared but did not love. If I was right, and he and Joséphine belonged together, what might this do to them? To me? His mouth was light, his touch simple. From the flowers outside I caught a wafting of lilac, brought in by the warm air from the braziers.

'Outside,' I told him softly. 'In the garden.'

He glanced at Anouk, still sleeping on the sofa, and nodded. Together we padded outside under the starry purple sky.

The garden was still warm in the glow of the braziers. The seringas and lilacs of Narcisse's trellis blanketed us beneath their scent. We lay on the grass like children. We made no promises, spoke no words of love though he was gentle, almost passionless, moving instead with a slow sweetness along my body, lapping my skin with fluttering movements of the tongue. Above his head the sky was purple-black like his eyes, and I could see the broad band of the Milky Way like a road around the world. I knew that this could be the only time between us, and felt only a dim melancholy at the thought. Instead a growing sense of *presence*, of completion filled me, overriding my loneliness, even my sorrow for Armande. There would be time for grieving later. For the moment, simple wonder; at myself lying naked in the grass, at the silent man beside me, at the immensity above and the immensity within. We lay for a long time, Roux and I, until our sweat cooled, and little insects ran across our bodies, and we smelt lavender and thyme from the flowerbed at our feet as, holding hands, we watched the unbearable slow wheeling of the sky.

Under his breath I could hear Roux singing a little song:

> *V'là l'bon vent, v'là l'joli vent*
> *V'là l'bon vent, ma mie m'appelle . . .*

The wind was inside me now, tugging at me with its relentless imperative. At the very centre, a small still space, miraculously untroubled, and the almost familiar sense of something *new*. This too is a kind of magic, one that my mother never understood, and yet I am more certain of this – this new, miraculous, living warmth inside me – than of anything I have done before. At last I understand why I drew the Lovers that night. Holding the knowledge close, I closed my eyes and tried to dream of her, as I did in those months before Anouk was born, of a little stranger with bright cheeks and snapping black eyes.

When I awoke, Roux was gone, and the wind had changed again.

37

Saturday, March 29
Easter Eve

HELP ME, *PÈRE*. HAVEN'T I PRAYED ENOUGH? SUFFERED enough for our sins? My penance has been exemplary. My head swims from lack of food and sleep. Is this not the time of redemption, when all sins are washed away? The silver is back on the altar, the candles lit in anticipation. Flowers, for the first time since the beginning of Lent, adorn the chapel. Even mad St Francis is crowned with lilies, and their scent is like clean flesh. We have waited so long, you and I, since your first stroke. Even then you would not speak to me, though you spoke to others. Then, last year, the second stroke. They tell me you are unreachable, but I know this to be pretence, a waiting game. You will awake in your own time.

They found Armande Voizin this morning. Stiff and still smiling in her bed, *père*; another one who has evaded us. I gave her the last rites though she would not have thanked me even if she had heard. Perhaps I am the only one who still derives comfort from such things.

She *meant* to die last night, arranged everything to the minutest detail, food, drink, company. Her family around her, deceived by her promises of reform. Her damnable arrogance! She will pay, promises Caro, twenty Masses, thirty Masses. Pray for her. Pray for us. I find I am still trembling with rage. I cannot answer her with moderation. The funeral is on Tuesday. I imagine her now, lying in state in the hospital mortuary, peonies at her head and with that smile still fixed on her white lips, and the thought fills me, not with pity or even satisfaction, but with a terrible, impotent fury.

Of course, we know who is behind this. The Rocher woman. Oh, Caro told me about that. She is the influence, *père*, the parasite which has invaded our garden. I should have listened to my instincts. Uprooted her the moment I set eyes on her. She who has balked me at every turn, laughing at me behind her shielded window, sending out corrupting suckers in every direction. I was a fool, *père*. Armande Voizin was killed because of my folly. Evil lives with us. Evil wears a winning smile and bright colours. When I was a child I used to listen in terror to the story of the gingerbread house, of the witch who tempted little children in and ate them. I look at her shop, all wrapped in shining papers like a present waiting to be unwrapped, and I wonder how many people, how many souls, she has already tempted beyond redemption. Armande Voizin. Joséphine Muscat. Paul-Marie Muscat. Julien Narcisse. Luc Clairmont. She has to be routed. Her brat too. In any way we can manage. Too late for niceties, *père*. My soul is already compromised. I wish I were sixteen again. I try to recall the savagery of sixteen, the inventiveness of the boy I once was. The boy who flung the bottle, and who put the matter behind him. But those days are over. I must be clever. I must not discredit my office. And yet if I fail . . .

What would Muscat do? Oh, he is brutal, contemptible in his way. And yet he saw the danger long before I did. What would he do? I must take Muscat as my model, Muscat the pig, brutal, but *cunning* as a pig.

What would he do?

The chocolate festival is tomorrow. On this depends her success or failure. Too late to turn the tide of public opinion against her. I must be seen to be blameless. Behind the secret window, thousands of chocolates wait to be sold. Eggs, animals, Easter nests wrapped in ribbon, gift boxes, baby rabbits in bright ruffles of Cellophane . . . Tomorrow a hundred children will awaken to the sound of Easter bells, and their first thought will not be *He is risen!* but *Chocolates! Easter chocolates!*

But what if there *were* no chocolates?

The thought is paralysing. For a second hot joy suffuses

me. The clever pig within me grins and prances. I could break into her house, it tells me. The back door is old and half-rotten. I could lever it open. Sneak into the shop with a cudgel. Chocolate is brittle, easily damaged. Five minutes among her gift-boxes would do it. She sleeps on the top floor. She might not hear. Besides, I would be quick. I could wear a mask too, so that if she saw . . . Everyone would suspect Muscat, a revenge attack. The man is not here to deny it, and besides—

Père, did you move? I was certain for a moment that your hand twitched, the first two fingers crooked as if in benediction. Again, that spasm, like a gunfighter dreaming past battles. A sign.

Praise the Lord. A sign.

38

Sunday, March 30
Easter Sunday, 4.00 a.m.

I BARELY SLEPT LAST NIGHT. HER WINDOW WAS LIT UNTIL two, and even then I dared not move in case she was lying awake in the darkness. In the armchair I dozed for a couple of hours, setting the alarm in case I overslept. I need not have worried. My sleep, such as it was, was shot through with pinpricks of dream so fleeting that I barely remembered them even as they stung me awake. I think I saw Armande – a *young* Armande, though obviously I never knew her then – running through the fields at the back of Les Marauds in a red dress, black hair flying. Or maybe it was Vianne, and I had somehow confused them. Then I dreamed of the fire at Les Marauds, of the slattern and her man, of the harsh red banks of the Tannes and of you, *père*, and my mother in the chancery ... All that summer's bitter vintage seeped through my dreams, and I, like a pig snouting for truffles, turning over more and more of the rotten delicacies and gorging, gorging.

At four I rise from the chair. I have slept in my clothes, discarding my soutane and collar. The Church has nothing to do with this business. I make coffee, very strong, but with no sugar, though technically my penance is over. I say technically. In my heart I know that Easter has not yet come. He is not yet risen. If I succeed today, *then* He will rise.

I find that I am trembling. I eat dry bread to give myself courage. The coffee is hot and bitter. When I have accomplished my task I promise myself a good meal; eggs, ham, sugar rolls from Poitou's. My mouth fills at the thought. I put on the radio to a station which plays classical music. 'Sheep may Safely Graze'. My mouth twists in a hard, dry grin of contempt. This is no time for pastorals. This is the hour of the pig, the cunning pig. Off with the music.

The time is five to five. Looking out of the window I can see the very first crack of light on the horizon. I have plenty of time. The curate will be here at six to ring the Easter carillon; I have more than enough time for my secret business. I put on the balaclava which I have laid aside for my purpose; in the mirror I look different, alarming. A saboteur. That makes me smile again. My mouth under the mask looks tough and cynical. I almost hope she sees me.

5.10 a.m.

The door is unlocked. I can hardly believe my luck. It shows her confidence, her insolent belief that no-one can withstand her. I discard the thick screwdriver with which I would have jimmied the door, and take up the heavy piece of wood – part of a lintel, *père*, that fell during the war – in both hands. The door opens into silence. Another of her red sachets swings above the doorway; I pull it down and drop it contemptuously onto the floor. For a time I am disoriented. The place has changed since it was a bakery, and in any case I am less familiar with the back part of the shop. Only a very faint reflection of light gleams from the tiled surfaces, and I am glad I thought to bring a torch. I switch it on now, and for a moment I am almost blinded by the whiteness of the enamelled surfaces, the tops, the sinks, the old ovens all shining with a moony glow in the torch's narrow beam. There are no chocolates to be seen. Of course. This is only the preparation area. I am not sure why I am surprised that the place is so clean; I imagined her a slattern, leaving pans unwashed and plates stacked in the sink and long black hairs in the cake mixture. Instead she is scrupulously tidy; rows of pans arranged on the shelves in order of size, copper with copper, enamel with enamel, porcelain bowls to hand and utensils – spoons, skillets – hanging from the whitewashed walls. On the scarred old table several stone bread pans are standing. In the centre, a vase with shaggy yellow dahlias cast a shock of shadows before them. For some reason the flowers enrage me. What right has she to flowers, when Armande Voizin lies dead? The pig inside me tips the flowers onto the table, grinning. I let him have his way. I need his ferocity for the task in hand.

5.20 a.m

The chocolates must be in the shop itself. Quietly I make my way through the kitchen and open the thick pine door into the front section of the building. To my left, stairs lead up into the living area. To my right, the counter, the shelves, the displays, the boxes . . . The smell of chocolate, though expected, is startling. The darkness seems to have intensified it so that for an instant the smell *is* the darkness, folding around me like a rich brown powder, stifling thought. The beam of my torch picks out clusters of brightness, metallic paper, ribbons, sparkling puffs of Cellophane. The cave of treasures is all around me. A thrill runs through my body. To be here, in the witch's house, unseen, an intruder. To touch her things in secret as she sleeps. I feel a compulsion to see the display window, to tear down the screen of paper and to be the first – absurd, as I intend to wreck the whole thing. But the compulsion will not be denied. I pad softly in my rubber soles, the heavy block of wood held loosely in my hand. I have plenty of time. Time enough to indulge my curiosity, if I want to. Besides, this moment is too precious to be squandered. I want to savour it.

5.30 a.m

Very gently I pull aside the film of paper which covers the window. It comes away with a small ripping sound, and I lay it aside, straining to hear any signs of activity from the floor above. There are none. My torchlight illuminates the display, and for a moment I almost forget why I am here. It is an amazement of riches, *glacé* fruits and marzipan flowers and mountains of loose chocolates of all shapes and colours, and rabbits, ducks, hens, chicks, lambs gazing out at me with merry-grave chocolate eyes like the terracotta armies of ancient China, and above it all a statue of a woman, graceful brown arms holding a sheaf of chocolate wheat, hair rippling. The detail is beautifully rendered, the hair added in a darker grade of chocolate, the eyes brushed on in white. The smell of chocolate is overwhelming, the rich fleshy scent of it which drags down the throat in an exquisite trail of sweetness. The wheatsheaf-woman smiles very slightly, as if contemplating mysteries.

Try me. Test me. Taste me.

Its song is louder than ever, here in the very nest of temptation. I could reach out a hand in any direction and pick up one of these forbidden fruits, taste its secret flesh. The thought pierces me in a thousand places.

Try me. Test me. Taste me.

No-one would be any the wiser.

Try me. Test me. Taste—

Why not?

5.40 a.m.

I will take the first thing which falls beneath my fingers. I must not lose myself in this distraction. A single chocolate – not theft, precisely, but *salvage*; alone of all its brethren it will survive the wreck. My hand lingers in spite of itself; a hovering dragonfly above a cluster of dainties. A Plexiglas tray with a lid protects them; the name of each piece is lettered on the lid in fine, cursive script. The names are entrancing. *Bitter orange cracknel. Apricot marzipan roll. Cerisette russe. White rum truffle. Manon blanc. Nipples of Venus.* I feel myself flushing beneath the mask. How could anyone *order* something with a name like that? And yet they look wonderful, plumply white in the light of my torch, tipped with darker chocolate. I take one from the top of the tray. I hold it beneath my nose; it smells of cream and vanilla. No-one will know. I realize that I have not eaten chocolate since I was a boy, more years ago than I can remember, and even then it was a cheap grade of *chocolat à croquer*, 15 per cent cocoa solids – twenty for the dark – with a sticky aftertaste of fat and sugar. Once or twice I bought Suchard from the supermarket, but, at five times the price of the other, it was a luxury I could seldom afford. This is different altogether; the brief resistance of the chocolate shell as it meets the lips, the soft truffle inside . . . There are *layers* of flavour like the bouquet of a fine wine, a slight bitterness, a richness like ground coffee; warmth brings the flavour to life and it fills my nostrils, a taste succubus which has me moaning.

5.45 a.m.

I try another after that, telling myself it will not matter. Again I linger over the names. *Crème de cassis. Three nut cluster.* I select a dark nugget from a tray marked *Eastern journey.* Crystallized ginger in a hard sugar shell, releasing a mouthful of liqueur like a concentration of spices, a breath of aromatic air where sandalwood and cinnamon and lime vie for attention with cedar and allspice. I take another, from a tray marked *Pêche au miel millefleurs.* A slice of peach steeped in honey and eau-de-vie, a crystallized peach sliver on the chocolate lid. I look at my watch. There is still time.

I know I should begin my righteous work in earnest. The display in the shop, though bewildering, is not enough to account for the hundreds of orders she has received. There must be another place where she keeps her gift boxes, her stores, the bulk of her business. The things here are just for show. I grab an *amandine* and stuff it into my mouth to aid thought. Then a caramel fondant. Then a *manon blanc*, fluffy with fresh cream and almond. So little time, when so many morsels remain to be tasted. I could do my work in five minutes, maybe less. As long as I know where to look. I'll take one more chocolate, for luck, before I go searching. Just one more.

5.55 a.m.

It is like one of my dreams. I roll in chocolates. I imagine myself in a field of chocolates, on a beach of chocolates, basking-rooting-gorging. I have no time to read the labels; I cram chocolates into my mouth at random. The pig loses his cleverness in the face of so much delight, becomes a pig again, and though something at the top of my mind screams at me to stop I cannot help myself. Once begun it cannot end. This has nothing to do with hunger; I force them down, mouth bulging, hands full. For a terrible instant I imagine Armande returning to haunt me, to curse me perhaps with her own peculiar affliction; the curse of death by gluttony. I can hear myself making *sounds* as I eat, moaning, keening sounds of ecstasy and despair, as if the pig within has finally found a voice.

6.00 a.m.

He is risen! The sound of the bells jangles me out of my enchantment. I find myself sitting on the floor, spilled chocolates around me as if I have indeed, as I imagined, rolled in them. The cudgel lies forgotten at my side. I have removed the restrictive mask. The window, cleared of its wrapping, gapes blankly with the first pale rays of morning.

He is risen! Drunkenly I stagger to my feet. In five minutes the early worshippers will begin to arrive for Mass. Already I must have been missed. I grab at my cudgel with fingers slimed with melted chocolate. Suddenly I know where she keeps her stock. The old cellar, cool and dry, where flour sacks were once kept. I can get there. I know I can.

He is risen!

I turn, holding my cudgel, desperate for time, time . . .

She is waiting for me, watching from behind the bead curtain. I have no way of knowing how long she has watched me. A tiny smile curves her lips. Very gently she takes the cudgel from my hand. Between her fingers she is holding something which looks like a charred piece of coloured paper. A card, maybe.

385

And that was how they saw me, *père*, crouching in the ruins of her window, face smeared with chocolate, eyes haggard. From nowhere people seemed to come running to her aid. Duplessis with his dog-lead in one hand, standing guard at the door. The Rocher woman at the back door with my cudgel crooked in her elbow. Poitou from across the road, up early for his baking, calling the curious in to see. The Clairmonts, like landed carp, staring. Narcisse shaking his fist. And the laughter. God! The laughter. And all the time the bells are ringing *He is risen* across St Jérôme's square.

He is risen.

39

Monday, March 31
Easter Monday

I SENT REYNAUD ON HIS WAY WHEN THE BELLS STOPPED ringing. He never said Mass. Instead he ran off into Les Marauds without a word. Few people missed him. Instead we began the festival early, with hot chocolate and cakes outside La Praline while I quickly cleared up the mess. Fortunately this was little; a few hundred chocolates spilled onto the floor, but none of our gift boxes damaged. A couple of adjustments to the display window and it looked as good as ever.

The festival was all we hoped for. Craft stalls, fanfares, Narcisse's band – surprisingly, he plays the saxophone with rakish virtuosity – jugglers, fire-eaters. The river people are back – for the day, at least – and the streets were alive with their variegated figures. Some set up stalls of their own, hair-beading and selling jam and honey, tattooing in henna or telling fortunes. Roux sold dolls he had carved from pieces of driftwood. Only the Clairmonts were missing, though I kept seeing Armande in my mind's eye, as if on such an occasion I could not imagine her being absent. A woman in a red scarf, the round curve of a bent back in a grey pinafore, a straw hat, gaily decorated with cherries, bobbing above the holiday crowd. She seemed to be everywhere. Strangely enough I found that I felt no grief. Merely a growing conviction that at any moment she might appear, lifting the lids of boxes to see what was inside, licking her fingers greedily or whooping with glee at the noise, the fun, the gaiety of it all. Once I was even sure I heard her voice – *wheee!* – just beside me as I leaned forward to reach a packet of chocolate raisins, though when I looked there was only space. My mother would have understood.

I delivered all my orders and sold the last gift box at four-fifteen. The Easter-egg hunt was won by Lucie Prudhomme, but all the entrants had *cornets-surprise*, with chocolates and toy trumpets and tambourines and streamers. A single *char*, with real flowers, advertised Narcisse's nursery. Some of the younger people dared start a dance under the severe gaze of St Jérôme, and the sun shone all day.

And yet, as I sit now with Anouk in our quiet house, a book of fairy tales in one hand, I feel uneasy. I tell myself that it is the anticlimax that inevitably follows a long-awaited event. Fatigue, perhaps, anxiety, Reynaud's intrusion at the last moment, the heat of the sun, the people . . . Grief too for Armande, emerging now as the sound of merriment abates, sorrow coloured with so many other conflicting things, loneliness, loss, disbelief and a kind of calm feeling of *rightness*. My dear Armande. You would have loved this so much. But you had your own fireworks, didn't you? Guillaume called late this evening, long after we had cleared away all signs of the festival. Anouk was getting ready for bed, her eyes still filled with carnival lights.

'Can I come in?' His dog has learned to sit at his command, and waits solemnly by the door. He is carrying something in one hand. A letter. 'Armande said I was to give you this. You know. After.'

I take the letter. Inside the envelope something small and hard rattles against the paper. 'Thank you.'

'I'll not stay.' He looks at me for a moment, then puts out his hand, a stilted, yet oddly touching gesture. His handshake is firm and cool. I feel stinging in my eyes; something bright falls onto the old man's sleeve – his or mine, I am not certain which.

'Goodnight, Vianne.'

'Goodnight, Guillaume.'

The envelope contains a single sheet of paper. I pull it

out, and something rolls with it onto the table – coins, I
think. The writing is large and effortful.

Dear Vianne,
   Thank you for everything. I know how you must feel.
Talk to Guillaume if you like – he understands better than
anyone else. I'm sorry I couldn't be at your festival, but
I've seen it so often in my mind that it doesn't really
matter. Kiss Anouk for me and give her one of the enclosed
– the other is for the next one, I think you'll know what I
mean.
   I'm tired now, and I can smell a change coming in the
wind. I think sleep will do me good. And who knows,
maybe we'll meet again some day.
Yours, Armande Voizin.
P.S. Don't bother going to the funeral, either of you. It's
Caro's party and I suppose she's entitled to it if that's the
kind of thing she likes. Instead invite all our friends around
to La Praline and have a pot of chocolate. I love you all.
A.

When I had finished I put down the sheet and look for
the rolling coins. I find one on the table and the other on
a chair; two gold sovereigns gleaming red-bright in my
hand. One for Anouk – and the other? Instinctively I
reach for the warm, still place inside myself, the secret
place I have not yet fully revealed even to myself.

*

Anouk's head rests gently on my shoulder. Almost asleep, she croons to Pantoufle as I read aloud. We have heard little of Pantoufle these past few weeks; usurped by more tangible playmates. It seems significant that he should return now the wind has changed. Something in me feels the inevitability of the change. My carefully built fantasy of permanence is like the sandcastles we used to build on the beach, waiting for a high tide. Even without the sea, the sun erodes them; by tomorrow they are almost gone. Even so I can feel a little anger, a little hurt. But the scent of the carnival draws me nevertheless, the moving wind, the hot wind from – where was it? The South? The East? America? England? It is only a matter of time. Lansquenet, with all its associations, seems less real to me somehow, already receding into memory. The machinery winds down; the mechanism is silent. Perhaps it is what I suspected from the first, that Reynaud and I are linked, that one balances the other and that without him I have no purpose here. Whatever it is, the *neediness* of the town is gone; I can feel satisfaction in its place, a full-bellied satiety with no more room for me. In homes everywhere in Lansquenet, couples are making love, children are playing, dogs barking, televisions blaring. Without us. Guillaume strokes his dog and watches *Casablanca*. Alone in his room, Luc reads Rimbaud aloud without a hint of a stammer. Roux and Joséphine, alone in their newly painted home, discover each other from the inside out, little by little. Radio-Gascogne ran an item on the chocolate festival this evening, proudly announcing *the festival of Lansquenet-sous-Tannes, a charming local tradition.* No longer will tourists drive through Lansquenet on their way to other places. I have put the invisible town on the map.

The wind smells of the sea, of ozone and frying, of the seafront at Juan-les-Pins, of pancakes and coconut oil and charcoal and sweat. So many places waiting for the wind to change. So many needy people. How long this time? Six months? A year? Anouk nestles her face into my shoulder and I hold her close, too hard, for she half-wakes and murmurs something accusing. La Céleste Praline will be a bakery once more. Or perhaps a *confiserie-pâtisserie,* with *guimauves* hanging from the ceiling like strings of pastel sausages and boxes of *pains d'épices* with *Souvenir de Lansquenet-sous-Tannes* stencilled across the lid. At least we have money, more than enough to start again somewhere else. Nice perhaps, or Cannes, London or Paris. Anouk mutters in her sleep. She feels it too.

And yet we have progressed. Not for us, the anonymity of hotel rooms, the flicker of neon, the move from North to South at the turn of a card. At last we have faced down the Black Man, Anouk and I, seen him at last for what he is: a fool to himself, a carnival mask. We cannot stay here for ever. But perhaps he has paved the way for us to stay elsewhere. Some seaside town, perhaps. Or a village by a river, with maize fields and vineyards. Our names will change. The name of our shop, too, will alter. La Truffe Enchantée, perhaps. Or Tentations Divines, in memory of Reynaud. And this time we can take so much of Lansquenet with us. I hold Armande's gift in the palm of my hand. The coins are heavy, solid to the touch. The gold is reddish, almost the colour of Roux's hair. Again, I wonder *how* she knew – exactly how far she could see. Another child – not fatherless this time, but a good man's child, even if he never knows it. I wonder if she will have his hair, his smoky eyes. I am already certain she will be a girl. I even know her name.

Other things we can leave behind. The Black Man is gone. My voice sounds different to me now, bolder, stronger. There is a note in it which, if I listen carefully, I can almost recognize. A note of defiance, even of glee. My fears are gone. You too are gone, *Maman*, though I will always hear you speaking to me. I need no longer be afraid of my face in the mirror. Anouk smiles in her sleep. I could stay here, *Maman*. We have a home, friends. The weathervane outside my window turns, turns. Imagine hearing it every week, every year, every season. Imagine looking out of my window on a winter's morning. The new voice inside me laughs, and the sound is almost like coming home. The new life inside me turns softly, sweetly. Anouk talks in her sleep, nonsense syllables. Her small hands clench against my arm.

'Please.' Her voice is muffled by my jumper. '*Maman*, sing me a song.' She opens her eyes. The Earth, seen from a great height, is the same blue-green shade.

'OK.'

She closes her eyes again, and I begin to sing softly:

> *V'là l'bon vent, v'là l'joli vent*
> *V'là l'bon vent, ma mie m'appelle.*

Hoping that this time it will remain a lullaby. That this time the wind will not hear. That this time – *please, just this once* – it will leave without us.